The Scarred Woman

A DEPARTMENT Q THRILLER

ALSO BY JUSSI ADLER-OLSEN

The Department Q Series

Mercy

Disgrace

Redemption

Guilt

Buried

The Hanging Girl

Standalone Novels

Alphabet House

JUSSI ADLER OLSEN

The Scarred Woman

A DEPARTMENT Q THRILLER

Translated by William Frost

Quercus

First published in the USA in 2017 by
Dutton
Penguin Random House
New York, United States

This edition first published in Great Britain in 2017 by

Quercus Editions Ltd
Carmelite House
50 Victoria Embankment
London EC4Y 0DZ

An Hachette UK company

A CIP catalogue record for this book is available
from the British Library

HB ISBN 978 1 78429 596 7
TPB ISBN 978 1 78429 599 8
EBOOK ISBN 978 1 78429 598 1

10 9 8 7 6 5 4 3 2 1

Printed and bound in Great Britain by Clays Ltd, St Ives plc

Dedicated to our wonderful "family" in Barcelona
Olaf Slott-Petersen, Annette Merrild, Arne Merrild Bertelsen, and
Michael Kirkegaard

PROLOGUE

Saturday, November 18th, 1995

She didn't know how long she had been kicking the sticky, withered leaves, only that her bare arms were now cold and that the shouting up at the house had become shrill, sounding so harsh and angry that it hurt her chest. Only just now, she had been about to cry, but that was something she really didn't want to do.

You'll get lines on your cheeks and that's ugly, Dorrit, her mother would say. She was good at reminding her of that sort of thing.

Dorrit looked at the wide, dark tracks she had left in the foliage on the lawn, then once more counted the windows and doors of the house. She knew perfectly well how many there were; it was just a way to pass the time. Two doors for the wings, fourteen large windows and four rectangular ones in the basement, and if she counted every pane, there were one hundred and forty-two.

I can count really high, she thought proudly. She was the only one in her class who could.

Then she heard the hinges of the basement door on the side wing squeak, which was rarely a good sign.

"I'm not going in," she whispered to herself when she saw the housemaid coming up from the basement stairwell, heading straight toward her.

At the far end of the garden where it was dark among the bushes, she often crouched down and hid, sometimes for hours if necessary, but this time the housemaid was too quick, the grip on her wrist tight and hard.

"You're crazy trudging about out here with those fine shoes on, Dorrit. Mrs. Zimmermann will be fuming when she sees how mucky they are. You know that."

She stood in front of the sofas in her stocking feet, feeling uncomfortable because the two women just stared at her as if they had no idea what she was doing in the drawing room.

Her grandmother's face was stern and full of foreboding, while her mother's was red-eyed and unattractive. Just as wrinkled as she had said Dorrit's would become.

"Not now, Dorrit, darling. We're speaking," her mother said.

She looked around. "Where's Daddy?" she asked.

The two women looked at each other. In a flash, her mother was like a scared little animal, cowering in a corner, and not for the first time.

"Go to the dining room, Dorrit. There are some magazines you can flick through," her grandmother dictated.

"Where's Daddy?" she asked again.

"We'll talk about that later. He's gone," answered her grandmother.

Dorrit took a careful step backward, watching her grandmother's gesticulations: *Go now!* they seemed to say.

She could just as well have stayed out in the garden.

In the dining room, plates with stale cauliflower stew and half-eaten pork patties still lay on the heavy side table. The forks and knives lay on the tablecloth, which was stained with wine from two overturned crystal glasses. It didn't seem at all like it normally did, and it was certainly not somewhere Dorrit wanted to be.

She turned around toward the hallway and its many gloomy and tall doors with worn handles. The large house was divided into several areas, and Dorrit thought she knew every corner. Up on the second floor, it smelled so strongly of her grandmother's powders and perfumes that the scent clung to one's clothes even after returning home. Up there, in the flickering light from the windows, there was nothing for Dorrit to do.

On the other hand, she felt right at home in the wing at the back of the first floor.

It had both a sour and sweet smell of tobacco from the drawn curtains, and heavy furniture of the sort one couldn't see anywhere else in Dorrit's world. Large, cushioned armchairs you could cuddle up in with your feet tucked under you, and sofas with decorated brown corduroy and carved black sides. That domain in the house was her grandfather's.

An hour ago, before her father had started arguing with her grandmother, all five of them had been happily sitting around the dining table, and Dorrit had thought that this day would softly wrap around her like a blanket.

And then her father had said something or other really wrong that caused her grandmother to immediately raise her eyebrows and her grandfather to stand up from the table.

"You'll have to sort this out yourselves," he had said, pulling up his pants and sneaking away. That's when they sent her out into the garden.

Dorrit carefully pushed open the door to his study. Along one wall there was a pair of brown dressers with shoe samples in open boxes, while on the opposite wall was her grandfather's carved desk, totally piled with papers covered with blue and red lines.

It smelled even stronger of tobacco here, though her grandfather wasn't in the gloomy room. It almost seemed as if the tobacco smoke came from over in the corner, from where a small shaft of light shone through a pair of bookshelves and rested across the writing chair.

Dorrit moved closer to see where the light came from. It was exciting because the narrow crack between the bookshelves revealed unknown territory.

"So, are they gone, then?" she heard her grandfather grunt from somewhere behind the shelves.

Dorrit pushed through the crack, entering a room she had never seen before, and there on an old leather chair with armrests by a long table sat her grandfather attentively leaning over something she couldn't see.

"Is that you, Rigmor?" he said in his distinctive voice. It was his German, which wouldn't disappear, her mother often said with irritation, but Dorrit was very fond of it.

The decor of the room was very different from that in the rest of the house. The walls in here were not bare but plastered with large and small photographs, and if one looked closely it became apparent that they were all of the same man in uniform in various situations.

In spite of the thick tobacco smoke, the room seemed lighter than the study. Her grandfather was sitting contentedly with his sleeves rolled up; she noticed the long, thick veins that coiled up his bare forearms. His movements were calm and relaxed. Gentle hands leafing through photographs, his eyes fixed on them with a scrutinizing stare. He looked so content sitting there that it made Dorrit smile. But in the next moment, as he suddenly swung the office chair around to face her, she realized that the usually friendly smile was distorted and frozen as if he had swallowed something bitter.

"Dorrit!" he said, standing halfway up with his arms outstretched, almost as if trying to hide what he had been perusing.

"Sorry, Opa. I didn't know where I was supposed to go." She looked around at the photographs on the walls. "I think the man in these photos looks like you."

He looked at her for a long time, as if considering what to say, before suddenly taking her hand and pulling her over to him and up onto his lap.

"Actually, you aren't allowed to be in here because this is Opa's secret room. But now that you're here, you might as well stay." He nodded toward the wall. "*Och, ja,* Dorrit, you're right. It is me in the photographs. They are from when I was a young man and a soldier in the German Army during the war."

Dorrit nodded. He looked handsome in his uniform. Black cap, black jacket, and black pants. Everything was black: belt, boots, holster, and gloves. Only the skull and crossbones and the smile with the pearly white teeth shone among all the black.

"Then you were a soldier, Opa?"

"*Jawohl.* You can see my pistol for yourself up there on the shelf. Parabellum 08, also known as a Luger. My best friend for many years."

Dorrit looked up at the shelf with fascination. The gun was grey-black with a brown holster beside it. There was also a small knife in a sheath beside something she didn't recognize but that resembled a softball bat, only with a black can at one end.

"Does the gun really shoot?" she asked.

"*Ja,* it has done many times, Dorrit."

"So you were a real soldier, Opa?"

He smiled. "*Ja,* your *Opa* was a very brave and talented soldier who did many things in World War II, so you can be proud of him."

"World war?"

He nodded. As far as Dorrit new, war could never be good. Not something that could make you smile.

She sat up a little and looked over her grandfather's shoulder so she could see what it was he had been looking at.

"*Nein,* you mustn't look at those pictures, Dorritchen," he said, putting his hand on the back of her neck to pull her back. "Maybe another time when you are grown up; those pictures aren't for children's eyes." She nodded but stretched forward a few centimeters more and this time wasn't pulled back.

When she saw a series of black-and-white photos in which a man with drooping shoulders was dragged over toward her grandfather, who in the following photos raised a gun and then shot the man in the back of the neck, she asked tentatively, "You were just playing, weren't you, Opa?"

He turned her face tenderly toward his and met her eyes.

"War isn't a game, Dorrit. You kill your enemies or you'd be killed yourself. You understand, don't you? If your *Opa* hadn't done everything he could back then to defend himself, why then, you and I wouldn't be sitting here today, would we?"

She shook her head slowly and moved closer to the table.

"And all these people wanted to kill you?"

She glanced over the photos; she didn't know what they were supposed to represent. They were horrifying. There were people falling down. Men and women hanging from ropes. There was a man being beaten on the back of the neck with a club. And in all of the pictures, there was her grandfather.

"Yes, they were. They were evil and loathsome. But that's nothing for you to worry about, *Schatz*. The war is over and there won't be another one. Trust your *Opa*. It all ended back then. *Alles ist vorbei*." He turned toward the photographs on the table and smiled, almost as if he took pleasure in seeing them. It was probably because he no longer had to be scared or defend himself against his enemies, she thought.

"That's good, Opa," she replied.

They heard the footsteps from the adjoining room almost simultaneously, managing to push themselves up from the chair before Dorrit's grandmother stood in the doorway between the shelves, staring at him.

"What's going on here?" she said harshly, grabbing Dorrit while giving them a piece of her mind. "There is nothing for Dorrit in here, Fritzl, didn't we agree on that?"

"*Alles in Ordnung, Liebling*. Dorrit has only just come in and is on her way out again. Isn't that right, little Dorrit?" he said calmly but with cold eyes. *You'll keep quiet if you don't want a scene,* she understood, so she nodded and followed obediently as her grandmother dragged her toward the study. Just as they were leaving the room she caught a glimpse of the wall around the doorway. It was also decorated. On one side of the door hung a large red flag with a large white circle in which a strange cross took up most of the space, and on the other side of the door there was a color photo of her grandfather, head held high and with his right arm raised toward the sky.

I will never forget this, she thought for the first time in her life.

"Take no notice of what your grandmother says, and forget what you saw in there with your grandfather. Promise me that, Dorrit; it is all just nonsense."

Dorrit's mother pushed her arms into her jacket sleeves, bending down in front of her.

"We're going home now, and we'll forget all about this, won't we, my sweet?"

"But, Mommy, why were you shouting like that in the sitting room? Is that why Daddy left? And where is he? Is he at home?"

She shook her head with a serious expression on her face. "No, Daddy and I aren't getting along at the moment, so he is somewhere else."

"But when is he coming back?"

"I don't know if he will, Dorrit. But you mustn't be upset about it. We don't need Daddy, because your grandfather and grandmother will look after us. You know that, don't you?" She smiled and caressed her cheeks. Her breath smelled of something strong. Similar to the clear liquid her grandfather poured in small glasses from time to time.

"Listen to me, Dorrit. You are so beautiful and wonderful. You're better and more intelligent than any other little girl in the whole world, so we'll manage just fine without Daddy, don't you think?"

She attempted a nod but her head just wouldn't budge.

"I think we should head home right now so we can turn on the television and see all the exquisite dresses the ladies are wearing to the prince's wedding with the beautiful Chinese girl, okay, Dorrit?"

"Then Alexandra will be a princess, right?"

"Yes, she will, just as soon as they are married. But until then she's just a normal girl who has found a real prince, and you'll also find your prince one day, sweetie. When you grow up, you'll be rich and famous because you're even better and prettier than Alexandra, and you can have whatever you want in the world. Just look at your blond hair and beautiful features. Does Alexandra have these things?"

Dorrit smiled. "And you'll always be there, won't you, Mommy?" She simply loved it when she could make her mother look as touched as she did now.

"Oh yes, my darling. And I would do anything for you."

1

Tuesday, April 26th, 2016

As always, her face bore traces of the night before. Her skin was dry and the dark circles under her eyes were more pronounced than they'd been when she went to bed.

Denise sneered at her reflection in the mirror. She had now spent an hour on damage control, but it was never good enough.

"You look and smell like a hooker," she said, mimicking her grandmother's voice as she applied her eyeliner one more time.

In the studio apartments around her, the noise signaled that the other tenants were waking up and that it would soon be evening again. It was a well-known cacophony of sounds: the chinking of bottles, the knocking on doors to bum cigarettes, and the constant traffic to and from the run-down toilet with shower that the contract described as exclusive.

The small society of Danish outcasts from one of the darker streets of Frederiksstaden was now set in motion for yet another evening with no real purpose.

After turning around a few times, she stepped toward the mirror to inspect her face close-up.

"Mirror, mirror, on the wall, who's the fairest of them all?" She laughed with an indulgent smile as she caressed her reflection with her fingertips. She puckered her lips, let her fingers slide up her hips, over her breasts, up to her neck and into her hair. She picked some fluff from her angora blouse and dabbed a little foundation on a couple of insufficiently covered blemishes on her face before stepping back with satisfaction. Her plucked and painted eyebrows together with NeuLash-enhanced eyelashes added to her overall appearance. The makeup, together with the glow of her irises, gave her a more intense look, adding with ease an extra element of aloofness.

In other words, she was ready to take on the world.

"I'm Denise," she practiced saying, tensing her throat. It was as deep as her voice could be.

"Denise," she whispered, slowly parting her lips and letting her chin drop toward her chest. The result was fantastic when she adopted this attitude. Some might interpret her look as submissive, but it was exactly the opposite. Wasn't it precisely at this angle that the hotspots—a woman's eyelashes and pupils—best caught the attention of those around her?

Totally in control. She nodded, screwing the lid of her face cream back on and piling her arsenal of cosmetics back in the bathroom cabinet.

After a quick look around the small room she realized that hours of hard work lay ahead of her: clearing away the laundry, making the bed, washing all the glasses, taking out the trash, and sorting all the bottles.

Fuck it, she thought, grabbing the duvet and shaking it and plumping the pillow, convincing herself that when one of her sugar daddies had made it this far, he wouldn't give a damn about the rest.

She sat on the edge of the bed and checked that her handbag had all the essentials she would need.

She nodded with satisfaction. She was ready to take on the world and all its desires.

An unwelcome sound made her turn to face the door. *Click, clack, click, clack,* came the limping, loathsome sound.

You're far too early, Mother, she thought as the door outside between the stairs and the corridor was pushed open.

It was almost eight o'clock, so why was she coming now? It was way past her dinnertime.

She counted the seconds, already feeling irritated as she got up from the bed when the knock came at the door.

"Honey!" she heard her mother shouting from the other side. "Won't you open the door?" Denise took deep breaths, remaining silent. If she didn't answer, her mother would surely just go.

"Denise, I know you're in there. Open up just for a moment. I have something important to tell you."

Denise sighed. "And why should I do that? I don't suppose you brought any dinner up with you?" she shouted.

"Not today, no. Oh, won't you come downstairs to eat, Denise? Just for today. Your grandmother is here!"

Denise rolled her eyes. So her grandmother was downstairs. The mere thought was enough to make her heart race and cause her to break out in a sweat.

"Grandmother can kiss my ass. I hate that bitch."

"Oh, Denise, you mustn't talk like that. Won't you just let me in for a moment? I really must speak with you."

"Not now. Just leave the dinner in front of the door, as usual." Apart from the man with the flabby skin who lived a few doors down the corridor, who had already downed his first beer of the day and was now sobbing in despair over his miserable existence, it was suddenly totally quiet out in the corridor. It wouldn't surprise her if everyone was pricking up their ears right at this moment, but what did she care? They could just ignore her mother like she did.

Denise filtered out the sound of her mother's pleas, concentrating instead on the whining coming from the loser down the hall. All the divorced men like him living in studio apartments were just so pathetic and laughable. How could they believe the future might be brighter given how they looked? They stank of unwashed clothes and drank themselves into oblivion in their pitiful loneliness. How could these cringeworthy idiots live with being so pathetic?

Denise snorted. How often had they stood in front of her door in an effort to tempt her with their small talk and cheap wine from Aldi, their eyes betraying hope of something else and more?

As if she would ever associate with men who lived in studio apartments.

"She's brought money with her for us, Denise," her mother said insistently.

Now she had Denise's attention.

"You simply have to come down with me because if you don't she won't give us anything for this month."

There was a pause before she spoke again.

"And then we *really* won't have anything, will we, Denise?" she said severely.

"Can't you shout a little louder so they can also hear you in the next building?" Denise retorted.

"Denise!" Her mother's voice was now quivering. "I'm warning you. If your grandmother doesn't give us that money, you'll have to go to the social services office because I haven't paid your rent for this month. Or maybe you thought I had?"

Denise took a deep breath, went over to the mirror, and put on her lipstick one final time. Ten minutes with the woman and then she was out of there. She had nothing but shit and confrontation coming her way. The bitch wouldn't leave her in peace for a second. She would just come with demand after demand. And if there was something Denise couldn't deal with, it was all the demands people put on her. It simply drained all the life and energy out of her.

It depleted her.

Down on the first floor in her mother's apartment there was a not un-expected stench of tinned mock turtle soup. Once in a while it might be cutlets only just past their sell-by date or rice pudding in sausage-shaped plastic packaging. There wasn't exactly entrecôte on the menu when her mother attempted to put on a spread, which the blemished silver-plated candlesticks with spluttering candles emphasized.

In this flickering artificial ambience the vulture was already seated at the center of the table, scowling and ready to attack. Denise was almost knocked out from the stench of her cheap perfume and powder, which no shop with any self-respect would demean itself to sell.

Now her grandmother parted her dry, red, blotchy lips. Maybe the vulture was preparing to smile, but Denise was not so easily fooled. She attempted to count to ten but this time made it to only three before the woman's verbal abuse began.

"Well! The little princess could finally find time to come down and say hello."

A dark and disapproving look came over the grandmother's face after a quick inspection of Denise's seminude midriff.

"Already plastered with makeup and I don't know what. No one will miss you coming, because that really would be a catastrophe, wouldn't it, Dorrit?"

"Would you stop calling me that? It's almost ten years since I changed my name."

"Since you ask so politely, yes, as it isn't something one is accustomed to from you. Then you think that name becomes you better, do you, . . . Denise? A little more French. It almost puts one in mind of the suggestively dressed ladies of the night, so, yes, maybe it is more fitting." She looked her up and down. "Then congratulations with the camouflage work, is all I can say. You've prepared yourself for the hunt, I wouldn't wonder."

Denise noticed how her mother tried to calm the mood with a slight touch of her hand on her grandmother's arm, as if that had *ever* worked. Even in that area her mother had always been weak.

"And what have you been up to, if one might inquire?" continued her grandmother. "There was something about a new course, or was it actually an internship?" She squinted. "Was it a job as a nail technician you wanted to try this time? I almost can't keep up with all the excitement in your life, so you'll have to help me. But wait, maybe you're not actually doing anything at the moment? Could that be it?"

Denise didn't answer. She just tried to keep her lips sealed. Her grandmother raised her eyebrows. "Oh yes, you're much too precious for work, aren't you?"

Why did she bother asking when she had all the answers? Why was she sitting there hiding behind her wiry grey hair in a mask of disgust? It made you want to spit at her. What stopped her from doing it?

"Denise has decided to enroll in a course to learn how to coach people," interjected her mother bravely.

The metamorphosis was enormous. Her grandmother's mouth was open, aghast; the wrinkles on her nose disappeared; and after a short pause the change was accompanied by a laugh that came so deep from within her rotten core that it made the hair on Denise's neck stand on end.

"Oh, that's what she's *decided,* is it? An interesting thought, Denise coaching other people. Just in what, exactly, if I might inquire? Is it actually possible to find anyone in this disturbed world who would want to be coached by someone who can do absolutely nothing besides dolling themselves up? In that case, the world must have come to a complete standstill."

"Mother—" Denise's mother attempted to interrupt.

"Be quiet, Birgit. Let me finish." She turned toward Denise. "I will be direct. I don't know anyone as lazy, talentless, or with so little sense of reality as you, Denise. Shall we agree that you actually can't do anything? Isn't it high time that you tried to get a job to fit your modest talents?" She waited for an answer, but none was forthcoming. She shook her head, leaving Denise in no doubt as to what was coming next.

"I have said it before and I have warned you, Denise. Maybe you think it is acceptable to just lie on your back? It's downright shocking. You're not as beautiful as you think, my dear, and certainly won't be in five years, I'm afraid."

Denise inhaled deeply through her nose. Two more minutes and she'd be out of here.

Now her grandmother turned to her mother with the same cold, contemptuous expression. "You were the same, Birgit. Thought only of yourself, never doing anything to get on in life. What would you have done without your father and me? If we hadn't paid for everything while you squandered life away in your self-obsessed megalomania?"

"I *have* worked, Mother." Her tone was pitiable. It was years since her ammunition of protests hadn't fallen on deaf ears.

It was now Denise's turn again, as her grandmother turned her attention back toward her, shaking her head.

"And as for you! You couldn't even get a job folding clothes, if that's what you think."

Denise turned around and disappeared into the kitchen with the poison from her grandmother trailing behind her.

If it was possible to see what was inside her grandmother, the ingredients could be laid out in equal measure of intense hatred, vengeance, and unending images of how different she thought everything had once been. Denise had heard the same fake nonsense over and over, and it was irritatingly hurtful every time. About what a good family she and her mother came from; about the golden years when her grandfather had had his shoe shop in Rødovre and earned really good money.

All a load of crap! Hadn't the women in this family always stayed at home and done their duty? Hadn't they been supported solely by their husbands, been meticulous about their appearance, and looked after the home?

Hell yes!

"Mother! You mustn't be too hard on her. She—"

"Denise is twenty-seven and is good for exactly nothing, Birgit. *Nothing!*" shouted the witch. "How do you two propose to survive when I'm not here anymore, can you answer me that? Don't for one second expect any significant inheritance from me. I have my own needs."

Something else they had heard a hundred times before. In a moment she would attack Denise's mother again. She would call her shabby and a failure, before accusing her of passing on all her negative qualities to her granddaughter.

Denise felt disgust and hatred right to the pit of her stomach. She hated the shrill voice, attacks, and demands. Hated her mother for being so weak and for not having been able to keep a man who could look after them all. Hated her grandmother precisely because that was what she had done.

Why wouldn't she just lie down and die?

"I'm out of here," said Denise coldly when she stepped back into the dining room.

"Oh, are you, now? Well then, you won't be having this." Her grandmother pulled a bundle of notes from her handbag and held it in front of them. One-thousand-kroner notes.

"Come and sit down now, Denise," her mother implored.

"Yes, come and sit down for a moment before you go out and sell yourself," came the next tirade from her grandmother. "Eat your mother's awful meal before you head out to find men to ply you with booze. But be careful, Denise, because the way you are, you'll never find a decent man who'll go for you! A cheap girl with fake hair and hair color, fake breasts, fake jewelry, and bad skin. Don't you think they'll see through you in a second, my dear? Or maybe you think a decent man can't tell the difference between elegance and your cheap appearance? Maybe you don't think that as soon as you open your bloodred mouth that he'll immediately discover that you know absolutely nothing and have nothing to say? That you're just a waste of space?"

"You don't know shit," snapped Denise. Why wouldn't she stop?

"Ah! Then tell me what you intend to do about *that* before you're *out of here,* as you so elegantly put it? Tell me, just so I know, because I'm dying to. What are your plans exactly? Perhaps to become a famous film star, like you rambled on about when you were young and much sweeter than now? Or perhaps you should become a world-famous painter? Just for the sake of curiosity, tell me what your next fad will be. What have you convinced your caseworker of this time? Have you maybe—"

"*Just shut up,*" shouted Denise as she leaned in over the table. "Shut up, you mean bitch. You're no better yourself. Can you do anything else other than spit out poison?"

If only it had worked. If only her grandmother had recoiled in silence, Denise would have been able to sit in peace for once and eat the abominable brown mess, but that wasn't how things went.

Her mother was shocked, digging her nails into the seat of her chair, but her grandmother was far from it.

"Shut up, you say? Is that all your feeble brain can come up with? Maybe you are under the impression that your lies and vulgarity can shock me? Well, let me tell you this. I think you'll both have to wait to receive my support until you offer me an explicit and unreserved apology."

Denise pushed herself away from the table so roughly that the tableware rattled. Should she give her grandmother the satisfaction of leaving them red-faced and empty-handed?

"Give my mother the money or I'll take it from you," she hissed. "Hand it over or you'll be sorry."

"Are you threatening me? Is that where we have ended up?" said her grandmother as she stood.

"Won't you two stop this? Just sit down," her mother begged. But no one sat down.

Denise could see all too clearly where this was leading. Her grandmother wouldn't give her a moment's peace. She had turned sixty-seven last summer and could hang on until at least ninety, the way she was going. A future of eternal criticism and arguments flashed before her.

Denise screwed her eyes tight shut. "Listen up, Grandma. I don't see any great difference between you and us. You married a nasty, wrinkled Nazi thirty years your senior and allowed him to take care of you. Is that any better?"

This gave her grandmother a jolt, causing her to take a step back as if she had been doused in something caustic.

"Isn't that the case?" screamed Denise, while her mother wailed and her grandmother walked over toward her jacket. "What is it we have to live up to? You? Give us the money, damn it!"

She snatched at the money, but her grandmother pushed it under her armpit.

Then Denise turned on her heel. She could hear the scene behind her when she slammed the door.

She stood momentarily with her back to the wall in the hallway, gasping for breath, while her mother was inside crying and spewing forth pleas. It would be to no avail; experience told her that. There would be no money before Denise made an appearance in a boring suburb with imploring eyes, cap in hand. She didn't intend to wait that long.

Not anymore.

There was a bottle of red Lambrusco in the freezer of her mini-fridge, she recalled. There normally weren't any facilities in these sorts of studio apartments besides a sink, a mirror, a bed, and a wardrobe made of laminated chipboard, but she couldn't live without her fridge. After all, it was after a couple of glasses of chilled wine that her sugar daddies were at their most generous.

She took the bottle from the freezer and noticed how heavy it was. As expected, the Lambrusco was completely frozen, but the cork was still intact, and the beautiful bottle hid a myriad of interesting uses.

2

Rose braked the scooter two hundred meters before the red light.

She suddenly couldn't remember the way. Even though she had taken the same route for so many years, it didn't look like it normally did today.

She looked around. Only ten minutes ago in Ballerup it had been the same, and now it was happening again. The coordination between her senses and her brain momentarily cut off. Her memory was playing tricks on her. Of course she knew that she couldn't drive through the viaduct and up on to Bispeengbuen on a scooter, which was allowed to travel at only thirty kilometers an hour. So where was it she was meant to turn? Was there a road a little farther along that went down toward Borups Allé? Maybe to the right?

In desperation, she rested the tips of her toes on the tarmac and pressed her lips together. "What's going on with you, Rose?" she said aloud, causing a passerby to shake her head before hurrying away.

She coughed a couple of times in frustration, feeling like she was about to throw up. She stared in bewilderment at the traffic, which resembled an endless chaos of playing pieces at war with one another. The deep humming of dozens of engines and even just the variety of colors of the vehicles caused her to break out in a cold sweat.

She closed her eyes and tried to remember what she could usually do blindfolded. For a moment, she considered turning around and driving home, but then she would have to cross the road, and how

would she manage to do that? When it came to it, could she even remember the way home? She shook her head. Why on earth should she
turn around when she was closer to the police headquarters than she
was to home? It didn't make any sense.

Rose had been in this state of confusion for several days now, and
suddenly it felt as if her body had become too small for everything it
was carrying. As if all the thoughts swarming in her head that she
couldn't cope with couldn't even be contained in several heads. If she
didn't break down when she was feeling like this, coming up instead
with all sorts of strange ideas to avoid it, she'd probably slowly
burn out.

Rose bit her cheek until it bled. Maybe the ward in Glostrup had
discharged her too early last time. One of her sisters had certainly
implied it, and there was no mistaking Assad's worried looks. Could
she really rule out that her sister might have been right? Maybe it
wasn't an alarming mix of depression and personality disorder that
were at the root of her breakdown. Was she basically just ins—?

"*Stop* these thoughts, Rose!" she blurted out, and once again a passerby turned around and stared at her.

She looked at him apologetically. It had been impressed on her that
she could call the psychiatrist if she feared a relapse. But was that
what was happening? Wasn't she just under a lot of pressure with
work, and wasn't she failing to get enough sleep? Wasn't it simply
stress?

Rose looked straight ahead and immediately recognized the broad
steps of Bellahøj Swimming Stadium and the high-rise buildings in the
background. A mild sense of relief came over her that she hadn't completely lost control, causing her to sigh and start the scooter.

Everything seemed to have fallen into place, but after a few minutes she was overtaken by a bike in low gear.

Rose looked down at the speedometer. She was doing only nineteen
kilometers an hour; apparently she hadn't even had the composure to
keep her hand on the throttle.

She wasn't really in control after all.

I really need to be careful today, she thought. *Keep to myself and try to calm my nerves.*

She dried her forehead with shaky hands, looking about attentively. Above all, she needed to make sure she didn't faint in traffic and find herself made into mincemeat by a turning truck. Surely she could manage that.

On good days, police HQ looked immensely appealing, with its light facade and imposing architecture, but today the innocent white appearance had taken on a greyish hue, the gaps between the columns more frightening and blacker than usual, almost as if they could swallow her whole.

She didn't say hello to the security guard like she normally did and only half registered the sweet look the secretary, Lis, gave her in the stairwell. It was one of those days.

It was quiet down in the cellar, where Department Q was located: no stench from Assad's mint tea, no blabbering from TV2 News on Carl's oversized flat-screen, no puzzled Gordon.

Thank God they haven't turned up yet, she thought, staggering into her office.

She slumped in front of her desk, pressing her diaphragm hard against it; it sometimes helped when she was feeling like this. It lessened the feeling of not being in control, and sometimes she also felt the benefit of pressing her clenched fist against her solar plexus.

It wasn't working just now. Friday the thirteenth, what else could she expect?

Rose stood up and closed the door to the hallway. If it was shut, the others would probably think she hadn't arrived.

Peace at last.

For now.

3

Monday, May 2nd, 2016

From the moment she walked into the social security office, Michelle's pulse quickened. The name alone had that effect despite being fairly neutral. In her opinion, names like Agony Office, Beggars' Institution, or Humiliation Center were much more fitting, but who in the public sector ever called things what they really are?

Michelle had been pushed from pillar to post in this demeaning system for years. First in Matthæusgade, then as far out as Gammel Køge Landevej, and now back to Vesterbro. Wherever she was sent, she was met with the same demands and wretched atmosphere, and nothing could erase this feeling. As far as she was concerned, they could put up as many new, polished counters with large numbers as they wanted, and provide computers so you could sit there and do their work for them—if you could figure out how to use them, that is.

The majority of people who came to this center were people she wasn't overly keen on. People who stared at her as if she was one of them. As if she would have anything to do with them in their shabby and unsightly clothes! They couldn't even manage to put an outfit together. Had she ever gone out without making an effort with her appearance? Without washing her hair or thinking about what jewelry went best together? No, she hadn't, and no matter what happened, she wouldn't dream of it.

If she hadn't had Patrick with her today, she would have just turned around at the entrance, even though she was well aware that she *had* to go in, partly because she needed to ask permission to go on vacation. Patrick had also reminded her about that.

Patrick was an apprentice electrician and Michelle's best trophy. If anyone doubted what sort of person she was, all they had to do was look at him, because he afforded her a certain status. Few were taller, broader, more muscular, or more stylishly tattooed than Patrick. No one she knew had darker or shinier hair. And it suited him to wear slim-fitting shirts. It really showed off how proud he was of his body and why he had good reason to feel that way.

Now she was sitting next to him in front of the useless caseworker, who like a ghost had followed her no matter what office Michelle was registered at. Someone in the waiting room had once said that she'd won a large sum of money. But if that was the case, why the hell didn't she just disappear from Michelle's life?

Her name was Anne-Line. A ridiculous name that only someone like her would have, so there her name was, Anne-Line Svendsen, on one of the typical metal signs on the edge of the table, and at which Michelle had been staring for the past twenty minutes. She hadn't even heard a word they were saying for the last five minutes.

"Do you agree with what Patrick has just said, Michelle?" Anne-Line Svendsen asked her now and then.

Michelle responded with a robotic nod. Would there be any reason not to? She and Patrick agreed on almost everything.

"Fine, Michelle. So you've said yes to being assigned a job at Berendsen?"

Michelle frowned. That wasn't why they'd come here. They'd come to make this woman understand that she simply couldn't cope with the stress of working and to get permission to take two weeks' vacation from her job search. Hadn't they explained a hundred times how much pressure and stress the system was putting her under? Didn't she understand what they were saying? Not everyone had had the same good fortune as this idiotic caseworker. If Michelle had been the one who had won the lottery, or whatever, would she be sitting here? Not a chance.

"Berendsen? Err, no, I don't think so," she answered.

Michelle looked imploringly at Patrick, but he was just glaring at her.

"What exactly is Berendsen?" she asked. "Is it a clothes store?"

Anne-Line smiled, and it didn't look good with her wine-stained teeth. Hadn't she ever heard of whitening?

"Well, yes. In some way it is clothes they are handling," she answered. Was she being patronizing?

"Berendsen is a well-reputed company that works primarily with washing bed linen for large companies and public institutions."

Michelle shook her head. She hadn't agreed to anything like this with Patrick; he knew that.

Anne-Line Svendsen knitted her unkempt eyebrows. "You don't seem to understand the seriousness of the situation, do you, Michelle?"

The woman turned her attention to Patrick. "You two do live together, so I assume, Patrick, that you're aware that Michelle has been illegally claiming benefits for almost six months. That's what we call fraud and it's a serious matter. Have you thought about that?"

Patrick pulled his sleeves up. The swelling from his new tattoos still hadn't gone down, which was probably why he seemed irritated.

"There must be a misunderstanding, because we don't live together. Not really. Michelle has a room out in Vanløse."

This information certainly didn't faze the caseworker. "I've spoken this morning with the family at Holmestien who rented out a room to Michelle. They inform me that Michelle hasn't paid her rent for the last five months, so she lives with you, shall we agree on that? We'll be deducting the benefits for the entire period from your wages, you must realize that, Patrick, and there will probably also be legal consequences. But presumably you're aware of the new rules."

Patrick slowly turned to direct a menacing look toward Michelle. There was something in his expression that she didn't like the look of.

"But . . ." Michelle frowned, even though it didn't look flattering. "We only came today to get permission to go on vacation. We've seen a really cheap last-minute deal leaving in two weeks, and Patrick can get the time off, so . . ." Michelle paused and bit her lip.

It was a mistake that she'd handed in the notice on the room. Or at least a mistake that she hadn't told Patrick about it, and this wouldn't be the last she'd hear of it; that was for sure. Up until now, Patrick had never laid a finger on her, which was one of the reasons she stayed with him, but just now it seemed like that situation might change.

"I see, but I don't think that's going to happen, Michelle. From Patrick's expression, it seems to me that you might have forgotten to tell him about the room. Isn't that right?" the hag continued.

Michelle nodded almost unnoticeably. Patrick suddenly stood up in front of the window, almost entirely blocking out the light. "There must be a mistake," he protested with a frown. "I'll drive out to see the family and find out why they're saying this."

He turned to face Michelle. What he said to her next wasn't to be understood as a suggestion but an order; that much was clear.

"Stay here, Michelle. Your caseworker has offered you a job, so I think you should have a chat with her about it, okay?"

She pressed her lips together as he angrily slammed the door behind him. How mean of him to abandon her in this situation. If she had had any inkling that the woman would check up on her living situation like this, she would never have given up the room. What on *earth* was she supposed to do now? They couldn't afford to lose that money, and *especially* not if there was going to be a fine on top of it.

If only Patrick could talk the family around, maybe she could rent the room again; they couldn't have any objection to that. As long as the rent was less than her benefits, it would still leave something, even if eighteen hundred kroner in rent was money she wouldn't have in her pocket.

She'd actually thought she could use that money on herself; that's why she'd done it. Wasn't Patrick happy with her appearance when she'd been to the hairdresser? Did he complain when she was wearing sexy new lingerie?

Ten minutes later, Michelle was sitting in the waiting room to compose herself and take in what had just happened. There would definitely be an investigation into the benefit fraud—the woman in the office had said as much—and they'd have to pay back a lot of money. She simply hadn't been able to deal with listening to how much it actually was. It made her feel queasy. But why did Anne-Line have to be like that? Was it because she wouldn't take that job at the laundry?

No way! Michelle shook her head, it was so depressing. She certainly wasn't going to get up at four every morning and take the S-train all the way to Helsingør to handle other people's shit-stained sheets. Much of it came directly from hospitals, where sick people had been using the linen. Who knew what they had wrong with them. It could be contagious, maybe even deadly. Hepatitis or Ebola or something like that. Just the thought made her nauseous.

No, they couldn't demand that of her. Not that.

"What did you expect, Michelle?" the woman had asked her caustically. "You haven't been able to handle a single job we've offered you. Neither have you completed any of the courses we've enrolled you in. Are you aware what a girl like you who doesn't contribute anything actually costs society? And on top of all that, now you want to go on vacation with the money you've fraudulently claimed? It can't go on like this, can it, now, Michelle?"

But why was she like this? What had Michelle ever done to her? Didn't she understand the mind-set of people like Michelle?

She was really good at looking after the apartment she shared with Patrick, making sure it was always clean and tidy. She did the laundry for both of them and could even turn her hand to a bit of cooking, and it was also her who did the shopping. Wasn't *that* worth anything?

"The social isn't going to pay for that, Michelle," Patrick had said, as if she didn't know that. But her mother and sister had always been homemakers, so why not her?

She looked down at her smart red suede boots, which she had

bought to look good for precisely this meeting, and to what avail? Michelle took a deep breath. This was all just too much to take in at once.

She scratched a little mark off her pants with her polished nails and smoothed down the sleeves of her blouse. She always did that when she couldn't keep up with what was going on.

Damn that snotty woman, Anne-Line Svendsen. If only she'd walk in front of a car and die.

Michelle looked around forlornly. Screw all the people sitting here, hanging about wearing worn-out shoes and hoods pulled down over their ears, looking like shit. It was their fault that there wasn't enough money to keep someone like Michelle on benefits. Good people like herself who didn't hurt anyone or drink or get so fat that they had to be hospitalized, who didn't stick needles in their arms or go around stealing from others. Who out of all the others sitting here could say that? She smiled at the thought, it was so stupid. Did any of these people do what they were supposed to do? Were any of them even respectable? Certainly not many.

She looked over at a pair of young women standing in the queue waiting for a number. They both appeared to be around her age, and she thought that in contrast to everyone else, they might be all right. At least the sort it was easier to identify with due to their super-nice clothes and attractive makeup.

When the two girls had taken their numbers, they looked around, catching sight of the two empty seats in the corner by Michelle, and sat down.

They exchanged respectful and knowing looks.

"Are you waiting too?" one of them asked, and five minutes later all three of them were chatting together as if they were old friends.

It was funny how much they had in common. The corner in the waiting room where they were sitting quickly became the center of good taste. Tight, light jeans and tops from Føtex or H&M, earrings, necklaces, rings and bracelets from Tiger or somewhat dubious shops on the side streets. All three of them had carefully styled hair extensions and high-heeled boots, but, as one of them said, once in a while you *could* also wear moonboots with fake fur. Yes, it was funny how alike they all were.

They had one further thing in common, much to Michelle's surprise. They were all fed up with being pushed around by the system and having all sorts of demands put upon them. And as if that wasn't enough, God help them, they all had the same caseworker: Anne-Line Svendsen.

Michelle laughed, throwing her head back. There was another girl sitting directly opposite them. Her face was furrowed and she had punk hair and eye makeup that was far too black: ugly through and through. She was staring at them in a tense and uncomfortable way, almost as if she was jealous. Michelle smiled to herself because that girl had every reason to be, with her weird fashion and odd mannerisms. She was tapping her feet as if she was hitting a drum pedal, and she looked like she was on speed or something, her glare becoming slowly more and more intense. Maybe she just needed a cigarette. Michelle knew the feeling well enough.

"Freaking weird that anyone here would want to associate with you three wet blankets," came the sudden tirade obviously directed at Michelle and the other two. "Shit is gold in comparison to people like you."

The girl next to Michelle seemed taken aback as she turned to face the punk. It was the one who had said her name was Jazmine and who was otherwise pretty cool, just not right now. But the second of the two girls, the one called Denise, reacted ice cool, giving the punk the finger, even though Jazmine tried to stop her.

"Where you come from, they probably haven't learned to tell the difference!" hissed Denise. "But shit sticks together, they say, and the first land the Nazis invaded was their own. Did you know that, you idiotic punk?"

Michelle shook her head. That was a weird thing to say.

In a split second, the mood changed; you could have cut the air with a knife. The punk girl clenched her fists. She looked like she was capable of doing anything at that moment. Michelle didn't like it one bit.

Then a number was called and the Jazmine girl breathed a sigh of relief when the punk gave in and stood up. But the look she sent their way as she walked over to the caseworker's office didn't bode well.

"Who the hell was that? It looked like you knew her," Denise asked Jazmine.

"Not someone you should give the finger to, I can tell you. She lives a few streets away from me and comes from Iceland. Her name's Birna and she's totally sick in the head. I mean, really screwed up."

4

Friday, May 13th, 2016

"**Yes, it was me** who did it. I bashed her head in with an iron rod. She really screamed but I didn't care, just kept hitting her."

Carl tapped the cigarette on the back of his hand, bringing it up to his lips a couple of times before putting it back down.

With his eyes screwed almost shut, he looked at the ID the man who sat opposite had handed him without being asked. Forty-two years old, but he looked at least fifteen years older.

"You hit her and she screamed, you say. But how hard did you hit her, Mogens? Can you show me? Stand up for a minute and demonstrate."

The slender man stood up. "You mean you want me to hit the air and pretend I'm holding the iron bar?"

Carl nodded, hiding a yawn as the man stood up. "Hit out just as you did at the time."

The man opened his mouth and screwed up his face in concentration: a pitiful sight. Sallow skin, shirt buttoned up incorrectly, pants hanging off his hips, the man grabbed his imaginary weapon and raised his arms, ready to strike.

When he let rip, his eyes opened wide with a perverse pleasure, as if he could see the body falling. He quivered momentarily, as if he had cum in his pants.

"That's how I did it," he said, smiling with relief.

"Thanks, Mogens," said Carl. "That was exactly how you killed the young substitute teacher from Bolman's Independent School in Østre Anlæg, right? And then she fell forward facedown?"

He nodded, looking at him remorsefully, like a naughty child.

"Assad, can you come in here?" Carl shouted out to the cellar hallway.

There was a sound of huffing and puffing from the corridor.

"And bring your Mexican coffee with you, Assad," shouted Carl. "I think Mogens Iversen is a bit thirsty." He looked at the man, whose face switched mechanically between friendly and subdued gratitude.

"But check first what information we have concerning the murder of Stephanie Gundersen in 2004," he shouted again.

He nodded to the man, who smiled and squinted with confidence. His expression seemed to suggest that in this moment they were almost colleagues. Two souls working together successfully to clear up an old murder case. Nothing less.

"And then you hit her again while she was lying on the grass, is that right, Mogens?"

"Yes. She screamed but I hit her three or four times more and then she just stopped. I don't remember exactly. It was twelve years ago, after all."

"Tell me, Mogens, why are you making this confession? And why now?"

His gaze faltered. His mouth hung open, quivering, revealing a set of hideous teeth in his lower jaw, which much to Carl's irritation reminded him that his own dentist had unsuccessfully tried to get hold of him three times to remind him of his yearly checkup.

It was obvious from the way the guy's diaphragm was shaking that he was fighting bravely with himself. It wouldn't surprise Carl if he suddenly started crying.

"I just couldn't keep it to myself any longer," he said, his jaw quivering.

Carl nodded while typing the man's social security number into their system. "I understand you, Mogens. A murder like that is an awful burden to carry alone, isn't it?"

He nodded gratefully.

"I can see here that you live in Næstved. That's quite a distance from Copenhagen—and from the scene of the crime in Østre Anlæg, I might add."

"I haven't always lived in Næstved," he said almost defensively. "I used to live in Copenhagen."

"But why have you come all the way here? You could just as easily have reported this gruesome crime at the local station."

"Because you're the ones who deal with the old cases. Even though it's a while ago since I read about you in the papers, it is still you lot, isn't it?"

Carl frowned. "Do you read many newspapers, Mogens?"

He tried to appear more serious than he was. "Isn't it our duty to keep up with the news and preserve the freedom of the press?" he asked.

"The woman you murdered . . . why did you do it? Did you know her? I can't imagine you've had any connection to Bolman's Independent School."

He dried his eyes. "She just walked past when it came over me."

"Came over you? Does that happen often, Mogens? Because if you've killed anyone else, now is the time to get it off your chest."

He shook his head without batting an eye.

Carl looked down over the screen. They had quite a bit of information on the man, so there was little doubt what he might come up with next.

Assad entered, placing a slim case file in front of him. He didn't look happy.

"That's four more shelves that've collapsed out in the hallway, Carl. We need to get more shelf space; they get too heavy otherwise."

Carl nodded. All this damn paperwork. They could burn the lot for all he cared.

He opened the case file. They hadn't received much down here in the cellar concerning the Stephanie Gundersen case. So it was presumably still in the spotlight up with homicide.

He turned to the last page, read the last few lines, and nodded to himself.

"You forgot the coffee, Assad," he said, still looking at the file.

Assad nodded. "For him?"

Carl winked. "So make it extra-extra-good. He needs it."

He turned toward the man while Assad disappeared out into the hallway.

"I can see you've been down here at headquarters before to make a confession in other cases, Mogens."

He nodded guiltily.

"And each time you've had such a flimsy knowledge of the nature of the case that you've been sent home, encouraged to seek psychological help and never come back again."

"Yes, that's true. But this time it *is* me who did it. You can trust me on that."

"And you couldn't just go up to homicide and tell them because they'd send you straight home with the same advice as before, am I right?"

He seemed thrilled that someone understood. "Yes, that's exactly what they'd do."

"Have you been to see a psychologist in the meantime, Mogens?"

"Yes, many times. And I've been admitted to the psychiatric ward at Dronninglund and the lot."

"The lot?"

"Yes, medication and so on." He looked almost proud.

"Right. Well, I can tell you that you're getting the same answer from me as you got upstairs in homicide. You're a sick man, Mogens, and if you come down here again with these false confessions, we'll have to detain you. I'm sure another stay in psychiatric would help you, but it's up to you."

Mogens frowned. Crazy thoughts rushed through his mind—that much was clear.

Lies seasoned with real remorse and a pinch of the facts he could have sneakily obtained were now mixed with desperation. But why? Carl had never understood people like Mogens.

"Don't say another word, Mogens. If you thought we wouldn't know about all this down here in the cellar, you were mistaken. And I also know that everything you've told us about the attack on this poor woman is downright wrong. The direction of the blow to the head, the angle the blow came from, how she fell after the attack, how many blows there were. You had nothing to do with this murder, and now it's time you went back home to Næstved, okay!?"

"Hi, here's that little Mexican coffee in a fancy cup à la Señor Assad," trolled Assad as he placed it in front of the man. "Sugar?" he asked.

Mogens nodded in silence, resembling a man robbed of his release just as he was about to orgasm.

"It's a good drink to send you off on your way, but you need to down it in one," Assad said smilingly. "It will be *so* good for you."

A hint of suspicion came over the man's face.

"If you don't do it, we'll arrest you for making a false statement, Mogens, so drink," Carl said harshly.

They both leaned in toward him, watching his reluctant grip on the cup as he brought it up toward his mouth.

"In one gulp!" Assad threatened.

His Adam's apple went up and down a couple of times as the coffee went down. It was just a question of time. Poor man.

"How much chili did you actually put in that cup, Assad?" asked Carl when they had cleaned up the remaining vomit from the table.

He shrugged his shoulders. "Not that much, but it was a fresh Carolina Reaper."

"And that's strong?"

"Yes, Carl. You saw him."

"Can it kill him?"

"Unlikely."

Carl smiled. Mogens Iversen would definitely not be bothering Department Q with that sort of nonsense again.

"Should I write the man's 'confession' in the report, Carl?"

He shook his head as he flicked through the paperwork. "I can see that it was one of Marcus Jacobsen's cases. It was too bad for him that he never managed to solve the case."

Assad nodded. "Did they ever find out what weapon was used to kill the woman?"

"Not as far as I can see. With some kind of blunt object, it says. We've heard that before."

Carl closed the case file. When the time came for homicide to archive the case, it would be their job to get to the bottom of it.

They would deal with that when the time came.

5

Anne-Line Svendsen wasn't exactly one of the happiest people you could meet, and there were plenty of reasons for this. As far as looks went, she'd been well enough endowed. A good head, an attractive enough appearance, and a body that in its day had turned men's heads. But she'd never learned to make the best of what she had, and as time went by, she'd also begun to doubt the usefulness of her physical attributes.

Anne-Line, or Anneli, as she liked to call herself, had never really managed to navigate life, as her father used to put it. When men walked by, she seemed to be looking left when they were standing on the right. When she bought clothes, she listened to what she wanted to hear rather than what the mirror showed her. When she chose what to study, she considered short-term over long-term financial gains. As time went on, she ended up in a situation she couldn't have imagined and certainly hadn't wished for.

Following a string of pitiable relationships, she was one of the 37 percent of Danes who lived alone; as a result, over the last few years, she had eaten too much and more often than not of the wrong sort of food, ending in a permanent state of disappointment about her amorphous body and almost unbearable tiredness. But the worst of all these miscalculations in life was the job she had ended up with. When she was younger, a sort of idealism had convinced her that working in the public benefits sector would aid society and also give her personal satisfaction. How could she have known back then that in the wake of the millennium there would be a series of reckless and badly thought through political decisions that now resulted in her being caught in a so-called collaboration between incompetent middle management and just as equally unrealistic political decision makers lacking in solidarity? Neither she nor her colleagues had had a chance to keep up with all the memos, directives, and analytical measures that had been thrust on them, leaving her working in a social security system that was totally misgoverned, often administered contrary to the law, and with a system for distributing social security benefits that could never work in practice. Many of her colleagues were suffering from stress, just like Anneli. She had had two months off work, lying under her duvet with dark, depressing thoughts and a total inability to concentrate on a single objective. When she finally returned to work, it was almost worse than before.

In this morass of political mismanagement, she not only was supposed to take care of the usual clients but had also been put in charge of what she regarded as a ticking time bomb in the system: a group of mostly young women who had never learned anything and who in all likelihood never would.

When Anneli went home from work she was dead tired and irritated. Not because she had been doing useful work but precisely because she hadn't. And today had been no different. In other words, it had been a terrible day.

She was shortly due to attend a routine mammogram at Copenhagen University Hospital, following which she intended to buy a couple of cakes to take home, put her feet up, and snuggle under a blanket before heading out to meet the girls from the office for their weekly yoga class at eight o'clock.

The truth was that Anneli hated any form of physical exercise and especially yoga. Her body ached all over afterward, so why on earth did she do it? When it came to it, she didn't even like her colleagues and knew for certain that the feeling was mutual. The only reason they didn't leave her out was that she could help with anything they were unsure about at work.

That was another side to Anneli.

"Have you ever experienced any discomfort in this area lately, Anne-Line?" the doctor asked as she examined the scan.

Anneli attempted a smile. She had taken part in this research project for ten years now, and the answer had never really changed.

"Only when you flatten my breast out like a pancake to take the scan," she answered dryly.

The doctor turned around. The normally expressionless face looked worried, sending an unexpected shiver down Anneli's spine.

"There's actually a lump in your right breast, Anne-Line."

Anneli held her breath. *Bad joke,* she thought in a moment of confusion.

Then the doctor turned back to face the screen. "Look here." She outlined a large mark with her pen before quickly typing something on the computer to bring up a new image.

"This scan is from last year, and there was nothing there then, Anne-Line. I'm afraid we'll have to escalate this from a routine check to treating it as an acute situation."

She didn't understand. The word "cancer" seemed to float past her. Such a shitty word.

"How come you're late?"

The four women smiled condescendingly, but she was used to it.

"Where on earth have you been? We've been twisting our bodies into all sorts of impossible positions."

She sat down at their regular table in the coffee shop and attempted a smile. "I just had so much to do today. I'm totally exhausted."

"Have a cake; that'll put a smile back on your face," said Ruth. She was the one who had worked at the social security office for twenty-two years before finally giving in and had now been working as an office assistant for a taxi company for six months. In many ways she was a bit peculiar, but she was certainly more competent than most.

Anneli wavered for a moment. Should she take this band of irrelevant people into her confidence and explain why she hadn't been able to find the energy to stretch toward the sun and free her mind to the sound of so-called world music? If she blurted it out, would she be able to control her feelings? She definitely wasn't going to start crying while the others were watching.

"Jesus, you don't seem well. Is anything wrong, Anne-Line?" asked Klara, the most approachable one.

She looked around at her colleagues, sitting there without makeup, their cake forks in full swing. What damn good would it do her if she ruined this lovely harmony with the harsh reality of her news? She didn't even know what sort of bloody lump she had.

"It's just those awful girls," she said.

"Oh, them again!" One of them nodded, looking bored. As if Anneli didn't know that no one should waste their energy on that subject, but what the hell else was she meant to talk about? She didn't have a husband at home she could complain about. No children she could boast about. No new exclusive curry-colored sofa she could show everyone a photo of and tell them just how expensive it had been.

"Yes, I know it's my problem, but it still makes me feel sick, okay? There are those in need and then there are those who are just full of it, sitting there blowing hot air, all dolled up in their boots, makeup, and hair extensions. You just can't find fault with those girls. Everything matches: bags, shoes, clothes. It's all bling, bling, bling!"

The description made the youngest of the group smile, but the rest of them just shrugged their shoulders. They were the diametrical opposite of the girls: the grey public servants who, when they finally did let their hair down, did no more than apply a little henna to their hair or wear black ankle boots with neat little studs. Of course they didn't care. Why would they? No one cared in this society anymore. They just turned a blind eye when it was time to act. How else could every-thing have gone so wrong?

"Don't take any notice of them, Anne-Line," said Ruth.

Don't take any notice? Easy enough for her to say now that she'd managed to escape that crap.

Anneli moved her hand slowly up to her breast. It suddenly felt as if the lump was huge. How hadn't she noticed it before? It was hope-fully just a side effect of the checkup.

Say something, anything. You just need to think about something else, she thought as her pulse raced.

"My brother's daughter Jeanette is the same," Klara said, saving her. "I can't tell you how often I've had to listen to my sister-in-law and brother talking about how beautiful, fantastic, and talented she was." She smiled wryly. "What talents? If she had any, she certainly never developed them. They fussed over her for years, and now she's exactly like you described, Anne-Line."

The feeling in her breast subsided a little, replaced by a strange warm sensation that brought forth her anger. Why couldn't this dis-ease take one of these useless wenches instead of her?

"So I assume Jeanette is now on benefits and has been given a long list of job offers and apprenticeships?" Anneli forced herself to ask.

Klara nodded. "She begged for a work placement at a hairdresser's for years, and when she finally got it she only lasted half a day."

A few of the others looked up. Clearly they were interested in what Klara had to say.

"Jeanette was told to clean up during her lunch break, which she protested and said was totally unfair, but that wasn't the excuse she came back home with!"

"What did she have to say for herself?" one of them asked.

"She said that she became *so* depressed listening to all the clients' problems. Simply couldn't deal with it!"

Anneli looked around. They sat there frowning, but this was An-neli's daily life. How often had she and the job center tried to find work placements and jobs for girls like Jeanette who couldn't cope with them when it came to it?

Why hadn't she just studied economics like her father had recommended? She could have been sitting with all the crooks in the parliament, enjoying the perks of the job instead of being burdened with this mismatch of dysfunctional girls and women. They were like dirty water in a bath, and Anneli wanted to pull the plug!

She had called four very well-dressed girls into a meeting today, all of whom had been unemployed for a long time. But instead of humility and basic ideas about how they might improve their situation, she was met with shameless demands for handouts from the public purse. It was really annoying, but, as always, Anneli had tried to lure them into her trap. If they didn't *want* to learn anything and couldn't hold down a placement, they'd have to accept the consequences. The law could help her that far.

Anneli's experience told her that these four harpies would be back before long with sick notes declaring them *unfit* for work, and the reasons would be myriad; when it came to that area there was no limit to their initiative: depression, dodgy knees, bad falls against the radiator with subsequent concussion, irritable bowel syndrome, and a long list of other ailments that could be neither observed nor checked. She had tried to get her line manager to take a stand against the doctors' ridiculous diagnoses, but the subject was strangely too sensitive, so the doctors continued writing undocumented sick notes, as if that was all they were good for.

One of the girls had turned up today without having extended her sick note because she had arrived too late at the doctor's surgery. And when Anneli had asked why, stressing how important it was to keep one's appointments, the bimbo had answered that she had been at a café with some friends and lost track of time. They were so socially inept and incompetent that they didn't even know when they should lie.

Anneli should have been shocked by the answer, but she was used to it. The worst of it was that it was girls like Amalie, Jazmine, whatever their names were, that were going to look after people like herself when she ended up in a nursing home one day.

Jesus Christ.

Anneli looked blankly into space.

When she ended up in a nursing home, she had thought, but who was to say that she would live that long? Hadn't the doctor implied that breast cancer of this sort should be taken very seriously? That even if they ended up removing the breast that the cancer might already have spread? That they didn't know yet?

"Why don't you just stop working as a caseworker?" said Ruth, dragging her back from her own thoughts. "You've got the money."

It was a really awkward question to answer. For almost ten years now, Anneli's circle had been under the impression that she had won a large sum of money on a scratch-off card, a delusion she had done nothing to stop. All at once she had unrightfully obtained a certain status that would have been impossible for her to achieve any other way. People still saw her as a small, boring, surly grey mouse. That was the reality of it. Only now, she was a grey mouse shrouded in mystery.

Why did she use so little of the fortune on herself, they would ask? Why did she still go around in cheap rags? Why didn't she buy expensive perfume or exotic vacations? Why, why, why? they asked.

She had cheered completely spontaneously when she scratched the card at work in the middle of the day; five hundred kroner was her record win. Her victory cry brought Ruth hurrying from the neighboring office to hear what all the commotion was about.

"I've won five hundred! Can you believe it? *Five* hundred!" Anneli had cheered.

Ruth was speechless. It was perhaps the first time she had seen Anneli smile.

"Have you heard? Anne-Line's won *five* hundred thousand!" the woman had suddenly screamed, resulting in the news spreading like wildfire throughout the entire office. Afterward, Anneli had bought cakes for everyone, thinking that she had nothing against the misunderstanding under which they were all living. It elevated her status, made her a little more visible. That she couldn't escape the lie and would later be teased for her persistence was another matter. Anneli weighed the situation and found the balance to be in favor of recognition rather than her alleged stinginess.

And now here was Ruth asking why she didn't just quit her job. What on earth could she answer? Maybe it was just a matter of time before the question answered itself. Before she was no longer in the land of the living.

"Stop working? And who would replace me?" she answered seriously. "A girl of Jeanette's age? A fat lot of good that would be."

"The first generation to be less educated than our parents!" agreed one of the others, who persisted in her belief that the bob was a fashionable haircut. "And who would employ someone who can do nothing?"

"*Paradise Hotel, Big Brother,* and *Survivor*!" one of them answered in jest.

But it was hard to see the funny side.

Anneli's cocktail of gin and tonic mixed with negative thoughts left her in a state where she could neither sleep nor stay awake.

If she had to leave this world, she was sure as hell not going to go alone. The thought of Michelle, Jazmine, Denise, or the violent punk Birna walking around laughing while she was rotting in her grave was just too depressing. The worst of it was that while she was trying to help them as best she could, she knew that they were sneering at her behind her back. Only today she had gone to call in one of her favorite clients, an elderly man who was unsteady on his feet and who had been unfit for work for almost six months, when she saw them sitting there comfortably and talking behind her back while the other clients laughed along. They said she was a miserable cow and that the only thing that could help a bitch like her was a couple of bottles of sleeping pills. Yes, they stopped when someone warned them that she had entered the waiting room, but they didn't wipe the smirks off their faces. The episode left her seething inside.

"Those damn scroungers need to be exterminated," she drawled listlessly.

One day she would head down to the side streets of Vesterbro and get her hands on a really heavy gun. And when bimbos like them were sitting waiting, she would walk out and shoot them one by one right in the middle of their powdered foreheads.

She laughed at the thought, staggering over to the display cabinet and grabbing the bottle of port. When the first four girls were down, writhing in their own blood, she would print out the client list and drive around to find and liquidate the rest of them until there were no more girls of that sort left in town.

Anneli smiled, taking another swig. It would certainly save little old Denmark a lot more money than it would lose keeping her on bread and water for the rest of her life. Especially if her life was to be as short as it seemed at the moment.

She burst out laughing at the thought. It would leave her yoga friends gawping when they read about it in the newspaper for sure.

The question was how many of them would actually visit her in prison.

Probably none.

She momentarily imagined the empty chair in the prison visiting room. Not exactly an appealing scene. Maybe it would be a better idea if she concentrated on eradicating the girls in a slightly more discreet way than simply gunning them down.

Anneli fluffed up the sofa cushion, making herself comfortable, with her glass resting on her chest.

6

Friday, May 13th, 2016

"Rose!" Carl gauged her blurred expression. She had appeared tired for some time now, but was this tiredness or was she just being contrary?

"Yeah, you probably don't want to hear this, but my patience has finally run out asking you to complete the report for the Habersaat case. I've begged you for it at least twenty-five times, and I can't be bothered reminding you about it anymore, okay? It will be exactly two years ago tomorrow that we cleared up the case of June Habersaat's death. *Two years,* Rose! Get with the program!"

She shrugged her shoulders. It was one of those days again where she pottered around in her own world doing her own thing.

"If you think it's so important, you can write it yourself, Mr. Mørck," she said.

Carl lowered his head. "You know full well that whoever starts a report in Department Q is the one who finishes it. How often do we need to discuss this? You've got all the notes in there, so just get it finished, Rose."

"Or what, Carl? You'll fire me?"

Their eyes met. "Listen here, missy! It's reports like this that justify the existence of Department Q. Or should I be equally ridiculous and ask if you're out to ruin the department?"

Rose responded again with the same provocative shrugging of her shoulders. "What do we need this report for? I don't get it. The murderer confessed and also happens to be dead. No one reads the reports, anyway."

"Very likely, Rose, but they're registered. And unfortunately, even though June Habersaat confessed to the murder of Alberte to Assad and myself just before she drew her last breath, it hasn't exactly been documented, has it? It's her word against the unmistakable fact that she didn't make a written statement to that effect. Of course she was the murderer, but we don't have hard evidence to back that up, so the case is still open in principle. That's how the system works, however idiotic it might sound."

"Right! Well then, maybe I can just report that we never solved the case."

"Damn it, Rose. Just get that shit finished before I lose my temper with you. I don't want to talk about it anymore. Finish that report so it makes our internal statistics look better. It's the only thing left in the case, now that we've cleared the cellar of all the material concerning it. Then we can put it behind us and move on with some of the other awful cases we've been boring ourselves with over the last few weeks."

"Put it behind us? That's easy for *you* to say, but what about me?"

"Stop, Rose! I want that report on my desk first thing tomorrow, got it?" He slammed his hand on the table so hard it hurt. He certainly hadn't needed to go that far.

She stood there fuming for a moment before rushing to her office, swearing as she went.

As expected, less than thirty seconds later Assad stood in front of him, eyes agog and resembling a question mark.

"I know, I know," said Carl, exhausted. "It's a complete mess with Rose, but there are always new cases waiting to be solved and archived. She's the one who always hounds us about that. We need to be on top of things with the old cases and keep up-to-date with the new ones. It's an important part of our work, so don't look at me like that. Rose just needs to do what's expected of her."

"Yeah, but it still wasn't very clever, Carl. I can scent that she's not happy."

Carl looked at him with confusion. "Scent! You mean sense, don't you, Assad? Scent is something else."

"Yeah, yeah, whatever you say. But keep in mind how much the Habersaat case affected her. It was due to that case that she had a breakdown and decided to have herself admitted to the psychiatric ward—and she's still under observation. Why else would it take her so long to write that report?"

Carl sighed. "As if I don't know that. The similarity between Christian Habersaat and her dad triggered something in her."

"Yeah, and then the hypnosis, Carl. Maybe she remembered everything about her dad too clearly after that. He was killed right in front of her."

Carl nodded. The hypnosis hadn't been good for any of them. Memories of events they'd rather forget had come to the surface. Carl had had sleepless nights and weird dreams for a long time after, and it was much the same for Assad. So it was reasonable to assume that memories of the terrible accident at the steel plant that cost Rose's dad his life had resurfaced during the hypnosis and plagued her ever since, even if she would never admit it.

"I think that report is going to take her back to a dark place, Carl. Do you think it's such a good idea? Can't I write it for her?"

Carl looked worried. He could imagine the result. Only Assad had ever understood what his reports actually contained.

"Assad, that's good of you, and of course we need to keep an eye out for Rose, but she needs to be able to cope with that assignment. I'm afraid I don't have time to discuss it further."

He looked at the clock. The witness statement in the district court was scheduled to start in twenty minutes, so he needed to get going. It was the final hearing before sentencing in one of their cases, and who was going to write up the report for that? Him, who else? Carl, who hated every form of routine except smoking and taking a nap with his feet up on the table.

He had just made it to the hallway when Rose, looking as white as a sheet, appeared in front of him and made it clear that if he pushed her to have anything to do with that report, she'd go home sick.

Maybe he mouthed off a few unchoice words, but blackmail wasn't going to cut it with him, and then he left.

The last thing he heard on his way up the stairs was Rose's shaky voice shouting that she'd do what he expected but that he would damn well have to live with the consequences.

7

Wednesday, May 11th, 2016

"**Haven't you got anything** in the fridge, Denise?"

He sprawled himself on the mattress without covering anything. His skin was glistening, his eyes wet, and he was still out of breath. "I'm dying of hunger here. You know how to drain a man of energy, honey."

Denise wrapped her kimono tightly around her. Rolf was the one of her sugar daddies who came closest to giving her a feeling of what one might call intimacy. The men were normally halfway out the door before they'd even come, but this one had no wife waiting for him at home and no job where he needed to be at any given time. She had met him on an all-inclusive vacation to Alanya, which turned out to be the cheapest holiday she had ever been on.

"Come on, you know I haven't, Rolf. You'll have to make do with the crumbs in that bag there."

She pointed at the crumpled paper bag as she walked over to the mirror.

Had his grip on her neck left a mark? Her other sugar daddies wouldn't be happy about that.

"Can't you pop down to your mother's and see what she's got? I'll pay you handsomely for it, sugar baby." He laughed. He was all right as far as that area was concerned.

She stroked the skin under her chin. There was a slight redness but nothing that would draw attention.

"All right then, but don't go expecting room service next time. This isn't a hotel, you know."

He tapped the sheet lazily, sending her a commanding look. A little resistance always turned him on, and the fee would reflect this.

It smelled stuffy down in the apartment and all the lamps were turned on. It was dark out on the street, but it was like daylight in here; her mother had kept it like this since her grandmother died. She seemed to be frozen in time.

Denise noticed her mother's arm first, hanging over the edge of the sofa holding a burned-out cigarette, a pile of ash on the carpet next to her, before noticing the rest of her pathetic decay. Her mouth was hanging open, her wrinkled face without makeup, and her hair matted with the woolen blanket under her. What else could you expect when you turned up unannounced?

The kitchen was complete chaos. Not just the usual, where the washing up, empty liquor bottles, packaging, and scattered food remains bore witness to laziness and a lack of discipline, but a totally surrealistic inferno of colors of the sort you would expect from rancid food, spread over the walls and every available surface. Her mother had apparently gone on a bender right in the middle of things; that's the way it was when she had been drinking and decided to sod the consequences. She'd have a chance to think about those when she sobered up.

Naturally, the fridge was almost empty. If she was going to feed Rolf, it would have to be with sour yogurt and eggs from God only knew when. It wasn't exactly what he'd paid for, but who knew what he'd want when he was ready for action again.

"Is that you, Denise?" croaked a rough voice from the sitting room.

She shook her head. She'd de damned if she was going to listen to her mother's drunken rambling at this time of night.

"Won't you come in here? I am awake."

Wasn't that exactly what she was afraid of?

They both looked at each other for a moment, neither of them with any particular sympathy.

"Where've you been the last couple of days?" her mother asked, with dried spit in the corners of her mouth.

Denise looked away. "Here and there."

"The coroners are finished, so your grandmother's body will be released soon. Will you come with me to the funeral director?"

She shrugged her shoulders. That would have to be answer enough for now if she wanted to avoid a discussion. After all, she had a man lying in bed upstairs on the top floor.

8

Thursday, May 12th, 2016

The crumpled newspaper on the kitchen table reminded him of what he had lost. In the space of four years, he had gone from being a happily married man, with a job that demanded respect and offered exciting challenges, to this abyss of loneliness. In these four years, his reduced status and increased lack of self-awareness had become more acute in a way he couldn't have predicted. He had been through an awful period of illness with the best friend he had ever had. He had witnessed his beloved wife wither away, holding her hand for months while she cried in agony, just as he had also held her hand when the pain shot through her one final time before allowing her to finally find peace. Since then, he had smoked sixty cigarettes a day and not done much else. Everything in the apartment smelled of stale tobacco, his fingers resembled mummified leather, and his lungs wheezed as if they had a puncture.

His elder daughter had warned him four times that if he didn't mend his ways he would soon be joining their mother in her grave, a statement hidden in the clouds of smoke, waiting for him to act on it. Maybe that was what he actually wanted—to smoke himself to death and free his tortured soul, eat until he popped and just let himself go. What other option did he have?

But then that newspaper had turned up from nowhere. The front page alone had thrown him off-balance. His curiosity awakened, he had put his cigarette down in the ashtray and picked up the newspaper from the pile under the mail slot. He even ventured the impossible, holding the newspaper half a meter in front of him in an attempt to read it without his reading glasses.

Marcus Jacobsen breathed heavily while reading. The time before everything terrible in his life had happened suddenly felt very present. Inadvertently, impulses shot through his brain synapses, which hadn't been in use for years. Repressed abstractions were woven together, creating new possibilities and images over which he had no control.

All the thoughts rushing through his head gave Marcus a headache, and what good were they anyway? There had been a time, before he retired, when he had had the power to follow his whims, but now he didn't even know if anyone would listen to him. But somewhere in his idle existence, there was still part of him that thought and worked as a crime investigator. He had had many successes in his decades on the force. And as head of homicide in the now defunct Department A, he had had a success rate that none of his predecessors had ever been able to match, so he had good reason to look back on his career with pride. But as anyone who has worked in homicide knows, it isn't the cases that were solved one thinks about in the quiet, dark hours, but those that weren't solved. These were the cases that constantly kept him awake at night, the ones that made him see the perpetrator around every corner. And dark thoughts about how the perpetrators of these murders of innocent victims still walked the street among normal law-abiding citizens gave Marcus goose bumps. Sympathy for those left behind who were unable to find closure gave rise to an irrational sense of shame for having let them down, something that pained him in particular. The torment of all the circumstantial evidence that couldn't be proved, and the leads that hadn't been spotted. But what good did this do him?

And then he quite literally fell over this front-page story in the pile of unread newspapers cluttering the floor in the corridor, reminding him that there would be no rest so long as people and their capacity for evil were given free rein.

He skimmed the report one more time. He had been wondering what to do about it for ten days now, but something had to happen. Of course, he knew that Lars Bjørn and his team at police HQ must have tried to link this murder to similar unsolved cases, but were they on the same track as him? That the coincidences that gnawed away at him between this new case and the old case were simply too obvious to be mere coincidences.

He read the article again, summarizing the facts.

The murder victim had been identified as the sixty-seven-year-old Rigmor Zimmermann. She had been found in the King's Garden in Copenhagen, behind a fashionable restaurant, and that it was murder was irrefutable. No one could hit the back of their own head with such force.

The postmortem revealed that the victim had suffered a single but deadly blow with a reasonably broad and rounded object. The newspaper characterized the victim as a perfectly average retired woman with a quiet and normal life. Ten thousand kroner had disappeared from her handbag, which her daughter could say with certainty had been in the bag when her mother left her apartment on Borgergade, shortly before she was attacked. As a result, the motive was seen as financial, with subsequent attack and murder, often referred to as a robbery murder. It was still unclear what the murder weapon had been, and probably as a result of the downpour and cold April weather, no one had witnessed the crime, which a waiter at Restaurant Orange-riet thought must have happened between quarter past eight—when he had popped out for a cigarette—and half an hour later, when he went out for another nicotine fix and found the body.

There were no other real facts reported, but Marcus could picture both the body and the crime scene. The victim's face was pressed down in the damp earth due to the force of the fall, and her body had also left an imprint on the ground. It had been a surprise attack from behind; the deceased hadn't stood a chance. Exactly the same circumstances he had been mulling over years ago. Back then the victim had been a temporary teacher at Bolman's Independent School, one

Stephanie Gundersen; she was quite a bit younger than this latest victim, but otherwise the most obvious difference was that the first body hadn't been urinated on.

Marcus sat for a moment, recalling the circumstances surrounding the discovery of the first victim. He thought about it a lot. And he was no stranger to convincing himself that thinking about it was pointless.

In his opinion, the murderer had struck again. The same area in the city, with only six to seven hundred meters between the two crime scenes.

He shook his head in frustration and regret. Why hadn't they called him so that he could have seen the crime scene while it was still fresh?

For some time he stared passively at his phone, which seemed to scream at him from where it lay on the edge of the kitchen table.

Pick me up and do something about it, it seemed to say.

Marcus looked away. The case was now seventeen days old, so it could wait a while more.

He nodded to himself, reaching out for the pack of cigarettes. He needed a couple more before he could know what the heck he was going to do.

9

Thursday, May 12th, 2016

"**Wow, this place is** super-nice," said Michelle, settling herself on a corner sofa and pulling her bag over.

Denise yawned, feeling the effects of last night, and looked around. She tried to see the place with Michelle's eyes. The café was only half-full, and the clientele, a small but mixed group of unemployed, students, and two women on maternity leave, were about as lively as a funeral cortege in the rain. Denise could think of cozier places than this run-down café, but this time it was Jazmine who had chosen the place.

"I really needed to get out of the house," continued Michelle. "Patrick's gone crazy at the moment; I almost don't dare speak to him. We were supposed to go on vacation together, too, but that isn't going to happen now."

"Why don't you just throw him out?" asked Denise.

"I can't; it's his apartment. Yeah, everything is his actually." Michelle sighed, nodding to herself. She obviously knew that she was in deep water. "I almost didn't come to meet you because I've got zero money and Patrick doesn't give me any."

Denise bent down toward the floor, pushing the bottle of wine in the bag a little to one side so she could get to her purse.

"He's an asshole, that Patrick. Forget him, Michelle. I can give you money," she said, pulling out her purse and noticing the expression on their faces when she opened it.

"Here, take it," she said, putting a note in front of Michelle from a bundle of one-thousand-kroner notes. "Now Patrick can just kiss your ass for the next week."

"Err, thanks. That's . . ." Michelle caressed the note with her fingers. "I don't know . . . I mean, I probably can't pay you back."

Denise waved her hand dismissively in the air.

"And if Patrick finds out . . . I don't know . . ."

"There was a lot of money in that purse," Jazmine said dryly. They clearly wanted to ask how she had come by so much money when she was on the dole just like them.

Denise scrutinized Jazmine's facial expression. Up until now, they had met each other only three times, and although she liked the others, the question was how much they liked *her*.

She smiled. "Let's just say I'm good at saving up."

Jazmine laughed sarcastically. It was apparent that she'd heard better lies than that. She suddenly turned her attention instinctively toward the door; Denise followed her gaze.

Jazmine looked worried when she saw the first girl who walked in through the café door. Squinting eyes, jaw muscles working away under her soft skin, and a definite frown. Like a hunted animal standing on its hind legs, she scanned the movements outside the door, and when the next girls came in she leaned in toward the other two.

"Do you remember the punk who was provoking us at the benefits office the first time we met?"

They nodded.

"The girls there are called Erika, Sugar, and Fanny, and when they're here, it's only a matter of time before Birna arrives. Just wait and see."

"Shouldn't we just go somewhere else?" Michelle asked nervously.

Denise shrugged her shoulders. She didn't give a damn about that black-clad nothing. She didn't scare her.

"They've got a gang: the Black Ladies," continued Jazmine. "They're known in the area, and not for anything good."

"I wonder why," said Denise as she inspected their totally hideous clothes and makeup. Black, yes, but not ladies.

They were far from being the only people in the café who only moments later noted Birna's arrival and the demonstrative way in which she slouched at the table with the rest of the gang. One of the women who was breastfeeding slowly put her breast back in her blouse and stood up, nodding to her friend. They put a couple of notes on the table, packed their belongings, and left without saying a word, avoiding any eye contact with the women in black, who were fidgeting in their seats, staring down everyone around them.

When their leader spotted Jazmine, she stood up from the table, staring directly at their group, making it clear that this area was out of bounds so long as she was there.

Denise took a quick drink from her cup before standing up just as demonstratively, despite Jazmine pulling on her sleeve. Standing in her high heels, she was taller than Birna, but this just made Birna clench her fists even harder.

"We're leaving," whispered Jazmine, getting up slowly. "They'll kill us if we stay. Come on."

Perhaps the gang misread Jazmine's reaction, because all at once the members of the Black Ladies stood up.

An unease spread in the area behind the bar, Denise observed. The two female bartenders stepped backward toward the stockroom while the male waiter turned his back on the guests and put his cell phone to his ear.

"Come on, Denise." Jazmine took her by the arm but Denise shook herself loose. Did they think they could order her about? That just because she was beautiful and feminine she was weak?

"They've been inside for GBH, Denise. Fanny, the one with the crew cut, has stabbed people," whispered Jazmine.

Denise smiled. Hadn't her granddad taught her what to do with enemies? If anyone here expected her to scamper away, they didn't know Denise or her background.

"One of them lives just three streets from me, so they know where to find me," Jazmine whispered again. "So let's get out of here."

Denise turned to Michelle, but she didn't look scared like Jazmine, just determined.

Birna stood in the middle of the floor glaring, but this had no effect on Denise. Perhaps it should have when Birna pulled out a bundle of keys from her pocket and one-by-one stuck the keys between her fingers, making a menacing knuckle-duster.

Denise smiled wryly, stepped out of her high heels, picked them up, and pointed the stilettos directly at her opponent.

"Birna, remember our agreement," shouted the man behind the bar, pointing his cell phone at her threateningly.

Birna reluctantly turned to face him, hesitated for a moment at the sight of the phone, and put the keys back in her pocket without batting an eye.

"You've got two minutes and then they'll be here," warned the waiter.

The other members of the gang stared in anticipation at their leader, but Birna didn't react. She simply turned to Denise with an ice-cold stare.

"Put your stilts back on, dolly bird," she said in her heavy Icelandic accent. "We'll be waiting for you, don't you worry. Then I'll shove those shoes so far down your throat that you won't know what hit you. And as for you, you Neanderthal." She turned to face Jazmine. "I know where you live, all right?"

"Get out of here, Birna. They're on their way," the waiter insisted.

She stared at him, giving him a thumbs-up. Then she waved her hand at her clique of girls and they all left without closing the door behind them.

Before Denise had managed to put her shoes back on, there was a deep humming sound from out on the street and the waiter walked over toward the entrance.

Three large motorbikes with pumped-up riders wearing leather vests and armbands spoke with the man from the café. Then they waved to each other before the motorcycles disappeared into the distance.

The waiter looked at Denise as he walked past her. His expression was respectful but not exactly friendly, and when a couple of the regular café patrons began clapping, he sent them a look that made them stop.

Denise was satisfied with herself for having taken the lead, but when she saw Jazmine's face, she realized that a power struggle between them might just become a reality.

"Yeah, sorry, Jazmine," she said appeasingly. "I couldn't help myself. Do you think it will be a problem for you?"

Jazmine scowled. Of course it was a problem. She took a deep breath, smiling faintly at Denise. The apology was apparently accepted.

"Shall we pay and get out of here?" said Denise, taking out her purse as Jazmine rested her hand on hers.

"Are we agreed that we're friends?" she asked.

In the background, Michelle nodded enthusiastically in consent.

"Yes, of course," answered Denise.

"So we're a team in everything, right? Decisions, actions, and what we want to do."

"Fine by me, yeah."

"All three of us have secrets, but it doesn't need to be like that forever. Are we also agreed on that?"

Denise hesitated. "Okay," she answered finally. Michelle's consent was more unreserved, but what the hell sort of secrets could she possibly have?

"Then I want to reveal one of my secrets. And I'm paying, okay?" She waited until they had both nodded in agreement before continuing. "I'm flat broke," she said with a laugh. "But it doesn't normally stop me."

She nodded in the direction of the corner. "See the one with the work pants? He's staring at us and has been ever since we arrived."

"I noticed," said Michelle. "Why does he think we're interested in him and his dirty pants? And why didn't he stand up for us when we were being threatened by that bimbo?"

"Have you noticed how he's been undressing us with his eyes?"

Denise turned around. The guy had a short thick neck and was smiling slyly at them from behind his half-empty beer bottle, while his friends leaned in over the table with folded arms. He was obviously the self-appointed pack leader.

Jazmine looked directly at the man, waving him over to them. He looked momentarily confused, but there was no doubting that he was interested.

"Watch and learn," whispered Jazmine as she raised her head toward the man when he stood before them in a haze of cheap aftershave.

"Hi," said Jazmine. "You look good. And that's why you're the one who'll pay our tab."

He looked taken aback, turning toward his friends, who sat back in their seats attentively.

He caught Jazmine's gaze again. "Pay? Why should I do that?"

"Because you've been eyeing us up. Haven't you been imagining what our pussies look like?"

He pulled his head back and was just about to protest when Jazmine interrupted.

"You can see mine, but then you'll have to pay. I've got a photo of it that my boyfriend took."

He smiled. He obviously knew what the deal was even if he wasn't entirely sure what it entailed.

"You'll just show me some other pussy you found on the Internet." He turned toward his friends and laughed. Out of earshot, they didn't fully understand what was going on but laughed back anyway.

"Are you in or not?" Jazmine took out her cell phone from her purse. "You just have to pay the bill. We don't have any money."

He stood for a moment, swaying in his work boots.

Denise tried to keep a straight face. Jazmine was totally cool and the man was caving in: brilliant to watch.

The bricklayer turned to the bar. "Waiter! How much do these ladies owe?" he shouted.

He checked the cash register. "One hundred and forty-two," he answered.

The guy turned toward Jazmine. "I don't normally pay to see

pussy, but I'm a gentleman and can't refuse to help ladies in distress."
He took out a plump wallet and found the money.

"Keep the change," he said, slamming the notes down on the bar.
How generous: eight kroner as a tip.

He's working on the side, thought Denise, staring at the wallet. She
had a builder sugar daddy who was much the same.

Jazmine held out her phone and let him have a good, thorough look.

He nodded, breathing a little heavier through his slightly dilated
nostrils. He alternated his gaze between Jazmine and the screen. *If you
want more than that, I'm game,* his expression said. Denise was impressed.

"If you want to see one where I'm not shaved, it'll be two hundred
extra," she offered.

The guy was apparently in his own world, his neck and ears flushed
with blood.

He put down two hundred on the table. "But then you have to send
it to my e-mail." He gave her the address letter by letter while
Jazmine typed.

When he heard a tone on his cell a few seconds later, he turned to
his friends, sent them a good-bye glance, and left.

"Do you think he's running straight home to jerk off?" Michelle
said, laughing.

It was easy money. Denise nodded appreciatively. "Was that your
secret?" she asked.

Jazmine shook her head. "Hell no. That was just a trick. I'll tell you
the secret later." She shoved the two hundred kroner in her back
pocket, packed her handbag, and suggested they leave.

But then a guy stood up from one of the tables by the bar and
slammed another two hundred kroner note in front of them.

"I saw what you did. I want in on it."

Jazmine smiled, taking her phone out of her bag.

Denise looked the man over. There were many reasons why he was
standing there. Even though he was no more than thirty-five, his face

had lost its glow. No ring on his finger to indicate a serious relationship. His clothes were nice enough but put together wrong. Dandruff on his unironed jacket. A typical guy with a permanent job and no one to come home to.

Denise didn't like him. Frustrated men could explode at any moment, which was exactly what happened.

In a surprising move, he grabbed Jazmine by the wrist so he could soak up the image on the screen in his own good time. Denise was about to intervene, but Jazmine shook her head. She'd deal with this herself.

"I want to see the whole body," said the guy. "Two hundred is too much for a few pubes."

Cocky, thought Denise, as alarm bells rang.

"Come on, bitch. Full frontal or I won't let go."

Jazmine wriggled loose, pulling her cell phone back. Even Michelle showed initiative, grabbing the two hundred kroner from the table and stashing it away.

Then the guy started shouting, calling them whores and thieves and saying they all needed a knock to the head.

That was when the waiter got involved, demonstrating that he could make things happen. He masterfully grabbed the man, asking him whether he should call the gang back or if he would leave the place quietly.

The guy managed to spit on the table before storming out the door.

The waiter shook his head, taking the cloth from his apron.

"Lively young women, aren't you," he said as he wiped away the spit. "A little too lively for a Thursday afternoon for my taste," he said. "So when that guy has reached the end of the street, I'd appreciate it if you'd find yourself another hunting ground."

It was difficult to argue with.

Five minutes later they were standing out on the street, bent over double laughing. Denise was about to say that they could learn a lot from each other but was interrupted by the unmistakable stench of aftershave from the bricklayer Jazmine had just pulled a number on. She turned toward the entrance of the building next to them just as the bricklayer stepped out.

Threatening, determined, and with lightning speed, he grabbed the strap of Jazmine's bag and, despite her attempts to pull away, managed to stick his hand in and pull out her cell phone.

"Give me the pin code or I'll smash your phone on the cobbles," he warned, raising it in the air above his head to show he meant business.

Jazmine's expression showed that she knew this was a fight she couldn't win, that the easy money would soon be back where it had come from, and that her cell phone was worth more than she stood to lose.

"Four-seven-one-one," she said, watching him type in the code and open her picture gallery. He scrolled back and forth before finding the file he was looking for. When he opened it, Jazmine's hand was already in her back pocket to get the money.

"I knew it!" he shouted. "You bitch, this isn't you!" He shoved a photo in her face of the woman who had provided the titillation. There was apparently a whole series.

Jazmine shrugged her shoulders. "We couldn't pay and you were the one who seemed most like a gentleman; wasn't that the word you used to describe yourself?"

Jazmine's smile, intended to accompany this carefree confession, was suddenly wiped off her face as the bricklayer lunged at her, knocking her flat to the ground.

He was just about to kick her where she lay but stopped mid-action and fell quietly to his knees. The bottle of wine Denise had brought to their get-together was obviously more than his bull-like neck could take.

The cobbles on the pavement by the canal on Gammel Strand were warm with the rays of the sun when they sat down under the railings side by side with another group of young people who were sitting with their legs against the wharf and the water beneath them. The summer sun was coming out and the light was sharp, so Jazmine's cheek wasn't easy to miss.

"Cheers," said Denise, passing on the bottle of red wine.

"And cheers to you." Jazmine gestured toward Denise, raising the bottle to her mouth and taking a good swig. "And also to you," she said to the bottle before passing it on to Michelle.

"You shouldn't have kicked him so hard when he was lying there, Jazmine," Michelle said quietly. "I didn't like him bleeding from his head. Why did you do it? He was already unconscious."

"I was raised badly," she offered.

They looked at each other for a moment and then Michelle started to laugh. "Selfies!" she shouted and pulled out her phone.

Denise smiled. "Watch you don't drop it in the water," she said as they nudged up closer to one another.

"We look damn good together, don't you think?" Michelle held out her cell at arm's length. "There aren't many here with better legs than us," she said, laughing.

Denise nodded. "That was a good one you pulled at the café, Jazmine. I think we have the makings of a good team."

"Then maybe we can call ourselves the White Ladies," Michelle said with a laugh. Two swigs and the red wine was already having an effect on her.

Denise smiled. "You were going to tell us a secret, Jazmine. How about now?"

"Okay. But I don't want to hear a bad word about it afterward. No judgment or shit. I've had enough of that from home, all right?"

They swore silently, raised their hands, and laughed. How bad could it be?

"When we met each other it was only the third time in six years that I'd gone to the social to beg, but I've actually been on benefits the whole time."

"How?" Michelle sounded especially interested. Not surprising in her situation.

"I make sure I'm pregnant and go through with the pregnancy. I've done it four times now."

Denise's head shot forward. "You've *what*?"

"Yeah, you heard. You look a state for a while—stomach, tits, and whatnot—but I've always regained my figure." She patted her flat stomach. Mother to four children and not a visible trace.

"Have you got a guy?" Michelle asked naively.

Jazmine laughed without making a sound. That was obviously the point.

"Adopted, all four. The system is simple. Get pregnant with some-one, complain about pelvic joint pain or some other bullshit, and the social will come to your rescue. When they start making noises about you finding work, you just get pregnant again. They remove the baby automatically after a while, and then you're pregnant again and saved one more time. It's been a few months now, so lately I've just been go-ing to the meetings at the social." She laughed.

Michelle reached out for the bottle. "I wouldn't be able to do *that*," she said. "I really dream about having kids even if it probably won't be with Patrick." She took a swig and turned to Jazmine. "So you don't know who the father is?"

Jazmine shrugged her shoulders. "Maybe for one of them, but it's completely irrelevant."

Denise followed the ripples on the water when yet another tour boat had sailed past them. Jazmine wasn't like anyone she'd met be-fore. A remarkable woman.

"Are you pregnant now?" she asked.

Jazmine shook her head. "But maybe in a week. Who knows?" She tried to force a smile. It was obvious that there were other scenarios she'd rather imagine.

Was she maybe thinking that it was time to consider new survival strategies?

"What about that girl gang? What if you're pregnant and they as-sault you? Have you thought about that?" asked Michelle.

She nodded. "I'm moving away from the area, anyway." She shrugged her shoulders apologetically. "Yeah, I still live at home. Haven't I mentioned that?"

They didn't answer, but then she hadn't expected them to.

"'Next time you're pregnant, I'll kick you out,' my mom shouts all the time." Jazmine pursed her lips. "I just need to find a place; then I'm out of there."

Denise nodded. Untenable living situations for all three of them.

"If you don't dream about having kids, what do you dream about, Jazmine?" asked Michelle. She obviously hadn't moved on.

Jazmine looked blank. Those sorts of dreams were obviously not something she mulled over on a daily basis.

"Choose whatever you want," Michelle suggested, trying to help her along.

"Okay. Then it's to beat up that lousy caseworker Anne-Line Svendsen and never have to go back to the social."

Denise laughed and Michelle nodded. "Yeah, just be totally free. Maybe some sort of reality TV show where you can win money; then you could do whatever you wanted."

Then they turned toward Denise with an encouraging look.

"Oh, is it my turn? But you've already mentioned everything. Win a load of money and sort out that bitch caseworker once and for all."

They looked at one another in silence, as if picturing how they could put an end to all their problems.

10

"Frustration" was a moderate word to describe Carl's state of mind after having waited in vain for more than half an hour in the courtroom. Copenhagen resembled a bombsite now more than ever due to the terrible coordination of roadworks and diversions as a result of building the metro; be that as it may, if he and the witnesses could manage to turn up on time despite the difficulties, then the damn judge should be able to manage it too.

All things considered, it was a real bummer of a case, and now it had been postponed again. And to make matters worse, it wasn't even a case within Carl's remit; he had just been on a routine investigation in the vicinity when the woman screamed for help from inside a house.

Carl glanced over at the glowering defendant. Three months earlier he had been standing in front of Carl with a claw hammer, threatening that if he didn't leave his property he'd plant the hammer in his head. It was one of the few times Carl had wished that he had had his service revolver with him. So he did what the man asked and left.

When he returned twenty minutes later with backup and kicked the door in, the man had already cracked his Filipino girlfriend's jaw and trampled on her, breaking every rib on her breastbone. Definitely not a pretty sight.

Carl thought again that if only he had heeded his basic training from the police academy and had his revolver in his holster under his jacket, he would have been able to prevent what happened.

No, it wouldn't happen again. After that incident he had been more particular about remembering to put on his shoulder holster. And now that ugly bugger was sitting there with his Neanderthal face, smirking at him as if he could get away without any punishment because the judge was a tardy slowpoke. True, the guy didn't have "idiot" written on his forehead, but it wasn't far off. At least four years was Carl's bet for what the guy would get for his violence, because it was certainly not his first offense. One just had to hope that someone would give him a good beating in the slammer so he could learn what it felt like to be battered so brutally.

"You need to go up to Lars Bjørn," the people in security informed him when he was back at HQ.

Carl frowned. Was he some sort of rookie to be ordered where to go and when? He'd just wasted an hour and a half on nothing; wasn't that enough for today?

"And Bjørn asked us to give him a heads-up when you were on your way, so just straight up the stairs and to the left, Carl." They laughed behind him.

What did he care what they had been asked to do?

Down in the basement corridor, Gordon was standing waving his arms. "We've got a problem," he managed to blurt out before noticing Carl's moody expression.

"But, err, maybe it's better if Assad explains it," he was quick to add.

Carl stopped. "Explain what?"

Gordon stared at the ceiling. "It's something to do with our department that Lars Bjørn came up with. Something about us not solving enough cases."

Carl looked surprised. It was only fourteen days ago that he had calculated the percentage of solved cases in Department Q as sixty-five over the last two years, which was in no way less than it had been in previous years. Viewed objectively, it was far more than what could be expected considering that their cases were those that the rest of the force had been unable to solve. A 65 percent success rate and 65 percent of perpetrators no longer loose on the streets. What was Bjørn talking about?

"Take this and put it on my desk." He shoved the legal papers into Gordon's arms, heading directly toward the endless stairs that led up from the basement.

He'd show Bjørn how to read statistics; that was for sure.

"Yes, Carl, unfortunately it is completely accurate." Lars Bjørn looked almost sad about it, but Carl hadn't fallen for that sort of emotional manipulation since his girlfriend in high school told him that she was pregnant by his best friend.

As expected, Bjørn's next sentence was uttered with much less empathy. "The parliamentary judicial committee have been analyzing the percentage of solved cases in different jurisdictions to facilitate a more satisfactory division of resources and strengthening of local workforces, and they have been scrutinizing special funding in particular. That is precisely where Department Q falls, so cuts have been made. One employee will be laid off and you'll relocate up here, in the event that the department isn't disbanded. That's their final word, Carl; I'm sorry, but I can't do anything about it."

Carl looked tiredly at him. "I have no idea what you're talking about. Our percentage of solved cases is sixty-five, and those cases we haven't yet solved are just waiting for a breakthrough. These are cases that everyone else has given up on and which would otherwise be left rotting in the archives if it weren't for us."

"Hmm. Sixty-five percent, you say. Where is that noted? I can't see that in my paperwork."

He rummaged around a little on the neatly ordered desk.

"Here!" A piece of paper was raised in the air, and Bjørn pointed at a number before passing it to Carl. "This is what Department Q has submitted. And this is what management have concluded from that. Percentage of solved cases, fifteen. Not quite sixty-five percent, now, is it, Carl? So, the conclusion is that you are too ineffective and that your department is costing society a lot of money that would be put to better use up here."

"*Fifteen* percent!" Carl looked shocked. "They're totally bonkers. And what do these mediocre idiots from Christiansborg know about what we cost and what we do? We might well be a couple of reports behind schedule, but that's all."

"A *couple* of reports? A fifty percent difference is not a *couple* of reports, Carl. You exaggerate as usual, but it will do you no good in this situation."

A sudden feeling of fire and brimstone harrowed Carl's nervous system. Could he be the one to blame for the situation?

"Firstly, that analysis is utter nonsense, and, secondly, you're the ones with your sticky fingers on most of the special funding allocated for Department Q—don't forget that, Lars Bjørn. So if *we* are closed down, it's to save less than a quarter of what the judicial committee think we cost. That paper isn't even worth wiping my ass with." He waved it angrily. "Where do you have these figures from, Lars?"

Bjørn threw his arms out. "Are you asking *me* that, Carl? You're the ones who have submitted the reports."

"Then you damn well haven't registered them properly."

"Well, opinion is divided on that matter, as you might well imagine. To deal with this unfortunate situation, I recommend that you lay off Rose Knudsen and that I move Gordon to my team, while you and Assad also move up here. Then we can see if you two can cope with a regime like ours that works in accordance with the law."

He smiled, probably aware that as far as this was concerned, Carl was certainly not going to follow orders. So what was his game?

"Once again, Carl, I am sorry. But the police commissioner has already reported to the judicial committee, so the decision is out of my hands."

Carl looked at his superior suspiciously. Had the man taken a course with the state department in delegating responsibility? Goddamn it, didn't Bjørn know better than to dance with those incompetent losers who only knew how to scratch the surface rather than finding out what lay beneath it?

"But listen, Carl, if you are so dissatisfied, then complain to the politicians," he said in conclusion.

Carl was furious, slamming the door so hard that the whole floor shook, causing Mrs. Sørensen's jaw to drop along with the papers she had just taken from the desk.

"You two," he shouted toward her and Lis, who was shredding papers. "Are you the ones who have submitted the wrong stats from us and are now in the process of killing off our department?"

They shook their heads in confusion.

He slammed down Bjørn's memo in front of them. "Have you written this?"

Lis leaned her pretty chest in toward the counter. "Yes, I have," she said without regret.

"But what you've written isn't right, Lis," he said, annoyed.

She turned toward her desk, bent down, and brought up a manila folder of the archived materials.

Carl tried to keep his wandering eyes in check. There was certainly more of her since she had given birth to her last child at the age of forty-six. Her body looked just as it should, but maybe one could help her along by burning off some of that baby belly. He breathed deeply. She had always been his first choice when he tuned in to his nighttime fantasies, and then she went and pulled this number on him.

"No," she said, her hand on a row of numbers. "I didn't understand it either, but look, what I wrote is correct. I'm sorry, Carl, but you've handed in exactly as many reports on closed and solved cases as I've noted here." She pointed at the number on the last line. Not a number Carl recognized.

"I've even embellished it a little, Carl, sweetie." There was that smile with the overlapping front teeth, whatever good it was just now.

Hearing the sound of steps behind him, Carl turned around. It was the police commissioner in his best suit on his way in to Lars Bjørn's office.

The nod he directed at Carl was extremely reserved. The chosen efficiency expert of police headquarters was obviously on one of his rare but fierce rounds.

"Where is Rose?" shouted Carl when he reached the final step on his way down to the cellar.

The echo from the empty corridor had hardly returned before Assad poked his curly mop of hair around the opening to his broom cupboard of an office.

"She isn't here, Carl. She left."

"Left? When?"

"Just after you went to court. At least two hours ago, so I wouldn't count on her coming back today. At least not imminently."

"Do you know anything about Rose not sending the reports on the cases we've cleared up—apart from the Habersaat case, obviously?"

"What cases? When?"

"Our man up on the Walk of Fame says that over the last twenty-four months, Rose has only delivered a fifth of the reports to homicide."

Assad looked shocked. Obviously he didn't know.

"Damn it, Assad, she's gone loopy." Carl walked determinedly to his desk, dialed Rose's home number, and let it ring until her automatic answering machine kicked in.

It wasn't a message he had heard before. Rose's answering-machine message was normally borderline hysterically bubbly, but this time the voice sounded unusually hoarse and sad.

"This is Rose Knudsen," it said. *"If you need me for anything, tough luck. Leave a message but don't count on me listening to it because that's just the way I am."* And then came the beep.

"Rose, come on, answer the phone; it's important," Carl said anyway. Maybe she was on the other end snarling, maybe even laughing, but he'd put a stop to that when he got hold of her. Because if it was Rose who had made such an outstandingly shoddy job of her reports, Department Q would be one employee down regardless.

"What about you, Gordon? Did you find any of Rose's documentation?"

He nodded, leaning in over Carl's computer. "I've sent it to you so you can see for yourself." He opened the file, scrolling down through the pages.

Carl was tight-lipped. Line for line, there was an exact account of which cases Department Q had been working on, which case numbers, the nature of the cases, and the dates when they were opened and closed and with what result. Green columns for cases solved, blue for those they were working on right now, purple for those they had put to one side, and red for those they had given up on. There was even a date for when the report was finished and forwarded to management. It was fair to say that viewers of the file would be met with a very positive impression, and all cases apart from the Habersaat case were checked with a tick. All according to the book.

"I don't know what this is all about, Carl, but our Rose has done what she was meant to," said Gordon, coming to her defense like a knight in shining armor.

"How has she delivered them?" came a voice from the door.

Gordon turned toward Assad, who was standing with a cup of sugar-filled tea in his hand.

"As an attachment sent on our intranet."

Assad nodded. "To what address? Have you checked, Gordon?"

He stretched out his lanky body, plodding back to Rose's office while mumbling to himself. He obviously hadn't.

Carl pricked his ears. Hard leather soles on the concrete floor wasn't a sound you normally heard down here. An ominous sound like that adopted by Hollywood actors when creating the illusion of a Nazi officer in second-rate war films could be replicated only by Mrs. Sørensen. Normal police workers wear rubber soles, unless they have a permanent seat in the domain of the police commissioner, and it definitely wasn't any of them.

"Goodness, it stinks here," was Mrs. Sørensen's first remark, her top lip drowning in small beads of sweat. The other day, it had been remarked that during her hot flashes, she sat with her feet in a tub of cold water under the desk. There was always a good story about Mrs. Sørensen's behavior, and they were seldom untrue.

"You'd better not drag this Middle Eastern smell with you upstairs to us," she continued, placing a plastic folder in front of him. "Here are the detailed statistics for your department. Over the last six months, we've as good as not received a single report from you, leading management to conclude that you haven't solved anything of significance in that time frame. But now Lis and I have begun to question that because we do follow what goes on here at headquarters, and thank goodness we do. We know that Department Q has had good publicity in the media concerning the cases you've worked on in that same time period, so something doesn't add up, I'll say that much."

She attempted a little smile but was obviously not in the habit because it didn't work.

"Look at this, Carl," said Gordon, bursting in. He put the printout on the table and pointed. "Rose has sent her files to both Lis and Catarina." He nodded to her. "Only to Lis in the beginning, and since Lis's maternity leave almost exclusively to Catarina Sørensen."

Mrs. Sørensen bent her sweaty body over the printout. "Yes," she said, nodding. "The address is right enough and, in principle, it is to me. The problem is that it is more than twenty months since that address has been active; I got divorced in the meantime and went back to my maiden name. The initials aren't CS anymore but CUS."

Carl put his head in his hands. Why wasn't there an automatic redirection from the old e-mail address to the new one? Was it sabotage or had the mess the rest of society lived in now come to them?

"What does CUS stand for?" asked Gordon.

"Catarina Underberg Sørensen," she answered with pathos.

"Why still Sørensen, when you've changed back to your maiden name?"

"Because, little Gordon, Underberg Sørensen *was* my maiden name."

"Oh. And you married a Sørensen and ended up being called the same just without the other part?"

"Yes, that's how my husband wanted it. He felt it was too posh with the other part." She momentarily tutted. "Or it was just because he was a miserable alcoholic and didn't want to have a nickname."

Gordon looked confused, obviously not understanding her last remark.

"Underberg is a German bitter, Gordon," she informed him surlily, as if it was of any interest to a man who rarely drank and could get plastered from aftershave fumes.

Just finished with a report of the sort that would put the police commissioner in his place, and which could also create an enemy for life, Carl leaned back and looked around. This humble basement corridor was his base until they carried him out in a box. He had everything here that he needed: an ashtray, a flat-screen with all the channels, and a desk with drawers you could put your feet up on. Where else could you find these necessities at police HQ?

Carl imagined the police commissioner's difficulty in explaining himself to the judicial committee and burst out laughing until the telephone rang.

"Is that Carl?" asked a bland voice, which he felt he ought to recognize but couldn't quite place.

"It's Marcus. Marcus Jacobsen," said the voice when the pause became too long.

"Marcus! Well, I'll be damned! I almost didn't recognize your voice," he blurted out.

Carl couldn't help but smile. Marcus Jacobsen, his old boss in homicide on the other end of the phone! A living example that Denmark was once led by people who were both serious and knew what they were doing like the back of their hand.

"Yeah, I know. The voice is a little hoarse, but it *is* me, Carl. I've just had my share of cigarettes since we last met!"

It must be three to four years since they had last spoken, so there was a slight sense of bad conscience creeping through the line. Carl knew Marcus had been through the mill of it lately, just not how it had all ended. That was the real mistake, because he ought to know.

After five minutes, the full extent of the catastrophe was explained. Marcus had been made a widower and was marked for life.

"I am really sorry to hear that, Marcus," Carl said, trying to find words of comfort in a brain that didn't normally deal with that sort of thing.

"Thanks, Carl, but that's not why I'm ringing. I think we need each other right now. I've just come across a case that I think we ought to talk about. Not because I'm trying to set you up on the case—the people on the Walk of Fame would be against it—but because the case reminds me of another one that has been niggling away at me for years. And maybe inadvertently because I've been reminded of how grateful I am that there is still someone at HQ who keeps their eyes open for cases that would otherwise be pushed in a corner."

Café Gammel Torv restaurant was where they had agreed to meet fifty minutes later.

Marcus was already sitting at his old table. He had grown older and was looking more tired, but maybe that wasn't so strange after the awful years before his wife eventually succumbed.

Now he was alone, and Carl knew firsthand what loneliness and a feeling of being abandoned could do to a man.

Not that their experiences were comparable.

Marcus took his hand as if they had been old friends and not colleagues at different stages of the career ladder.

Perhaps out of politeness and perhaps because of a desire to immerse himself in the reality of police headquarters, he asked Carl how things had been recently with Department Q.

The question was like fuel to Carl's fire, causing him to burst out with such frustration that it almost made the jelly on the pâté wobble.

Marcus Jacobsen nodded; no one knew better than him that the constellation of Carl and Lars Bjørn's totally different personalities could easily result in something explosive.

"But Lars Bjørn is actually an all right guy, Carl. I can't imagine that he's behind this number. Even though old e-mail addresses normally are forwarded to a new one. Could the police commissioner be behind this?"

Carl couldn't see the logic. What on earth would the commissioner get out of it?

"But what does an old former head of homicide know about politics? Still, I'd look into it if I were you." He nodded to the waiter, indicating that he could pour another schnapps, downed it in one, and cleared his throat. "What do you know about the murder of Rigmor Zimmermann?"

Carl followed Marcus's lead, downing his drink in one. It was one of those types of schnapps that tied the intestine in knots.

"Just the right schnapps for my mother-in-law," Carl said, coughing and drying away the tears from the corners of his eyes. "What do I know? Not too much, actually. They're investigating the case up on the second floor, so it's outside my remit. But the woman was murdered in the King's Garden, right? Was it three weeks ago?"

"Err, almost. Tuesday, the 26th of April, at approximately quarter past eight in the evening, to be more precise."

"She was in her mid-sixties, as far as I remember, and it was a robbery murder. Wasn't there a few thousand kroner missing from her purse?"

"Ten thousand, according to the daughter, yes." Marcus nodded.

"The murder weapon wasn't found, but it was a blunt instrument, and that's just about all I know. I've had enough to do with my own cases, but I might just know what you're thinking. I almost got goose bumps when you called, Marcus, because it was just a couple of hours after I'd spoken with a certain Mogens Iversen. Maybe you remember him as the guy who confessed to all sorts of crimes?"

After the slightest of pauses, Marcus nodded. There was no one at headquarters—well, apart from Hardy—who could match his total recall.

"And Iversen also confessed to the murder of that substitute teacher, Stephanie Gundersen. I'm sure he got the idea after reading about the attack on Rigmor Zimmermann because I can imagine how the papers have drawn the connection between the two attacks. Of course, I threw the idiot out afterward."

"The papers? No, no one has seriously connected the two cases, as far as I know, but we didn't release many details at the time about the murder of Stephanie."

"Okay. Then let's just say that you and I know that there are a few similarities between the two cases. But you ought to know that the Stephanie Gundersen case hasn't been passed on to me. I do have a slim case file about it, but the bulk of the material is up with Bjørn."

"Do you still have Hardy living with you?"

Carl smiled at the change of topic. "Yeah, I won't be rid of him until the day he finds a woman who is turned on by wheelchairs and wiping saliva and snot." He regretted the joke straightaway—it was a bad call.

"No, jokes aside, things are the same with Hardy," he continued. "He's still living with me and it's going great. He's actually become quite mobile. It's almost miraculous what he can manage with the two fingers he's got a little sensation in. But why are you asking about that?"

"Back at the time of the Stephanie Gundersen case, Hardy came to me with some information about her and the school where she was a substitute teacher. Apparently, Hardy had met her before. Maybe you didn't know?"

"Err, no. He wasn't investigating it anyway, because in 2004 he was with me and . . ."

"Hardy was never afraid to give his colleagues a helping hand. A fine man. Really sad what happened to him."

Carl smiled, tilting his head. "I think I understand, Marcus. Your purpose is clear."

He smiled and stood up. "Really! That genuinely pleases me, Inspector Carl Mørck. Very much so," he said, pushing a few pieces of paper with notes over toward him. "I hope you have a good Whitsun."

11

Wednesday, May 11th, to Friday, May 20th, 2016

What no one around Anneli knew was that the Anne-Line Svendsen they thought they knew, for better or for worse, had, in reality, not existed for quite a few days.

Her usual day-to-day life had recently been altered by both worry and excessive anger, during which time she had repeatedly begun to reevaluate her current life and self-image. From having been a conscientious citizen and employee whose ideals included being community-minded and having a positive work ethic, she had become a genuine Mr. Hyde, lost in her most base instincts as she decided on the course of events that would determine her future and possibly short-lived life.

Following her diagnosis with cancer, she had experienced a couple of days weighed down by a fear of death, which had manifested itself in a sort of passive anger that was once again directed at those damn young women who totally cheated society, wasting both their own and other people's time. With that and the way they had mocked her in mind, Anneli defined her simple mantra:

Why on earth should they be allowed to live when I can't? And it helped.

Anneli was almost smiling on the way to the hospital to receive her sentence, because the decision had definitely been made.

If she was going to die, then they would damn well die too.

The consultation was one long blur because Anneli was unable to concentrate on all the unreal and real words. Terms such as "sentinel lymph nodes," "scintigraphy," "X-ray," "electrocardiography," and "chemo" passed by. She just waited for the final and ultimate sentence.

"Your malignant tumor is estrogen-receptor-negative, so we can't treat you with hormone therapy," the doctor had said, adding an explanation that the tumor had a malignancy level of three, which was the most dangerous type, but that the tumor was small because it had been found so early and that with an operation everything would probably be fine.

Such a long sentence ending with "everything would probably be fine" was ominous.

Probably! What the hell was "probably" supposed to mean?

Everything went very quickly on the day of the operation. Wednesday morning at eight o'clock she had called in sick to work with influenza. The anesthetic was at nine, the operation was over a few hours later, and she was home by late afternoon. Altogether radical changes in the quiet life she had otherwise led up until this point, and Anneli couldn't quite keep up.

The results were ready on Friday the 13th of all days, a couple of days after the operation.

"It wasn't cancer in the sentinel lymph node," she was told as her heart raced. "The evidence suggests that there is a good chance you'll have a long and healthy life, Anne-Line Svendsen." The doctor couldn't help but smile a little. "We have performed breast-conserving surgery and you can expect a speedy recovery if you follow our advice carefully. Then we'll have a look at your future treatment."

"No, I'm still not quite myself; it's a really bad case of influenza, this one. Of course I can come into the office, but I'm worried I'll give it to everyone else. Why don't I wait until sometime next week to come back? At least then I *ought* to be over the worst."

The answer from her line manager was a little hesitant; it wasn't a good idea to put other people at risk, so she should try to get herself as well as possible; they would look forward to her being back again after Whitsun.

Anneli hung up, feeling the beginning of a smile. She had been marked for death and had therefore decided to take her revenge on those girls who were of no value to society, and now she might not die after all. She would go to radiation therapy, get dry skin, and expect to be utterly exhausted, but what did that have to do with her vendetta against women like Jazmine and Camilla and Michelle, and whatever the hell they were called? Nothing!

A vendetta is a vendetta, and as she saw it, she should stick with it.

That evening, against the advice of the doctors, she emptied most of the contents of a cognac bottle, which some merciful soul had left at her place after the only get-together she had ever had.

Intoxicated by fermented grapes from a dusty bottle, she regained all her indignation and anger. From this day forth, she was finished with playing the victim. She would attend her treatment without mentioning anything at work, and if anyone asked, in the event that she arrived late in the morning after her treatment, she would say that she had been to the psychologist to deal with latent stress issues. At least it was something every center manager would be able to understand.

She laughed again, holding the half-empty glass up to the light emanating from the hanging lamp.

No, no, from now on she would think of only herself and her own needs. No more nice girl who hardly ever lied or went against the rules. Gone was the woman who thought she would collapse under the strain and who had already been thinking about a place to be buried. From now on, she was going to live life and take no nonsense from anyone.

Beautiful scenes danced before her in her drunkenness. She saw them in front of her—the girls and their idiotic mothers, who had neglected their offspring, making them useless, and whom she would now cause to fall down in shock.

"They're *absolutely worthless*!" she shouted, making even the storm windows shake.

She lay on her side on the sofa, doubled up with laughter cramps, stopping only when the scar from the operation began to throb. She swallowed a couple more painkillers and wrapped herself in her old quilt.

Tomorrow, she would quietly and calmly come up with a way to wipe out those broads, and then she would get hold of an address list of the most superfluous and useless girls in greater Copenhagen.

There were fifty printouts from Google in front of her, all detailing the simplest and safest way to steal a car. A mass of exciting information and many things that seemed very obvious when one had read the advice and learned the techniques a car thief needed to know by heart to ensure nothing went wrong. If one knew these basic sentences like the back of one's hand, then one had the essentials necessary to gain access to a locked car without a key, and also how to get it started.

The only crime she could think of that she had committed up until this point was when she neglected to tell the checkout staff in the supermarket if she was given too much change. *Fuck that,* she'd always thought, because public employees like Anneli didn't have much to play with to start. But to steal cars with the intention of using them to kill was a totally different matter. The thought made her giddy.

She thought of the idea after seeing a crime report that had been all over the media. A murderer on Bornholm had deliberately driven into a girl so brutally that she had been flung up into a tree. She could picture the scene. It was a murder that had taken twenty years and a lot of luck to solve, and that was on the sparsely populated island of Bornholm. So if one were to do the same in a densely populated city like Copenhagen and took the right precautions, who on earth would work out that it was her?

With good preparation and meticulousness, it will all be fine, she thought. And she was both meticulous and well prepared.

It was alpha and omega that one didn't use a car that could be traced back, which was why it was necessary to steal one—something she now knew quite a bit about.

Whether one was a professional or an amateur in the field, the first step was to ensure that the car wasn't fitted with an alarm. The easiest way to check was to push the car roughly when walking past. If an alarm went off, the idea was to skip the next ten cars and try again with the eleventh. Only when an old banger had been spotted and proven not to have an alarm could step two be brought into play.

Were there any security cameras in the vicinity? People at windows or on the street, passersby on bikes or mopeds or in cars who might notice her when she got under way? All very logical for a young entrepreneurial car thief, but not for a so-called respectable woman in her prime.

Following this, the make and state of the vehicle should be thoroughly inspected. Anneli had no plans to sell the car to a mechanic in Lodz or strip it of airbags and expensive GPS equipment, so expensive vehicles were of no interest to her. She just needed any old car that was reasonably reliable, and which could be rammed directly into a human for an easy kill.

When that had been done, it was her intention to leave the car in some random place far from the crime scene.

The most important thing of all was that it was an easy car to steal. An older model where the steering lock could be wrenched apart, or which could even be started with a screwdriver stuck in the ignition. It certainly shouldn't be a vehicle with an immobilizer, but she could check that on her smartphone. And then there were the basics, like checking whether the tires were flat. If there were any items in the car that might lead to problems, like a child safety seat with a child in it, for example. And then whether or not it was possible to maneuver the car out of the parking lot quick enough. Was there even enough room to get out of the parking space? Anneli needed at least forty centimeters in front of and behind the car, but that wasn't that unusual.

Anneli smiled as she went through her checklist. Where would she run if she was caught red-handed? And if she didn't make it, what story would she come up with?

Anneli practiced. "Gooood, isn't that my car? I wondered why the key wasn't working. Oh no, God, if that isn't my car, then *where* have

I parked mine?' Wouldn't most people believe she was a law-abiding but confused woman? That she had panicked or was maybe slightly senile?

Anneli completely forgot the pain she was in that Saturday. She just popped pills and emptied the liquor cabinet, reading so much that she became dizzy. It was decades since she had felt so warm inside, so ready for action and full of life. So it couldn't be totally wrong.

The next day she made her first attempt.

Using Google Street View, she picked a large parking lot in Herlev, where she reasoned that the vehicles wouldn't be as fancy and unapproachable as in Holte or Hørsholm, for example.

While she was still on the S-train, Anneli began to feel a tingling sensation in her body. All the other passengers suddenly seemed so grey and insignificant. Young people laughing or kissing didn't irritate her like they usually did, and she almost felt sorry for the women her own age who would be returning home to their families and domestic chores at some point.

Then she patted the bag where the screwdriver, inflatable cushion, little crowbar, emergency hammer, and thin, expensive nylon string from Silvan waited for her.

The feeling was almost like being reborn.

Anneli looked around. It was a quiet Sunday the day after the Eurovision Song Contest. It probably didn't affect the mood out here in the suburbs that Denmark had been knocked out; it was just as dull and quiet as always.

The goal for the day wasn't to actually steal a car but just to get as far as gaining access and sitting in the vehicle. She wasn't in a rush at the moment because safety had to come first. She would take the next step later in the week, attempting to short-circuit the ignition and go for a drive. She was setting the pace.

She found a promising Suzuki Alto with rust marks under the doors that looked like it had already been stolen. There was limited activity around her; it was the time when most normal people were relaxing with breakfast or busying themselves preparing the Whitsun lunch.

The grey wreck was parked between a couple of older BMWs, the type that neither steel rims nor noisy stereos could improve. It was a good quiet place to give the Suzuki a knock.

It rocked silently on the wheels: no alarm.

There were three options. Either the one with the string, which could be forced through the crack in the passenger door and down to grab hold of the locking tab on the door; the more difficult option with the inflatable cushion, which could be pushed in the door of the trunk to force it up, allowing one to kick down the passenger seats; or then there was the more simple option of smashing a window.

Anneli was more in the mood for smashing windows.

She had learned on the Internet that the best way to do it was with a short hit down in the corner of the window, so that was what she did. Firstly with the flat side of the hammer, which didn't work, and then a hit with the pointy end.

Not too hard, she reminded herself. She shouldn't risk her hand going through and cutting herself.

After the third attempt, she concluded that the window was irregular and therefore impossible to smash.

Then she tried the door handle. She ought to have tried that earlier: It opened.

After a few hours of breaking into different vehicles using different methods, she concluded objectively that with her pronounced lack of dexterity, everything pointed to smashing windows as the best method. All the fuss with string and inflatable cushions didn't work for her. The string broke or the loop that was meant to go around the door lock became tangled, and the cushion punctured on the first attempt. At least you knew where you were when it came to smashing windows.

And all you had to do afterward was poke the broken glass out through the window frame and brush the shards of glass from the passenger seat onto the floor. Nobody would take any notice of the open window in this warm May weather, so long as the weather stayed as it was. And if one wanted to use the car multiple times and try to hide the fact that it was stolen, it was easy enough to get hold of strong see-through plastic.

She was also able to conclude that her tools, and in particular the hammer, weren't the best for the job. Therefore, a pointy carbon thingamabob like they suggested on the Internet would have to be the next thing she got hold of. And then there was the issue with the ignition. She tried once to press a screwdriver hard in the ignition and turn it, but *that* hadn't sounded good.

Smaller and pointier screwdrivers next time and a better technique, she thought.

She still had homework to do.

It took Anneli until the following Friday before she began to feel experienced enough. The week had passed with a little work during the day and breaking into cars in different parts of town during the rest of the day. And she had now been successful in starting the cars using different methods.

When finally sitting in a car one hadn't personally paid for and taking a street corner at full speed, the adrenaline rush felt extrapowerful. With a racing pulse and heightened senses in full swing, it was an altogether younger version of Anne-Line Svendsen sitting behind the wheel, or so it felt anyway. Sight and hearing were sharpened, as was the ability to quickly assess the surroundings, and the skin became warm and elastic.

Anneli suddenly felt shrewd and sly. Like someone who hadn't yet reached her full potential; like a woman able to match a man in almost anything.

In other words, Anneli had become someone else.

On her kitchen table there was now a list of young women whom she had had professional contact with in recent years.

They were girls and women for whom nothing but their own needs meant anything. Everything around them seemed like it must be just for them. They scrounged off the feelings and charity of the world around them. Anneli hated every last one of them. In fact, hate wasn't a strong enough word.

It had been a bit of a job finding relevant information from the other social security offices where she had worked in recent years. She needed a professional reason to check them first, but Anneli turned a blind eye to that regulation and now had fifty names to choose from, which satisfied her.

They were the ones the world was going to be rid of.

Midweek, she had made a list of priorities. First on the list were those who had irritated her the most, which was a mixed group from the three social security offices, so there wouldn't be any immediate murder pattern, and then those who had been fleecing the system for years.

Anneli lit a cigarette and leaned back in the kitchen chair. If the police ever caught up with her, she would face her punishment with her head held high. She had nothing at home to hold her back and no one in society to stop her: Her relationships were dull and superficial. On the other hand, in prison she would get what mattered most for the majority of people: security, regular meals, routines, and lots of time to read good books. Far away from wretched work and stress. And there might even be some people in prison whom she would get on better with than those on the outside. Why not?

Well, if that was the alternative, it wasn't the worst.

She printed out maps of Copenhagen's different housing areas and marked with a pencil where the girls lived. *Don't shit on your own doorstep,* she thought, selecting the girls who lived close to her in Østerbro and placing them at the bottom of the pile.

After some consideration, she chose Michelle Hansen as her first victim. Firstly, the girl was less intelligent and therefore presumably easier to outwit, and, secondly, she was a demanding and irritating rat who could bring Anneli out in a rash just from thinking about her.

She knew that the girl lived with her boyfriend, Patrick Pettersson, and that the building was so hidden among the labyrinth of small streets in the North West district that you could count on the traffic being limited, giving her peace to execute her plan. There didn't seem to be any impediment to her taking the next step.

She threw her cigarettes in the bag and headed out into the morning traffic. Now she was going to find a car.

The hunt was on.

12

Friday, May 20th, 2016

When Michelle turned twenty-seven, she suddenly felt old. Twenty-six was already bordering on old, but twenty-*seven*! That was nearly thirty, and years since she had been the age at which all the stars had their breakthrough. She thought about Amy Winehouse, Kurt Cobain, and all the other celebrities who had died at her age, and about everything they had achieved.

And then they just died. Before their time.

Michelle, on the other hand, was alive and kicking and hadn't achieved anything other than living in a studio apartment in the North West district with Patrick. Admittedly, she was still somewhat in love with him, but was that all there was to life? Hadn't she always been told that she was destined for great things? And yet now here she was, twenty-seven years old. What had happened to those great things?

All the TV appearances she had never been offered tormented her. Not that she had tried to draw much attention to herself, but still. Why wasn't there someone who had discovered her on the street, just like that Natalya Averina from Roskilde? Or like Kate Moss, Charlize Theron, Jennifer Lawrence, Toni Braxton, or Natalie Portman? She did look better than most people, and she could also sing, according to her mother.

Now she was twenty-seven, so things needed to happen soon. Patrick had been on one reality show, and she had fallen for him initially when she saw him on-screen, even though he had been voted off in the second episode. At least she had managed to get him after stalking him for a few weeks, so something had worked out. And if he could get on TV, then so could she, feminine and beautiful as she was. Every morning she spent almost half an hour shaving her legs, arms, and crotch, half an hour on her hair, and half an hour doing her face, followed by time spent selecting an outfit. Didn't she still have a flat stomach? Didn't her breast implants make her look great? Didn't she have at least as good a sense of fashion as those bitches who were cast in shows as if from thin air?

Yes, something would have to happen soon. And if she couldn't become famous, she would have to become rich. Marry a billionaire or something like that. You certainly wouldn't become rich as a florist, nail stylist, or makeup artist, and definitely not as a washerwoman in Helsingør. Didn't they understand that at all? Patrick, her stepdad, and her caseworker were all out to get her. But why? She was destined for something greater. A few months ago she had gone on sick leave for stress because they all demanded too much from her. And now it was all coming back to bite her for the umpteenth time, what with all the crazy hassle with Patrick's apartment, the fraud, and everything else.

Did it mean that her future was just this studio apartment? Would she have to rush to work early every morning and develop unsightly wrinkles from lack of sleep? Would she have to listen to Patrick's whining year in and year out? She couldn't deny how hard he worked, putting in extra hours in the evening for cash-in-hand jobs when he wasn't otherwise working as a bouncer at Victoria—the nightclub where they had kissed for the first time. But why couldn't he just come up with a great idea that would make them rich so that they could have a lovely house with nice furniture, freshly ironed tablecloths, and a couple of beautiful children?

Okay, she understood that when he came with her to social services, it was to try to help them have a little more luxury. She needed to bring in some dough, he always said, but what good did her small change do them? Patrick had material needs that her small wage could never cover. The gym three times a week, fancy clothes, and lots of pairs of cowboy boots. And cars. Okay, he already had a car—an Alfa Romeo with light-colored seats—and she appreciated it when he could be bothered to take her out for a drive. But now he would rather have another car, newer and more expensive, and that was without doubt what he would buy with the money she earned. It just wasn't fair.

She looked down at her left hand. She had a small discreet tattoo of Patrick's name at the base of her thumb, and Patrick had a tattoo of her name on his biceps exactly where two muscle groups fought for power, and it looked super-hot. But was that all?

Next year she would turn twenty-eight, and if nothing had happened by then, she would leave him and find another man who valued her assets more tangibly.

Michelle looked over at him lying there, half-covered in the bed-sheet, stretching his naked lower body. It was actually only in bed that things felt really good with him, now that she thought about it.

"Hi," he said, rubbing his eyes. "What's the time?"

"You've got half an hour before you have to go," she answered.

"Damn!" He yawned. "And what will you be doing today? Popping down to social services to say sorry to your caseworker?"

"No, I'm doing something else. So not today, Patrick."

He leaned up on his elbows. "*What* did you say? Something else? Damn it, you don't have anything more important to do, you stupid bitch!"

She gasped for breath. *Stupid bitch?* She wasn't going to let anyone talk to her like that.

"You can't get away with calling me a stupid bitch, I'll tell you that much!"

"What are you going to do about it, Michelle? There seems to be something very important that you don't understand, so you must be a stupid bitch. It's almost three weeks since your caseworker charged us with fraud. And there are two reminders on the table that you haven't even bothered to open. And why are you now getting letters in the mail from social services—aren't you checking the damn e-mails they send you? It could be important. Have you thought about that? I bet they're fines or summons or bills or some other shit."

"You can just open them yourself and have a look if you're that interested."

"They've got *your* bloody name on them, so why don't you do it yourself? Why the hell should I get more mixed up in that shit? Damn it, Michelle, get a grip or I'll kick you out. Don't think I won't."

She swallowed a couple of times. It was all too much at once. She stood up from the dressing table and was just about to shout something at him but knew that if she did, she'd pay for it ten times over.

Michelle stared down at the floor. If she didn't keep it together she'd tear up and that would ruin her perfect makeup.

She staggered the fifteen steps out to the bathroom and slammed the door behind her. She didn't want Patrick to see how he could throw her off-balance.

"Don't be in there too long," he shouted from the bed. "I need to get in there in a minute."

The mirror revealed all too clearly the effect he had on her. There was already a wrinkle on her forehead. Didn't he know what it cost to have something like that corrected with Botox? Idiot!

Michelle grabbed the edge of the sink. She was actually feeling quite queasy just now. As if all the horrible words were in the pit of her stomach and she was about to throw them up.

She bit her lip, feeling a burning sensation in her throat. "Kick you out," he'd said. "Kick you out!"

Her!

She vomited violently without warning, but she didn't make a sound. There was no way she was going to let him know how he made her feel or that he could get to her so much that she threw up. She had done it a few times before, but standing there with heartburn and the remains of yesterday's dinner in the corners of her mouth, she made up her mind that this would be the last time.

When Patrick had finally left, she systematically rummaged through all his belongings. She found a few hundred kroner here and there, and some cigarettes in his jacket pocket even though he said he had quit because it was too expensive and that she ought to do the same. She also found some condoms in the small pockets of his Levi's.

What did he want with condoms? She was bloody well on the pill and terrified of getting blood clots from them. So what did he need condoms for?

She tore up a couple of them and threw them on the bed. Then he would be able to work out for himself why she wasn't there when he came back.

Michelle looked around, wondering what to take with her. No way was she going to move back to her family, even if it was just for a short while, because Stephan was there—the idiot her mother had been seeing for three years. He was a complete psycho. Didn't her so-called stepfather want her to work for him in his rotten garage for a measly fourteen thousand a month? Did he really expect *her* to get oily and dirty for fourteen thousand a month?

As if he was doing her a favor.

She sat for a moment and stared at the wallpaper, trying to see everything from the outside. Why was she so bad at this sort of thing? Why couldn't she just do what was best for herself? She really needed some support and good advice.

Then she thought of Denise and Jazmine, who were both so focused. What would they do in her situation?

Michelle walked down the street feeling positive. She had called the girls and they were meeting in town in an hour. She felt ready to lay all her cards on the table. Perhaps they could help her, and one of them might even have an idea about where she could find a decent place to sleep for a while.

She smiled and noticed the red car a little farther down the street pulling out from where it was parked. The driver was probably someone not so different from her, albeit without all the demands she was subjected to. Someone who took herself seriously.

She nodded. In a few months *she* would probably have her own car. Just before she left the apartment, she had checked Facebook and seen that there was another casting for a TV show that she was definitely better suited for than the person who had posted the link. It was a totally new concept—nothing Michelle had heard of before—something about girls on a farm having to fend for themselves and that sort of thing. *That* was definitely something she could do—but she wouldn't tell the producers that. She would just play dumb, pretending not to even know how to boil a potato or anything. Play dumb and look amazing while showing off her tits and ass. They'd take her without a doubt.

She crossed the street. There was also another reality show looking for contestants. *Dream Date* it was called or s—

She looked instinctively over her shoulder, but it was already too late. The car was suddenly there, a bright red blotch in the middle of the street, coming quickly at her with the engine roaring in low gear.

The woman behind the windshield looked directly at her while jerking the wheel toward her—a face that made Michelle throw out her hand protectively in panic.

But her hand couldn't stop the car.

She was woken by a faint throbbing in her arm. She tried to open her eyes and sit up but her body wouldn't budge.

I'm lying with my mouth open, aren't I? she thought as smells and sounds she couldn't place smothered her like a heavy blanket.

"Michelle, listen." She felt a soft tug on her good arm. "You've been in an accident, but it's not serious. Can you open your eyes?"

She mumbled something or other. It was just a silly dream.

But then someone patted her on the cheek. "Wake up now, Michelle. There's someone here who wants to talk to you."

She took a deep breath that pulled her out of her daze.

A bright white light surrounded a face that was looking directly down at her.

"You're at Copenhagen University Hospital, Michelle, and you're okay. You've been very lucky."

She saw now that it was a nurse. She had freckles just like Michelle had once had.

A man was standing behind her nodding with a friendly smile.

"The police are here to ask you a few questions, Michelle."

The man stepped forward. "Hello, my name is Preben Harbæk. I'm a police sergeant from Bellahøj Police Station. I'd like to ask you a few questions about what you can remember from the accident."

Michelle crinkled her nose. There was a strong smell and the light was far too bright.

"Where am I?" she asked. "Am I in the hospital?"

The man nodded. "You were in a hit-and-run accident, Michelle. Can you remember that?"

"I'm meeting Denise and Jazmine. Can I please go?" She tried to support herself on her elbows again, but it made her head hurt. "I need to talk to them."

The nurse looked at her insistently. "You need to stay where you are, Michelle. You have a deep gash in the back of your neck and you have a lot of stitches. The friends you were meant to be meeting are in the waiting room. They called your cell phone to ask why you hadn't arrived." She looked serious—but why, if Jazmine and Denise were outside waiting?

"You've been here for three hours and we need to keep you under observation for concussion because you took a heavy blow to the head when you hit the pavement. You were lying unconscious when some-one from the neighborhood found you. You've lost a lot of blood."

Michelle didn't understand everything, but she nodded. At least Jazmine and Denise were here. Now she could tell them that she had left Patrick.

"Do you understand how serious this is, Michelle?" asked the policeman.

She nodded and answered his questions as best she could. Yes, she had seen the car. It was red and not too big. It drove right at her as she was crossing the road. When she realized the danger she had tried to stop it with her hand. Was that why it hurt so much?

The policeman nodded. "But it is miraculously not broken," he said. "You must really be a strong girl."

She liked that he said that. He was okay. Other than that, she had nothing to add.

"They say you need to stay here for a few days, Michelle." Jazmine looked around the room. It was apparent that she didn't feel comfortable, but then the place did smell pretty disgusting. Only a screen separated her bed from her neighbor's, and there was a bad smell emanating from there. Over by the sink and mirror there was a trolley with the bedpan the nurse's aid had just taken from her bed. So all in all the place wasn't exactly appealing.

"We'll come and visit every day," said Denise. She didn't really seem to mind the place or the stench.

"We would've brought flowers, but then we thought we'd rather use the money in the cafeteria," said Jazmine. "Are you allowed to get out of bed?"

Michelle didn't know so she just shrugged.

"I've left Patrick," she said casually. "Would you mind checking if that's my bag over there?" She pointed over at the pile on the chair and they nodded. That was good.

"I don't want him coming here. Can you let them know out there?"

They nodded.

"Then maybe I have somewhere you can live that won't cost you anything," said Denise. "And there's room for you too, Jazmine."

Michelle looked at her gratefully. Brilliant.

"For a while anyway," she added.

Michelle pursed her lips. That was awesome, but then she'd known all along that those two would sort everything out for her.

"What happened? They said you were run over. What did you say to the police?" asked Denise.

She explained everything about the car.

"It wasn't Patrick, was it?" asked Denise.

"No," she said with a laugh. What kind of a question was that? Hadn't she just said that it was a small, old, red rust bucket? As if Patrick would be seen dead in something like that.

"Patrick drives an Alfa Romeo. It's bigger and black."

"Drivers are psychos," said Jazmine.

Then came the thing she just had to say. "But I do think I recognized the face of the woman in the car."

They went silent as if they expected a complete description on top of her explanation.

"Have you told the police?" asked Denise.

"No." Michelle kicked her blanket off. It felt suffocating.

She nodded over to the screen separating the person in the next bed. It was none of her business what she was about to say.

"I was just about to tell the policeman," she whispered, "but I wanted to ask you first what you think I should do." She put her finger to her mouth to remind them to keep their voices down.

"What do you mean?" Denise whispered.

"I think it was Anne-Line Svendsen behind the wheel."

She got the reactions she had hoped for: shock, disbelief, and confusion.

"Christ! Are you sure?" asked Denise.

She shrugged. "I think so. At least it was someone who looked like her. Even the sweater."

Denise and Jazmine looked at each other. Didn't they believe her?

"Do you think I should report it?" she asked.

They sat for a while staring blankly. All three of them hated Anne-Line Svendsen. Three claimants whose lives the bitch had made difficult for years.

Michelle was sure that she was thinking the same as they were just now. *If* it really was Anne-Line Svendsen, who would believe a girl like her? Why would a caseworker who on top of everything else had won a huge sum of money do something like that? She could see the problem.

I'm the one who's committed fraud, she thought. And wasn't it extremely risky to make false accusations? Wouldn't there be severe consequences? Yes, that much she knew from TV shows.

"I have a meeting with her on Monday," said Jazmine a moment later. "So I'll just ask her straight out if it was her who did it."

Denise nodded. "Okay. 'Straight to the point,' as my granddad always said."

"But if she denies it—and she will—what do we do then?" asked Jazmine. "Any suggestions?"

Denise smiled but said nothing.

13

In Allerød, the barbecue was already in full swing, and while before there had been a mild aroma of smoke from the neighbor's garden, now the entire parking lot was covered in a thick haze that smelled strongly of burned meat.

"Howdy, Morten and Hardy!" shouted Carl, throwing his jacket in the hallway. "Are you also having a barbecue?"

There was a faint humming from Hardy's electric wheelchair as he approached. He was dressed in white from top to toe—a stark contrast to his gloomy expression.

"Anything wrong?" asked Carl.

"Mika has just been here."

"Oh! Are you having treatment with him on Fridays now? I thought . . ."

"Mika has been here with Morten's stuff. They've split up. Morten's sitting in a corner of the sitting room in a right state, I can tell you. He needs his friends around him just now, so I've told him that he can move back into the basement, okay?"

Carl nodded. "What the . . ." He put his hand on Hardy's shoulder. It was a good thing that at least Morten and Hardy had each other.

The rejected lover was huddled up in the corner of the sofa looking as dejected as someone who had just received a death sentence. Ashen, tearful, and by all appearances totally exhausted.

"Hi, mate, what's this I hear?" asked Carl.

Perhaps he should have approached the subject more delicately, because the result was that Morten jumped up and threw his arms around Carl with a guttural wail as the tears streamed down his face.

"There, there!" was the only thing he could think of to say.

"I can hardly bear to think about it," Morten sobbed in Carl's ear. "I'm so miserable! And at Whitsun of all times. We were supposed to be going to Sweden together."

"Tell me what happened, Morten." He held him at arm's length and looked directly into his tearful eyes.

"Mika wants to study medicine," he cried, snot running from his nose. It didn't really sound so drastic.

"And he says he doesn't have time for a serious relationship anymore. But I know there must be another reason."

Carl sighed. Now they'd have to clear the basement again so Morten could move back to his old quarters. His stepson's things would have to go. And not too soon. How many years had it been since Jesper actually moved out?

"You can stay in the basement if you want," he said, trying to change the subject. "Jesper still has some stuff down there, but I'll get him to . . ."

Morten nodded and thanked him, wiping his eyes with the back of his hand like a little boy. His once plump body looked starved, Carl noticed now for the first time. He almost didn't recognize him.

"Are you ill, Morten?" he asked tentatively.

Morten grimaced. "Yes. I'm dying of a broken heart. Where in the world will I find a guy as divine as Mika? I won't, because he's a dream. Heavenly. So groomed and handsome and extremely adventurous in bed. He has the stamina, strength, and dominance of a stallion. If only you knew how . . ."

Carl held up the palms of his hands to stop him. "Thanks, Morten. You don't need to explain further. I think I get it."

After dinner, which Morten had managed to serve despite his

recurring hysterics and tears, though he himself had been unable to muster the appetite to eat, Hardy looked intensely at Carl. A look Carl knew only too well. It was the look of a seasoned investigator.

"Yeah, yeah, Hardy. You're right. I *do* actually have something to tell you," he said. "I've met up with Marcus."

Hardy nodded without seeming surprised. Had they already spoken?

"I think I know why, Carl," he said. "I was just waiting for it to happen, but I'd anticipated you being the one to start the ball rolling."

"I'm confused. Help me out here. What are you talking about?"

Hardy pulled at his control, moving his chair a bit away from the dining table. "Coincidences, Carl. The attack in the King's Garden in 2016 and the attack in Østre Anlæg in 2004. Am I right?"

Carl nodded. "Okay, spot on. But if you have any more of these well-founded hunches, give me a heads-up straightaway, all right?"

Hardy had had this hunch for almost three weeks, he said. Three weeks in the life of a man with a lot of time on his hands and no one to disturb his mysterious train of thought. He had laboriously thought through and listed the details of the attack on Stephanie Gundersen twelve years ago and that on Rigmor Zimmermann almost three weeks ago, finding the coincidences noticeably significant.

"We could also take the trouble to focus on the differences between the two attacks, but there aren't many. The most notable is probably that Rigmor Zimmermann's body had been urinated on but not Gundersen's. And the urine was from a man, Tomas told me."

Carl nodded. Of course he had spoken to the canteen manager at HQ, Tomas Laursen, the former and usually well-informed forensic technician.

"Okay, so the theory is that Rigmor Zimmermann was killed by a man?

"But was that also the case with Stephanie Gundersen? I don't know much about that case, and Marcus Jacobsen said that it was all kept a bit hush-hush back then."

"That it was supposedly a man who murdered Stephanie Gundersen? No, not exactly. The blow to her head was severe and delivered with extreme force, but as they never figured out what murder weapon was used, they could never determine how heavy or effective it was. So it's impossible to conclude anything specific about the fatal blow that would indicate the gender of the killer."

"Hardy, I can tell by your face that *you* think it's the same killer. Am I right?"

He shook his head again. "Who knows? But the coincidences are significant."

Carl got it now. Hardy wouldn't let either case go before the question had been answered.

"But there was also another difference between the two murders," he added.

"Are you thinking about the victims' ages? There must have been thirty-five years between them."

"No. I'm thinking about the fatal blows again. In Gundersen's case, the back of her head was bashed halfway into her brain, whereas the blow that killed Rigmor Zimmermann was more precise and controlled. A blow to the back of the head a little farther down toward the neck bones, almost cutting the spinal cord in two but not damaging the skull quite so severely."

They both nodded. There could be many reasons for that. A different murderer, differences in the weight and surface of the murder weapons, or simply that the murderer had become more skilled.

"But, Hardy, you know just as well as I do that there isn't much I can do about the Zimmermann case because it's still up with homicide. And this is not the time for me to make waves with Bjørn."

He explained the current situation with Bjørn and the cutbacks facing Department Q.

At this, Morten suddenly stopped in his mission of almost scrubbing the enamel off a pot. "Then you need to steal the Zimmermann case from Lars Bjørn, Carl," he shouted from the kitchen. "Man up and solve both cases. That's *my* advice."

Rich coming from him.

Carl shook his head and looked at Hardy, who just smiled. He obviously agreed with Morten.

———

After a few peaceful days off without any worry other than Morten's occasional crying fits, Carl was back in his office discussing with Assad whether to take on the Gundersen case even though it hadn't reached the depths of the cellar yet. Both Hardy and Marcus were eager for him to look into it, but Carl was still a little skeptical.

"What if we start at the other end with the Zimmermann case?" asked Assad.

"Hmm. That particular case is still well and truly up on the second floor," said Carl. But he could sense that he was growing increasingly curious. It was certainly more interesting than what they were otherwise engaged with.

"We could bring Laursen on board, Carl. He keeps talking about how boring it is in the canteen."

Carl nodded. *Yeah, why not?* he thought as Rose arrived in a getup none of them had seen before.

She almost jumped down the stairs to the cellar in her bright trainers and skinny jeans, introducing herself as Rose's sister Vicky Knudsen while smoothing down her cropped hair.

Gordon, who had stuck his head out of his office, stood gawping. "What on earth are you doi—" Assad pulled at his arm, stopping him midsentence.

"Would you come with me for a minute, Gordon, while Carl talks with Vicky? I think you and I need a good cup of coffee," insisted Assad.

Gordon was about to protest but suddenly raised his lanky leg in pain due to the full force of Assad's pointy boot against his shin. He got the message.

Carl sighed about the absurdity of the situation but invited Vicky into his office. If he had to get used to another one of her disguises, he would first have to explain to this self-created reincarnation, or Rose, that she couldn't expect to be able to just barge in from the street and be reckoned with if she wasn't an employee at HQ.

"I know what you're going to say," the transformed woman pre-empted him. Maybe it wasn't quite as bad as the time when Rose had imitated her sister Yrsa.

"I'm Rose's younger sister. The second of four girls."

Carl nodded. Rose, Vicky, Yrsa, and Lise-Marie. He had heard about them enough, and according to Rose, Vicky was the most carefree and vivacious of them all. This would be fun.

"If you think that I've come here to be drowned in meaningless work in your musty catacombs like Yrsa, you're much mistaken. I'm only here to tell you that you need to treat my sister Rose with more respect. Don't tease her and don't assign her depressing or boring work, or work that brings back unpleasant memories for that matter, okay? She's been feeling like shit over Whitsun because of you lot."

"I—"

"I'm giving you the opportunity to apologize on behalf of Department Q for all the stress you've put Rose under, and then I'll head over to her with your apology. And I sincerely hope for your sake that Rose, the most efficient employee in this pool of stupor, can find a grain of mercy in her abused soul."

Then she stood up and looked at Carl energetically with her fists clenched on her hips and a fierce expression. Any lover of B movies would have been impressed.

"Then I apologize profusely!" said Carl without hesitation.

"What just happened there, Carl? Did she leave?" Assad's eyebrows twitched with concern.

"Yes. I'm worried that Rose is even more disturbed than last time." He sighed. "I don't know what that character who was just here was thinking, but my gut feeling is that, in the moment, Rose firmly believed that she was Vicky. I just don't know what to make of it, Assad. Maybe it was all just an act."

Assad took a deep breath and placed a big pile of printouts on Carl's desk. It was so obvious how hard it was on him when there was trouble with Rose. The two of them had worked well together for seven years now, but lately there had been one issue after another, what with Rose being committed and her mood swings. You never knew where you were with her.

"Do you think this is the end of the line for Department Q?" Assad asked with a frown. "Because if Rose doesn't come back, we might as well do what Bjørn says. That is, if you aren't thinking of using those," he said, pointing to the pile of printouts.

His expression seemed to be daring Carl. Surprisingly enough, he didn't look like a man who had given up.

"He's busy just now," said Lis, to no avail, as Carl stormed past the desk and burst into Bjørn's office like a madman. While the door was still swinging on its hinges, he slammed down Assad's printouts of Rose's reports on the table between Bjørn and his visitor, whoever that was.

"*Now* you can damn well read some reports you haven't tampered with, Bjørn. You can't run rings around me."

The head of homicide remained surprisingly calm, looking at his visitor. "Allow me to introduce you to one of our most creative investigators," he said calmly, pointing from one to the other. "Carl Mørck, head of Department Q, our team in the cellar who investigate all the cold cases."

Bjørn's visitor nodded to Carl. An annoying type. Red beard, saggy belly, and glasses, all of which seemed to have been with him for years.

"And Carl, this is Olaf Borg-Pedersen, the producer of *Station 3*. I'm sure you're familiar with the brilliant show."

The man offered his sweaty hand. "Pleased to meet you," he said. "Yes, we know *exactly* who *you* are."

Carl didn't give a damn what he knew and turned to face his boss. "Have a good look through this lot, Bjørn, and I'll look forward to a brilliant explanation about how you could have got it so wrong."

Bjørn nodded approvingly. "A really stubborn, snappy dog we have in our pack here," he said to his visitor. He turned toward Carl. "But if you've got something to complain about, I suggest you talk directly with the police commissioner. I'm sure he'll be glad of the update."

Carl frowned. What the hell was Bjørn up to?

Then he took the pile of papers from the table and left without shutting the door behind him.

Now what? he thought as he leaned up against the wall in the archway. Several of his colleagues from homicide walked past without Carl returning their perfunctory greetings.

Why on earth hadn't Bjørn reacted more severely to Carl's aggressive attack? Of course, he had probably held himself in check because of his visitor, but it still felt different from usual. Was this about the relationship between Bjørn and the police commissioner? Had Carl become Bjørn's puppet—a useful idiot chosen to lead a revolt against their boss so that Bjørn didn't have to do it himself?

His eyes moved toward the police commissioner's office.

He would have to put it to the test.

"No, you can't talk to him now, Mørck. The police commissioner is in a meeting with the judicial committee," said one of the commissioner's two well-kept secretaries. "But I can schedule a meeting for you. What about May 26th at quarter past one?"

Did she just say the 26th? I'll show her where she can stick her quarter past one meeting in nine days, he thought, grabbing the door handle and entering the office.

A group of faces turned inquisitively toward him from across the eight-meter-long oak table. The police commander was sitting at the end of the table, erect and expressionless in his leather chair; the police commissioner was standing over by the bookcases frowning, while the group of politicians were sitting with their usual arrogant expressions, annoyed at not being taken seriously.

"I'm sorry, he slipped past me," apologized the secretary from behind him, but Carl couldn't care less.

"Okay," he said with a menacing voice as he looked around. "Now that the whole gang is present, I want to make it clear that the percentage of solved cases from Department Q over the past year has been no less than sixty-five."

He slammed Rose's reports down on the table.

"I don't know who it is up here in the tower that came up with the idea of sabotaging our figures, but if there's anyone present who dares to voice the opinion that Department Q should be disbanded or subjected to cutbacks, you should know that it won't happen without a fight."

Carl noticed the confused expression of the police commissioner, but then the police commander—an authoritative man with a stoic face and large eyebrows—stood up and addressed the group.

"Excuse me a moment while I discuss this matter with Inspector Carl Mørck."

Carl laughed all the way down to the basement. What a drama.

Clearly he had brought something to the table that the high and mighty on the committee did *not* know about. They had been close to disbanding a department that carried out effective investigations and had solved many cases, and someone had to take the fall for this mistake. Carl pictured the police commissioner's face and laughed again. The police commissioner alone would be held responsible for this. In polite circles, one would call it a loss of prestige, but Carl called it being in deep shit.

"We've got visitors, Carl," said Assad as soon as he met him in the hallway.

"Aren't you going to ask me how it went?"

"Yes, I . . . So how did it go?"

"Well! Now that you ask, I think Lars Bjørn pulled a number on our commissioner, because I'm dead certain that Bjørn was fully aware of the real percentages but still allowed the wrong information to make its way to the commissioner's office. And the commissioner took the bait, giving instructions to Bjørn to cut back Department Q, and subsequently informed the politicians about the changes."

"Okay, sorry if this is a stupid question, but why would Bjørn do that?" asked Assad.

"I'm fairly certain that Lars Bjørn has always defended Department

Q to the commissioner and has now stressed that he was right that Department Q is justified despite the large running costs. Because I don't think Bjørn has told him that his department snatches more than half our budget. But now the police commissioner knows that he needs to be careful about giving explicit orders to Bjørn. It's a mutiny against the police commissioner, Assad, and Bjørn knows me. I react when I'm provoked enough, and then it hits the fan."

Assad frowned. "It wasn't very nice of Bjørn to use us."

"No, but I'm planning to take revenge."

"How? Are you going to stroke him the wrong way?"

"You mean rub him the wrong way, Assad." Carl smiled. "Yes, something like that. In a way, Bjørn stole our figures for his own ends, wouldn't you say? So then it's also okay if I steal some cases from homicide for *my* ends, when and if it suits me."

Assad raised his hand to give Carl a high five. He was in.

"Who did you say was waiting for me?" Carl asked.

"I definitely didn't say anything about who it was, Carl."

Carl shook his head. While Assad was finally picking up on the finer nuances of Danish, no one was perfect.

He had only managed to reach the doorway to his office before the full horror of the situation was revealed.

Sitting in Carl's office chair was none other than the renowned red-bearded TV man Olaf Borg-Pedersen, looking as if he ought to have something to say for himself.

"Haven't you taken a wrong turn?" asked Carl. "The toilets are down the corridor."

"Ha-ha. No, Lars Bjørn has spoken so highly of you that we decided together that *Station 3* would shadow Department Q and watch you at work for a few days. Just a small film crew of three men. Me, a cameraman, and a sound technician. Won't it be fun?"

Carl glared and was about to give him a piece of his mind but thought better of it. Maybe this would present him with an opportunity for sabotage and Lars Bjørn would be sorry.

"Yes, it sounds like fun." He nodded with his eyes fixed on the notes Marcus Jacobsen had given him and which were now scattered unread on his desk. "Actually, we're investigating a case that might interest you. A very current murder case that could be perfect for your program, and which I happen to think is connected to one of our cold cases."

That caught his attention.

"I'll let you know when we get started."

"We're really worried about Rose, Carl."

There they stood, the oddest pair you could find at HQ. The short, squat, and dark Assad, with masculinity oozing from his jet-black stubble, standing next to Gordon, looking pale and as tall as a giraffe in comparison, and who was still waiting for his first real shave. The worry in the faces, however, was identical. It was genuinely touching.

"I'm sure she'll appreciate it, guys," he said.

"We thought we'd drive over there now, didn't we, Assad?" said Gordon.

He nodded. "Yes, we need to see how she's doing, Carl. Maybe she needs to be admitted again."

"All right, you two," he said soothingly. "Try not to worry. It's probably not so bad. Let Rose cool off. She said what she had to say. I'm sure she'll be back to her old self tomorrow."

"Yeah, maybe, Carl, and then again maybe not," said Assad. He didn't look convinced.

Carl knew where he was coming from.

"Time will tell," he said.

14

The perfume bottles stood close together in a neat row on the bathroom shelf. One for Vicky, one for Yrsa, and one for Lise-Marie, the way Rose had arranged them. Three very different and delicate scents that each bore witness to personal style and some measure of elegance, which wasn't something one would accuse Rose of possessing much of.

Each bottle had a sticker with one of the sisters' names on it. And when Rose sprayed one of these scents on the back of her wrist, it was normally only a matter of seconds before she could mimic the personality and identity of that sister down to the smallest detail.

It had always been that way with the scents of the women Rose had grown up with. When she was a child, she had mimicked her grandmother and mother by spraying her wrists with eau de cologne or Chanel No. 5, respectively, and later in life also all her sisters with each of their perfumes. Only her own perfume had an almost anonymous scent because "it's easier to dress when naked," as her pale Danish teacher always used to say with a hint of irony.

Earlier today, like so many times before, she had splashed herself with Vicky's perfume, and carried by this scent she had taken the S-train into the city to give Carl a piece of her mind. Prior to that, she had been to the hairdresser to have her hair cropped so short that even Vicky would have found it daring. She had bought a blouse from Malene Birger and a pair of jeans that were so tight around the crotch that anyone except Vicky would have found them obscene. When she arrived at police HQ dressed and acting like Vicky, she had shown her ID card to the puzzled security guard and made her way down to Carl, where she had spent five memorable minutes letting rip to Carl about how hard, unfair, and insensitive he always was with Rose, her beloved sister.

In Rose's experience a disguise often had the same effect on people as alcohol, as they both strengthened courage as well as the characteristics that didn't normally see the light of day.

She knew full well that Carl wouldn't be easily fooled, even though she had once managed to convince him for several days that she was her sister Yrsa, but that didn't matter. People were still more willing to listen to a cry for help if it was expressed by someone else or by people one pretended to be.

Afterward, she had felt great for about an hour, because Carl deserved no better. But then things took a turn for the worse.

She had only just arrived back at Stenløse Station when the all-consuming blackout hit her like a bolt of lightning from a clear sky. She couldn't remember what happened in the following hours. She just suddenly came to in her sitting room, having wet herself and with her expensive blouse pulled halfway down her shoulders and torn up to her bellybutton.

This had made Rose scared. Not just confused and uneasy like she had felt so many times before when her dark side had taken over, but soaked in complete and irrational anxiety. These blackouts were rare and superficial, but this time it was different. It almost felt as if a liquid had spread in her brain, killing her cells, and that there were membranes growing on her senses.

"Either this is going to kill me or I'm really going crazy," she whispered.

"But just think about it. You've hardly had any sleep or anything to drink in the last four days, and you haven't eaten anything. What did you expect?" she argued.

She wolfed down the remains in the fridge and drank liters of water in an attempt to feel better, but every time she tried to swallow it felt as if an internal vacuum sucked her further into herself. It made her nausea ten times worse than when she needed to be sick.

When evening came, she walked like a zombie from room to room, spitting on the bare walls. She saw faces deep within staring intensely at her from everywhere: the paneling, the walls, the tiles in the bathroom, and the cupboard doors in the kitchen.

Make the sign of the cross over us if you want to block out evil, screamed the surfaces. *Protect yourself against the inescapable abysses if you can, but hurry, you don't have much time.*

Rose found all the pens and pencils she could find in her drawers and placed them in front of her. Slowly and carefully, she chose a couple of bundles of black and red permanent markers and began to cover the walls with words that for a brief moment could keep all her terrible thoughts at bay.

After many hours in this daze, with aching wrists and stiff neck muscles, she put the permanent marker in her other hand and continued. She didn't allow herself any rest the entire night. She didn't even stop when she needed the toilet. It wasn't the first time today she had wet herself, so why should she worry if she did it again? She was driven by the fear of a harsher reality overpowering her if she didn't continue. She was constantly looking for bare surfaces to cover with her message, and eventually only the mirrors, fridge, and ceilings were left.

By that time, Rose's hands were shaking uncontrollably and her eyes wouldn't stop blinking. Her gag reflex had almost taken over her breathing and her head was swinging from side to side like a clock pendulum.

When Rose had written throughout the night and the dawn light revealed the walls and surfaces of the apartment daubed with a horrible message of powerlessness, her body was almost out of control. When she looked at herself in the hallway mirror between the myriad red and black lines and noticed how the Rose she otherwise knew so well now unmistakably reminded her of the distorted faces and lost souls in locked wards, it finally dawned on her that if she didn't do something about this now she would perish.

When she rang the psychiatric ward pleading for immediate help in a quivering voice, they recommended that she just take a taxi and find her own way there. They tried to sound upbeat and optimistic, maybe in the hope that it would have some effect on her and encourage her to find some willpower.

It was only when she began to scream down the telephone that the gravity of the situation became apparent, and an ambulance was sent for her.

15

Carl sat glued to the screen in amazement. With more than a million regular viewers, the crime documentary program *Station 3* had become the most popular continually running program in Danish TV history. Other programs of that sort had a serious approach, carefully presented the police work, and were happy to lend a hand in the investigation where possible. *Station 3* had an altogether different agenda, doing its best to explain criminal behavior based on the motto that all criminal acts were the result of poor social background, which was why the program often ended up glorifying the criminals.

The program Carl had just seen was no exception. It had started with a so-called exhaustive study of Hitler's background, concluding that he had been neglected and that the Second World War could have been avoided if his childhood had been more harmonious. As if that was news to anyone. Then the focus switched to the behavior of fifteen American serial killers, which without exception was the result of a string of parallel punishments in their youth. Time after time, it was made clear that police work was nothing more than a social effort aimed at helping these criminals to avoid this otherwise unavoidable destiny at an early point in their lives.

It was apparent to any fool, and yet the professional psychologists and other consultants on the program made good money from analyzing violent criminals, murderers, fraudsters, and other scum as victims, while eloquent journalists used their dubious talents to interview the criminals about the abuse they had been subjected to themselves.

Carl shook his head. Why the hell didn't they ever ask how these criminals could explain away all the terrible abuse they had inflicted? Serious matters were turned into entertainment, allowing politicians to sit back and breathe a sigh of relief because Denmark's most popular TV program conveyed the impression that something was being done about the situation.

Carl pressed eject and momentarily held the DVD that the TV company had given him before throwing it in the wastebasket. What the hell had Bjørn imagined that he could contribute to that infantile show? Now it seemed even more stupid to him that he had jumped on that bandwagon.

He turned to Assad, who was standing behind him. "What can we say about that rubbish, Assad?"

He shook his head. "Well, Carl, you might as well ask why camels have such big feet."

Carl pulled a face. Couldn't those bloody camels find somewhere else to go?

"Big feet?" He took a deep breath. "In order not to sink down in the sand, I assume. But what on earth do big camel feet have to do with that TV show, Assad?"

"The answer is that camels have big feet so they can dance the fandango on poisonous snakes if the vermin are stupid enough to slither past."

"And?"

"Just like camels, you and I also have big feet, Carl. Didn't you know that?"

Carl looked down at Assad's small duck-like feet and took a deep breath. "So you think Bjørn assigned us to the job to make things difficult for *Station 3*?"

Assad gave him a thumbs-up with his scarred thumb.

"I don't want to play at being a camel to make Bjørn feel better," he said, reaching out for the landline. No, if anyone was going to play the camel, it was going to be Bjørn.

As soon as he put his hand on the telephone, it rang.

"Yes?" he snarled. There was never any peace to get things finished around here.

"Hello, my name is Vicky Knudsen," said a subdued voice. "I'm Rose's younger sister."

Carl's face changed. This should be interesting. He grabbed the extra receiver and gave it to Assad.

"Well, hello, Vicky. Carl Mørck speaking," he said with a hint of sarcasm. "How is Rose today? Did you give her my apology?"

It went silent at the other end of the line. Surely she knew now that he had seen through her.

"I don't understand. What apology?"

Assad signaled to Carl to tone it down. Was his desire to attack really that obvious?

"I'm calling because Rose is in an awful state," she continued.

"I'll say," whispered Carl with his hand over the receiver, but Assad wasn't listening.

"Rose has been admitted to the psychiatric center in Glostrup again as an emergency measure, so I'm calling to let you know that she won't be ready to come back to work for a while. I'll make sure that the center sends you her sick note."

Carl was just about to protest and say that now things had gone far enough, but the next few sentences he heard stopped him.

"A couple of our friends saw her sitting on a bench outside Matas in Egedal shopping center yesterday, shaking all over. They tried to take her home with them but she told them to get lost. Then they called me and said that I had better come down there. I looked for her with our younger sister Lise-Marie all over the whole shopping center, but we weren't the ones to find her—that was a parking attendant, we were told later. He'd found her on the ground in a puddle of pee, half asleep against a car parked in the farthest parking bay wearing a blouse she had almost pulled off. He was also the one who helped her home.

"Then this morning our mom called to say that the psychiatric center had contacted her and that Rose had been admitted again. Of course, I called them immediately, and the head psychiatric nurse told me that they'd found an S-train ticket in her pocket, which had been validated at Copenhagen Central Station. So we think that she must've walked from the station in Stenløse and perhaps stopped on the way home to buy groceries, which she normally does in Meny supermarket. But when the parking attendant found her, she had no groceries with her so she probably hadn't done that."

"I'm sorry to hear that, Vicky," he heard himself say while Assad nodded along. It really was very sad.

"Is there anything we can do? Do you think we could visit her?" Assad nodded again, but slower this time and with sharp, reproachful eyes.

Carl got the message. It was true. He should have allowed Gordon and Assad to drive over to Rose's apartment yesterday.

"Visit? No, unfortunately not. The doctors have created a treatment plan for her and would rather she wasn't disturbed."

"She hasn't been committed, has she?"

"No, but she's not likely to want to leave the institution as long as she is in this state, they say. She's ready to receive treatment."

"Okay. Let us know if anything changes."

There was a pause at the other end as if she were picking up the courage to say something else. Probably not anything that would soften the blow of the already sad news.

"Actually, I'm not only calling to tell you this," she finally said. "My sisters and I would appreciate it if you'd come over to Rose's apartment. I'm calling from there. And remember she'd moved one floor up."

"Do you mean now?"

"Yes, please, that would be good. We thought we'd just get some clothes for Rose and hadn't at all expected the sight that met us. We've spoken about whether you or someone from your team might be able to come and help us understand what's going on with Rose."

Rose's bright red Vespa was parked in the parking lot at Sandal-sparken, next to the bicycle stands under a couple of budding trees, conveying nothing but peacefulness and normality. Rose had lived for more than ten years in this yellow block cocooned in open-air walk-ways without ever having expressed any dissatisfaction. That fact in particular was difficult to understand given the sight that met Carl and Assad when Vicky, who wasn't at all unlike the woman Rose had pre-tended to be the day before, opened the door.

"Why did Rose move up here? Isn't this apartment similar to the old one?" asked Carl, scanning the surroundings.

"Yes. But she can see the church from here, which she couldn't re-ally from the ground floor. Not because she's religious or anything; she just thought it was nicer," answered Vicky before showing them into the sitting room. "What do you make of this?"

Carl swallowed hard. What a miserable chaos and indescribable mess. Now he understood better why Rose's perfume was sometimes quite strong, even though it still couldn't overpower the stuffy smell. In fact, the apartment looked like it was home to a hoarder who had been robbed by someone who had ransacked everything. Cardboard packaging everywhere. Moving boxes half-packed with the contents of drawers. Dirty dishes piled up on the coffee table. Dining table covered in leftovers and take-away boxes. Books thrown down from the bookcase, blankets and duvets ripped to shreds, and sofas and chairs with torn upholstery. Not a surface had been spared.

It was a very different sight from the apartment Carl and Assad had visited a few years ago.

Vicky pointed at the walls. "That's what shocked us the most."

Carl heard Assad behind him mumbling a few words in Arabic. If Carl had been able to, he would probably have done the same, because he couldn't find words to express his shock. Rose had ferociously written the same sentence over and over in varying sizes on every inch of every wall.

YOU DO NOT BELONG HERE

He understood exactly why Rose's sister had called.

"Have you informed the psychiatrists about this?" asked Assad.

Vicky nodded. "We've e-mailed them photos of most of the apartment. Lise-Marie is in the bedroom photographing the rest just now."

"Is it the same in there?"

"Everywhere. The bathroom, the kitchen. Even on the inside of the fridge."

"Do you have any idea how long it's been like this?" asked Carl. He simply couldn't associate this chaos with the otherwise extremely structured person who ordered everyone around in Department Q on a daily basis.

"I don't know. We haven't been up in the apartment since our mom came home from Spain."

"I seem to recall Rose mentioning that. It was at Christmastime, right? So almost five months ago."

Vicky nodded with a forlorn expression. It obviously plagued her that she and her sisters hadn't been there for Rose. They weren't the only ones.

"Come in here a minute," shouted Lise-Marie from the bedroom. She sounded somewhat desperate.

They were met by a similarly graffiti-covered room, where Lise-Marie was sitting cross-legged and crying on the bed, the camera on the duvet in front of her. In her lap she had a small cardboard box full of grey notebooks with dark spines.

"Oh, Vicky, it's terrible," exclaimed Lise-Marie. "Look! Rose just kept on and on. Even after Dad's death."

Vicky sat on the edge of the bed, picked up one of the notebooks, and opened it.

A moment later, her expression changed as if she had been slapped.

"It can't be true," she said, while her younger sister hid her face in her hands as the tears streamed from her eyes.

Vicky picked up a few more notebooks and turned to Carl. "She always did this when we were children. We just thought it'd stopped when our dad died. Here's the first one she wrote."

She passed a notebook to Carl: "1990" was written on the front with a permanent marker.

Assad looked over Carl's shoulder as he opened it.

Had it been graphic design, it would have been interesting. But as it was, it could only be sad and shocking.

He leafed through the notebook. Just the same thing again and again. Every page was covered with the same sentence, written with the characteristic capital letters of a ten-year-old. Close together and uneven.

"SHUT UP SHUT UP SHUT UP," written page after page.

Assad reached out to take another notebook, which had "1995" written on the front in black and white on the back.

He opened it, holding it out so that Carl could also see.

"I CAN'T HEAR YOU I CAN'T HEAR YOU I CAN'T HEAR YOU," was written on page after page.

Carl and Assad looked at each other.

"Rose and our dad didn't get along," said Vicky.

"That's a hell of an understatement," said Lise-Marie. Apparently the younger sister had gained enough composure to join the conversation.

"I know." Vicky looked exhausted. "Our dad was killed in a work-related accident at the steel plant in 1999. After that, we never saw Rose with her notebooks. And yet here they are."

She threw one of them over to Carl, who caught it in midair.

On the front was written "2010," and like the others it was completely covered with a single sentence, only now in a more adult hand.

"LEAVE ME ALONE LEAVE ME ALONE LEAVE ME ALONE
LEAVE ME ALONE."

"I wonder if this might be her way of communicating with your dad, dead or alive," said Assad.

The others all nodded.

"It's totally messed up," cried the youngest.

Vicky was more composed, nothing like the wild and witty girl Rose always spoke about. "Dad bullied her," she said calmly. "We don't know exactly what he did when it was at its worst because she never told us, but we've always known that she hated him for it. So much that it's difficult to imagine."

Carl frowned. "Bullied her, you say? Do you mean he abused her? Sexually, I mean."

They both shook their heads. Their dad wasn't like that. He was all bark and no bite. At least that was what they claimed.

"I just don't understand why it didn't stop when Dad died. But here are all the notebooks. And now all the writing on the walls." Vicky nodded at the walls. The writing was so dense that there was hardly an empty surface.

"It doesn't make any sense." Lise-Marie sniffled.

"Come out here, Carl," Assad shouted from the hallway.

He was standing in front of the mirror looking at the bureau. Despite its diminutive size, it was piled high with books. Wide and flat like atlases—though that wasn't what they were.

"I looked through the pile, Carl, and you won't believe it."

He picked up the one on the top, a medium-sized book with a hard cover.

"Copenhagen Police HQ," it was called, and Carl knew it well. It was an overview of the police headquarters in Copenhagen, and rather detailed apart from the glaring absence of Department Q in the cellar.

It left no doubt about their status in the grand scheme.

"Look!" Assad pointed at the next book in the pile, approximately one and a half centimeters thick and bound in shirting like the many others piled underneath in different colors.

He opened the book on the first page. "Look at the title. She's called it 'Bag lady.'"

Assad turned the page and pointed at a photo of a young woman.

"She's created a personal ID card for all those involved in the case," he said, pointing at the writing underneath: "Kirsten-Marie Lassen, alias Kimmie."

Carl read further.

"Summary: lives in a small brick house by the train line parallel to Ingerslevsgade. Has lived on the street for eleven years. Gave birth to a stillborn child some years back. Father lives in Monte Carlo. Mother, Kassandra Lassen, lives in Ordrup. No siblings."

He scanned the page. It contained all the important information about the person in the first case Rose had been involved in.

He leafed quickly through the following pages. No one was forgotten, with photos, biographies, and newspaper clippings of the most important events in their lives.

"There are more than forty cases in the pile, Carl. All cases that Rose has worked on in Department Q, and she's given them names. For example, 'Message in a Bottle,' 'Scandal on Sprogø,' and 'Marco,' just to name a few."

He pulled out a rust-red scrapbook from the bottom of the pile.

"I think this one will interest you more than the others, Carl." Carl opened it. "The Hanging Girl," she had named it.

"It's the Habersaat case, Carl. Have a look at the next page."

Carl turned the page and saw a face he didn't recognize.

"It looks like Habersaat, but I suppose it isn't," he said.

"No, but read the text underneath, and go to the next page."

"Arne Knudsen—12.12.1952–5.18.1999," was written under the photo. "Okay," said Carl and turned to the next page, where there was a photo of Christian Habersaat.

"Turn the page back and forth; then you'll see it."

He did and it was true. Seen one after the other, the resemblance was striking. The eyes were almost identical, except that Arne Knudsen's were totally expressionless.

"I think Rose's dad was a very unpleasant man," said Carl.

"She must've been really crazy to cut up all the furniture and tear everything to bits," said Assad, sitting as usual with his feet up on the dashboard.

They had been driving for ten minutes without saying a word, but someone had to break the silence.

"Yes, more crazy than we could've imagined," admitted Carl.

"Now I'm wondering what her dad did to her," continued Assad. "Why only her and not the other daughters?"

"I asked Vicky about it, but you probably didn't hear. If there was any sign that he was about to bully her sisters, Rose stopped him in his tracks."

"How? Why couldn't she stop him when he was going for her?"

"Good question, Assad. None of the sisters could answer that either."

"It's like camels. No one has any idea why they do what they do."

"I'm not sure I appreciate the comparison, Assad."

"That's because you don't respect camels enough, Carl. But they are the ones who get people safely across the desert, remember."

Respect for camels? He shook his head. He'd need to find some respect for them even if just to get some peace.

They were silent for the remainder of the journey, struggling with their own thoughts and self-reproach. Why the hell hadn't they been more involved in Rose's life?

Carl sighed. Now he had three cases to focus on: the murder of a woman twelve years ago, a three-week-old murder case, and now the death of what they knew as Rose's personality.

He no longer knew which of these cases to prioritize.

16

Friday, May 20th, to Monday, May 23rd, 2016

Anneli undressed in a daze and lay down on the bed, still shaking from the cocktail of exhilaration and adrenaline from murdering Michelle out in the North West district. It was really an unknown sensation for this nice girl who for almost fifty years had been something of a Goody Two-shoes, having never hurt anyone or anything. How could she have known how good it would feel to play judge and jury over people's lives? It was like uninhibited sex that you hadn't expected. Like eager hands on your body that awoke latent desires that seemed otherwise forbidden. She had once refrained from rejecting a man next to her in the cinema who had put his hand on her thigh uninvited. Just let him do what he wanted while she lost herself in the on-screen embraces that would never be hers anyway. And now, as she lay there touching herself, recalling the effect he had had on her when he pushed his hand all the way up to her crotch and how she had controlled her orgasm in silent ecstasy, her body was struggling to cope with the inconceivable fact that she had killed another human being.

Michelle Hansen had been exactly the easy victim that Anneli had expected. She had plodded across the street without looking and naively tried to defend herself with her arm, but it was already too late.

Anneli had anticipated feeling nervous about what she had planned to do. That she would have felt sick to her stomach and that her heart would have been pounding, but up until the moment she put her foot down on the accelerator, there had been no reaction at all of that sort.

A huge, ten-second injection of adrenaline was all she experienced, and then it was over.

Maybe Anneli had thought that the impact would feel different, but the dull thud when she hit the body didn't measure up to the sight of Michelle Hansen's body being flung backward and her head hitting the pavement.

Their eyes had met for a split second before the impact, and that had been the biggest satisfaction. The fact that the girl had drawn her last breath knowing that she had been targeted, that the driver was someone she knew, and that she got what she deserved.

The small Peugeot Anneli had chosen had been surprisingly suitable and easy to maneuver, so she reckoned that if she was going to go after her next victim this weekend, she could use it again.

With Michelle Hansen's terrified face still fresh in her mind, Anneli forgot about the cancer, pain, and anxiety, resting her head back on her pillow. In reality, it was maybe a sort of divine gesture that this stupid girl could give another person such heavenly pleasure with her last gaze. Perhaps fate had somehow chosen both victim and perpetrator for this symbiotic act. One by giving her life, the other by taking it.

Anneli woke feeling rested and her mind occupied with the project. In just one day, she would have disposed of another expendable human being, and what a great thought that was. Of course, she was well aware that it was wrong in a societal sense. Taking the law into one's own hands, not to mention murder, was illegal. But when she thought about the thousands of hours these parasitic girls had spent on making fools of her and the system, wasn't it about time and good for everyone that someone finally took action? And considering the moral decline in Denmark at present, there were many other things that deserved harsher criticism than her little vendetta. The politicians were acting like pigs, taking society for a ride with stopgap measures and insane ideologies that were better suited to dictatorships. What did a few petty murders matter compared to the character assassination of an entire nation?

She sat down in her small kitchen with the hideous cupboard doors and, slowly and steadily, in the comfort of her own little world, built up a feeling of justified indignation and omnipotent power. In this tiny, humble room, she temporarily represented all the executive power in the world, and no one could argue against her.

She had wanted to celebrate the media coverage of Michelle's death by spoiling herself today, buying things she otherwise didn't allow herself, indulging herself with something nice to eat, and only then planning the details of her next retaliation.

But when she turned on her computer to check the news and found the headline she was looking for, she felt a violent stab in her chest, and any feeling of euphoria was gone.

"Young female victim of a hit-and-run in Copenhagen's North West district miraculously survives," it read.

Anneli froze. She read the text over and over before collecting herself enough to click on the link to read the full story.

The victim's name was not mentioned—of course it wasn't—but there couldn't be any doubt that it was Michelle Hansen.

In her desperation, she searched the text for the words "in critical condition" but didn't find them. She was in shock. Couldn't even breathe.

Everything went black and she fell backward onto the kitchen floor.

When she woke she managed to push herself up into the corner next to the fridge. Her head was full of unpleasant questions.

Had Michelle Hansen really seen her face? How could she have when the windshield was so filthy and it was only a question of a split second? And even if she had seen her, like she had initially hoped, what would that even prove? Anneli knew that middle-aged women with faces like hers were a dime a dozen, so she could just deny it. Explain it away by saying that the girl must have imagined it or was purposely trying to frame her because she hated her. That she was nothing but a drain on society and that she was trying to get revenge in this petty way because Anneli had made things difficult for her.

Anneli convinced herself that no one else could have seen her. The street had been completely empty, and even if there might have been witnesses who had been looking out of their windows, it would be impossible for them to identify her.

Pensively, she reached out for a bottle of red wine and unscrewed the cap. What if someone had managed to see the number plates? The thought made her hand shake when she poured, because then the police would already be searching for the car.

She emptied the glass in a few gulps while thinking.

How could she find out if the car had been reported missing? And if it had, was it parked far enough away from her home on Webersgade?

Anneli assessed the situation over and over. There was so much that felt wrong just now. First and foremost that Michelle Hansen was still alive, but also that this could hinder her entire project.

"No," she shouted out after her third glass. Now she had finally felt alive. Had finally felt the joy of life rushing through her veins. She wasn't about to give that up. Not even at the risk of being caught.

So Anneli got dressed without having a shower first and stepped out determinedly into the gentle sunshine toward the street where she had parked the red Peugeot.

She waited until the street was empty. Then she removed the plastic from the broken side window, opened the door, got in the car, and forced the screwdriver into the ignition.

Anneli had a plan that was not only smart but also simple. She needed to find out if the police had been informed about the number plate of the car involved in the hit-and-run. And what better way to find out than to park the car in a public place where there would be a lot of traffic and police presence? Then it would only be a question of time before she knew if they were looking for it.

During the two hours when Anneli kept an eye on the parked car from a distance, at least four patrol cars had driven slowly past it. And as nothing had happened, she bought a parking ticket with some spare change and left the car. If it was still parked on Griffenfeldsgade tomorrow, she could keep her weapon of choice.

Senta Berger had named herself after a famous Austrian film star, which Anneli had struggled to get used to. Senta had formerly been called Anja Olsen, which she changed to Oline Anjou before eventually deciding on this glamorous name that she could by no means live up to. She had been Anneli's client throughout the years, in which the girl had gone from being an annoying, self-promoting, and demanding eighteen-year-old to being an insipid, glitter-covered, and pompous pest of twenty-eight.

The mere thought of Senta made Anneli feel nauseous, and therefore she had been happy when she was reassigned to another office and could leave the harpy to be judged by others. But even if she was rid of the sight of this odd Barbie imitation in her professional life, she constantly saw her in town.

Senta was always carrying shopping bags from various clothing stores and lived for nothing else but this urge to waste public money, which, even hours after these chance meetings, accentuated Anneli's natural indignation and anger. So it was no coincidence that Anneli picked Senta's profile from her list of parasitic girls, which would now ultimately end in Senta Berger's death.

Anneli took her time. The day after Saturday night's parties that kind of girl rarely ventured out before late afternoon, so Anneli leaned back in the car seat with her thermos, concentrating on the door from which she expected the girl to appear.

If she was with someone, Anneli would wait until another day, and the same applied if there was any other sort of obstacle.

On a Sunday afternoon, it was as dead out here in Valby as in a restaurant in Lyngby on New Year's Eve. Once in a while someone ventured out to buy Danish pastries for their coffee or a cyclist took a shortcut down toward Vigerslevvej, but otherwise absolutely nothing was happening. It was just as it should be.

Approaching five o'clock she saw movement in Senta Berger's apartment. The curtains were opened and she could see the outline of a figure behind the window.

Anneli screwed the lid back on her thermos and pulled on her gloves. Less than fifteen minutes later, the main door opened and Senta pranced out with a fake designer bag, miniskirt, leather boots up to her thighs, and a scarlet faux-fur cape.

She was killed a hundred meters farther down the street on the sidewalk. The stupid bitch had apparently turned up the volume on her headphones, because she didn't manage to react before her body was crushed against the wall of the building.

This time the victim was definitely dead, but it was still with a sense of frustration that Anneli reversed the car onto the road and left the neighborhood. Damn it, the girl was supposed to have noticed her executioner just before her mind went blank and her brain was splattered on the wall. Then she would have acknowledged a lifetime of mistakes and misuse at the moment of death—that was supposed to be the beauty of it.

That was what excited Anneli. So no, she wasn't satisfied. It hadn't gone exactly to plan this time either.

She drove the car to the car wash and remained in the car as the brushes attempted to rip off the plastic from the side window. When the wash was finished, she mopped up the soapy water that had seeped into the car and wiped down all the areas she might have touched.

She had decided to use the car only one last time. Not only did she have to be careful in choosing her victims to make sure that there was no recognizable pattern; she also had to be careful about her choice of murder weapon.

Just like last time, she would park the car on Griffenfeldsgade. Whether the car was wanted for being stolen or for being used as a getaway vehicle was one and the same; the only question was whether or not the police were keeping an eye on it. All she had to do now was put enough coins in the parking meter and come back every day to renew the parking ticket. If the police had not noticed it in the meantime, she could use it again.

She put the thermos, a few hairs, some cracker crumbs, and a couple of used tissues in a plastic bag and slammed the door. It wouldn't be long before her next mission, and *this* time she would make sure her victim turned around.

Even if she had to use the horn.

The radiotherapy building outside the main entrance to Copenhagen University Hospital was almost hidden by the chaos of portable buildings and hectic activity. Anneli followed the signs to entrance 39 and then walked down several flights of stairs while thinking about radiation danger and the sixties bunkers built to protect from nuclear attacks. *Calm down, Anneli. They want what's best for you,* she said to herself, entering a waiting room of unexpected proportions with information desks, an aquarium, sofas, flat-screen TVs, and sunbeams falling softly down through the skylight and hitting the myriad green plants. Down here on this early Monday morning, all the patients waiting to receive radiation treatment were gathered, and despite the unfortunate reasons for them being here, the atmosphere felt secure and comforting. Everyone was here for the same reason, bound together by fate, each of them with small dots tattooed on their bodies so the nurses and radiographers could locate precisely where they should have their treatment. They were down here to give life a chance, just like Anneli would be here five times a week for the next four to five weeks.

If it turned out that contrary to expectation neither radiation nor chemo could get rid of the cancer, she would speed up her murder rate. From a rational point of view, she could manage to kill dozens of these women if she put in the effort. And if the police closed in on her, the solution could be to kill several girls a day, because the consequences were clear. Whether she killed one or forty women was all the same in a country where the ultimate sentence was life imprisonment. She had seen how comfortably those murderers who society didn't dare release lived in psychiatric wards. And if *that* was the worst that could happen, she could handle it.

Anneli smiled to herself when they called her in for her radio-therapy, and she was still smiling an hour later when she was sitting on her office chair advising clients.

After a couple of rare satisfactory meetings, it was finally Jazmine Jørgensen's turn.

You're in for it, thought Anneli with some delight when the wench sat down and turned her head toward the window, probably completely uninterested in the fact that Anneli was the one setting the agenda.

If only she knew how Anneli felt about that attitude.

Over the last few years, Jazmine Jørgensen had gotten off the hook with pregnancies, related afflictions, and maternity leave, without fulfilling any of her obligations. Now she had been referred to a psychologist, and if she didn't accept the offer of more radical prevention, she would be called in to a meeting about what they should do with her.

However, Anneli didn't imagine it would come to that. In a few months, Jazmine Jørgensen would be in her grave anyway—pregnant or not.

Over the next few minutes, Anneli explained the framework for their future collaboration, including job search courses, prevention, and budgeting, and as expected, Jazmine didn't look away from the window or the street outside for a moment. Provocative, yes, but it increased Anneli's feeling of fighting for justice.

She pushed a sheet of paper across the table to inform the silly girl in more detail about what she had just told her. Finally, Jazmine turned to face her.

For a young woman like her who no matter what always tried to look her best, her face was suddenly extremely cold and charmless.

Behind the painted facade of eyeliner, foundation, and lipstick, there was more to this pretty doll face than Anneli had noticed before. Defiance that bordered on something aggressively sly. A hint of resolve that exceeded the usual demand for money, and a stubborn rejection of having to work for it.

"Have you heard that Michelle Hansen is going to be okay?" asked the girl, dryly and unexpectedly. Nothing in her expression changed; she just stared hatefully at Anneli, who unwillingly reacted with an almost unnoticeable twitch of her head and thankfully nothing else. But inside, Anneli was all but collected. Chaotic thoughts and defense mechanisms, mixed with tempered caution and a lack of understanding, rushed through her.

How much did this nasty bitch know?

"Michelle Hansen, you say?" she said hesitantly. "What's happened to Michelle? Do you know her?" she asked, as if she didn't know. As if Michelle hadn't been one of the three girls who had spoken behind her back in the waiting room. That wasn't something you just forgot.

They sized each other up, Anneli looking quizzical while Jazmine resembled a dog ready to bare its teeth.

She's waiting for you to make a move, Anneli, so be careful! she thought.

"You're not answering me, Jazmine, and I'm not sure I quite follow. What do you mean by saying Michelle will 'be okay'? What will be okay?"

Jazmine still didn't say anything. She just stared at Anneli, as if expecting that the slightest twitch of an eye or a beating pulse on her neck would give her away.

Anneli breathed calmly despite everything inside her screaming to high heaven that this couldn't be happening. She was cornered and the only thing she could do was impress on herself that no one in the world could prove her crimes. Thank God that as far as she knew no one had seen her in connection with the hit-and-run attacks on Michelle Hansen or Senta Berger.

"Isn't there something about you and red cars being a good match?" asked the girl coldly.

Anneli smiled as best she could. "Jazmine, are you sure you're feeling quite all right? Take this piece of paper home and read it carefully." She pushed the paper another couple of centimeters toward the girl. "And by the way, my car is blue and black. A nice little Ka. Do you know them?"

And while she indicated that Jazmine Jørgensen could leave, she decided that she had used the red car for the last time and that it might be a good idea to keep an eye on this girl's movements and whom she saw.

But no matter what, this meeting meant that Jazmine immediately moved up a few places on her list.

17

Thursday, May 19th, 2016

"This is where Rigmor Zimmermann was found."

Tomas Laursen pointed at an outline on the grass that was almost gone.

Carl smiled. Assad had had the brilliant idea to lure the police HQ canteen manager with them to the King's Garden. Tomas had long since stepped down as a forensic technician, but there was nothing wrong with his eyes.

"Do we know which entrance she took into the park?" asked Assad. "Was it the one down there?"

Carl looked along the wrought-iron railings to Kronprinsessegade down toward the farthest corner of the park. He nodded. Given that the woman had left her daughter's apartment at the bottom of the Borgergade neighborhood in heavy rain, it was most likely that she had used the entrance from Sølvgade so she could take a shortcut to the exit out to Gothersgade.

"I don't really get it," continued Assad. "She lived out in Stenløse and used to take the S-train. Do we have any idea why she walked toward Nørreport Station rather than the metro at Kongens Nytorv or Østerport Station? That would've made more sense."

Tomas Laursen leafed through the already rather extensive police report. Amazing that he had managed to get it out from homicide.

Now he shook his head. "No, we don't know."

"But what does the daughter say? Maybe she knows," said Carl.

"We have a copy of what she told the police, which isn't much. So our colleagues haven't really touched on that either," said Laursen.

It's a fairly elementary question, so why the hell haven't they asked it? thought Carl.

"Who's in charge of the investigation?" he then asked.

"Pasgård."

Carl sighed. You'd be hard-pressed to find a more self-glorifying, superficial jerk.

"Yes, I know what you're thinking." Tomas nodded. "But he's also *almost* as big a whiner as you, Carl. He won't like it one bit when he hears that you're investigating his case."

"Then we'll just have to keep it a secret," suggested Assad.

Laursen nodded and knelt down next to the outline to investigate the grass. The park keeper had followed the police order to the letter, refraining from cutting the grass in a three-meter radius around the scene, which had resulted in that grass growing slightly longer than the grass around it.

"Hmm," said Laursen, holding up a single withered leaf he had found half a meter from the outline.

Carl noticed that both Assad and Laursen looked puzzled and followed their gaze, slowly scanning the flower beds and the wrought-iron railings down toward Sølvgade. Now he saw it too. It was well observed. The leaf didn't come from any of the bushes or trees near where she had been found.

"Could the leaf have been here for more than three weeks?" asked Assad.

Laursen shrugged. "Possibly, yes. The crime scene is some distance from the paths, and there hasn't been any wind to speak of for weeks." Then he shook his head. "On the other hand, it could've been on the bottom of someone's shoe or left here by a dog at any time since the murder. What type of leaf is it anyway? Do you know, Carl?"

Where the hell should he know that from? He wasn't a bloody gardener or botanist.

"I'm just going for a walk," said Assad, which was a bit of an understatement given that he started running, looking like a cross between a French bulldog and someone who had just shat himself, the way he darted along the path toward the Sølvgade entrance.

Carl gawped.

"I can see that the leaf has been flattened. So it might very well have been under a shoe," said Laursen, with his behind sticking in the air and his nose pressed down to the ground.

Carl was just about to say that they probably wouldn't get much more out of this crime scene because all the leads, not to mention the body, were long since gone.

"On the other hand, I've spotted some very fine furrows on the surface of the leaf. And shoes don't have narrow furrows like that, and neither do dogs," continued Laursen, laughing. His sense of humor had always been odd.

"And?"

Laursen leafed through the report again and pointed to a photo of the body. "And so it could be from these," he said, tapping the pants on the body. "Narrow-ribbed corduroy. Very popular with elderly ladies who don't update their wardrobe from one day to the next," he said.

Carl took the leaf and studied it closely. Laursen was right.

"Perhaps we'll learn more when our sprinter crosses the line," he said, pointing at Assad, who was running toward them at full speed like a stampeding gnu.

He was out of breath but proud. "Here," he said, thrusting a leaf in their faces. "There are lots of leaves like this down there in the thicket just to the left of the entrance behind the bicycle stands."

All at once, Tomas Laursen's face broke out in a smile. It was a long time since Carl had seen him so thrilled.

"Bloody brilliant!" cheered the canteen manager. "Now we know where that male urine came from. Yeah, we know quite a lot all of a sudden."

Assad nodded. "I also read that she had dog shit on her shoes."

"Yes, but there was no gravel in the shit," said Laursen. "So it's more likely that she stepped in that outside the garden."

Carl didn't follow at all.

"So you actually believe that you've just described the course of events more or less? That would really be a breakthrough." Carl was skeptical.

Laursen laughed. "Hell yes. It almost makes me want to join the force again."

"So you think that Rigmor Zimmermann wanted to take a shortcut through the park but had already begun running on the sidewalk outside the park? And what makes you think that?"

"She was a classy lady, right? Smart handmade shoes from Scarosso, and she'd even been married to a shoe shop owner and must have known quality when she saw it. Exclusive shoes like that cost more than two thousand kroner, let me tell you," said Laursen.

"Right up the prime minister's street," Assad said with a laugh.

"And she wouldn't voluntarily smear those shoes with dog shit, is that what you're telling me?" asked Carl, smiling at his own powers of deduction. But then again, who the hell would ever purposely step in dog shit?

Laursen gave him a thumbs-up.

Assad nodded. "She ran along the sidewalk without looking where she was going. It was also pouring that night, so I agree with Laursen."

It was exactly like watching an old film with Sherlock Holmes and Watson showing off.

"And she didn't watch her step, resulting in her stepping in dog shit with her smart, expensive shoes. Not because she was in a rush but because she felt threatened. Is that where you two are going with this?"

Two thumbs-up.

He followed them down to the thicket and looked at it for a moment. Not a bad hiding place when it came to it.

"Okay, let's sum up. Rigmor Zimmermann ran because she felt threatened. Ran into the King's Garden . . ."

"Rosenborg Castle Gardens, Carl," interjected Assad.

"It's the same bloody park, Assad."

Assad's dark eyebrows leapt in the air.

"And then she ran into *Rosenborg Castle Gardens*," he corrected himself to keep the peace while looking at Assad. Apparently that name made Assad feel more comfortable. "And then she hid in this thicket, where the ground is covered with the same leaves as the one we found at the crime scene. It's probably a place where a lot of people piss."

"Yes, the smell gives that away, Carl. You can smell it from a distance, but then it is just at the entrance to the park and handy for those who are bursting," concluded Laursen.

"Hmm. You say that the coroner found the urine on the right buttock and thigh of the body, and now you're concluding that it's because she was hiding in the bushes." Carl nodded to himself. "But why didn't the perpetrator attack her right here? Is it because they didn't see her and ran past her?"

Laursen smiled triumphantly. Finally they were on the same wavelength, it seemed.

"Presumably, yes," said Laursen. "And then Rigmor Zimmermann sat there for a while until she felt sure the coast was clear and continued down the path. But that's just a theory. We can't know for sure."

He was right about that.

"Then you also think that the perpetrator hid down by the restaurant in the meantime and jumped out right at the moment Zimmermann walked past?"

There were those bloody thumbs in the air again.

Carl laughed, shaking his head. "Perhaps you two ought to start writing crime novels, given that you build your conclusions and theories on dog shit and withered leaves."

"Nevertheless, it's highly likely, Carl." Laursen looked at him with subdued complacency, which actually suited him. "In my years as a forensic technician, I learned that mysteries can suddenly be solved on the basis of the wildest theories. Do you know what I mean?"

Carl nodded. He knew that better than anyone. He just couldn't help but smile. If there was any truth to this hypothesis, a certain Inspector Pasgård would kick himself.

"Ahh, there you are," shouted a male voice across the lawn. "Gordon was right, then. Would you mind going back to the place where the woman was found?"

There were three men. The cameraman, the sound technician, and the bloody annoying Olaf Borg-Pedersen from *Station 3* himself. What the hell were they doing here and why had Gordon told them where they were? He was in for it now.

When they were standing back at the crime scene, Borg-Pedersen gestured to his sound technician, who produced some sort of equipment from his bag.

"We've brought a can of white spray paint so we can redraw the outline of the position of the body. Do you want the honor, or shall I?"

Carl frowned. "If you so much as spray a single drop, I'll damn well empty the entire can in your face. Are you out of your mind? This is a crime scene."

Olaf Borg-Pedersen was clearly a man with years of experience in handling obstinate people, so without hesitation he put his hand in his pocket to reveal three Yankie chocolate bars.

"Low blood sugar?" he said.

Only Assad accepted the offer. Taking all three of them, in fact.

There were lots of names on the intercom, and the name Zimmermann appeared twice. Birgit F. Zimmermann on the ground floor was the one they had come to talk to, but there was also a Denise F. Zimmermann on the fifth floor, whom Carl had never heard of.

"Can you believe it?" he said, pressing the buzzer. "Those TV guys were completely delusional, thinking that they could be present when we are questioning someone."

"I guess, but even so, Carl. You should've thought twice before kicking that TV producer in the shin. I'm not sure he believed it was an accident," said Laursen.

Carl smiled wryly at Assad. Wasn't it just the sort of alternative but extremely effective method of communication he had used to shut up

Gordon? Assad smiled back and shrugged. As long as it worked, what was the problem?

They pressed the buzzer several times again before a drawling female voice finally answered.

"Police," said Laursen. A clumsy introduction, but then communication had never been his strong point—he was a technician after all.

"Hello, Mrs. Zimmermann," Carl said in a friendlier tone. "We'd appreciate it if you could spare us five minutes of your time."

There was a crackling buzzing sound at the door, and Carl gave Laursen a knowing look as he pushed open the door to the entrance. *Let me do the talking,* his look had indicated.

She opened the door wide wearing a kimono that was opened almost just as wide, revealing her pale skin and wrinkled panty hose. It was already obvious from the stench of alcohol on her breath how she spent her days.

"Yes, sorry we didn't inform you we were coming beforehand, Mrs. Zimmermann. I apologize. But we just happened to be in the neighborhood," said Carl.

She stared at the three men as she swayed a little from side to side. She found it especially hard to take her eyes off Assad.

"Lovely to meet you," said Assad, offering his hand with a twinkle in his eye. He had a way with women, especially if they were a bit tipsy.

"Excuse the mess. I've had a lot on my plate lately," she said, attempting to clear some space on the sofa. A few indefinable objects fell to the floor, and then they sat down.

Carl began by offering his condolences. It must have been hard losing her mother in that terrible way.

She attempted to nod normally, struggling to keep her eyes open so that she could follow the conversation.

Carl looked around the room, counting at least twenty-five empty wine bottles as well as numerous liquor bottles spread across the floor, cabinets, and shelves. She certainly hadn't been holding back.

"Birgit Zimmermann, we'd like to ask you if you have any idea why your mother chose to walk through the King's Gar . . ." Carl looked at Assad. ". . . I mean through *Rosenborg Castle Gardens* instead of walking to the metro at Kongens Nytorv or up to Østerport Station. Do you know?"

She cocked her head. "She thought it was nice in the park."

"So she always did that?"

The woman smiled, revealing front teeth covered with lipstick.

"Yes," she said, nodding excessively before composing herself enough to continue. "And she did her shopping in Netto supermarket."

"At Nørreport Station?"

"Yes, exactly! Always!"

It took fifteen minutes before they admitted to themselves that the timing wasn't optimal if they wanted to go into more complex questions.

Carl signaled to the others that it was maybe time to go, but then Assad jumped in.

"Why was your mother walking around with so much money? You said she was carrying ten thousand kroner, but how did you know that, Birgit?" Assad took her hand, which made her flinch, but he didn't let go.

"Well, she showed me the money. Mother really liked cash—and she bragged about it."

Nice one, Assad, Carl said with a look. "Did she also boast about her money to strangers?" he then asked.

Birgit Zimmermann lowered her head and let it bounce against her chest a couple of times. Was she silently laughing?

"My mother always boasted, ha-ha. To all and everyone." She was now openly laughing. "She shouldn't have done that."

Touché, thought Carl.

"Did your mother also have money lying around at home?" asked Assad.

She shook her head. "Not as such. She wasn't stupid, my mother. You can say a lot about her, but she wasn't stupid."

Carl turned to Laursen. "Do you know if the mother's home was searched?" Carl asked in a hushed tone.

Laursen nodded. "They didn't find anything to help in the case."

"Was it Pasgård?"

Laursen nodded. Apart from Børge Bak back in the day, there was hardly anyone Carl respected less.

Carl turned toward the woman. "You wouldn't happen to have an extra key to your mother's apartment, would you, Birgit?"

She huffed a couple of times, as if he was putting her to a lot of bother. They needed to hurry things along before she fell asleep.

Then she suddenly lifted her head, answering with surprising clarity that she did because her mother was always losing her keys. She had once had ten sets cut, and there were still four sets in the drawer.

She gave them a single set but insisted on seeing their ID first. When she had scrutinized Carl's, he passed it behind his back to Laursen so she would see the same one again. She seemed satisfied with this. She forgot about Assad.

"Just one final thing, Birgit Zimmermann," said Carl when they were standing in the doorway. "Denise Zimmermann, is that a relative of yours?"

She nodded joylessly.

"A daughter?" asked Assad.

She turned awkwardly toward him.

"She isn't home," she said. "I haven't spoken with her since the funeral."

Back at HQ, Carl sat down heavily in his chair, staring at all the papers on his desk. Two piles were current cases that could wait, so he put them to one side. Then there was a case Rose wanted him to look at, so he threw that one in the corner. The rest of the papers were just notes and various printouts and other miscellaneous things people thought might interest him. Most of it normally ended up in the trash, but he couldn't just throw Marcus's notes away. It was apparent that the case was nagging away at him and that he was bound to see connections whenever the chance presented itself. That's just the way it was with retired policemen. Carl had seen it all before. But did he want to get involved? Wasn't he just going to end up down a blind alley like those before him? And wouldn't he just disappoint Marcus, leaving the man without any hope of the case being solved, which would cause him to withdraw into himself? That was Carl's biggest fear.

He reached for a color printout. "Stephanie Gundersen," someone had written in block capitals at the bottom.

He noticed the eyes in particular. Slightly slanting, green, and without doubt piercing and enchanting.

Why would anyone kill a girl like her?

Was it because the eyes weren't enchanting but rather bewitching? That was probably the question.

18

Monday, May 23rd, 2016

It was deadly quiet in the S-train car because almost all the passengers were surfing on their smartphones and iPads. Some were enthusiastic and concentrated, while others were just scrolling their thumbs over the screen in the desperate hope for some form of contact.

Contact wasn't the first thing on Jazmine's mind when she looked at her telephone. She counted the days on her Google calendar since her last period, and everything indicated that she would soon be ovulating, so a decision had to be made.

What was she meant to do? If she got pregnant again she would without doubt be thrown out of the house, but what did that really matter? Social services would just have to step in if that was the case.

The thought made her smile. Then Anne-Line Svendsen could stick all her admonitions, plans, restrictions, and whatever else she could come up with right up her fat ass. Once she was pregnant and complained of back trouble, she'd be home free again. It wasn't like they could make her have an abortion.

Jazmine had hardly noticed her last pregnancy even though she had told the doctor a different story. No morning sickness and no remorse when they came to collect the baby, so that was easy enough. All the same, this time it seemed shortsighted to do it again. Because when the next baby was handed over and she was again thrown into the benefits system, she would suddenly have turned thirty. *Thirty!* So even though she didn't have any expectation of being saved by a knight in shining armor, she would suddenly have deflated the currency she had always cherished and which had always been her safest bet when it came to invoking the miracle: her youth.

Because who would want a woman of thirty who has had five children with God knows who and given them all up for adoption? Yeah, or four children, for that matter, she thought soberly.

She looked up at the other passengers. Was there anyone here who she would even care to have as her husband the way things had turned out for her? And was there anyone in here who would want her for that matter? Maybe the guy over in the corner, who looked thirty-five and was moving clumsily around on his seat as if he was smothered in Vaseline. But should she really waste her time and life on someone like him? That would be pointless.

Jazmine shook her head and opened the dating app that gave the quickest results. Victoria Milan was supposed to be for people in steady relationships looking for a bit on the side—and Jazmine wasn't exactly in the target group—but why should she care? If she could arrange casual sex with a decent man who understood the importance of personal hygiene and didn't cause her any trouble, and whom she might be able to extort some money out of by showing him her pregnant stomach, then the website was just what she needed. The site also had a panic button you could press if partners of the users suddenly came and looked over their shoulder. Perfect for Jazmine, especially because up until now she had been living in a tiny apartment where the dining table was the only space where you could surf the Internet. She had sometimes used the panic button when her mother came snooping. *Pow!* And no one could see that date.

She logged onto her brilliantly disguised profile and looked over the prospects. If she could choose for herself, she would find a man who was nothing special. It would make it much easier for her to give up the baby when it turned out not to be particularly beautiful. And besides, in her experience, ordinary men were just better lovers than the good-looking ones.

The thought made her smile. Those nerdy guys really did go the extra mile.

"So what did she say?" asked Michelle, impatiently tugging at Jazmine's sleeve. Despite the abrasions and bandaging on the back of her head, she looked much better now that she was up and dressed in her own clothes.

"Wait," said Denise, pointing to the duty nurse who was just popping her head around the corner.

"All the best, Michelle. Look after yourself," the nurse said, handing her a bottle of tablets. "Take two of these a couple of times a day if you still get headaches, but come and see us if you feel at any time that something else is wrong, okay?" Michelle nodded and the nurse shook her hand somewhat formally.

"Come on, then. Out with it, Jazmine," said Michelle when the nurse had gone.

Jazmine nodded questioningly to the screen separating them from the other bed.

"The skunk who was lying there? No, she was discharged this morning." Michelle wrinkled her nose, turning her attention back to Jazmine. "Did you get Anne-Line to reveal anything? What did you say to her?"

"In the middle of all the usual caseworker crap she always comes out with, I told her that you would be okay and then asked her if she had a preference for driving red cars."

"*God,* you didn't!" Michelle put her hand to her mouth.

Jazmine nodded. "Yup. Of course she reacted—we would have done the same—but I don't think she seemed shaken."

"You don't think it was her I saw?"

Jazmine shrugged. "No, I don't think so."

Michelle seemed momentarily uneasy on hearing this but nodded anyway. She collected her belongings and went with the others out into the reception area that divided the ward's four units, where there was an information desk, a waiting area, and elevators. From the panorama windows looking out over a vast part of northern Copenhagen, the light was pouring in as if it was the middle of summer, and almost everyone in the waiting room was sitting facing the view of the city rooftops.

"God, there's Patrick," whispered Michelle worriedly, pointing over toward the sofa, where a big bundle of muscles was sitting sprawled out with his sleeves rolled up and looking like a body builder.

Jazmine looked over at him. He must have just arrived, because he hadn't been there when she and Denise were sitting there.

Denise reacted quickly, standing in front of Michelle, but it was already too late. He obviously had an animal instinct and had sensed prey, standing up in the same split second he caught sight of them. Six steps later, he was standing next to them staring at Michelle as if he was ready to give her another reason to stay on ward 32, or whatever it was called.

"What the hell do you think you're doing, Michelle? Why couldn't I visit you?"

Michelle grabbed Denise's arm, hiding behind it. She was obviously scared of him, which Jazmine could easily understand.

"Who are these bitches?" he asked angrily.

"Denise and Jazmine, not that that's any of your business," she said quietly.

"What Michelle is trying to tell you is that she's moved out," Denise answered on her behalf. "She doesn't want to live with you anymore."

Two wrinkles appeared between his eyes. He wasn't satisfied with that answer.

"Fuck you, bitch. Until Michelle has paid what she owes me, you should keep your nose out of our business," he said, pushing Denise away from Michelle and up against the wall.

A few of the people in the waiting room shuffled in their seats at the commotion, and a nurse at the information desk looked up. Maybe that was why he lowered his arm.

"What does she owe you money for? For living with you and waiting on you hand and foot?" asked Denise without batting an eye. "Did you think it was free to have sex with a girl like Michelle?"

Michelle looked worried now, and Jazmine shared her worry. Maybe it would be wise if Denise toned it down a bit.

"You look big enough to understand the basic principles, buster, but maybe you haven't had enough experience with women," she continued.

The guy smiled. Apparently he was too smart to let himself be provoked in front of all these witnesses. He turned toward Michelle instead.

"I couldn't give a damn what you do. But if you move out, you need to pay your share of the rent for February, March, April, and May, Michelle. Six thousand, that was what we agreed, do you understand me? Once you've paid, you can fuck off wherever you want, but not before, got it?"

Michelle said nothing, but her hand on Jazmine's arm was shaking. *How do you expect me to do that?* her expression seemed to say.

Then Denise stood between them again. For a moment the big guy and she stood staring at each other. If they had been anywhere else it would have ended badly.

Denise pushed him in the chest fearlessly a couple of times. "You can get half now and that's your lot," she said. "Or you can just fuck off with nothing."

She put her hand in her bag and pulled out three one-thousand-kroner notes.

"Don't expect too much," said Denise as she put the key in the lock. "My grandmother was just a stupid old bitch, so the furniture is ugly and the place stinks of cheap perfume."

Jazmine nodded. Denise had said the same thing ten times on the way here, as if it bothered her how the apartment looked or smelled. As long as there was a bed to sleep on until she found something else, she was happy and could see that Michelle felt the same.

"Oh my God, there are photos of you over there and there, Denise. And is that your mother?" exclaimed Michelle excitedly. She pointed at a black-and-white photo of a beautiful, shapely woman who had been cut out from another photo and placed on a color photo background of a park.

Denise nodded. "Yes, but that's from ages ago. She doesn't exactly look like that now."

"Why has the photo been cut out like that?"

"Because my dad was standing next to her and my grandparents didn't waste any time erasing him from our lives."

"Oh." Michelle appeared to be really sad for having asked. "But where is he now? Do you see him?"

"He was an American and a former soldier. My grandmother couldn't stand him, and my mother didn't back him up, so he went back and joined the army again."

"Then why do you have your mother's name and not his? Weren't they married?"

Denise snorted. "What do you think? Of course they were, and I do have my father's surname. Denise Frank Zimmermann."

"That's weird—it's a boy's name. Can it also be a surname? I had no idea. Do you write to each other?" Michelle continued.

Denise smiled wryly. "A bit hard seeing as he was blown to smithereens by a roadside bomb in Afghanistan just before Christmas 2002. Great Christmas present, right?"

This information didn't dull Michelle's curiosity.

"He's dead? Then in some way it was your grandmother's fault," said Jazmine.

Denise pointed accusingly at a faded photo of her. "That's exactly what it was."

Jazmine looked around the sitting room. Nice furniture if you liked oak tables and smooth brown leather. Personally, she preferred the modern Scandinavian style.

Not that she would ever be able afford furniture like that, but at least she had taste.

The apartment had enough rooms for them each to have their own bedroom, she realized with satisfaction, and there was also a dining room and large sitting room with panorama windows looking out over a broad canopied balcony, a lawn, and behind that another block of apartments like the one they were in. Far better conditions than what she was used to.

She walked through the hallway to the bathroom to inspect it—there was no more important a room in an apartment. It wasn't terribly big, but it would do. Washing machine, tumble dryer, and a couple of bathroom cabinets that could be cleared of all the woman's old junk, so that would be fine. The mirror was enormous. In fact it took up the whole recess where the sink stood, so they wouldn't even need to use it one at a time.

"Was your grandmother disabled, Denise?" she asked when they were sitting back together in the sitting room.

"Why do you ask that?"

"There are grab rails on the wall and armrests on the toilet that go up and down. Did she have trouble walking?"

"Her!? No, she was always on the move when she had the chance. They are from the former owners, I suppose."

"What about your granddad? He didn't use them either?"

"He was already dead when she moved out here. It was a long time ago and he was a lot older than her."

"Okay, but that doesn't matter," said Michelle. Was she thinking about the grab rails or the old man? It wasn't always clear what she was thinking.

"Who pays for the apartment?" asked Jazmine.

Denise lit a cigarette, blowing the smoke in the air.

"The mortgage has been paid off already. All the other costs are simply deducted from her account. The probate court are taking care of the money, and there's a lot of it. My grandfather had a shoe business with a monopoly selling some exclusive brands, but my grandmother sold most of the shit in one fell swoop when he died. I expect to inherit half when they've finalized her estate, and then we can find somewhere else to live. There's no way I want to stay here. I *hate* this place."

"What about food and stuff?" asked Jazmine. "Michelle isn't earning anything and if I don't take a job I'll lose my benefits." She bit her cheek and took a cigarette from the table. "I'm ovulating this week so I'm considering getting myself knocked up."

Jazmine pulled out her smartphone, placed it on the table, opened her dating account, and pointed at a photo. "I've got a date with him tonight. At his place, actually. His wife is at a school reunion somewhere in darkest Jutland, so we've got the place to ourselves."

"Him?" Michelle gawped, and Jazmine could only agree, because he certainly wasn't handsome. But as the man's wife was pregnant, there was nothing wrong with his sperm.

"I really don't think you should do that." For once, Michelle looked grown up. "What about in a year's time?"

Denise also looked critical.

Jazmine looked at the smoke from her cigarette, but she never found an answer there. "What do you mean 'in a year's time'?" she asked.

Denise put her cigarette butt in a vase of withered tulips standing in the middle of the table. "Okay, Jazmine. If you insist on using your body to have kids, why not earn a bomb doing it? It's pathetic that you're willing to settle for benefits while you're pregnant. Find a couple who can't have children. The way you look, which is bloody good by the way, you could easily earn a hundred and fifty thousand kroner under the table as a surrogate. Haven't you considered that?"

Jazmine nodded.

"Well, then! Isn't that a better solution?"

"No, not for me. I don't want to know anything about the kid. It's just a piece of meat I hand over as far as I'm concerned, okay?"

Jazmine could sense that Michelle was appalled. But what the hell did she know about how it felt if you looked the child in the eyes? Jazmine had tried that once, and there was *no* way she would do it again.

"Okay, I get your point," said Denise. "But then you should do what I do. Find a few sugar daddies. You can choose the guys yourself; there's enough of them. They might be a bit on the older side, but they can be very generous. If you only sleep with each one once a month, you can easily earn five thousand out of them if you make an effort. One or two of those a week and you've got it made. Where do you think I get my money from? And it isn't just when you're twenty-eight, let me tell you. You've got years in you yet."

Michelle began to fiddle with her lace collar. She seemed uncomfortable at the way the conversation was developing. "That's prostitution, Denise," she said. "And what you're doing, Jazmine! That's even worse."

"Okay. But then I don't know what you call the situation you had with Patrick," said Denise. "What we saw at the hospital didn't exactly look like love. But okay, Michelle, if you can come up with a better way to earn that kind of money, let me know. I'm up for anything."

"Anything?" asked Jazmine.

"Just name it. As long as I don't get fucked over. No pun intended."

Jazmine laughed and put out her cigarette. Time to put her to the test. "Even murder?"

Michelle almost dropped the cup she was holding, but Denise just sat there grinning. "Murder! What do you mean?"

She thought for a moment. "Kill someone. Someone who has a lot of money lying around at home."

"Ha-ha, you're very creative, Jazmine. And who should we begin with? One of the fashion queens? Or an art dealer?" asked Denise.

Maybe she was saying it for a laugh; Jazmine couldn't figure it out.

"I don't know if people like that have cash lying around, but we could just start with Anne-Line."

"Christ! Of course," blurted out Michelle excitedly. "I've heard she once won a couple of million, so she must have some cash lying around. But do we need to kill her? You're just kidding, right?"

"Are you telling me that Anne-Line has money? You wouldn't think it to look at her." Denise's dimples showed in both cheeks. "Actually a rather creative suggestion, Jazmine. If we kill her, it will be two birds with one stone: most importantly the money but also that we get rid of her. Quite an interesting thought. Ha-ha, but not very realistic."

"Maybe we could settle for blackmailing her. That would be better in case her money is in the bank," said Michelle. "If you and Jazmine tell her that you're going to testify that you saw her when she tried to run me over, don't you think she'll cough up?"

Jazmine and Denise looked at each other: They were impressed.

19

Monday, May 23rd, 2016

Carl stood for a moment looking at the notice board in the situation room. It looked like Assad, Gordon, and Laursen had been busy, because it was full of information.

Some of the information they had pinned to the board he hadn't seen before. Photos of Rigmor Zimmermann's body where it was found on the ground with the back of her head bashed in. A photo of a proud married couple and some employees in front of a shoe shop in Rødovre. Some journals from Hvidovre Hospital concerning several of Rigmor Zimmermann's hospital admissions: surgical removal of the uterus, stitches to a minor lesion on her head, and the relocation of a dislocated shoulder.

Then there was a map of the woman's movements from Borgergade to where the body was found, a few photos of the bushes in the King's Garden that Assad had taken with his smartphone, a fact list that increasingly conflicted with the investigation that had been carried out on the second floor, and Rigmor Zimmermann's postmortem report. Finally, there was Fritzl Zimmermann's death certificate and other more or less insignificant things that Carl didn't think belonged there.

All things considered, they were beginning to flesh out the Zimmermann case. But the problem was that they had no suspect in sight and the case was de facto not theirs and wouldn't become theirs either. If they continued with this, he alone would bear the responsibility.

Most of all he wanted to include Marcus Jacobsen in their

discoveries. But didn't he risk the retired head of homicide telling him to follow the chain of command? That he wouldn't understand Carl's attempt to get involved in his colleagues' work up there on the second floor?

"Are you going to report anything to Bjørn about our discoveries, Carl?" asked Tomas Laursen pertinently.

Assad and Carl looked at each other. Carl nodded to Assad, indicating that he could answer. That took the heat off him for the time being.

"Surely they have enough work on their hands up there with another case at the moment," answered Assad.

It was good that Assad yielded on behalf of Department Q, but what was he talking about? What case?

"Haven't you read the newspaper today?" Assad said, preempting Carl's question. "Bring it here, Gordon."

A pair of bony hands placed the newspaper on the desk. The lanky specter was beginning to look like a stick insect. Didn't he eat anything?

Carl scanned the front page. CONNECTION BETWEEN HIT-AND-RUN VICTIMS? read the headline, and beneath it were photos of the two women involved in the incidents over the last few days.

Carl read the captions. *Michelle Hansen, jobseeker, 27 years old. Severely injured following a hit-and-run on May 20th. Senta Berger, jobseeker, 28 years old. Killed in a hit-and-run on May 22nd.*

"The paper has made a connection between the two victims," said Gordon eagerly. "Not surprising when you look closer."

Carl looked at the faces skeptically. Yes, they were born in the same year and were both good-looking, but so what? There were lots of hit-and-runs in Denmark today, where the drivers were too cowardly to take responsibility. Usually because they were under the influence of drugs or alcohol. To hell with that shit.

"Just look at the earrings, Carl. They're almost identical. And the blouse is the same, bought at H&M, only in two different colors," continued Gordon.

"Yeah, and they're both made up like spitting images," added

Assad. His imagery was perhaps a little mixed up, but he was right. Even their makeup was similar; Carl could see that.

"The rouge on the cheeks, the lipstick and eyebrows, and the well-cut hair with highlights," continued Assad. "If I'd been with them at the same time, I wouldn't have been able to tell the difference after five minutes."

Laursen nodded. "There are certainly similarities, buuuut . . ."

Once again, Laursen and Carl were on the same wavelength. Coincidences like this were common enough.

Carl smiled cheekily. "Okay, Assad. So you think that our colleagues up on the second floor are looking at the paper and connecting these two incidents?"

"I know they are," said Gordon. "I was upstairs asking Lis about something and she told me that they've already assigned a team to the case. A cyclist saw a red Peugeot tearing down the street where Michelle Hansen was hit, and a similar car was spotted parked with its motor running for over an hour on the street where the other girl was killed. Lars Bjørn has sent several teams out to the area to question people all day. I think Pasgård's team was among them."

"Hallelujah," said Assad.

Carl looked at the front page of the newspaper again. "I can't bloody believe that they're prioritizing this! But regardless of what they're running around doing today, I seriously doubt that it'll bring homicide to a standstill. Uniform will take care of this until there is evidence of murder." He turned to Laursen. "But, Tomas. If *you* don't say anything to Pasgård and his team who are investigating the Zimmermann case, then I think I can damn well forget it too."

Laursen patted Carl's shoulder on his way out. "Then let's hope you get there first, Carl."

"Sure. What could stop me?"

He turned toward Assad and Gordon. There were several things in the case that needed clarification. Their assumption was that Rigmor Zimmermann had felt that someone was following her just before the murder and had therefore tried to hide. They also assumed that it might be because she had a bad habit of flashing her cash a bit too boldly and openly. The question remained how they could establish her movements from the daughter's apartment to the scene of the crime. Had she gone in somewhere and opened her purse under the nose of someone she shouldn't have? Or was it a coincidence that the killer had found both a victim and loot? But if the killer had just been a random person, why had she run? Had the person tried to attack her farther down the street? And was it even likely in a place where so many people walked and lived?

There were a lot of unanswered questions even in this small area of the investigation, so Assad and Gordon would be kept busy visiting dozens of buildings, shops, and cafés.

"Tell him what else you've been up to, Gordon," Assad said with a grin.

Carl turned to face the lad. What had he done *now* that he didn't dare mention himself?

Gordon took a deep breath. "I know we haven't agreed on this, Carl, but I took a taxi to Stenløse."

Carl frowned. "To Stenløse! With your own money, I assume."

He didn't answer. So he had had his fingers in the taxi vouchers.

"Rose's youngest sister has let me borrow all of Rose's notebooks," he said. "She met me at the apartment."

"I see. And of course Lise-Marie begged you on her knees to come and get them, is that it? Why didn't she come down here with them herself if it was so important for her?"

"It wasn't quite like that." Was he pretending to be embarrassed? That man could be so annoying. "It was actually my idea."

Carl felt his blood pressure rising, but just before he exploded, Assad jumped in.

"Look, Carl. Gordon has organized all the information."

He placed Rose's collection of notebooks and a sheet of letter-sized paper on the desk.

Carl looked at the piece of paper—a chronological collection of what were undoubtedly frightening phrases filled most of the page.

It read:

1990 SHUT UP

1991 HATE YOU

1992 BLOODY HATE YOU

1993 BLOODY HATE YOU—I AM SCARED

1994 SCARED

1995 I CAN'T HEAR YOU

1996 HELP MOM—BITCH

1997 ALONE HELL

1998 DIE

1999 DIE—HELP ME

2000 BLACK HELL

2001 DARK

2002 ONLY GREY—DON'T WANT TO THINK

2003 DON'T WANT TO THINK—AM NOT

2004 WHITE LIGHT

2005 YELLOW LIGHT

2006 I AM GOOD

2007 DEAF

2008 LAUGHTER STOPPED?

2009 GET LOST, SHIT!

2010 LEAVE ME ALONE

2011 I AM OKAY, OKAY?

2012 LOOK AT ME NOW, BASTARD!

2013 I AM FREE

2014 I AM FREE—IT ISN'T HAPPENING—AWAY

2015 I'M DROWNING

2016 I'M DROWNING NOW

"These are the sentences that Rose has written in the notebooks." Gordon pointed to the front covers: 1990 to 2016. They were all there.

"As we already know, each notebook is filled with a phrase that is repeated over and over, and it's these phrases that I've systematized on this sheet. In total, there are ninety-six pages of these phrases per notebook, with the exception of a few that Rose didn't fill completely."

Gordon opened the notebook on the top of the pile, the one from 1990, where she had written over and over again: "SHUT UP SHUT UP."

"She started every new day by drawing a thin line under the first word," he said. "So four lines on one page cover approximately four days, as you can see."

He pointed at a random page. It was just as he said; thin lines separated the days, and each day with the same number of phrases. Rose had obviously had a very systematic approach even as a ten-year-old.

"I've counted the lines. There are in fact three hundred and sixty-five lines because she has also drawn a line under the first word of the last paragraph on the last day of the year."

"What about the leaping years?" asked Assad.

"They're called leap years," Carl corrected him.

He looked confused. "Leap years! That doesn't make any sense," he said dryly.

"Anyway, it's a good question, Assad," said Gordon. "She had those covered too. In the seven leap years that there have been since 1990, she inserted an extra day. She even drew a circle around the words written on the leap day."

"Of course she did. That's our Rose," grunted Carl.

Gordon nodded. He seemed proud on Rose's behalf, but then he was also her biggest fan and admirer. And all the feelings that came with that.

"Why seven? Haven't there only been six of those . . . leap years?"

"Today is May 20th, Assad. We *have* had February. And 2016 is a leap year."

Assad looked at Carl as if he had been accused of being dim-witted. "I was actually thinking about the year 2000, Carl. Years divided by a hundred aren't leap years; I know that much."

"True, Assad, but if the year can be divided by four hundred, then it *is* a leap year. Don't you recall all the discussion there was about it back in 2000? It was repeated over and over."

"Okay." He nodded, looking thoughtful rather than hurt. "Maybe it's because I wasn't in Denmark around that time."

"And people didn't think about leap years where you were?"

"Not really," he said.

"And where *were* you?" asked Carl.

Assad broke the eye contact between them. "Oh, you know, here and there."

Carl waited. That was obviously all he was going to get out of him this time.

"Anyway, I chose to list what she has written down year for year," interrupted Gordon. "And it says a lot about how she was feeling in those periods."

Carl skimmed over the page. "She doesn't seem to have been well in 2000. Poor girl." Then he pointed at 2002. "I can see that there are two different phrases in some of the years, and three in 2014. Why is that? Have you also figured that out, Gordon?"

"Yes and no. I don't know exactly why they change, but it's possible to count the days and work out exactly when the phrases change, so we can assume that something significant must have happened in her life on those days."

Carl scrutinized the page further. Five of the years had two different phrases, while only one had three.

"We do know why the change occurred in 2014, right, Carl?" said Assad. "She chose to use a new phrase just after the hypnosis, isn't that right, Gordon?"

He nodded looking slightly surprised. "Yes, exactly. And it's actually the only year that has a few empty days in the middle. She starts off writing: 'IT ISN'T HAPPENING IT ISN'T HAPPENING.' Then we have three empty days, which she just marks with separating lines, and then for the rest of the year the phrase: 'AWAY AWAY AWAY.'"

"All very peculiar," observed Assad. "What happens when a new year begins? Does she just come up with new phrases every time?"

Gordon's expression changed. It was very difficult to see how this really affected him. On the one hand, he was serious like a relief worker coming to the last-minute rescue of someone in peril, and on the other hand, like an elated boy who had just scored his first girlfriend.

"That's a brilliant question, Assad. She actually starts all twenty-seven years except four with a new sentence on January 1st."

Assad and Carl stared at the years, especially 1998 and 1999. DIE! It made them feel uneasy. Could it really be their Rose who in such an agitated frame of mind had written "DIE DIE DIE DIE" again and again every day for a year and a half?

"It's almost sick," said Carl. "How can a young woman sit night after night and write this terrible stuff? And then suddenly turn on a dime and constantly cry for help? What was going on in her head?"

"Really scary," Assad said quietly.

"Have you also worked out on which date the phrases change in 1999, Gordon?" asked Carl.

"It was May 18th," answered Gordon immediately. He looked proud and had every reason to be.

"Jesus Christ, no," sighed Carl.

Gordon looked confused. "Did anything special happen on that day?" he asked.

Carl nodded, pointing to a thin yellow folder hidden between two binders with white indexes on the back.

REGULATIONS was written on them. That was one way to make sure that no one in Department Q would come anywhere near the yellow folder.

Gordon reached out for the yellow folder and handed it to Carl.

"Here's your explanation," he said, pulling out a page from a newspaper from the folder and laying it out on the desk.

He pointed at the date on the top of the page—May 19th,

1999—and ran his finger down the page, stopping at one of the minor news stories.

47-YEAR-OLD MAN KILLED IN STEEL PLANT ACCIDENT, it read.

Carl let his finger slide down the text to the victim's name.

"As you can see, the man was called Arne Knudsen," he said. "And that was Rose's dad."

They stood speechless for a moment, digesting what they had just read, their eyes moving from the article to Gordon's sheet.

"I think we can agree that Rose's notebooks are a collected statement of her state of mind throughout more than twenty-six years," said Carl, pinning Gordon's sheet to the notice board.

"You probably don't want it hanging there when Rose comes back," said Gordon.

Assad nodded. "Of course not, she'd never forgive us—or her sisters."

Carl agreed, but it would have to stay for now.

"We know from her sisters, Vicky and Lise-Marie, that Rose's dad was always after her and that Rose sought escape in these notebooks when she was alone in her room at night," he said. "Apparently, it was a form of therapy for her, but something indicates that it didn't help her in the long run."

"Did he hit her?" Gordon clenched his fists, but it didn't look very menacing.

"No, not according to her sisters. And neither did he abuse her sexually," said Assad.

"Then the bastard was all mouth?" Gordon's face had turned scarlet. It actually suited him.

"Yes, again according to her sisters," answered Carl. "He terrorized her without mercy. We just don't know how, so we need to find out. We can conclude that there wasn't a single day in more than twenty-six years when this systematic harassment didn't affect her, leaving her with deep mental scars."

"I just can't believe that this is the Rose we know," said Assad. "Can you?"

Carl sighed. It was hard.

They stood in front of Gordon's sheet, studying it closely. Just like the others, Carl examined each line carefully before moving on to the next.

At least twenty minutes passed before anyone said anything. They had all taken mental notes based on their reading. Carl had felt a stab to his heart at least ten times thinking about Rose's self-initiated and lonely therapy. Years of silently screaming for help.

He sighed. It really was surprisingly hard to think about this woman whom they thought they knew so well but who for all these years had had to live with overshadowing and profound emotions that she was able to deal with only through writing all these harsh phrases.

Oh, Rose, thought Carl. Despite the way she had been feeling inside, she had still had the energy to help and support him when he was down. And on top of that, she had found the strength every day to engage wholeheartedly with the tough cases they worked on in Department Q. So long as she had had this safe system to come home to, she had been able to cope with all the negativity she had inside.

Intelligent, clever Rose. Everyone's annoying, wonderful, tortured Rose. And now she had been admitted again. Ultimately, her system hadn't been enough for her.

"Listen," said Carl.

The other two looked up.

"There is no doubt that her relationship to her dad determined her choice of words. But can't we also agree that when a phrase changes in the middle of a year, it must be related to a very specific event, and for many years at the beginning they only change for the worse?"

They both nodded.

"And we can deduct that there have also been positive developments later on. A nightmare in 2000 slowly becomes easier over the following years, ending with the phrase, 'I AM GOOD.' So if we want to understand what happened to Rose, which of course we do, our task is to uncover the events that triggered either bad or good phrases.

The development is most prominent when her dad died in '99: from something completely irreconcilable to almost the opposite."

"What do you think? Is she talking to herself or her dad when she writes?" asked Gordon.

"Yeah, that's what we need to ask for help in working out from those who knew her best back then."

"Then we'll have to talk to her sisters again. Perhaps they know what happened in the years when the phrases suddenly changed."

Carl nodded.

Gordon had regained his natural pâté-colored hue. Apparently, he was at his best when he looked most ill. Carl had never thought about that before.

"What if we speak to a psychologist to get their interpretation of Rose's varying states of mind? Then we'll also have someone who can pass on the results to her psychiatrists in Glostrup," suggested Gordon.

"Good idea. We'll need to talk to Mona, won't we, Carl?" For once Assad had wiped the smile off his face when talking about her.

Carl folded his hands, resting his chin on his knuckles. Even though he and Mona were working in the same building, it had been several years since he had really spoken with her. And even though he wanted to, she appeared so unapproachable and fragile that it seemed like a risky undertaking. Of course he had asked Lis if she was ill, but Lis had said she wasn't.

Carl tried not to frown but without success. "Okay, Gordon. You call the sisters now that you've developed such a rapport with them. Maybe some of them will have time to come to the meeting. Assad, you organize that meeting. Tomorrow if possible, okay? Have a word with Mona and fill her in on the situation."

There was Assad's cheeky smile. "And what about you, Carl? Are you going home to slack off or would you rather visit the second floor to see what you can find out about the Zimmermann case?" asked Assad, looking mischievous.

Why the hell did he even ask when he already knew the answer?

20

Tuesday, May 24th, 2016

They had been standing for a long time in front of the bathroom mirror. Jazmine and Denise in front, Michelle in the middle behind them, chatting away like old friends while they commented on and touched one another's hair. They looked smashing. If Michelle had not been living with them, she would have simply copied them. Jazmine's method of accentuating her high cheekbones with a soft brush, Denise's totally cool way of pushing up her breasts, and all sorts of things she thought made them different from her.

"My guy gave me four thousand yesterday," said Denise. "What about yours, Jazmine?"

She shrugged. "He wouldn't give me anything at first. He actually got pissed off and said it wasn't that kind of dating site, but then he threw me two thousand anyway because he was horny. But when I gave him a condom he demanded one thousand back, the idiot, and I had no choice because he looked like he meant it."

Michelle stuck her head in between them. "But you said you were going to try and get pregnant with him?"

Jazmine raised an eyebrow in the mirror. "Not with him; he was too ugly. Not that it matters, but I would have wanted more money out of him on the spot."

Michelle looked at her face. Would she be able to do what the others were doing? And would anyone want her the way she looked now?

Two black eyes, a bandage on the back of her head, and a bloodshot right eye.

"Do you think this will go away?" she asked, pointing at her eye. "I've heard that blood in the eye can turn the whites brown if it doesn't heal quickly enough."

Denise turned around, dangling her eyeliner in midair.

"Where on earth have you heard that? Do you also believe in fairies?"

An unpleasant feeling of being revealed as an idiot came over her. Were *they* now going to be the ones to belittle her? Wasn't she just as good as them? Didn't they actually like her? If she hadn't been extremely lucky, she would be lying in a coffin now instead of being here. Didn't they even think about that? Didn't they consider that she had nothing and that she wasn't like them? She couldn't sleep with strange men like *they* did. Did that make her stupid too?

In a way, Michelle knew that she wasn't quite as clever as her parents had led her to believe. Maybe they weren't as clever as they thought they were either. Her upbringing in the small, modest, light concrete house in Tune had certainly sheltered her from the reality that while she was walking around in her own fairy-tale world, thinking about her complexion, hair, and matching clothes, many of the other girls on her street had slowly and almost imperceptibly stepped out of the fairy-tale world and started to develop their skills.

The first time her confidence suffered a blow that really hurt was when she, in all earnestness, claimed that Ebola was a city in Italy, and later the same night that the past had been in black and white because she had seen it like that lots of times in films. These and other blunders had resulted in harsh and nasty comments about her intelligence, and the looks alone were enough to make her feel deeply ashamed—a feeling she had often felt ever since. She had a tendency to express herself with words that made sense to her but which didn't actually exist. And when she was called out, she had learned to disarm her critics with a laughter that she thought showed that she was in on the joke. However, the reality was that she felt deeply hurt when these things happened. And over time she had learned only to talk about things she knew about and otherwise keep her mouth shut in the company of people she didn't know, losing herself in her own fantasy world.

A world in which a handsome knight in shining armor came riding on a white horse. In which she was rich, adored, and waited on hand and foot. She was fully aware that she was good-looking and a nice person, and that that was what all knights were looking for. She knew that from romance novels, quoting proudly from them when she spoke with Denise and Jazmine over breakfast. The way they spoke about prostituting themselves in one way or another! It was up to her to show them a different path.

Denise looked up from her yogurt. "A knight? Do you really think they exist?" she said. "Because I don't—not anymore."

"But why not? There are plenty of nice guys in the world," said Michelle.

"We'll be thirty soon, Michelle. That ship has sailed, all right?"

Michelle shook her head. No, it wasn't all right. It was unthinkable.

She sat up straight. "Do you want to play truth?" she said, attempting to change the subject, pushing the plate of breakfast rolls to one side with a smile.

"Don't you mean truth or dare?" asked Jazmine.

"No, let's play without the dare. That's only fun if you're playing with guys. Just truth." She laughed. "Can I start? The one with the worst answer does the dishes."

"Worst answer? And who gets to decide that?" asked Denise.

"We'll know when we hear it. Are you in?"

The others nodded.

"Okay, Jazmine, what's the worst thing you've done in your life, apart from giving those babies away?" She noticed Jazmine's expression, realizing that she hadn't needed to say the last bit. She had just wanted to make sure that they didn't have to touch on the subject again.

"I'm not answering that," she said.

They were already ruining the game, making Michelle feel unsure if it would be a good idea for her to live with them. But what other option did she have?

"Come on," said Denise. "Out with it, Jazmine."

She drummed on the table with the tips of her fingers and took a deep breath. "I slept with my mom's boyfriend. He was the first guy I got pregnant with," she said with a cheeky smile, throwing her head back.

"Oh my God," said Michelle, looking at Denise's raised eyebrows. "Did she find out?"

Jazmine smiled, revealing the dimples on her cheeks.

"And that was the end of that affair, right?" Denise said, laughing.

Jazmine nodded again. "You can be sure of that! For both of us!"

Michelle was delighted. You really got to know each other with this game.

"What about you, Denise? What's the worst you've done?"

It was apparent that she would have to think hard about this by the way she inspected her bright red nails.

"To myself or someone else?" she asked, tilting her head to one side.

"That's up to you. There are no rules about that."

"Lots of things, I think. I steal from my sugar daddies if I can get away with it. For example, yesterday I stole a picture of this guy's wife. Sometimes, if I want to be shot of them, I blackmail them, and they get the photo back and disappear once they've paid up."

"That doesn't sound like the worst you can come up with," Jazmine said dryly.

A roguish smile spread over Denise's face. "If you say the worst thing you've done, Michelle, I'll come up with something better in a bit."

Michelle bit her bottom lip. She didn't know how to get the words out.

"It's soooo embarrassing!"

"Come on, your turn," Jazmine said, sounding annoyed and pushing her dirty plate over toward her. "Otherwise you can just start washing up now."

"Yeah, yeah. Give me a second." She hid the bottom of her face in her hand. "If I could get a job as an erotic model, I really think I could imagine sleeping with the photographer. It would round things off."

"What sort of shit is that to come out with, Michelle? Start washing up!" Jazmine looked sternly at her. "You make *us* come up with something real and then spout out some bullshit. What do you think we'd do in that situation? Do you think it was fun for me to fuck that ugly bloke yesterday and demand money for it?"

"At least it was better than getting pregnant again, wasn't it?" said Denise.

Jazmine nodded. "Come on, Michelle, don't be such a silly cow. Tell us what you've done that's soooo embarrassing."

Michelle looked away. "I love watching *Paradise Island*."

"Shut up, you little Goody Two-shoes, you can—"

"And often dream about being on the show."

Jazmine was about to get up. "*You're* doing the dishes."

"And if Patrick isn't at home, I masturbate all the way through the show. I take off all my clothes and touch myself while watching it. It feels really hot."

Jazmine made herself comfortable again. "Okay, crazy! You get credit for that, you little slut." She smiled.

Michelle was back in the game.

"I know it's because I've been so sick of Patrick. In a way, I hate him just now. All night while you two were partying, I was thinking about how I could take my revenge. Tell his boss that he steals cables and sockets and uses them to make money on the side. Or slash the tires of that car he loves so much. Or just slash it all the way around. Or I could make sure he would make a fool of himself at the club where he works. He'd hate that more than anything. He—"

"Well," Jazmine interrupted her, which didn't feel nice. "Are we getting anything from you, Denise?"

She nodded while considering her answer. "The worst I've done? I'd probably say it's that I lie all the time. That no one can trust me, and that goes for you two as well."

Michelle frowned. What a horrible thing to say.

"But now I'll tell you something else that will definitely be bad enough."

"Out with it, then!" Jazmine's expectations were clearly high, but not Michelle's. Denise had just said that she would lie about everything and to everyone. So what was the point of listening to her?

"I think we should help Michelle."

Michelle frowned again. Was she taking the piss? Was she now the butt of another joke?

"Okay, we'll do it. But what's that got to do with the game?" asked Jazmine.

"If Michelle goes along with my idea, you'll be the one washing the dishes, Jazmine." She turned to face Michelle. "As things stand now, you don't contribute anything at all around here, do you, Michelle? I'm only talking about money, okay? So now you're going to tell us how to get our hands on some, and whatever you say, we'll do it."

Michelle was totally confused. "What do you want me to say? I don't know how we can get hold of any; otherwise I would've done it already. You know Patrick kicked me—"

"Say anything, Michelle. You suggested we should rob Anne-Line Svendsen. So is that what we're doing?"

"No, that was just a—"

"Are we going to Patrick's apartment to steal everything we can lay our hands on?"

Michelle took a deep breath. "Hell no, he'd know it was me."

"Then what, Michelle? *I'm* willing to do whatever you say—even if it's really bad."

Jazmine laughed. She was obviously in. Michelle didn't like it at all. What was she meant to come up with?

"You mentioned before that Patrick steals from his boss. Maybe you could blackmail him," suggested Jazmine.

"No!" She shook her head. "I don't dare. He'll kill me if I do anything like that."

"What a jolly nice guy that Patrick must be. But what's the name of the club where he works as a doorman, Michelle, and when is he there?" asked Jazmine.

Michelle shook her head more and more violently. "He's there on Wednesdays and Fridays, but what difference does it make? He won't give me any money, if that's what you think. And we can't do anything to him because there are cameras and everything."

"I asked you what club."

"It's not really a club, more of a venue really."

"What venue, Michelle?"

"Victoria, out in Sydhavnen."

Jazmine sat back and lit another cigarette. "Victoria? Okay. I've been there loads of times to pick up guys. It's a really good concept because they're also open Monday to Thursday. Actually, they're the only place that is apart from a few city clubs and gay bars. They make you buy something to drink, but as long as you buy a Zombie you can sip it for the rest of the night—unless some guy picks you up and pays for the rest of the evening. But how long has Patrick been working there? I don't remember seeing him."

Michelle tried to remember. She wasn't good at keeping track of time.

"Never mind," said Denise, brushing the question aside. "Tell us everything you know. What the entrance is like, and how you get to the office. When they open and close, and what it's like on a Wednesday, for example. Are there many guests, and what are they like? Tell us everything we can find on the Internet and everything we can't. And afterward you can fill us in with whatever else you know, Jazmine."

"Why do you need to know all that? Are you planning for us to rob the place?" She smiled. It was all just a joke, wasn't it?

But Denise and Jazmine sat silently just a little too long for comfort.

21

Tuesday, May 24th, 2016

Carl and Hardy were worn out from Morten's constant hysterics. How did you tell a guy who was forty kilos overweight and usually a happy-go-lucky sort that there comes a time when significant weight loss is the order of the day if you want to hold on to a body-building, muscle-bulging, testosterone-fueled, encyclopedically knowledgeable, and out-standingly charming lover? As everyone knows, all roads lead to Rome, but there are at least as many potholes in the unhappy and broken heart of an oversensitive man. No matter what Hardy and Carl thought of to distract Morten from his hurt pride, it was like sticking voodoo pins in his all-consuming jealousy and apparently incurable misery.

So it was understandable when, following yet another night of Morten's heartrending sobbing every ten minutes, Hardy finally broke.

"I'm going out for a while," he said at the crack of dawn. "Tell Morten that I'm going to have my wheelchair battery recharged and I won't be back before dinner."

Carl nodded. Wise man.

Carl was also feeling tired as he began his day, taking the spiral stairs at HQ up to the second floor to see if he could gather any new information on the Zimmermann case.

When a new case with an investigative aspect ended up in homi-cide, you could sense it in the same irrational way as you could smell and feel the promise of snow in the air before it fell. Good colleagues lifted their heads slightly higher and straightened their backs, and their eyes became a little more alert. Although they had very little evidence to go on, the homicide unit almost collectively sensed that there might be a latent lunatic on the loose intent on killing people in hit-and-run attacks. Every hallway was buzzing with determination and a desire to make a difference, because if their hunch was right, a focused and skilled effort could save lives.

"What the hell do you know that's causing such a stir?" asked Carl when Bente Hansen passed him in the hallway. She had recently been appointed superintendent and was one of the few colleagues Carl respected.

"That's a good question, but you don't look away when Terje Ploug has a hunch. He's set up two interdepartmental teams to look for similarities between the two hit-and-runs, and they've already hit on a few things."

"Like what?"

"A red Peugeot was used in both incidents, model 106 we think— the slightly boxy one—and it might well be the same one that was used in both attacks. That the last attack was a deliberate act by the driver. That there were no skid marks in either case. That the residents in the area where the first incident happened think they saw a car that fits the description parked for some time on the street at some distance from the curb. That the victims looked and dressed alike, were the same age, and were both on benefits."

"Okay, but there are undeniably quite a few of that sort in Denmark today, and the shops sell the clothes they sell. Can you show me one household that doesn't have some piece of clothing from H&M in its wardrobe?"

She nodded. "Anyway, now they're keeping an eye out for a red car like that. All patrol cars have to report if they spot an older model of a red Peugeot, especially if there are marks indicating that it might have been involved in a hit-and-run."

"So now there are ten people in homicide waiting for that?"

Bente Hansen elbowed him in the stomach. "Always caustic and ironic, Carl Mørck. It's a good thing that there are some people in this country who don't change as the wind blows."

Was that a compliment?

He smiled at her and set a course for the front desk, behind which Mrs. Sørensen's grumpy face was just visible. Why was she sitting down, and why there?

"Who can I talk to about the Zimmermann case apart from Pasgård?" he asked innocently.

She demonstratively pushed a couple of pieces of paper to one side. "This isn't exactly an information service for state employees who don't want to follow the chain of command, is it, now, Carl Mørck?"

"Is Gert on Pasgård's team?"

She raised her head a little, her fringe sticking to her forehead, and the beginning of a frown on her face revealing her lower teeth. Annoyance wasn't enough to describe the state Carl assumed she was in.

"What the hell do you want, Carl? Do you want me to spell it out, put it up in lights, carve it in marble, or weld it in huge letters? *Follow the chain of command, okay?*"

This outburst made Carl realize what was really going on. Mrs. Sørensen was having hot flashes again, sitting with her feet in a basin of ice-cold water behind the desk. She was a dragon on the loose, the witch of Bloksbjerg, and a pack of stampeding wild animals that were after blood, all at the same time. Pure poison.

Carl backed away. From now on and until this menopausal hell was over, he would quietly find the easiest shortcut past the fury.

"Hi, Janus," he shouted when HQ's head of communications came trudging out from the Walk of Fame dressed to impress. Apparently it was time for him and the head of homicide to coordinate their opinions on how to deal with the media theories about the victims of the hit-and-run driver.

"Can you give me a quick breakdown of the developments in the Zimmermann case, Janus? There are some alarm bells ringing with us downstairs, so maybe—"

"Talk to Pasgård; he's in charge of that case." He waved over to Mrs. Sørensen, who responded with a tired expression, which was perhaps meant to demonstrate some form of respect.

Carl was again standing cap in hand when Lis came prancing out of Lars Bjørn's office, gracefully holding the door for Janus Staal.

"Do you know anything about the developments in the Zimmermann case, Lis?" he asked.

She giggled. "And who might have told you that I've just taken the minutes? Pasgård is in with Bjørn just now." She looked over at Mrs. Sørensen, who was waving her hands dismissively.

"Lis, listen. We have a case that might be connected to that case, and you know how Pasgård and I feel about one another."

She nodded. "Let me tell you something, Carl. The investigation is going in different directions, and Pasgård is well aware that there was an attack some years back that might resemble the one on Rigmor Zimmermann. And in that connection, they've been in contact with Marcus Jacobsen, who told them that you and he had discussed the circumstances of both murders. And Pasgård is fuming about it. So if I were you, I'd make myself scarce and mind my own business before he comes out, any second."

Okay. He would have to take up the gauntlet on this one. Bloody annoying that they'd dragged Marcus into the case. It was a good thing he hadn't kept Marcus informed about what they had discovered in the King's Garden. He would have to keep his cards close from now on if he was going to avoid them stealing everything from him.

Pasgård looked like he was ready to breathe fire when he opened the door. A split second later, when he saw Carl standing there with his arms crossed, he revealed his infamous lack of charm.

"*You!* Keep your hands off my cases, you fool. You'd better believe that I'll make your life hell, and you can count on a huge bollocking from Bjørn."

"But surely not as huge as your ego, Passy?" said Carl.

Not only did he screw up his eyes, but his entire face—mouth, nose, and eyes—seemed to be clenched. Carl didn't catch what Pasgård shouted at him at full force in the next moment, but it was enough for Bjørn to open his door.

"I'll handle this, Pasgård," he said calmly, waving Carl into his office.

The head of communications, who was already sitting at the desk, nodded at Carl as he sat down to receive a bigger than normal official reprimand.

"Janus has informed me that there are some issues with our joint project, Carl," it began.

Carl looked confused. "Joint project"? What was this about *now*?

"Carl, you need to understand that Olaf Borg-Pedersen reports to me. Public relations and the commissioner himself have chosen you to assist them in this project with *Station 3,* which we all hope will differentiate itself from the usual angle where everyone sympathizes with the criminals."

Carl sighed.

"You might well sigh, Carl, but starting tomorrow you'll show a little more willingness with the TV crew, okay?"

What the hell was he supposed to answer? Now things would seriously be messed up.

"Hold on a minute. That TV crew wanted to shadow me during a questioning, and that's where we draw the line."

The head of communications nodded. "Of course we do, but instead of just saying no, you need to offer them a constructive alternative, right, Mørck?"

"I'm not with you."

"Say to them: 'No, you can't come with me for this, but tomorrow we can do such and such.' It gives them a little something, you know?"

Carl sighed.

"We know that you've been sticking your nose in Pasgård's work, Carl," said Bjørn. "Why else would you have been seen standing with Tomas Laursen in the King's Garden at the Zimmermann crime scene? But tell me, what did you find, Carl?"

Carl was looking out of the window. The view was the best thing about this office.

"Out with it, Carl!"

"Okay, okay." He sighed. "We found an explanation for the urine the technicians found on the victim, and we also think that the victim was being followed by the perpetrator."

"See what I told you, Janus?" said Bjørn.

They nodded to each other and smiled. What the hell were they up to? Did they maybe actually want the case solved?

"We need to head up to Mona in ten minutes, Carl," said Assad when Carl was back in his office. "Did you have any luck upstairs?"

"Yeah, we've been unofficially chosen to stick our noses in the Zimmermann case because we're the only ones who can put *Station 3* in their place. Turns out *Station 3* requested to follow that case and Pasgård is the last person they want in front of a camera. Everyone would hate the police by the time he was finished."

Assad's jaw dropped.

"They also think you've gained a status as our ethnic wonderboy over the years and believe it's time we showed off our diverseness."

"You mean diversity, don't you, Carl?"

Now it was Carl's jaw that fell victim to gravity. Diversity? Was that the way you said it?

"Well then, we should just do what they say, Carl. My charm will see us through." Assad laughed for a moment before scrutinizing Carl's face. "Are you sure you're okay?"

"Hell no, Assad. I don't want those idiots following us around for the next two weeks."

"That's not what I meant. I was thinking about how we're meeting with Mona now."

"We're what?"

"I thought you didn't hear what I said. Mona is waiting for us. And Rose's sister Yrsa is with her up in the office. The other two sisters were at work."

22

Tuesday, May 24th, 2016

The newspaper stand outside the kiosk on Vesterbro Torv was conspicuous. Not only did the morning and afternoon papers mention the hit-and-run incidents, but the tabloid *DK* had really gone to town in reporting the top story of the day concerning the female victims. They didn't leave anything to the imagination about what their focus was. It was pure drama.

They had all used the same photos of Michelle Hansen and Senta Berger, but in a very misleading way. Readers were presented with the news of uncannily similar attacks on two young, healthy women that had resulted in an outpouring of emotion and outrage.

Jobseekers was written under their names again. Anneli snorted. Nothing could be further from the truth. The reality was that they were a couple of scrounging slime bags whom no one should give a second thought. And it infuriated Anneli that she had helped them achieve the unmerited fame that they had always thought they were entitled to.

Why couldn't they just call a spade a spade? Write that the girls were leeches, scroungers, and bloodsuckers of the worst sort? Parasites that should just be trampled underfoot and forgotten about. Why didn't journalists do some research on the people they were writing about and what they stood for before churning out this rubbish about how charming and popular they were?

They weren't bloody popular. Certainly not with her, so who were they popular with?

Since returning from her radiation therapy, she had just been sitting behind her desk, thinking the same thing over and over. What if Jazmine or Michelle had seen the newsstands or the front pages of the bloody newspapers and decided to talk to the police? She tried to imagine the situation where a couple of investigators suddenly turned up to have a word with her. But hadn't her confrontation with Jazmine yesterday proved that she could cope with the pressure? She thought it had. If the police came down on her, she would just say that she didn't know anything about it and that she would be as shocked as anyone if it turned out that the attacks really were planned. And then she would remember to say that this was particularly difficult for her because she knew both the girls. That although it had been a few years since she had last seen Senta Berger, she was a nice girl who hadn't deserved to die like this.

Anneli laughed at the thought, covering her mouth so they wouldn't hear her in the hallway. Someone might ask what was so funny—there wasn't exactly much to laugh about in this department.

Anneli considered her next move, trying to forget the horrible feeling that they could suddenly be closing in on her and her crimes.

She had considered killing her next victim this evening and already knew who it should be. She wasn't a pretty girl, which was a clever move considering the newspaper description of the other two girls' beautiful looks. Her new victim had steadily and stubbornly changed over the years from a demanding girl with too high an opinion of herself to an unpleasant, overweight brat with bad manners and a fashion sense that even girls in the former USSR would have turned their noses up at.

She called herself Roberta in an attempt to hide her real name, Bertha. And she was one of Anneli's many aversions, having bled more money out of the system than anyone else in her time as a caseworker. The number of boots she had asked to have money to replace over the years because they had split on account of her fat calves. Her gifted ability to ignore warnings, fobbing it off as forgetfulness. Not a single plan to get her back to work had resulted in anything other than excuses. And she had taken sanctions and reduced benefits on the chin, borrowing money all over the place when she could find someone who would help her out. The result was that she had managed to incur painful debts of more than one and a half million kroner when Anneli had applied for a transfer. That was four years ago, so it wouldn't come as any surprise if the debt had more than doubled in size since then.

A quick search online and Anneli had found her. She was still living on the same side street off Amagerbrogade in a block of small apartments with plenty of pubs nearby. Anneli was sure that she could find her in one of these pubs, sprawled out on a barstool with a wall of cigarette smoke between her beer glass and the man next to her, whom she had probably roped into paying the bill.

Anneli had once turned up for a home visit with Bertha Lind only to find a locked door and nobody home. Having done the rounds of the local pubs, she eventually found her in Café Nordpolen, where they had a short argument about breaching agreements. Since then, Anneli had not gone out of her way to help her.

No, Bertha Lind was no paragon of virtue and no role model either. It was unlikely that she would get the same front-page coverage as the other more attractive victims.

The problem now, however, was that with all this newspaper coverage, the jack was out of the box, so to speak. She would have to re-evaluate her plan. Bertha would have to wait for now.

When she finished work, she made a quick decision and cycled to Sydhavnen, where Jazmine lived.

She stood outside the red building for half an hour, sizing it up and observing the surroundings. When she killed Jazmine in a hit-and-run, it certainly couldn't take place here. In part because Borgmester Christiansens Gade was far too busy, even at the end where it was closed off, and partly because there was a constant stream of people on the other side doing their shopping in Fakta or just hanging around in the square. So Anneli had to keep to her original plan to just keep an eye on the girl and then improvise later. At some time or other, one of Jazmine's habits or vices would reveal a weak spot and inspire an idea of where the hit-and-run could take place.

She looked up at the third floor, where Jazmine had always been registered as living. According to the records, the only other person living there was her mother, Karen-Louise Jørgensen. Surely a woman who had had to put up with her fair share, what with all the pregnancies Jazmine had involved her in. But wasn't Karen-Louise Jørgensen the one who had raised this little devil, and wasn't she responsible for the way she had turned out? So there was no reason to feel sorry for her either.

But what if Jazmine didn't live there anymore? What if like so many others she used her parents' address while actually living with some guy or other who didn't want to lose his government housing money? Maybe Anneli would be lucky and discover that Jazmine had moved to an address that was more remote.

She searched for the mother's telephone number on her smartphone and pressed dial. After a short pause, she had contact.

"I'd like to talk with Jazmine," she said, disguising her voice.

"Do you, now? And who might you be?" Her voice sounded very affected. A bit odd for this neighborhood.

"Uh, I'm her friend, Henriette."

"Henriette? I've never heard Jazmine mention a Henriette. But you're calling in vain, Henriette. Jazmine doesn't live here anymore."

Anneli nodded. So her intuition had been right.

"Really? That's a shame. Where can I get hold of her, then?"

"You are the second girl who's asked for Jazmine today, but at least you speak Danish properly. Why are you asking? What do you want with her?"

It was a very direct question. What the hell did it have to do with her? Jazmine was a grown woman.

She could see Jazmine's mother step forward, standing with her cell phone at the window. Wearing a dressing gown at this time of day. What a role model.

"I borrowed some money from Jazmine when I needed to buy some Christmas presents, and now that I finally have some money again I want to pay her back."

"That sounds odd. Jazmine never has any money. How much?"

"Sorry?"

"How much do you owe her?"

"Two thousand two hundred," she blurted out.

It went silent for a moment at the other end. "Two thousand two hundred, you said?" came the response. "Listen, Henriette, Jazmine owes me a lot of money, so you can just give it to me."

Anneli was taken aback. She was one determined bitch.

"Okay, I can do that. But I'll need to call Jazmine first and tell her."

She sounded disappointed. "You do that, then. Good-bye."

No, no, no, you can't hang up, that won't help me one bit, Anneli screamed inside. "I live out in Vanløse," she blurted out. "Isn't it close by? Then I can tell her in person."

"I have no idea if it's close by. She has just moved to Stenløse, and I don't know exactly where that is, just like I told the other person who called. I think Jazmine is still having her mail delivered here, so I'll see her sooner or later, and then I can just tell her that you gave me the money."

"Stenløse? Actually, yes, I think I heard something about that. On Lilletoftvej, right?" She had no idea if there was a road with that name in Stenløse, but nothing ventured, nothing gained.

"No, that's not it. Of course, she didn't tell me directly. Why would she? After all, I'm just her mother. But I overheard her speaking to someone on her cell. Something about sandals, as far as I could hear. But remember to give the money to me, okay? Don't give it to her."

When Anneli looked up "Sandal" and "Stenløse" on the Internet, all she found was a homeowners' association in Sandalsparken, which, now that she was standing here, she realized was a huge area. Two long blocks containing approximately one hundred apartments. How on earth was she supposed to find out which one Jazmine lived in when she wasn't registered as living there—unless she found her dancing along the walkways? It wouldn't be a good idea to trudge around for hours on end until the early hours. Should she just call the bitch and come up with some excuse or other about a cheap TV package or something? The risk that she wouldn't bite was significant, and it might sow the seed of suspicion.

She looked dejectedly at the first block of apartments. There were names on every buzzer, according to the rules of the association, but there were just so many. Then she thought she could just check the residents on the Internet instead but realized there was little chance that Jazmine would have changed her details online already. Of course, she could take each doorway in turn, checking the mailboxes one by one, but again, the chances that Jazmine had put her name on the mailbox were minimal.

Anneli sighed. She had an opportunity within her grasp, and that was better than nothing.

She began at entrance A, at one end of the first block of apartments, checking the names on the silver-colored mailboxes that hung in clusters in the hallway. And then just when she was about to give up—because this obviously wasn't the sort of association where people simply stuck impromptu names on the mailboxes—she caught sight of a name in entrance B that made her heart skip a beat.

Two birds with one stone, she thought immediately.

Because there on the mailbox, written as per the rules of the association, was the name "Rigmor Zimmermann."

A surname that, while it wasn't Jazmine's, was the surname of someone else high up on Anneli's death list.

23

Tuesday, May 24th, 2016

Even outside her office, the scent was unmistakable. Sensual bygone days and months reached Carl's nostrils, sending his mind into a state of alert. Why hadn't he worn a smarter shirt? Why hadn't he borrowed one of Morten's vanilla-scented deodorants and given his armpits a quick wipe? Why hadn't he . . . ?

"Hi, Carl. Hi, Assad," came the voice that had once been able to bring him to his knees.

She was sitting in a room without a desk but with four armchairs, smiling at him through her red lips as if they had seen each other yesterday.

He nodded to her and Yrsa—that was all he could manage—and sat down with a lump in his throat so big that it would be hard to utter a sound.

Mona was her usual self and yet different. Her body was still slender and desirable, but he saw her face in a new light, even though the differences were minimal. Her red lips were thinner, the small wrinkles above her top lip deeper, the skin on her face looser, but all in all more tempting to caress.

His Mona had aged. His Mona who had lived for years without him. What had time done to her?

He clung for one second to the short-lived but intense smile she sent him, and gasped for breath. Like a blow, he felt it inside, and it was almost physically painful.

Had she noticed his reaction? He certainly hoped not.

She turned to Rose's sister, sitting in the armchair next to her.

"Yrsa and I have gone through Gordon Taylor's list and the accompanying timeline of when Rose Knudsen changed the phrases in her mantra notebooks, as we might call them. Yrsa has a lot to add, judging from what I've already heard. Would you, Yrsa? I will support you along the way and add my own comments when necessary."

The red-haired imitation of a character from a Tim Burton film nodded, seeming genuinely affected by the situation. *Please excuse me if I start to cry,* her eyes seemed to say. Then she took a deep breath and began.

"You'll know a lot of this already, but I don't know exactly what you know, so I'll just sketch out the details. It's quite strange, but this is actually the first time I've really considered exactly what Rose has written. The things Gordon has noticed make sense to me now."

She placed the sheet with all the phrases in front of them. Carl knew them almost by heart.

"My dad started hounding Rose when I was seven years old, Vicky eight, Lise-Marie five, and Rose nine. I don't know why, but it was as if something or other happened in 1989 that made him single her out. From 1990 to 1993, it became worse and worse. When Rose begins writing that she is 'scared' in 1993, it is about the time she begins isolating herself in her room. Actually, there was a time when she also locked the door, only opening up for me or my big sister Vicky. We'd bring her food because she had to eat something. We had to keep knocking and give her reassurances that Dad wasn't standing outside before she'd open. She only ever left her room to go to school or the toilet, and the latter only if everyone else was asleep."

"Can you give a few examples of the psychological terror your dad inflicted on Rose?" said Mona.

"Well, he did it in so many different ways. Rose could do no right in his eyes, and he put her down at every opportunity. Crushed her by calling her ugly, saying that no one in the whole world wanted her and that it would have been better if she'd never been born. That sort of thing. The rest of us blocked it out because we couldn't stand hearing it. So I am afraid a lot of it is repressed now. We have discussed it, Lise-Marie, Vicky, and I, and we just don't remember much at all. It's really . . ." She swallowed a couple of times, suppressing her desire to cry, but her eyes gave away how sad she was that they had noticed so little of Rose's misery.

"Go on, Yrsa," said Mona.

"Okay. In '95 you can see that Rose goes on the defensive. Can't you sense it when she writes 'I can't hear you'?" She looked questioningly at them.

"So you think these phrases are a sort of internal conversation with your dad, and that it continued even after his death?" asked Carl.

Yrsa nodded. "Yes, without doubt. And Rose changes in '95 from being a timid and scared Rose to one who dares to stand up for herself, and there's no doubt in my mind that it's because of a new girl who started in her class in the middle of the previous year. As far as I can recall, her name was Karoline. A cool girl who listened to rap and hip-hop artists like 2Pac, Shaggy, and 8Ball while the rest of us girls were crazy about boy bands like Take That and Boyzone. She came from Vesterbro and refused to fit in, which rubbed off on Rose. Suddenly our sister was wearing the type of clothes that annoyed our dad most of all, and began covering her ears when he went for her."

Carl saw it all too clearly. "And yet he didn't hit her?"

"No, he was more sophisticated than that. He would forbid our mom from cleaning Rose's room, or he'd punish her by stopping her allowance, or find all manner of ways to favor the rest of us."

"And the rest of you thought that was okay?" asked Carl.

She shrugged her shoulders with an evasive air. "Back then, we thought Rose didn't care. That she was fine in her own way."

"What about your mom?" asked Assad.

Yrsa pursed her lips, sitting silently for half a minute before she was composed enough to continue. Her eyes searched about the room, avoiding direct eye contact with them, which continued for some time after she began speaking again.

"Our mom was always on our dad's side. I mean, not seriously, but in the way that she would never contradict him or take Rose's side. And when she finally did stand up for Rose this one time, he just directed his tyranny at her—that was the price for her rebellion. You can see it in 1996 where our mom gave up and started going after Rose just like our dad. In hindsight, she just followed in his wake."

"Then that's why Rose is screaming for help from your mom in that year's notebook. But did she get that help?"

"Our mom moved out, leaving Rose almost defenseless. She has hated our mom for that ever since."

"She writes 'Bitch' when your mom moves out."

Yrsa confirmed with a nod, looking down at the floor.

Mona interrupted. "We can see that Rose was feeling worse from then on. And even though she did well in high school, the harassment only became worse and worse. In the end she didn't dare to do anything other than what her dad demanded. And when she was asked to pay full board and lodging for staying at home after graduating high school, she accepted an office job at the steel plant where her dad worked. Half a year later, he died in a tragic accident at the plant, and Rose was standing next to him when he was crushed by a steel slab. 'Help me,' she writes after that."

"Why do you think she does that, Yrsa?"

She turned to face Carl, looking dead tired. Perhaps her and her sisters' passive role had hit her in all its horror. She certainly couldn't answer.

Again, it was Mona who came to her aid. "Yrsa has explained to me that she and her sisters didn't know for certain because Rose moved away at that time. But there is no doubt that Rose was in permanent shock and suffering from depression of some sort. Sadly, she didn't seek treatment, so her depression worsened. A sort of gloom and guilt that made her do the strangest things. She began going to pubs to pick up men. She slept with anyone. Had a series of one-night stands. And she adopted different personalities when she was with these men. She didn't want to be herself anymore."

"Suicidal thoughts?" asked Carl.

"Maybe not in the beginning, right, Yrsa?"

She shook her head. "No. She tried to escape from herself by dressing up like us. She pretended she was someone else, maybe because our dad hadn't bullied us and we had actually had a fairly normal family life, which was thanks to Rose, because she always intervened and took the battles for us," she said quietly. "It was worst at the millennium. On New Year's Eve all four of us girls were together for once. We all had our partners with us, but Rose was alone and definitely not feeling well. It was just after we had sung 'Auld Lang Syne' that Rose declared that she was fed up with everything and that this year would be her last. A few weeks later, at Lise-Marie's birthday bash, we saw her playing with a pair of scissors as if she might cut her wrists with them."

Yrsa sighed. "Back then it was only a threat, and not like last year when she was committed to Nordvang psychiatric center having almost cut both her arteries." She dried her eyes and regained her composure. "Anyway, we managed to persuade her to see a psychologist back then. In fact, that was down to Lise-Marie, our youngest sister, who she has always been closest to."

"Okay. I wonder if the psychologist from back then is someone who might be able to help us understand all this," said Carl. "Do you remember the name, Yrsa?"

"The girls tried to talk with him, but he said he couldn't due to patient confidentiality, Carl. Yrsa has told me who he is. I used to know him. Benito Dion was competent and actually taught us cognitive—"

"You said 'was.' Is he still alive?"

Mona shook her head. "And even if he was, he'd be over a hundred today."

Damn it!

Carl took a deep breath and scanned the list of Rose's phrases. "I can see that over the next few years, she slowly returns to a more normal state of mind—from 'black hell' to 'dark' and then to 'grey.' Then she implores herself not 'to think' and not to exist at all. 'I don't exist,' she writes. But what happens in 2004 where there is suddenly a change in tone with 'white light'? Do you know, Yrsa?"

"No, but I think Gordon figured that out. She started at the police academy and was doing really well and felt happy about everything until she failed the academy driving test."

And yet she wasn't entirely normal, thought Carl. Hadn't he heard how her promiscuous behavior at the academy had become a burden? That she was legendary for being an easy lay?

"But she didn't have a total relapse back to 'hell' when she was kicked out? She seemed more stable, right?" he asked.

"She found a good office job at Station City, don't you remember?" said Assad, interrupting his train of thought. Carl had totally forgotten that he was there.

"At that point she becomes 'deaf' to your dad, I can see." Carl pointed at 2007. "I think we can work out the rest of her phrases, but perhaps Gordon has already done that?"

Mona nodded. "Her appointment in 2008 with Department Q made her stronger, and now she's almost mocking her dad. 'Laughter stopped?' and even more pronounced in 2009, 'Get lost, shit!'"

"I don't know if you remember, but the following year she suddenly came to work dressed as Yrsa, and managed to pull it off for several days. In fact, she was so good at mimicking someone else that she had us completely fooled. Was it just an act to tease us, or do you interpret that as a relapse, Mona?"

It was the first time in years he had spoken to her directly by name. It sounded strangely unfamiliar in his mouth. It almost felt intimidating. Far too intimate. What the hell was going on? "But don't you remember that you two had just had a squabble, Carl?" asked Assad. "She reacted as if you'd bullied her."

"I didn't, did I?"

Mona shook her head. "We'll probably never know. But seen from the outside, and no matter what, working with you has had an extremely positive influence on her," she offered. "And then came the case, which Gordon has explained to us, where a certain Christian Habersaat who shot himself on Bornholm resembled the girls' dad so much that Rose almost had a breakdown. In the long run, it could have had a beneficial effect, but then you all made the fatal decision to visit a hypnotist, where her repressed emotions rose to the surface at once, causing her to require psychiatric help for the first time since she has been working here, am I right?"

Carl pursed his lips. This didn't make for easy listening. "Yes, but I just put it down to hysteria or one of Rose's usual moods, which would be over quick enough. We've been through a lot together over the years, so how were we supposed to know that it was so serious?"

"She writes, 'I'm drowning.' That event probably hit her harder than you knew, Carl. You can't be blamed for that."

"No, but then, she didn't say anything."

He leaned forward, trying to remember. Did he recall things as they really had been? Had she never said anything?

"With the benefit of hindsight, I have the feeling that Assad was more alert all along." He turned to face him. "What do you think, Assad?"

Curly hesitated momentarily, stroking his hairy left arm with his right hand. It was obvious that he was trying to answer as delicately as possible.

"I did try to stop you when you assigned the Habersaat report to her, remember? But I didn't know all this or I'd have been more in-sistent."

Carl nodded. And then there was the message she had written all over the walls of her home: "You do not belong here." Her father had returned to her life.

The effect of his tyranny had no end.

"What now, Mona?" he asked dejectedly.

She tilted her head to one side, almost exuding tenderness.

"I'll write a report to Rose's psychiatrists about what we know, and you do what you do best, Carl. Find the girl who made Rose rebellious. Find out about the nature of the dad's psychological harassment. Maybe this friend knows what started it all. And finally, you and Assad need to do all you can to find out what really happened at that steel plant."

24

Wednesday, May 25th, 2016

"You say you haven't come in to work, so why are you here?" asked her manager with obvious skepticism in her voice.

Anneli looked at her blankly. She was one to speak. When had she last done a day's work that could make her team nod in acknowledgment? Certainly not in her current position. In fact, things were easier when the woman was away on one of her usual management courses in some exotic location or other with the rest of the municipal crooks. At least then they could get on with the important work. Anneli had had a few managers like her over the years, but she took the cake. Charmless and totally out of touch with the circulars and legislation informing them what they could and couldn't do. In short, she was the most expendable person in the department and yet the one they couldn't avoid.

"I'm working a little from home to keep up to date, but I needed to check up on a few things at the office," said Anneli, thinking about the case files of several potential victims.

"Working from home? Yes, you do appear to have had a good deal of what we might term sporadic absence, for want of a better phrase, Anne-Line."

The manager squinted so her eyelashes hid her pupils. In was at moments like this that you had to be most on guard. It was less than five weeks since the woman had attended an excruciatingly expensive efficiency course in Bromölla, Sweden, to learn what a consistent employee policy could do for her popularity with her boss, and which signals to send to scare her subordinates. Four colleagues had been demoted to crappy jobs since she had taken that course, and it could be Anneli's turn any second.

"Well, we appear to be at the point where a doctor's note would be appropriate if you feel you can't manage a normal working week, Anne-Line." She forced a smile, which she had obviously also learned. "You can come and talk to me anytime if you have something you need to discuss, but you know that already, I assume?" She was well aware that this offer was risk-free.

"Thank you. But I've just been working from home while I get over this bout of flu, and I don't think I'm behind with anything."

That swiped the smile off her manager's face. "No, Anne-Line, but people need to know that you'll be here when they've made appointments with you."

She nodded. "That's why I've conducted some of my meetings over the telephone," she lied.

"Have you, now? And I'm sure you'll be giving me a written record of these meetings, won't you?" she said, adjusting Anneli's desk nameplate.

She hadn't heard the last from her.

Anneli looked out of the window, watching sharp rays of sun struggling to shine through the dirty glass and into this futile Sisyphean world. All the bickering and nonsense that took place in the adjacent offices didn't interest her at all anymore. Her colleagues felt like shadows blocking out the light. That was the thought she had had while undergoing her usual fifteen minutes of radiation treatment. Of course, she did have some good clients who really needed help and who cooperated to the best of their ability to better their situation, even though it was often in vain. There were just very few of them at the moment, and as the days went by most of the cases on her desk seemed more and more irrelevant, because after her diagnosis and the new project, Anneli was no longer interested in stopgaps.

Over the last few days she had reluctantly had to force herself to slow down, because planning and preparing the next murders took time. Just trying to find a suitable car had taken five hours last night, but now that was arranged. The battered black Honda Civic she had found out in Tåstrup was perfect for her needs.

It was an inconspicuous, low, dark car with tinted windows—almost the ideal murder weapon. In fact this morning she had been sitting in the Honda for an hour without being noticed in the parking lot on Præstegårdsvej next to Sandalsparken so she could observe the comings and goings in the neighborhood.

In this blessed calm, she concluded that it was of no real consequence if there were witnesses when she hit her victim. What did it matter if they took down the number plate if she was going to use the car only once? She knew how to make a quick getaway and where she was going to park the car in Ølstykke, which was a good five kilometers from there.

All in all, she felt well prepared and intoxicated just thinking about it. She would make her move as soon as an opportunity presented itself to do away with the Zimmermann girl or Jazmine, no doubt about that. Naturally, there could be problems. What would she do if both girls turned up together, maybe even arm in arm? Just the sort of thing spoiled brats like them did. In that case, the impact would cause serious damage to the front of the car, and there was also the risk that one or both of the bodies would be thrown up on the hood and smash the windshield. It wasn't unheard of.

She smiled, feeling prepared even for this eventuality. With a scarf around her head and neck and sunglasses to protect her eyes, the shards of glass posed no problem.

Yes, she believed that she had considered every eventuality. Even though she had read about cars involved in collisions with wild animals where the beast had come straight through the windshield, maiming the driver, this situation was different. Deer had a tendency to panic and jump up, but she didn't anticipate this sort of athletic reaction from Denise or Jazmine. And especially not if she hit them from behind.

She could just picture it.

That evening after work, she backed into a parking space opposite the building so she had a clear view up to the apartment and the walkway. Whether the bitches were coming or going made no difference. She would hit them all the same.

She laughed at her wickedness and thought that there was nothing more meaningful at this moment than sitting in this godforsaken place in a stolen car with the radio on the lowest volume while keeping her eyes on the first floor. Because up there were two of the girls Anneli was looking most forward to killing.

There had been activity up on the walkway a few times. And if one of the girls made an appearance, Anneli's plan was to start the engine and let it run idle. It was such an aesthetic and powerful humming. A sound that promised action. Only the sound of fighter helicopters above a dense jungle could match it. This whirring sound of death had been the pulse of the Vietnam War. Poetic, rhythmic, and also comforting, it could be claimed for those who had been on the right side of the front. She closed her eyes for a moment, calling to mind the well-known scenes, and therefore failed to notice the UPS delivery vehicle until it stopped right in front of her, blocking her way out and no less importantly her view to the girls' apartment and the sidewalk in front of the main door.

When the deliveryman had walked past their apartment up on the walkway, a figure appeared from the door behind him. Anneli didn't manage to see whether it was Denise or Jazmine, but it had to be one of them considering the conspicuous outfit.

Damn that delivery van blocking her exit.

Anneli leaned forward over the wheel in frustration, as if that would result in the deliveryman returning quicker.

When he finally showed up, he got in the van and sorted through some paperwork for a few minutes before finally putting the van in gear and driving off.

Anneli gave up on the idea of driving in the direction that the girl from the apartment had gone. Egedal shopping center was only a few minutes away, so she had probably already disappeared into the labyrinth of shops.

Instead, she decided to pull out to the edge of the road so she wouldn't end up in the same situation as before.

Then she scratched the spot where the radiation therapy had damaged her skin and waited.

She first saw the approaching figure with shopping bags at the same time as an elderly woman with a dog crossed the parking lot. Right there, as if on command, the dog stopped on the sidewalk next to Anneli to do its business.

Damn mongrel, she thought. The woman was fumbling for a dog-waste bag just as the young woman was approaching.

"Get the hell out of here and just leave the shit where it is," she said, sitting back in her seat. The bags the girl was carrying were dangling around her legs as if they weren't full. She looked grotesque in her ridiculously high heels and a very fake-looking leopard-print jacket.

Tarted up for a night on the town even when she's doing the shopping, she thought as the girl turned her face in Anneli's direction.

Anneli gasped. It was Michelle.

She froze. Good God! *So Michelle lives there too,* she thought as the implications of that possibility dawned on her. If the three girls were living together in the apartment, it could easily be a lethal cocktail.

What had Michelle told the others? Did she still suspect her? And if so, what were the consequences?

Just one word from them to the authorities and she would be under suspicion.

Of course, she could deny the accusation, referring to the girls' dishonesty and aversion to her. But what good would that do when it came to it? Her meddlesome boss could confirm that her behavior had changed lately. They could easily find out that over the years she had been in contact with the girls she had hit. Her so-called friends from work could confirm that she had missed the yoga class last week and would eagerly say how much she hated that type of client. The police experts would probably be able to check her computer and trace her search history no matter how much she tried to delete it. Perhaps they could even find traces of her DNA despite her best efforts to clean the Peugeot.

Those girls could really cause her a lot of problems.

Anneli turned off the engine and considered the situation.

Apparently Michelle had now left her boyfriend, so maybe there were some problems on the home front that could point the finger of suspicion in his direction if anything were to happen to Michelle or one of the other girls.

Could that be the reason why Michelle had left Patrick? Did she suspect her imbecile boyfriend of trying to kill her? Was Anneli even a suspect?

For a moment she imagined all three girls appearing on the street together so she could solve this situation once and for all. A quick acceleration and one determined aim were all that would be needed. Of course the vehicle she had stolen was too light to kill all three of them, so she would have to run them over several times before she could be sure they were dead.

Anneli smiled and began laughing at the thought. It was so amusing to imagine those three stupid girls flattened out on the road. Her laughter rose and rose until her body began to shake.

She caught herself in the rearview mirror: open mouth, bared teeth, and a hysterical look in her eyes. That put a damper on her amusement.

She looked down at herself, noticing that her body seemed to have taken on a life of its own. Her hands were drumming on her thighs, her knees knocking together like pistons, and her feet tapping on the mat like drumsticks. It looked completely insane, but it wasn't unpleasant. Rather, it felt pleasurable, as if she had taken some sort of aphrodisiac.

Have I developed brain metastases? Am I going crazy? she thought and started to laugh again. It was all so comical and fantastic. An old caseworker like her whom no one reckoned with. To think of the power she suddenly wielded. What undeniable and potent power.

Anneli looked up at the roof of the car. The euphoric state she was in demanded action. If it couldn't be those three damn girls up there in the apartment, she could easily find someone else.

Anneli felt that her intuition was right. In fact, she could not remember ever feeling better.

She looked at her watch. It was very late, but if she drove off now she could make Bertha Lind her next victim.

A dark shadow appeared as a taxi stopped a few meters in front of her car. Simultaneously, the door opened up on the walkway and three women appeared.

As they got into the taxi, Anneli was certain. Even though two of them were almost unrecognizable with all the makeup and their hair dyed black, there could be no doubt. It was Denise, Jazmine, and Michelle dolled up for a night on the town.

When the taxi drove off, Anneli put the Honda in gear and followed.

25

Wednesday, May 25th, 2016

"**Stop calling me when** you're drunk, Mother. How often do I have to tell you? I can smell your breath through the receiver."

"Why do you say things like that, Denise? You know I'm just feeling sad." She sniffled once to emphasize her point.

"You're disgusting, Mother. What do you want?"

"But where are you? I haven't heard from you for days, and the police have been here. They wanted to talk to you, and I didn't know where you were."

"The police? What about?" Denise held her breath and sat back in her chair.

"They just wanted to talk to you about your grandmother."

"I don't want to talk to anyone about my grandmother, got it? I've got nothing to do with that, and you'd better not make them think otherwise. What have you told them?"

"Nothing about you. Where are you, Denise? I can come and meet you wherever you are."

"No, you can't. I've moved in with a guy in . . . Slagelse. And it's none of your business."

"But—"

Denise hung up and looked at Michelle, who was sneaking out of her room. She looked very plain without makeup. Her eyes looked small and the contours of her face were undefined. She was destined to look like a shadow of her younger self when she got old. She would become flabby from eating all the wrong things and would look like a cow in clothes that she was far too old to wear. It was a real shame.

"Hi, Denise." It looked like Michelle was trying to smile, but after their discussion the previous night it would take more than that to establish genuine intimacy between them. She felt much more on the same wavelength as Jazmine. She understood the situation and how screwed they were if they didn't create a new life for themselves. That the ship had sailed for these little girls, that reality, their bad choices, lack of education, and untapped talents had caught up with them. That was something a pathetic creature like Michelle could never understand.

"Cool that you chose Coldplay, Denise," said Michelle as the phone rang again with the ringtone for her mother.

Denise shook her head and immediately rejected the call, went to her settings, and blocked the number once and for all.

That was *that* sorted. Case closed.

"Shut up, Michelle. I know full well what the difference is between theft, a simple robbery, and armed robbery. But *nothing* is going to go wrong if you just do what we say. So shut up with all your crap."

Michelle's eyes looked like a mess of ash-grey, the color smeared on her eyelids, lashes, and even under her eyes. If anything, she resembled a silent film star suffering from TB. If she planned to go out like this tonight, she would definitely get attention.

"You've told us everything you know about the place. What the manager's office looks like, where they keep the money for admission and drinks throughout the night, and how to get to the office. We'll be careful, Michelle, don't worry. We'll wait until the coast is clear and be quick. Yes, it's theft, but no more than that."

"But what if someone comes? What'll you do then?"

"We'll threaten them, of course."

"But then it's a robbery." She pointed at the iPad. "Look! It says on Wikipedia that you can get up to six years for robbery. *Six* years! Then we'll suddenly be in our mid-thirties and our lives will as good as be over."

"You shouldn't believe everything you read on Wikipedia, Michelle!"

Jazmine took the iPad from her and looked at the page. "We've got no priors, so it won't be that bad."

"Yes, but look further down." Michelle was almost shaking. This didn't bode well for tonight. She looked at Denise. "I saw the way you pummeled that brickie to the ground, and I wouldn't be surprised if you did something like that again. That changes everything, Denise. Then we can get up to ten years."

Denise grabbed her arm. "Relax, Michelle. Nothing has happened. What's any of that got to do with you? Nothing! You just have to chat with Patrick while we do the dirty work, okay?"

Michelle looked away. "Are you telling me that if anything goes wrong, you'll take all the blame?"

"Of course. What else?" Denise looked at Jazmine. She just had to nod. And she did.

"Good, then we're agreed. And now we need to find some treasure in the apartment."

"Treasure?" Michelle didn't follow.

"My grandfather had a pistol, and I am sure my grandmother has kept it. I just don't know where. I think it must be somewhere in the apartment."

When it came to it, Denise didn't know her grandmother's apartment very well. The few times she and her mother had been invited there, the sitting rooms had always been full of her grandmother's friends chattering away, but always with their eyes peeled, making it impossible to snoop around. But now that the wardrobes were unattended, Denise took the opportunity to rummage through piles of frumpy skirt suits and cardigans from a bygone age.

"Throw all that junk on the floor and we can bag it up later," she said. "We can sell it to secondhand shops in Østerbro if they'll take it." She sounded doubtful.

"I think it's disgusting rummaging through people's old clothes.

They smell of moth balls and I've heard they're unhealthy for the skin," said Michelle.

Unlike her, Jazmine seemed to relish the job at hand. Shoe boxes, hats, underwear, boxes of tissue paper, torn nylon stockings, and garters of all sizes flew out of the wardrobes. Jazmine was hunting for treasure, and everything else was junk.

They looked under the beds, checked in sewing boxes, pulled out drawers, moved furniture, and when they had been through all the rooms they sat down and looked around. What had before resembled the home of an elderly woman was now revealed as the site of shameless hoarding by a woman who had long lost any sense of reality. "Why do old people have so much worthless crap?" said Jazmine dryly.

Denise was annoyed. Could her grandmother really have parted with her grandfather's belongings? The photos from the war, the pistol, the medals and military badges? And if she had, what could they use as a threat if they were caught red-handed with the loot? The situation looked bleak. She had at least expected to find a box of jewelry, stocks and bonds, or some cash in a plastic bag from the days when her grandmother jetted about on package holidays with her decrepit husband. But all they had found was crap, as Jazmine put it.

"That's the only place left to look," said Michelle, pointing at the balcony, which resembled a junkyard full of pots and plants still in their wrapping, and garden furniture waiting for warmer days that their owner would never enjoy. A few years ago, sliding glass partitions had been installed on the balcony with the intent of being opened once in a while. Now they were so dirty that you could hardly see out of them.

"Allow me," said Jazmine.

Denise looked at her with growing admiration. Compared to Michelle, she looked slight and delicate. But if anyone could match Denise's resolve, it was Jazmine.

A moment later, she was out on the balcony. The sound of clattering and banging, accompanied by exclamations that were anything but feminine, told them that she was hard at work.

"I think what we're doing is wrong," said Michelle.

Then sod off home back to Patrick, thought Denise. If only she would shut up. While Denise had to admit that it was due to Michelle that they had joined forces, she now seemed extraneous.

Once they had robbed the bloody nightclub, she and Jazmine would have to discuss Michelle's role.

They heard a sigh from the balcony and saw Jazmine get up from the floor with her hair tangled and lipstick smeared on her cheek.

"Come out here and help me," she said.

All the things were hidden in a heavy, rectangular, sun-bleached hay-box, covered by women's magazines from the eighties.

They knelt down around the box to look at what Jazmine had found. Denise had never seen the box before but knew what it must contain.

"This stuff is really old," said Jazmine, pulling out piles of *Neues Volk, Der Stürmer, Signal,* and *Das Schwarze Korps* from the box. "Isn't this Nazi stuff? Why would anyone keep stuff like this?"

"Because my grandfather was a Nazi," answered Denise. She hadn't mentioned it to anyone outside the family since she had blurted it out to a teacher when she was ten and received a couple of slaps to the face, against all regulations. Strangely enough, it didn't mean anything to her now. The dust had settled and now she was in charge of the legacy.

"What about your grandmother?" asked Michelle.

"What about her? I guess she was—"

"Ewww, what's this," said Jazmine, dropping a couple of photographs on the floor, which made Michelle jump.

"God, they're horrible. Let's not look at those," Michelle moaned.

"That's my grandfather," said Denise, pointing at a photo where he was placing a noose around the neck of a young woman who was standing on a stool. "Nice guy, right?"

"I don't like it, Denise. I don't like being here knowing that that sort of people have lived here."

"*We* live here, Michelle. Get a grip."

"I don't know if I can go through with tonight. It just seems so scary. Do we *have* to do it?"

Denise looked at her angrily. "What else do you propose? Do you expect me and Jazmine to provide for you? Do you think we enjoy doing what we do just to keep you fed? Would you spread your legs for our sake, Michelle?"

She shook her head. Of course she wouldn't. The little Goody Two-shoes.

"Here's a flag," said Jazmine. "Bloody hell, Denise. It's a Nazi flag."

"What?" asked Michelle.

"There's something heavy wrapped in it."

Denise nodded. "Allow me."

She carefully unfolded the flag on the sitting room floor, exposing a hand grenade with a wooden handle, an empty magazine and a whole box of cartridges, and a greasy pistol wrapped in fabric.

"Look," said Jazmine.

She held up a piece of cardboard with drawings of the pistol they had just unpacked and with "Parabellum 08" written on it.

Denise looked attentively at the drawing, which had a cross-sectional view and instructions, and held out the empty magazine with room for seven cartridges in front of her. She weighed it in her hand and pushed it up in the butt of the pistol. There was a satisfying click, and suddenly she could feel that the weapon had the right balance.

"This is the same pistol that he's using there," she said, pointing to a photo of her grandfather executing a prisoner with a shot to the back of the head.

"Ugh, that's disgusting," said Michelle. "You're not bringing that thing with you."

"There aren't any cartridges in it, Michelle. It's just to scare people."

"Look!" said Jazmine, pointing at a device on the top left side of the pistol. "The drawing refers to it as a *Sicherung,* so if we want to fool anyone, Denise, we'll have to click it up."

Denise found the safety and flicked it up and down. When it was down the word *"Gesichert"* could be seen engraved in the metal. It was so simple and cool. She weighed it in her hand once more. It felt exactly right—as if she was on top of the world and could decide everything.

"It's a real pistol, Denise," said Michelle sulkily. "They come down hard on you if you threaten someone with one of those, so we aren't taking it with us, are we?"

But they did.

Michelle was silent in the taxi, clenching her handbag against her chest. It was only when they were dropped off a few hundred meters from the closed-down factory building where the Victoria nightclub was located that she finally revealed her state of mind.

"I just feel so lousy. I don't understand what we're doing. Why don't we just go home again before it's too late?"

Neither Jazmine nor Denise answered. They had gone over this already, so what did she think?

Denise looked at Jazmine. The lipstick, fake eyelashes, huge black eyebrows, dyed hair, masses of eyeliner, and just as much foundation made it almost impossible to see who was underneath. It was an efficient disguise created with the minimum of resources.

"Goddamn it, you look cool, Jazmine. How about me?" Denise turned her face up toward a streetlight.

"Perfect. Stunning, like an eighties film star."

They laughed while Michelle pointed at Denise's handbag.

"Are you absolutely sure that the pistol isn't loaded? Because if it is and things go wrong, it'll cost another four years in jail. At least!"

"Of course it isn't. You saw yourself that the magazine was empty," answered Denise, straightening the scarf around her neck and observing the traffic on Sydhavnsgade. If it stayed as busy as it was now, it would take only a few minutes after it was all over before they were sitting in a taxi again.

"I know I've told you that Patrick and the others usually don't frisk girls, but I don't like this. I really don't like this . . . ," repeated

Michelle over the next fifty meters. If only she'd swallow her tongue. That chickenshit!

When they turned the corner, they followed the crowd to the entrance. The mood was high and many people were laughing. The pre-parties had done their job.

"I think we're the bloody oldest people here," sighed Jazmine.

Denise nodded. In the flickering light from the streetlamps, many of them looked only just old enough to drink and get past Patrick.

"It can only be to our advantage if Patrick is going to be busy checking IDs," said Denise. She turned to Michelle. "I hope you're right that he won't recognize us from the hospital."

"If only you could see yourselves. You're not easy to recognize. But if I'm wrong, we'll just leave again, okay?"

Jazmine sighed. "We've gone over this a hundred times, Michelle. Of course we will. We're not stupid!"

"Okay, sorry. Anyway, Patrick is actually fairly nearsighted, but he won't admit it, so I've never seen him with glasses. If you pull your neck scarves up a bit to reveal your cleavages like we discussed, he probably won't notice anything else." She considered what she had said for a moment. "The bastard," she added.

Jazmine looked at her watch. "It's only twelve, Michelle. Do you even think there's any money in the cashbox at this time?"

She nodded. "It's Wednesday and most people have to get up early tomorrow, so the doors opened at eleven."

She pointed at the security cameras. In a few seconds they would be visible on the screen.

Over at the entrance, Patrick was already in full swing, looking slightly threatening like the bulwark against unwanted guests he was employed to be. His tattoos were visible on his bare forearms and his sleeves were rolled up to his biceps, displaying what you would have to contend with if you were after trouble. Not to mention the black gloves and boots no one in their right mind would want to be on the receiving end of.

This image of a completely indifferent bouncer-robot admitted the guests one by one, frisked a few of the men, refused to let people in with plastic bags, and now and then demanded to see someone's ID. Those he knew were waved in without further ado. There was no doubt who was in charge.

"Wait!" Michelle grabbed Denise's arm. "I think we have some help," she whispered and pointed over to a group of determined guys crossing the road, who looked like they might be immigrants. Maybe one of them was old enough to gain entry, but not the others. Early beard growth rarely disguised immaturity in Denise's experience, and no doubt in Patrick's too.

It was clear that he had already spotted the problem the way he instinctively took a step forward and pulled out a walkie-talkie from his pocket to speak to one of his colleagues.

"This is it," whispered Michelle. "Walk behind me."

"Hi, Patrick," she said clearly and loudly, as if she had overcome the worst of her nerves.

An obvious look of confusion spread over Patrick's otherwise determined face. Two totally different problems were obviously more than he was used to handling at once, which allowed Jazmine and Denise to walk straight past him.

A few steps and they were inside, while Michelle remained outside to distract Patrick.

The room was grey and raw. It was impossible to say what it had formerly been used for because now it just resembled a dirty storeroom with bare concrete walls. Where there had once been doors, there were now just openings. The banisters had been removed and replaced with shutter boards. The fixtures and fittings—and anything else of any value—had been removed.

The whole sorry place will be demolished within a year, thought Denise. An era was coming to an end in Sydhavnen for all the small private businesses. It had simply become too expensive because of its proximity to the docks and the refreshing breeze over the harbor area.

They paid the entrance fee and pushed past people dancing in an attempt to cross the dance floor. A lot of guys looked their way, but tonight their minds were on something altogether different.

The DJ was already going crazy, and the mass of people and concrete floor appeared to be burning up under the laser-light show. The blasting volume was enough to render any meaningful communication impossible, so Denise just pushed through the crowd in Jazmine's slipstream.

Jazmine had said that a few years back she had been up in the office with the acting manager, who had been more than willing to accept her offer of a sexual encounter.

She later heard that he had ended up in his grave due to an excess use of methamphetamine and cocaine, so it was a good thing she didn't get pregnant by him like she'd intended. It would probably have damaged the embryo, she thought. And deformed children were harder to get rid of, so who would take the risk?

They reached the other side of the dance floor and entered an icy-cold corridor lit by fluorescent lighting at least ten feet above them on the ceiling. And then they were stopped.

The security guard, who in stature was a clone of Patrick, barred their path and asked what they were doing there, much as they had anticipated he would.

"Hi, mate! Lucky we found you." Denise pointed at his walkie-talkie. "Didn't you hear that Patrick needs help out there? There's some bother with a group of immigrant guys."

He looked skeptical, but the serious expression on Denise's face made him reach down for his walkie-talkie anyway.

"Get a move on, big guy," shouted Jazmine. "Do you really think he's got time to chat on the phone just now?"

He put his overly pumped body in motion and set off.

Jazmine nodded toward a metal staircase at the end of the corridor.

"Just now there's at least one person in the office watching the security cameras, so there's no doubt that we've been spotted," said Jazmine. She indicated with her head toward the ceiling. "Don't look up, but there's a camera there. I waved at it last time I was here."

Denise held on to the iron banister, and copying Jazmine, she pulled her neck scarf up around her lower face.

As they opened the door to the office, they were hit by a wall of sound. A couple were standing making out by the far wall, the woman with her hands all over the man without the faintest hint of shame.

Denise looked around quickly and then moved with the stealth of a cat over to the couple. The row of monitors on the side wall looked like flickering wallpaper, and one of them clearly showed that the situation at the entrance was already under control. Right there in the middle of the screen stood Michelle with a guilty expression next to her ex-boyfriend while he divided his professionally threatening attention between her and the constant stream of arriving guests.

Despite a minor scrap, it appeared that Michelle was managing to play her part, thank God.

Now the monitors revealed that the guard they had encountered before had reached the entrance. He shouted something to Patrick, who shook his head in confusion and pointed at another security guy standing nearby.

The guy looked frustrated. He would soon be back at his post in the corridor, presumably to try to prevent his boss from being disturbed.

"Open the safe!" shouted Denise suddenly into the ear of the love-sick man, causing both him and the woman he was kissing to jump in the air, with the unfortunate result that she bit his tongue. He spun around fuming, the blood running from the corners of his mouth.

"Who the fuck are you?" He seemed to be hissing inarticulately as he lunged in vain to grab the neck scarf covering Denise's lower face.

"Did you hear what I said?!" she demanded. "Now!"

The girl behind him was laughing hysterically but stopped immediately when Denise pointed a black pistol at the face of her guy and made a point of releasing the safety.

"Unlock the safe and my helper will take the money. We'll tie you up before leaving, so if you do as you're told you'll survive," she finished, smiling behind her perfect disguise.

Five minutes later they were standing in the corridor again with their neck scarves down around their necks and the bag so full of bills that it made all this worthwhile.

The guard, who was back at his designated spot, must have known something was up, but Denise remained cool.

"Your boss told me to tell you that you're one hell of a guy. Did you manage to help Patrick?"

He looked confused but still nodded.

When they arrived back at the entrance, Patrick and Michelle had stopped bickering. One look between Denise and Michelle and the message was clear. Michelle could wrap things up.

"You're right, Patrick," said Michelle ingratiatingly while Jazmine and Denise slipped behind her and out toward the road. "I'll pop by tomorrow and give you the rest of the money, all right, honey?" she cooed.

The three of them had agreed to meet in the alleyway between Victoria and the next building. Denise and Jazmine waited ten meters down the alleyway in the gloomy, hazy light and the stench of piss.

Relieved, Denise leaned the back of her head against the concrete wall, which was vibrating from the beat of the music. "That was fucking crazy!" she gasped with her blood pumping full of adrenaline. Not even scoring her first sugar daddy and lying in bed with a strange man had given her this rush.

She put her hand to her chest. "Is your heart pounding like crazy too, Jazmine?" she asked.

Her friend replied with an ecstatic grin on her face: "Fuck, yeah! I think I pissed my pants when he lunged for your scarf."

"God, yeah, that could easily have gone wrong, but it *didn't*, Jazmine," she said, laughing. "Did you see his face when I released the safety on the pistol? Fuck, he looked stupid. And now they're lying up there with gaffer tape all over their faces with their hands and feet tied, trying to figure out what the hell just hit them." She held her stomach. The whole operation had taken five minutes.

It couldn't get better than this.

"How much do you think we got, Jazmine?" she asked.

"No idea, but I totally emptied the safe. Thousands, I think. Wanna check?"

She stuck her hand down in the bag and pulled out a handful of crumpled notes. Most of them were two-hundred-kroner notes, but there were also five-hundred- and one-thousand-kroner notes.

Jazmine laughed. *"Fuck!* I think there's over a hundred thousand. Look!"

Denise shushed her. In between the buildings out toward the road, a sharp black silhouette appeared against the background of the streetlight. Someone had spotted them, and it was someone who was both slimmer and shorter than Michelle.

"What the fuck are you bitches up to?" shouted a voice with an accent as a female figure stepped toward them.

Denise had seen her before. It was Birna.

Jazmine gasped for air and Denise could understand why, because Jazmine had not had the composure to put the money back in the bag and was standing there fully exposed, a criminal caught red-handed.

Birna's eyes were glued to the money.

"That's not your money, is it, now?" she said threateningly, taking a single step forward. "You can just hand it over now. Now!" she said, gesturing with her hand that she meant business.

Does she think I'm stupid? thought Denise, provocatively putting one hand behind her ear. "Sorry, I can't really hear you through all the noise. What are you saying, punk?"

"Is this bitch hard of hearing, Jazmine?" said the punk. "Or do you think she's trying to provoke me?"

She turned toward Denise. "Bloody hell, you two look more like me than I do myself with all that coal around your eyes. Are you trying to make sure no one knows who you are?" She smiled sarcastically. "But now I know, so if you don't want any trouble, just hand it over." She pointed at Denise. "Listen up, bitch, if you give me any cheek again, you'll regret it. Hand over the money."

Denise shook her head. This was definitely not part of the plan. "I don't know what it is you think you know, but don't be a fool, Birna. Isn't that your name?" Denise put her hand in her pocket. "Haven't I told you to stay away from us?"

The smile on the punk's face vanished in a split second. "Okay, if that's how you want to play. It's your funeral." She turned toward Jazmine. "Come on, Jazmine, you know me. Tell that cunt that she'd better show me some respect." Then she slowly and calmly produced a switchblade from her pocket and released it. "Otherwise she'll regret it. Tell her, Jazmine."

She didn't wait for an answer but stepped up to Denise and waved the blade directly at her abdomen. The blade was sharp and double-edged and Denise quickly realized that it would sink in deeply without any resistance if she carried out her threat.

"What are you even doing here, Birna? You're not the clubbing type, are you?" asked Denise coldly without taking her eyes off the knife.

"What do you mean, shit face? This is our patch and we rule here. Jazmine knows that, don't you, Tinker Bell?"

Denise looked up toward the road. Was Birna expecting reinforcements from her gang? Hell no. The punk was all alone. And Denise would be damned if she was going to put up with her threats. They had planned and executed everything to the letter, and there was no way an ugly genderless nobody was going to ruin it now.

"I'm sorry, but this doesn't appear to be your day, Birna," she said, slowly pulling the pistol out of her pocket. "If you want to save your sorry life, I'll give you a thousand kroner here and now, and then you need to beat it. And if you so much as utter *one* word to anyone, I'll come and find you, okay?"

The punk drew back against the wall, weighing up what it was Denise was holding in her hand. Then she smiled and raised her head as if she had figured out that there was no way whatever it was could pose a real threat.

"Hey, what's going on?" sounded a horrified voice from the top of the alley. It was Michelle, innocent and out of place with her handbag over her shoulder.

"Nice! Is she also in on it? You fucking surprise me," the punk said with a laugh. And then without warning she lunged toward Denise with a roar, pointing the knife directly at her.

"I'll shoot," Denise tried to warn her, but it didn't stop Birna. And instinctively, Denise pulled the trigger, as if that would help.

The bang, which echoed between the concrete walls and resulted in a cloud of residue and a hole the size of a coin in the Icelandic girl's chest, was drowned in the noise from the club even before the punk had collapsed.

Denise stood with her hand pointing up from the recoil. She didn't understand. Had there been a cartridge in the magazine, and why hadn't she checked? She could have looked at the drawing to see how it all worked.

Jazmine and Denise stood gobsmacked, looking at the lifeless body and the blood seeping out onto the dry asphalt.

"What the *hell* is going on? You said it wasn't loaded, Denise!" sobbed Michelle in horror, staggering toward them.

"We need to get out of here," shouted Jazmine.

Denise tried to shake off the shock. This was bad, really bad. The hole in the wall, the blood on her shoes, the smoking pistol in her hand, and the girl who was still breathing while the blood was flowing out from under her armpit.

"The bullet went straight through her," she stammered.

"Come on! Can't you see she's still breathing? We have to drag her out onto the sidewalk or she'll just bleed to death," pleaded Michelle.

Denise put the pistol back in the bag mechanically and bent down to grab one of Birna's feet while Jazmine grabbed the other. Then they dragged her up to the end of the alleyway so that the streetlight just hit her legs.

They didn't look back over their shoulders as they disappeared up toward Sydhavnsgade.

The last thing Michelle said before they got in the taxi was that the whole thing was terrible, and that the queasy feeling in her stomach made her feel like she was going to be sick. That everything was spinning in her head and that she even thought she had caught a glimpse of Anne-Line.

26

It's more the rule than the exception, thought Carl.

The sheet underneath him had come off the mattress. The pillow was on the floor. Everything that had been on his nightstand had been knocked off. He had been sleeping badly for a long time now, and last night was Mona's fault.

She just wouldn't disappear from his head. Not least the meeting with her at HQ and the visible changes in her appearance had hit a nerve with him. The soft, loose skin around her neck and mouth. The way her hips had become broader. The visible veins on the backs of her hands. All this had aroused him and kept him awake. This was about the tenth time she had caused him to break down, and despite his repeated attempts, he just couldn't get her out of his mind. He had had short-lived affairs with women he had met in bars and cafés, at conferences and training courses. Even monthlong attempts at more serious relationships. But all of these experiences had been meaningless as soon as he thought about Mona.

He thought over and over about what she thought of him. He would have to find out once and for all.

"I found more of Jesper's stuff in the basement. Can I put it up in the attic?" asked Morten while he was feeding Hardy at the breakfast table.

Carl nodded, but inside he was shaking his head. Despite his pleas, his stepson still had a pile of shit down there. The guy had turned twenty-five a couple of months ago. He had graduated high school and was now nearing the end of his business degree. So what the hell was wrong with wanting to know how old your kids should be before you could expect them to *really* move out?

"Have you found anything to link the Zimmermann case and the murder of Stephanie Gundersen, Carl?" said Hardy, slurping.

"We're working on it," he answered, "but Rose's case and condition are taking up a lot of our energy just now. It seems we've become quite attached. You often only realize things like that when disaster *has* struck."

"That's true. I just thought it was important for you to solve those cases before Pasgård."

Carl allowed himself to smile. "As long as Pasgård is wasting energy looking for a man who pissed on the body, we can take it easy."

"If you ask me, you need to start making some headway, Carl. Marcus Jacobsen called yesterday to ask how far you've come. He's betting on both teams, you should understand. Solving the Stephanie case is all that matters to him just now."

"That's the thing, Hardy. Isn't it just a little bit *too* critical for him? I can't get that thought out of my mind."

Hardy thought for a moment, whispering to himself. He always did this when he was unsure about something. The quiet argument for and against. "You know what? I think you should call Rigmor Zimmermann's daughter," said Hardy. "You mentioned that Rigmor had withdrawn ten thousand kroner before she was murdered. I think Birgit Zimmermann can shed a bit more light on what the victim wanted with so much money. Catch her off guard this morning. As I understand from Marcus, she doesn't hold back from visiting the bars every night these days."

"Where does Marcus know that from?"

Hardy smiled. "Even an old circus horse needs a shot in the ring once in a while!"

Was he talking about himself now? Anything else would be weird.

Carl gave him a pat on the shoulder. Not that the paralyzed man could feel it, but all the same.

"Ow! That hurt," said Hardy unexpectedly.

Carl froze and Hardy looked shocked.

It couldn't be. Apart from a couple of fingers, Hardy had been paralyzed from the neck down for almost seven years. How—

"Just kidding, Carl," Hardy said, laughing.

Carl gulped twice.

"Yeah, sorry, mate. I couldn't resist."

Carl sighed. "Don't do that again, Hardy. You actually gave me a shock."

"Life is only as much fun as you make it," he said dryly, while Carl looked over at Morten, who was struggling up the stairs from the basement carrying Jesper's junk. It was true enough. There wasn't much to laugh about in the house at the moment.

Carl took a deep breath. For a split second he had been so happy, because wouldn't it be amazing if Hardy . . .

He took out his phone. It was probably optimistic to believe that he could catch Birgit Zimmermann with a clear head this early in the day, but at least he did what Hardy had recommended.

There was an answer at the other end surprisingly quickly, albeit the only giveaway at first was the sound of bottles clinking in the background.

"Yeees, hello," came a drawling voice at the other end.

Carl introduced himself.

"Yeees, hello," she said again. "Anyone there?"

"I think the idiot is holding the receiver upside down," he said dejectedly to Hardy.

"Hey, who are you calling an idiot? Who are you?" came the grumpy reply.

Carl calmly hung up.

"Ha-ha, that was a stupid remark to make, wasn't it?" Hardy said, laughing. It was nice to see him laugh. "Let me try," he continued. "You dial the number, put it on speakerphone, and hold it for me."

Hardy nodded when the woman answered with a torrent of abuse that was so outdated the phrases were extinct.

"Oh, I believe you must be mistaken, Mrs. Zimmermann. I don't know who you think I am, but you're speaking to Head of Department Valdemar Uhlendorff from the probate court. We are handling the will of your deceased mother, Rigmor Zimmermann, and have a few questions to ask you in that connection. Is that something you could help me with?"

The silence made it clear how confused the woman was and how hard she was struggling to appear composed despite her hangover.

"Of course, I'll . . . try," she said affectedly.

"Thank you. We know that your mother withdrew ten thousand kroner shortly before her sad demise. And according to you, she still had the money when she visited you shortly before the fatal attack. Do you have any idea at all what she needed the money for, Birgit Zimmermann? We're always concerned to make sure we don't overlook any claims, and we wouldn't want anything concerning your mother to arise and have to be settled at a later date. Did your mother owe money to anyone as far as you know? Maybe a private individual who she intended to pay the same day? Or could she have been considering a special purchase that she didn't manage to make?"

This time the silence was significantly long. Had she fallen asleep or was she simply searching her dimmed brain?

"A purchase, I believe," she finally answered. "Perhaps a fur coat that she had been talking about."

It definitely didn't sound convincing. Where would you buy a fur coat that late?

"We know that she often used her Visa card, so we find it odd that she would have such a large amount of cash on her person. But maybe she just liked to have ready cash on her. Is that the case?"

"Yes," she answered quickly.

"But ten thousand kroner? That's quite a lot."

"I'm afraid I can't help you further," she said in a quivering voice. Had she started crying?

She hung up.

They looked at each other.

"Good work, Hardy."

"Out of the mouths of babes and drunkards, as the phrase might as well be. She was lying, but you know that, I assume?"

Carl nodded. "Buy a fur coat with cash? The daughter is creative, I'll give her that." Carl smiled. He had spent two minutes of blissful nostalgia watching the man do what he did best like back in the old days.

"You called yourself Uhlendorff? Where the heck did that come from?"

"I know a guy who bought a holiday house where there had once lived an Uhlendorff. But can we agree that you need to scrutinize both Rigmor and Birgit Zimmermann's more recent bank history? There could well be correlations between withdrawals and deposits."

Carl nodded. "Yes, she might have brought the money for her daughter. But then why would she still have it on her *after* leaving her daughter's apartment? Can you tell me that?"

"Tell me, is it you or me who's being paid for police work, Carl? Just asking."

They both turned their faces toward Morten, who was standing on the staircase to the first floor gasping for breath, barely visible underneath the black rubbish bags he was carrying.

"I found some of Mika's old gym clothes down there. Can I put those in the attic too, Carl?" asked Morten, his face bright red from walking up and down the ladder.

"Yes, if you can find any room."

"There's enough room. Apart from all Jesper's belongings and a lot of boxes with Vigga's jigsaws and that sort of thing, there's only a pair of skis and a locked suitcase up there. Do you have any idea what's in it, Carl?"

He frowned. "That's probably something of Vigga's as well. I'll check it someday. You wouldn't want a severed corpse up there without knowing, would you?" He laughed at Morten's reaction. There certainly wasn't anything wrong with his imagination.

"What would you rather do today, Assad? Trudge around with Gordon in the area around the King's Garden and check for places where Rigmor Zimmermann might have flashed her cash, or try to find a current or former employee at the steel plant who knows about the circumstances surrounding Rose's dad's accident?"

Assad looked at him as if he was stupid. "Don't you think I know what you're up to, Carl? Do I look like a camel cow that just lost its calf?"

"Uh, I'm not sure I . . ."

"When the camel cow is grieving, it doesn't produce milk. Just lies down flat on the ground and nothing in the world can get it up again. Not until it gets a hard slap on the ass."

"Uh . . ."

"Of course the last one, Carl."

Now he didn't follow at all.

"I'll find that man from the steel plant, okay? And you can just drop that idea with Gordon. He already looked around there yesterday just after we'd seen Mona. Didn't he tell you he was going to do that?"

Carl was speechless.

"Yes, that's right," confirmed Gordon a minute later in the situation room. "I visited every kiosk, bar, restaurant, and even the hot-dog van. Everywhere between Store Kongensgade and Kronprinsessegade and between Gothersgade and Fredericiagade. I showed them all a photo of Rigmor Zimmermann, and a few of them recognized her without any hesitation but hadn't seen her for some time. So I have no explanation as to why she might have waved her money in front of anyone in that area."

Carl was taken aback. The guy must have rushed from place to place in order to visit them all within that time. Finally there was an advantage to his abnormally long legs.

"I'm trying to track down Rose's friend from school," he continued. "I called Rose's old school and the secretary was able to confirm that a new girl joined Rose's class in 1994. Her name was Karoline, like Yrsa told us in Mona's office. The school doesn't have the records anymore, but one of the old teachers remembers both Rose and Karoline. He even remembers that Karoline's surname was Stavnsager."

Carl gave him a thumbs-up.

"Yeah, I haven't found anyone under that name yet, but I'll get there, Carl. We owe that to Rose, don't we?"

An hour later Assad was standing in Carl's doorway.

"I've found a former employee from the steel plant. His name's Leo Andresen and he's a member of a historical society for retired employees up there. He said he'd try to find someone who was there in section W15 when Rose's dad was killed."

Carl looked up from his paperwork.

"A lot has happened up there since then, Carl. The plant was taken over by Russians in 2002. The company was split up into separate companies, and there are only three hundred employees left from the thousands that used to work there. He said that there has been billions invested in the place, so it looks very different today."

"That's hardly surprising given that the accident happened seventeen years ago, Assad. But what about the section you mentioned? Is that still intact so we can inspect the scene of the accident?"

He shrugged. Apparently he had not asked. He really wasn't in top form.

"Leo Andresen said he'd check it out. He remembers the accident well, even though he didn't work with the people involved. He worked with high voltage, I think he said, which was based elsewhere. That plant is huge."

"Then we'll have to keep our fingers crossed that he finds someone who knows a bit more."

Carl pushed the documents he had been looking at in front of Assad.

"These are two account statements, and don't ask me how I got hold of them."

He drew circles around various figures around the turn of each month on both statements. "Look here, and there, and there."

Carl tapped on a few of the circles. "These are Rigmor Zimmermann's withdrawals since January 1st. As you can see, there are large cash withdrawals at the end of every month. And then look here."

He pointed at a couple of figures on the other statement.

"This is the daughter's account. Funnily enough, in the same period a slightly smaller amount is deposited in her account just *after* the start of the month. So Birgit Zimmermann probably had her hands on her mother's money before depositing it in her account, from where she had set up direct debit payments to take care of her and Denise's rent, utilities, and so on. At least that's what the figures seem to suggest."

Assad's eyes lit up. "Score," he said quietly.

Carl nodded. "Exactly. And what does this tell us? I wonder if Rigmor Zimmermann was supporting her daughter and granddaughter long-term."

"And she obviously didn't this month because she was killed on April 26th." Assad had the same calm look in his eyes as when he stood up from his prayer rug. He counted on his fingers as he tallied up the facts.

"One. According to Birgit Zimmermann, her mother was carrying the money when she visited her on April 26th.

"Two. The money hasn't been deposited in Birgit's account, and therefore a lot of bills haven't been paid for May.

"Three. It seems reasonable to conclude that the daughter didn't receive the money the day Rigmor Zimmermann was killed.

"Four. Something happened that day that made Rigmor Zimmermann decide not to give her daughter the money like she normally did.

"Five. We don't know why!"

"I completely agree, Assad. And six: Does this help us in any way given that we don't know anything about the relationship between Rigmor and Birgit Zimmermann?

"Of course, we'll have to confront Birgit with the facts, but I also think you need to investigate further into her mother's background. Who *was* Rigmor Zimmermann? Was she supporting her daughter because she expected something in return? And did she hold back the money on April 26th because she didn't get what she wanted? Was it a form of blackmail? Or was it a question of simply changing procedure?"

"What do you mean?"

"Why would you give someone cash in that way? I'm thinking it might be because the receiver wouldn't necessarily have to pay tax on the amount. But what if Rigmor Zimmermann got cold feet? That she suddenly realized that the connection *we* have just made was one the tax authorities could just as easily make. And what if she didn't dare take that risk anymore? Maybe she thought she shouldn't be the one to pay for the daughter and granddaughter's social fraud."

"Could that have happened?"

"Maybe if the amount was big enough. But no, I don't think that was likely. But *she* might have thought it was. It's also a possibility that Rigmor Zimmermann intended to pay the money into her daughter's account directly from then on. Perhaps she knew about her daughter's alcohol problem and didn't want to risk the money being used in the wrong way."

"But couldn't Birgit Zimmermann just have withdrawn the money and spent it on booze afterward?" asked Assad.

Of course, he was right. There were a lot of aspects to this otherwise simple calculation.

"In any case, the mother had enough money to support her daughter and granddaughter, I can see." Assad pointed at the main balance. There was more than six million.

Carl nodded. That alone was motive enough to wish her dead.

"Do we suspect Birgit Zimmermann, Carl?"

"I don't know, Assad. Check the background of these three Zimmermann women. Find out as much as you can, Assad, and give me the number of that guy from the steel plant. I'll go and visit him."

"His name is Leo M. Andresen and he used to be the union rep and head of one of the sections at the plant, Carl. So be nice."

That was some insinuation. Wasn't he always nice to people?

Although he was retired, the former union representative Leo M. Andresen had a youthful voice and an even younger-sounding vocabulary, which made it difficult to determine his age over the phone.

"Let's just meet up here when I've found someone who's a bit more down with the current setup, Carl Mørck. There are enough of us old steel boys to create an army. Anyway, if I find someone, we'll take a quick round of the plant and check out where the guy kicked the bucket."

"Err, thank you! So the site of the accident still exists? I was under the impression that there had been a lot of changes at the plant?"

He laughed. "Yeah, W15 has been expanded in every imaginable way—you're not wrong there. The slabs come straight from Russia now that we no longer mound them ourselves, so there isn't the same need for space as there used to be. But the part of the section where Arne Knudsen met his end looks more or less the same."

"So you get the finished product from Russia?"

"Not quite. We import the steel slabs from Russia and roll them into plates."

"I see, so that's the only thing they do at the plant now?"

"Yeah, I wouldn't say only; there's more to it than that. They receive the steel from Russia in big slabs and heat them up to around twelve hundred degrees Celsius and then roll them into plates of different sizes and only to order."

Carl had more questions, but then someone in the background shouted, "Leo, coffee's ready," and the man said good-bye.

A perfect example of how a pensioner's day could drastically change from one second to the next.

27

Thursday, May 26th, 2016

Michelle sat on the edge of the sofa with her head in her hands. It was all just so horrible that she had been crying most of the night. As soon as they had come home, she had done everything she could to make them understand how serious the situation was. That they had committed armed robbery and then shot a girl.

That it had already been reported on the radio.

But they just laughed at her, celebrated with warm champagne, and said that she should go back to Patrick with the couple of thousand he believed she owed him. And if she listened to him and played dumb when he told her what had happened at the club, no one was going to suspect her.

And as for Birna, she shouldn't worry about her at all. She only got what she deserved. But Michelle couldn't calm down, and it wasn't only because of that. Only six days ago, she had almost been killed in a hit-and-run, and it was almost a miracle that she was still able to be up and about in spite of her pain and injuries. But had the other two taken this into account? No, they hadn't. Now they had been living in the apartment together for three days and what had happened? Michelle had not done anything other than clean up after them. Was that okay when she was the one who had been in the hospital and still had occasional headaches? She didn't think so.

There were clothes scattered all over the apartment. The lids had not been put back on the makeup. There was toothpaste on the mirror, hair in the sink, and smeared-out phone numbers for their sugar daddies on the bathroom tiles. They didn't flush the toilet. They didn't cook, leaving that job to Michelle, who also had to do the dishes afterward. All in all, they were nothing like the two girls she had thought they were. The cool girls she had met at the job center were just a couple of slobs on the home front, she thought.

Denise had even brought one of her sugar daddies home late one night, even though they had agreed that they would not do that, leaving Michelle unable to sleep because of the noise. That kind of thing gave her even more of a headache. In fact, she couldn't deal with it at all.

And then yesterday! Despite their reassurances, it had ended very, very badly. And to make matters worse, it seemed like they didn't give a damn. The pistol had just been thrown back in the haybox on the balcony. Hadn't they considered that if Birna died, the pistol would be a murder weapon? If Jazmine could find it in the box, so could the police. Michelle couldn't bear it.

She looked up at the TV screen and began shaking as she thought about the consequences. Those two good-for-nothings were sleeping in their rooms even though it was well past ten, while TV2 News talked about nothing other than the robbery and the woman who had been shot. There was no news about whether Birna was dead or alive. Didn't they normally give that information?

There was money scattered everywhere because Jazmine and Denise had thrown it in the air, letting it rain down on them in their drunken state. The money was definitely a plus, but how was she going to explain to Patrick that she could suddenly pay him what she owed him? It was the end of the month, when she usually did not have any money left. And didn't he know her well enough to sense when something was wrong? Yes, he did.

And when she thought about him, and how long they had been together, she couldn't help crying again. Why had she even left him? And why hadn't she just taken that job at the laundry when that was what he wanted?

The TV screen now showed a reporter in a grey parka in front of

Victoria with a microphone in his hand. His lips were moving and the camera was alternating between him and the club.

Michelle turned up the volume.

"The two women who were wearing scarves over their faces got away with more than one hundred and sixty-five thousand kroner. They have been recorded by various security cameras and even though they seem to have known where they were, and disguised their faces, an approximate description of their age and height has been established. Based on the women's movements and dress, police experts believe them both to be ethnic Danes in their twenties with athletic builds, one being around one hundred and seventy centimeters tall and the second slightly taller. According to the club manager and security guard, they both have blue eyes."

Michelle watched with bated breath as the news channel showed videos of Jazmine and Denise seen from all angles. Thankfully their faces weren't visible, as the reporter had said, and the clothes they were wearing could have belonged to anyone, which comforted her a little.

"The police are now working on a more detailed description based on the eyewitness account of one of the bouncers, who was the only person to see them without their faces covered." The reporter turned toward the other camera. "The suspects are believed to have escaped up toward Sydhavnsgade. Police are now attempting to trace their movements by making inquiries with taxi companies and going through various security camera recordings from S-train stations and elsewhere in the vicinity."

He turned back toward the first camera. "The police have yet to make any connection between the robbery and the shooting in the alleyway behind the nightclub. But according to the manager of the club, who was held hostage by the women, the pistol used was a Parabellum, also known as a Luger—an iconic nine-millimeter handgun from the Second World War—which fits the caliber of the weapon used in the alleyway shooting."

They showed a photo of the type of pistol, which Michelle recognized as the same as the one in the box on the balcony.

"The young female victim was known to the police. They have identified her as the twenty-two-year-old Birna Sigurdardottir, who has been arrested several times for violence and disturbing the peace. The police are therefore not ruling out that she may have been involved in the robbery and perhaps even the person behind the whole plan. The police are currently questioning two women who are believed to be members of a gang led by Birna Sigurdardottir, and who together with her have committed several violent attacks on other women in the Southwest district of Copenhagen where the robbery took place."

Michelle shook her head. There were so many people looking for them. What would her mother and stepfather say if they knew that she had been involved? The thought sent a shiver down her spine. And how would everyone she knew react if they found out that she had been involved in all this?

"According to doctors at Copenhagen University Hospital, Birna Sigurdardottir remains in critical condition. Police have therefore been unable to question her and, if her condition does not improve, may find themselves unable to do so at a later date." Michelle stared at the screen. If she died, it would be murder. And if she didn't, Birna knew who they were. She would at least be able to identify Jazmine, and then the game would be up. If the police found Jazmine and came down hard on her, Michelle was convinced that she wouldn't be able to keep quiet.

Whatever happened, things just couldn't get any worse.

Michelle looked at her watch. The reporter would soon be wrapping up his report because it was just before eleven and time for the commercials. "Based on the perpetrators' apparent knowledge of Victoria nightclub, the police assume that the robbery was an inside job. In that connection, several employees at the club have been taken in for questioning. We will return when there's further news in the case."

Michelle sat back on the sofa. God, what if they had taken Patrick in for questioning?

She pursed her lips. She just had to get out of here. Home to Patrick. While she was gathering her things together, she wondered how much money she could take with her, because nothing had been decided on that front. Maybe the other two would become impossible if she took any at all.

In the end, she decided to take the twenty-thousand-kroner bundle lying on the coffee table. It was insignificant compared to the total of one hundred and sixty-five thousand. But if she kept the money well hidden and gave Patrick only a little, it couldn't do any harm.

She knocked on Denise's door and went in even though there was no sign of life.

Denise was lying on the bed half-unconscious, fully dressed, with her mouth wide open and her makeup smeared all over the pillow. She looked like a cheap hooker. There was a second pillow tucked between her legs and money scattered around her and on the floor. The sight genuinely shocked Michelle.

"I'm going now, Denise," she said. "And I won't be back, okay?"

"Y'okay," mumbled Denise. She didn't even bother to open her eyes.

Down on the street, Michelle tried to think about things that were at least slightly positive in the middle of this damn mess.

The first and best thing was that Patrick could testify that she had *not* taken part in the robbery and that no one knew that she and the two other girls had moved in together. It was also a plus that Denise had made sure the taxi couldn't be traced back to here. They had taken a taxi from Sydhavnen to City Hall Square, and from there they had walked to Ørsteds Park, where they had ditched the scarves and their jackets in front of a homeless woman sleeping on a bench. From there they had taken a bus to Østerport Station, and then on to Stenløse with a different taxi company.

On the way to Stenløse, Jazmine and Denise had acted as if nothing was wrong, chatting away about the great food they had eaten at a local restaurant. They were finally dropped off at the other side of Stenløse Station and walked home from there.

Anyway, Michelle doubted that anyone would suspect a girl who had just been the victim of a hit-and-run driver to be behind a robbery.

And then there was Jazmine and Denise. If Birna woke up, or if the police made a connection to them, would they be able to keep quiet or would they squeal? And if they did, would they take her down with them even though they had promised not to?

Michelle felt nervous. She had almost reached the station. Should she turn around and go back to them to agree what the plan was? She stopped, considering her options. They had said themselves that she should go back to Patrick and settle things. So wasn't that what she should do?

But what if the police really *had* taken him in for questioning? Then he wouldn't be at home. She had to find out before she did anything else.

She took her cell from her bag. If he answered his phone, that was a good thing. Then she could tell him she was coming with the money so he wouldn't be surprised when she turned up. Michelle smiled. Perhaps he would even be happy. He might even be waiting for her and try to convince her to stay. Hadn't there been a glimmer of hope between them yesterday? She was sure there had been.

Then she heard a thud that made her turn around to face a black car hurtling directly toward her.

The last thing she saw was the same familiar face behind the wheel.

28

Thursday, May 26th, 2016

Rose stared at the wall.

When she fixed her gaze on the pale yellow surface and sat completely still, a vacuum appeared around her that drained all consciousness from her. In this state, she was neither awake nor sleeping. Her breathing was imperceptible and her senses in hibernation. She was just one of the living dead.

But then when she was awoken by sounds in the hallway, a domino effect of thoughts tumbled through her mind, and as insignificant as they might be, they left her defenseless. The sound of a door opening or closing, the whimpering from another patient, or footsteps was all it took before Rose had to gasp for breath and started crying.

She had been prescribed medication to sedate her and medication that sent her into a deep, dreamless sleep. And yet these reactions returned at the slightest disturbance.

Before Rose had been admitted, she had been through weeks of sleepless nights. An almost inhuman accumulation of dark hours that she could suppress only by tormenting herself in multiple ways.

Rose knew full well why it had to be like that. Because if she let her guard down for even one second, she was thrown into a torrent of images of her father's screaming mouth and his blinking, almost astonished eyes in the moment he was killed. And in those moments she had inevitably yelled at the ceiling that he should leave her alone and scratched her skin to numb the pain of these eternally grinding thoughts for a few seconds.

"You do not belong here," she had begun mumbling after some time. And when her voice had given out after many hours, she had thought instead while writing.

After four days of having hardly slept or eaten, she had begged to be admitted.

Like usual, Rose knew where she was but had trouble keeping track of time. She had been told that she had been there for nine days, but it might as well have been five weeks. And the doctors, whom she knew so well from the last time she had been committed, stubbornly kept assuring her that her perception of time was of no importance. As long as she made progress in her treatment, however insignificant it might seem, there was nothing to worry about.

But Rose knew that they were lying. That this time they would do everything to ignore her integrity, forcing and intensifying the treatment so they would eventually have full control over her.

Rose sensed their distance from her in their expressions when she sought refuge in her tears, but the nurses seemed to find it especially difficult to maintain their poker faces. They didn't exude pity or sympathy like last time, but rather the kind of irritation experienced by a professional when things don't go as planned.

During her therapy sessions, they had emphasized that Rose was there voluntarily and that she should say only as much as she felt comfortable with about her sense of loneliness, being bullied, having been betrayed by her mother, and the loss of her childhood.

Obviously she didn't allow them access to her darkest place, because that was hers and hers alone. In that place the truth about her father's death lay buried, and the shame and shock caused by her part in the tragedy was not something that should be stirred.

No, Rose kept her distance. That was her specialty. If only they could find a medication that would make her hatred, guilty conscience, and sorrow disappear, she would be satisfied.

They collected her in the common room where she was crying, and she thought they would take her to her room to prevent her from up-setting the other patients, but instead they took her to see the chief physician in his office.

In the office, she was also met by an assistant physician whom she didn't like at all, the charge nurse, and one of the younger physicians who was in charge of prescribing medication. They all looked serious, and Rose knew that the day had come when she would once more be confronted with the offer of electroconvulsive therapy.

But she wasn't about to let anyone mess with her brain. The things she had experienced in her life should not just be shocked out of her system. Whatever spark or creativity remained in her shouldn't be dulled. If they couldn't find medication that could make her feel calm inside, she didn't want to be there at all. She had committed an offense and done things she wasn't proud of, and that was a fact they couldn't erase.

She would just have to learn to live with it. That was all there was to it.

The chief physician looked at her with the sort of steady expression you could learn. Manipulation came in many forms, but even if they tried their hardest, they couldn't fool an investigator who spent most of her time dealing with lies and evil.

"Rose," he said in a soft voice. "I've asked you here today because we've obtained some information that affects our understanding of your situation and what we can do to better it." He held out a pack of tissues but she didn't take them.

Rose frowned, wiped her eyes with the back of her hand, and turned toward the wall, staring intensely while trying to calm herself down. She hadn't seen this coming. Information, he had said? But there wasn't going to be any talk about information unless it came from her. That was for sure.

She began to stand up, thinking that now was as good a time as any to go back to her room and stare at the wall. She could think about what to do next later.

"Sit down and listen to what I have to say, Rose. I know it can feel extremely intimidating, but everyone just wants what's best for you. You do know that, don't you? Your sisters have come forward with some information about what you have written and your colleagues at police HQ have analyzed it. They've created a timeline, so to speak, of your life since you were ten based on your changing mantras."

Rose sat back down. She had lost her focus and felt trapped. Her eyes welled up and her jaw tensed.

She slowly turned toward him, and despite his welcoming and friendly attitude, she could easily see through him. He had seriously let her down, the shit. He had failed to inform her about the development and neglected to tell her that he was in possession of new information that he ought to have asked her permission to use. She had felt tortured for days and now he dragged her into the actual torture chamber.

"I'm going to place a sheet of paper in front of you with a list of the phrases you've written in your notebooks every year since you were a girl, Rose. Take a look at it and tell me what you feel."

Rose wasn't listening. She was just thinking that she should have burned the notebooks when she had the chance and committed suicide before the insanity took hold. Because now it was as big a threat as ever. The situation itself indicated as much.

There was a cabinet with glass doors next to where she was sitting. God only knew what the doctor kept in there, but she couldn't bring herself to look at it. Two days ago she had turned her head toward it and seen her reflection in the glass, and it had seemed so unreal that it terrified her. Was it really her own image she saw in the glass door, reflecting not only her face but also the thoughts that had been going through her head? Had the reflection of those eyes been the same eyes she knew were on her face, transmitting the impression to her brain? These impossible questions were driving her crazy. The incomprehensible fact of even existing made her feel dizzy, as if she was on something.

"Are you with us, Rose?" The chief physician gestured toward her, causing Rose to turn her head in his direction. It almost seemed as if his forehead was touching hers and that the room was smaller than ever.

It's because there are so many of us in here, she thought. *The room is the same as always. It really is.*

"Listen to me, Rose. These phrases you've written make it clear that you've attempted to protect yourself against your dad's psychological abuse through an internal dialogue with him. We roughly know when and why you switched between the different phrases, but we can't know exactly what was going on inside you. I think you've been searching for answers that could help you escape the darkness that surrounded you. And this is what we need to deal with now, once and for all, so you can free yourself from your compulsive thoughts. Are you willing to work with us, Rose?"

"Work with him," he said, as if they were colleagues.

Rose's arms felt limp, so she simply glanced across at the sheet on up toward the ceiling. She could clearly sense the way the four other people present were staring at her in anticipation. Perhaps they were waiting for this damn shit to cause her to have a breakdown. Perhaps they thought that these phrases and systems would suck the thoughts out of her and leave the answers to their questions rotating in the air around them. As if their maneuver would make her burst out with the information her medicine and their saccharine talk, admonitions, warnings, and pleas had failed to elicit. As if this was a truth serum— pure scopolamine in paper form.

She locked eyes with the chief physician.

"Do you love me?" she asked him with exaggerated clarity.

It wasn't only the chief physician who looked confused.

"Do you love me, Sven Thisted? Can you say that you do?"

He searched for the words. Stammered that of course he did, just like he loved everyone who entrusted him with their innermost thoughts. Like those who needed help and those—

"Please spare me your bloody doctor talk." She turned toward the others. "What do you say? Have you got a better answer?"

It was the nurse who took the role of the oracle.

"No, Rose, and you shouldn't expect that from us. The word 'love' is too big, too intimate, don't you understand?"

Rose nodded, stood up, walked over to the woman, and embraced her. Of course she misunderstood and patted Rose comfortingly on the shoulder, but this was not Rose's intention. She embraced her so that the contrast was all the greater when she turned toward the three doctors and hissed directly in their faces, sending a cloud of spit around them.

"Traitors, that's what you are! And *nothing* in the world is going to bring me back to a place where well-paid, healthy, condescending quacks who don't love me have secret thoughts that are more dangerous for me than the ones I have myself."

The chief practitioner attempted to appear indulgent, but this stopped immediately when she stepped toward him and slapped him in the face, causing the other two doctors to move back in their chairs.

When she walked past the medical secretary's desk in the corridor, the woman just managed to tell her that there was an Assad on the line asking to speak with her.

Rose swung around. "Oh, is he, now!" she screamed. "Well, you can tell him to go to hell and make sure he tells the rest of them to leave me in peace."

It hurt, but those who had betrayed her and pried into her life were no longer part of her world.

Fifty minutes later, Rose was on her way to where the taxis waited in front of Glostrup Hospital. She could sense that she was too drowsy for this because the medicine she still had in her body made everything seem like it was happening in slow motion and affected her sense of distance.

She felt that if she threw up she would fall over and not be able to get up again, so she squeezed her throat with her free hand, which strangely enough seemed to help.

But the situation was bad. From a rational point of view, she would probably never function normally again, so everything was fucked up, to say the least. Why not just get it over with? She had saved enough pills over the last few years to commit suicide. Just one glass of water and a few gulps and all these horrible thoughts would follow her to her grave.

She gave the driver a five-hundred-kroner tip, which made her feel momentarily happy. And walking up the stairs to her apartment, she thought about a poor crippled beggar with really deformed legs whom she had seen at the Cathedral Square in Barcelona. As she was leaving this world anyway, wouldn't it be a good idea if all her worldly possessions were distributed among unfortunate people like him? Not that she had much to give, but what if instead of ruining her organs with sleeping pills, she slit her wrists instead? She could leave a note stating that she wished to donate all her organs, and then call an ambulance while bleeding to death. How long should she wait to call the ambulance before losing consciousness if she didn't want to run the risk of them arriving in time to save her? That was the question.

She unlocked her apartment door, feeling confused about all these possibilities and obligations, and was immediately hit by the walls covered in her own writing: "YOU DO NOT BELONG HERE." You do not belong here.

The words hit her like a sledgehammer. Who was talking to whom? Was it her cursing her father or was it him cursing her?

Rose let her travel bag fall on the floor and held a hand to her chest. A pressure from inside was pushing her tongue up against her palate, blocking her throat. The choking feeling was so strong that her heart was beating like a pneumatic drill to oxygenate her body. With eyes wide open, she looked around the apartment, realizing how she had been stabbed in the back. Candle drippers had been put on her chandeliers. Clean tablecloths on the tables. Scrapbooks containing her Department Q cases had been stacked in a completely regular pile on the chest of drawers under the mirror. Chairs were suddenly upright. Sticky and sugary marks had been wiped off her stereo, floors, and carpets.

She clenched her fists, gasping for breath, No one should enter another person's home and decide what was normal and how the person living there ought to behave within her own four walls. Her dirty laundry, unwashed dishes, rubbish and papers on the floor, and complete powerlessness were all hers and hers alone. And no one should mess with it.

How the hell was she supposed to function in this clinically purged and violated home?

Rose stepped backward away from this poison, all the way out onto the walkway, where she leaned up against the railing and let her tears pour forth.

When her legs began to feel numb, she went over to her neighbor's door. In the years Rose had lived here, a sort of connection had been established between them. Not a friendship as such, but more like a mother-daughter relationship, which unlike anything Rose had experienced entailed a certain feeling of security and confidentiality. Even though it had been a while, the way she was feeling made her sure it was the right thing to do to ring the doorbell.

Unaware of how long she had been waiting outside her neighbor's door without anyone answering, she was suddenly aware of one of her other neighbors walking directly toward her.

"Are you looking for Zimmermann, Rose?"

She nodded.

"I don't know where you've been lately, but I'm sorry to say that Rigmor is dead." She hesitated for a moment. "She was murdered, Rose. It was three weeks ago today. Didn't you know? You're with the police, after all."

Rose stared up at the sky. Toward the eternally unknowable. She momentarily disappeared from the world, and when she returned it was as if the world disappeared from her.

"Yes, it's terrible," said the woman. "Really terrible. And then that young girl who was killed in a hit-and-run just around the corner earlier today. But maybe you didn't know that either?"

29

Thursday, May 26th, 2016

Assad was looking down in the dumps when Carl found him rolling up his prayer rug on the cellar floor of the claustrophobic office.

"You look sad, Assad. What's up?" he asked.

"Up where, Carl? Why do you ask?" He shook his head. "I called the hospital to ask how Rose is doing and I heard her screaming and shouting in the background that I should go to hell and that we should leave her alone."

"Heard?"

"Yes, she obviously knew that it was me on the other end. I just wanted to ask when we could visit her. She must have walked past as I called."

Carl patted his mate on the shoulder. He hadn't deserved to hear that.

"Well, I guess we're going to have to respect that, Assad. If it makes Rose feel worse that we contact her, we're not doing her any favors by trying."

Assad hung his head. He was feeling terrible. There was no doubt that he was very fond of Rose. Now Carl would have to try to lift his spirits. This wasn't helping anyone.

"Has Assad told you what she shouted at him?"

Gordon's face said it all. So he had.

"It's my fault that she's reacting like this," he said quietly. "I shouldn't have pried in her notebooks."

"She'll come around, Gordon. We've been through similar with Rose before."

"I doubt it."

So did Carl, but he said, "Come on, Gordon, you did what you needed to do. Unlike me. I should've asked her before we went looking around her apartment and handed your notes over to the psychiatrists. That was unprofessional."

"If you'd asked her first, she would've just said no!"

Carl pointed his finger at him. "Exactly! You're not as dumb as you look, and that's saying something."

Gordon smoothed out his notes with his spindly fingers, which were long enough to easily hold a basketball in one hand. The little weight he had managed to put on over the last few years had disappeared almost overnight since Rose had been admitted. The formerly pink bags under his eyes had turned dark, and his freckled skin was as white as whipped cream. No one could claim that it was a particularly aesthetic look.

"As we already know," he continued in an attempt to sound like he had things under control, "Rigmor Zimmermann's husband had a shoe shop in Rødovre with the monopoly on a fancy brand in Denmark. When he died in 2004 he left a large sum of money. Rigmor Zimmermann sold the business, the house, cars, and everything else, and moved into an apartment. After that she moved around a bit, and strangely enough is registered at her daughter's address. I think it's just a case of her never having updated her details."

Carl looked at Gordon. "Why are you investigating Rigmor Zimmermann? Weren't you supposed to find Rose's friend Karoline? Wasn't this Assad's assignment?"

"We're mixing things up a bit, Carl. We have to now that Rose isn't on the team. Assad is looking into Fritzl Zimmermann's background, and we've asked the national register to check up on the Karoline woman. We should get an answer later today."

"Why is Assad checking up on the husband? He hasn't got anything to do with the bloody case."

"That's exactly what Assad is checking. He thinks it seems a bit strange that he died exactly one day after Stephanie Gundersen was found murdered in Østre Anlæg."

"He *what*?"

"Exactly, Carl. That was Assad's reaction when he found out. Look here." There came those spindly fingers again. "Stephanie Gundersen was found murdered on June 7th, 2004, and Fritzl Zimmermann drowned on June 8th, 2004."

"Drowned?"

"Yes, in Damhus Lake. Fell on his face sitting in his wheelchair, eighty-six years old. He'd been using it since he suffered a blood clot six months earlier. As far as we know, he was fine upstairs but didn't have the energy to maneuver the chair himself."

"So how did he get there?"

"His wife went out with him every night, but that evening she'd nipped home to fetch him a sweater. When she came back she found the wheelchair in shallow water and her husband a few meters farther out."

"How the hell do you drown in shallow water in Damhus Lake? The place must be swarming with people at that time of year."

"The police report doesn't mention anything about that. But given that she went home for a sweater, it must have been cold that night. So maybe it was too cold for people to be out walking."

"Find out."

"Err, okay. But I have already. Summer 2004 was really cold and rainy. In fact, it wasn't until the beginning of August that we had the first real day of summer. A depressing record!"

Carl tried to recall that summer. It was the year before Vigga left him. They were supposed to have gone on a camping holiday to Umbria, but a case popped up, meaning that Carl had to stay in the country, so he had booked a summerhouse down by Køge instead, much to Vigga's annoyance. He remembered that summer well, and there was nothing romantic about it. If there had been, he might have been able to make her stay.

"Carl, are you listening?" said Gordon.

He looked up at Gordon's pale face.

"The wife said she left him down by the lakeshore, like she had done so often before. She couldn't rule out that her husband might have somehow managed to release the brake, and so the police couldn't rule out suicide. After all, he was eighty-six and could no longer run his business. In that situation, it isn't hard to imagine that someone could grow tired of life."

Carl nodded, but what the hell did this have to do with anything? They seemed to have gone off on something of a tangent.

The telephone saved him from continuing with this conversation.

"Mørck," he said authoritatively, waving Gordon out of the room.

"Are you the police guy?"

"I should think so. Who am I speaking to?"

"You might not want to speak with me if I tell you who I am."

Carl leaned forward. The voice was gruff and dark, almost as if he had put something over the receiver.

"That depends on what you have to tell me." Carl grabbed a notepad. "Try me."

"I hear you've spoken to Leo Andresen about Arne Knudsen's accident at the plant, and I just want to say that there is nothing suspicious about it. Even though we all hated the bastard Arne Knudsen and all laughed under our breath when he was squashed, it doesn't change the fact that it was an accident."

"Have I led you to believe that we think otherwise?" answered Carl. But now his suspicion was aroused. "You see, we're just investigating the case to help one of our colleagues, who was very affected by it."

"You're talking about Rose Knudsen, right?"

"I can't tell you as long as I don't know who you are or why you're calling."

"Rose was a lovely and sweet girl. She really was. She was everyone's Rose, except for her dad's, that is, the nasty bastard."

"Now, just a minute—"

"Of course it was a shock for her. She saw it happen. No number of investigations can change that, as I'm sure you'll agree. That was all I wanted to let you know."

Then he hung up.

Damn it. Why was the man trying to convince him that it was an accident? Carl's experience told him that people did that when the opposite was true. Had he just spoken to a man who had something to hide? Was he afraid that Rose would be implicated? Or was he more involved in the case than he was willing to admit?

Damn it. He could do with Rose here just now. No one knew the many mysteries of the HQ internal telephone system like her.

He had to make do with calling Lis in admin. "I know it's normally Rose's job, but can you find out who just called me, Lis?"

She seemed stressed, but it took her only three minutes to get back to him.

"The telephone is registered in the name of one of my idols, Carl."

"Ahh, so his name is Carl Mørck. What a coincidence."

Her laugh gave Carl butterflies. There was nothing as sexy as a woman laughing.

"Nooo. His name is Benny Andersson, like that guy from Abba. He's a bit tubby today, but back then when he was still playing, my God, he was charming. All he had to do was drop me a line back then when he and Anni-Frid split up, and I'd have been there in a flash."

She gave Carl the man's number and address while Carl tried to shake off the image Lis had given him.

"We're going for a drive, Assad," he shouted down the corridor.

"Do you remember the Nuremberg trials, Carl?"

He nodded. It wasn't hard to recall the black-and-white images of those bastards from the Second World War sitting in rows wearing Bakelite headphones while listening to accusations about their atrocious war crimes. Göring, Ribbentrop, Rosenberg, Frank, Streicher, and all the others waiting for the gallows. There had never been a Christmas at his aunt Abelone's house in Brovst when he had not looked at photos of the hauntingly displayed bodies in a history book, shuddering in horror. Strangely enough, despite the theme of the book, he had nothing but happy memories of a bygone childhood when he thought of those Christmases.

"There were also many smaller war tribunals like that around the world after the war, but I'm sure you know that?"

Carl looked at the GPS. Straight ahead for a few kilometers.

"Yes, they had them wherever there had been war crimes. The Balkans, Japan, Poland, France, and Denmark too. But why do you bring it up, Assad?"

"Because Fritzl Zimmermann was one of the people the Polish wanted executed."

Carl raised his eyebrows and briefly looked at Assad. "Rigmor Zimmermann's husband?"

"Exactly!"

"What had he done?"

"They couldn't prove anything because apparently he was one of the people who managed to erase the traces of their atrocities. No survivors. Full stop."

"They couldn't prove *what*, Assad?"

"That Fritzl Zimmermann was actually Sturmbannführer Bernd Krause, who was directly involved in executing captured Allied soldiers in France and later on civilians in Poland and Romania. I've read that they had convincing evidence against him in the form of photos and witness statements." He took his feet down from the dashboard and rummaged around in the briefcase on the floor.

"I don't understand. Witness statements? Didn't you just say he'd erased all traces and that there were no survivors to document his involvement?"

"Yeah, the main witnesses were two Totenkopf officers, but Fritzl Zimmermann's defense lawyer managed to convince the judges that their statements were unreliable because they wanted to pin their own war crimes on someone else, and therefore the case was dismissed. The other two were hanged for their crimes in 1946."

"And what about the photographs that pointed to Fritzl Zimmermann?"

"I've seen a couple of them but I'll spare you for now, Carl. The executions were extremely brutal, but the defense lawyer managed to prove that some of them had been doctored and that the man they showed wasn't Zimmermann. So he was acquitted."

"Acquitted just like that?"

"Yes. And later a death certificate was found stating that Sturmbannführer Bernd Krause had died from diphtheria on February 27th, 1953, in a POW camp in Sverdlovsk in the Urals."

"And meanwhile Fritzl had reinvented himself as a shoe retailer?"

"Yes, he started off small in Kiel and then worked his way up with a few shops in Southern Jutland before setting up business in Rødovre, west of Copenhagen."

"And where is all this information coming from, Assad? You've not had much time to research."

"I know someone with good contacts at the Simon Wiesenthal Center in Austria."

"But don't they only hold information about crimes committed against Jews?"

"Yes, many of Bernd Krause's victims were Jews. They kept a record of the whole case, and at the center they're convinced about Fritzl Zimmermann's guilt and identity."

"Was he still wanted when he was living and working in Denmark?"

"It doesn't say anything specific in the paperwork, but my friend was under the impression that 'someone'"—he made quotation marks with his fingers in the air—"had broken into his villa twice to look for evidence of his involvement. When they didn't find anything, the case was shelved."

"A break-in in Rødovre?"

"Don't underestimate the Israelis. Maybe you remember that they kidnapped Adolf Eichmann in Argentina and brought him back for trial in Israel?"

Carl nodded. Red light in front of him and then a right turn.

"And what can we use all this information for, Assad?" he said, putting the car in neutral.

"Among the photos that were mailed to me was this one, Carl. You'll understand when you see it."

He handed Carl a print so he could see it up close.

It was an unusually clear photo showing a black-clad officer seen from behind. Both his hands were clenching a short, blunt club, and his arms were raised above his shoulder, ready to smash the club into the back of the head of a poor tied-up victim standing in front of him.

On the ground to the right of the man lay three bodies with their heads smashed in. To the left of the victim stood another two bound men awaiting their fate.

"Fuck," whispered Carl. He swallowed a couple of times and pushed the photo away. There had been a time when people had thought that this kind of evil could never happen again, but all it did was remind him of the reality in large parts of the world today. How could this be allowed to happen over and over again?

"What are you thinking, Assad?"

"That Stephanie Gundersen and Rigmor Zimmermann were murdered in exactly this way. What more is there to say? Is it a coincidence? I don't think so." He pointed at the traffic light. "It's green, Carl."

Carl looked up. All of a sudden a Danish provincial town like this seemed so immensely distant from everything.

"But Stephanie Gundersen was murdered in 2004, and by that time Fritzl Zimmermann was eighty-six, very weak, and wheelchair bound, so he can't possibly have been the perpetrator," he thought out loud. "Not to mention the possibility of him killing his wife given that she died more than ten years after him."

"I'm just saying that I think there's a connection. Maybe Marcus is right."

Carl nodded. It was an impressive amount of information to have found in such a short time. And thinking about it, Assad had delivered the whole torrent without so much as making one of his usual linguistic blunders. It was remarkable how well-spoken he suddenly was.

He looked at Assad, who was staring pensively at the houses they drove past. Full of wisdom.

Who the hell are *you, Assad?* he thought, turning right.

The number from which the anonymous call to Department Q had been made was registered to an address in one of the more humble neighborhoods in the vicinity of the steel plant. A quick glance over the state of the house and the mess around it was enough to invoke Carl's prejudice.

"Do you think he collects scrap metal?" asked Assad. Carl nodded. What was it about all these defunct lawnmowers, bicycles, car wrecks, and other rusty vehicles that brought out the hoarder and protective instincts in certain types of men?

The guy who opened the door blended in naturally in this hopeless jumble of bad taste. Never had a tracksuit been in more need of a wash. Never had an unkempt mane of hair looked greasier. There was no doubt that keeping a distance would be better for their health.

"Who are you?" said the man with breath that could kill. Carl took a step back, giving the man the opportunity to slam the door in their faces if he wanted to.

"I'm the man you called"—Carl looked at his watch—"exactly fifty-two minutes ago."

"Called? I have no idea what you're talking about."

"Your name is Benny Andersson, and Assad here is recording your voice for the voice-recognition program as we speak. Show him the recorder, Assad."

He nudged Assad with his elbow and Curly was resolute enough to conceal his confusion and produce his smartphone from his pocket.

"Just a second; it's just processing," he said while the skunk looked at the cell with obvious skepticism.

"Yes, it's a match. He is the guy we recorded at HQ," said Assad with his eyes fixed on the empty phone display. "You've been caught out, Benny," he said without looking up from the phone. He pressed a few buttons, pretending to exit the program, and put the cell phone back in his pocket.

"Well, Benny," said Carl with a rare authority in his voice. "We've established that it was you who made an anonymous call to an investigator at police HQ an hour ago. We have come to determine whether there was any criminal intent behind your call. May we come in so we can have a chat, or would you rather come with us now to police HQ in Copenhagen?"

He didn't have a chance to answer, as Assad was already pushing at the door with all his weight.

Carl had gasped for breath a couple of times when he walked into the extremely stuffy house, but as soon as he had grown accustomed to the stench, he came down hard on Benny Andersson. Within the space of two minutes he had made the situation crystal clear. The accusations of malicious intent, a hidden agenda, and insinuations and secrets that could all come back to bite him. Only then did Carl change tack.

"You say that you liked Rose? But what's that got to do with her dad's death? Can you explain?"

The man stretched out his grubby fingers, fumbling for a cigar butt in a full ashtray, and lit it.

"Can I ask if an inspector like you has ever worked in a steel plant?"

"Of course I haven't."

"No, I thought not. So you can't possibly understand what it's like. The stark contrasts the work exposed us to every day: the huge buildings where small, vulnerable people were trying to master the powerful machines; the struggle against the heat, which was sometimes so strong that it felt suffocating and you had to go outside to cool down in the wind from the fjord; the knowledge that the work was dangerous and could destroy you in a matter of seconds, contrasted with the feeling of your sleeping child's soft cheek against your hardened fingertips. It's impossible to understand how savage it can be when you haven't tried it yourself. And of course some of us turned hard like the steel we were working with while others turned soft like butter."

Carl was surprised by the articulate monologue. Had the guy studied rhetoric in his youth?

"I don't think you should underestimate everyone else's work, Andersson. Police work can be quite savage too, so of course I can relate to what you're saying."

"Yes, or being stationed as a soldier. Or being a paramedic or fireman," interjected Assad.

"Maybe, but it's still not the same, because in that line of work you have to be prepared for what might happen, but not everyone is at a plant like this. And I don't think Rose was. In that work environment it was a blessing for the rest of us to have her there. There's the contrast again, you see? Because when a young, vulnerable girl like Rose ends up in such a brutal place, where everything is so savage—the steel, the mill, the heat—and where the men are so hardened and hardy, the contrast can become too much. Rose was too young and unprepared for that place; that's all I'm saying."

"What was your job at the plant, Benny?" asked Carl.

"Sometimes I was sitting in the control cabin managing the rolling mill at the old control desk. Other times I was in charge of inspecting the workstations."

"That sounds like a very responsible position to hold."

"All employees have responsible positions. A workplace like that can be very dangerous if someone screws up."

"And Rose's dad screwed up?"

"You'll have to ask someone else about that. I didn't see what happened."

"But what exactly did happen?"

"Ask someone else. I said I didn't see it."

"Shouldn't we just take him with us to HQ, Carl?" asked Assad.

Carl nodded. "I know that you and others have been informed by

Leo that we're investigating this case and that we would like to know more about the accident. I just don't understand your interest in it. Why you made an anonymous call and why you're being so uncooperative. So now my suggestion to you, Benny Andersson, is that you either start cooperating with us here in the lovely odor of your home or you put your jacket on, come with us, and wave good-bye to home sweet home for the next twenty-four hours. Which do you prefer?"

Please don't choose the latter, thought Carl, thinking about how this guy would ruin his backseat.

"Are you going to arrest me? For what?"

"We'll work that out. No one makes an anonymous call in the way you did without trying to cover something up. You hinted on the phone that Rose was involved in her dad's death. But what did you mean by that?" he pressed him to answer.

"I certainly did not."

"That's not how we see it." Assad leaned fearlessly forward over the sticky coffee table. "You should understand that Rose is a well-liked colleague of ours and we don't wish her any harm. So now I'm going to count down from six, and if you don't tell us what you know before I get to zero, I'll take that old chicken bone lying over there in a layer of stale sauce and stuff it down your throat. Six, five, four . . ."

"Ha-ha, you sound ridiculous. Do you think you can threaten me with that, you . . . ?"

He obviously had something racist on the tip of his tongue when Assad finished the countdown and got up to grab the chicken bone.

"Hey," shouted Benny Andersson as Assad picked up a jagged wing bone. "Stop right there. You'll have to ask someone else what really happened because, as I said, I don't know. All I can say is that Arne Knudsen was standing under the overhead crane in the old section when one of the magnets failed while lifting a ten-ton steel slab."

"I thought he was pulled into a machine."

"No, that's what they wrote in the newspapers, wherever the hell they got that information from. But it was the magnet that failed."

"So the steel slab fell on him?" asked Carl while Assad dropped the bone and returned to his grubby seat.

"Yes, and it completely crushed him from here down."

He pointed at a spot just beneath his breastbone.

"And he died on the spot?"

"Not from the way he was screaming, no. But it didn't take long. His entire lower body was squashed."

"I see. That sounds unpleasant. And what was Rose doing in that section that she's never told us about? Her sister once told me that she was a summer temp."

He laughed. "Summer temp? No, she certainly wasn't. She was on an apprenticeship as a feeder operator."

Carl and Assad both shook their heads. A feeder operator?

"That's the person who decides which slabs go in the furnace before they are transported to the rolling mill."

"Slabs are the big pieces of metal that are rolled into steel plate," explained Carl to Assad, recalling Leo Andresen's words. "And what was your role in this process, Benny?"

"When the slab came out red-hot from the furnace on the other side, I was sometimes the one who took over and did the rolling."

"And was that your job on this particular day?"

He nodded.

"And yet you didn't witness the accident?"

"Well, I couldn't have, could I? I was on the other side of the furnace."

Carl sighed as he tried in vain to picture the scenario.

There was no way to avoid it: Leo Andresen would just have to give them a guided tour.

30

Thursday, May 26th, 2016

Rose hadn't wasted any time. Cups smashed in confusion, souvenirs thrown off the shelves in frustration, furniture tossed around the room in anger. It took only a few minutes to vandalize most of the sitting room. It should have felt good, but it didn't. All she saw was Rigmor Zimmermann's face.

How often had Rigmor been there for Rose when her loneliness had become too much? How often had she bought groceries for Rose when she had gone a whole weekend without the energy to do so much as open her blinds? And now that Rose needed her most, she wasn't here anymore. And why?

Murdered, they said. But how? And by whom?

She picked up her laptop from the floor, switched it on, and realized with a certain irrational sense of relief that she could still log on to the Internet even though the screen was smashed. She sat down and entered the password to access the internal police home page.

There was little information to find about her neighbor, but she managed to find enough to discover not only that she was dead but also where and how.

"Severe trauma to the neck bones and the back of the head," the report read coldly. Where had she been when all this happened? Had she just been absorbed in her own problems in her apartment for two weeks without realizing that everything was quiet next door?

"What sort of person have you become, Rose?" she asked herself without crying. She couldn't even produce tears.

When her phone rang in her back pocket, she was back where she had been half an hour ago. Finished with existence. Out of sync with life.

The phone rang five times within the next few minutes before she finally took it out and looked at the display.

It was her mother calling from Spain. There was no one in the world she felt less inclined to talk with about her present situation. The hospital must have contacted her, so it wouldn't be long before she called Rose's sisters.

Rose looked at her watch. How much time did she have? Twenty to twenty-five minutes before her sisters turned up demanding an explanation as to why she had left the hospital.

"I can't let that happen!" she shouted while she considered smashing the phone so hard against the wall that it would break into pieces.

She took a deep breath while she wondered what she should write. Then she pressed MESSAGES and began texting:

Dear Mom, I'm on the train just now to Malmö. The connection is bad so I'm texting instead of calling. Don't worry about me. I'm fine. I discharged myself today because a good friend in Blekinge has offered to let me stay in their lovely house for a while. It will do me good. Will be in touch when back. Rose

One tap and the message was sent. She put down the phone in front of her, and safe in the knowledge that her mother wouldn't take it any further, she pulled out a drawer and took out a couple of sheets of paper and a pen. Then she went to the bathroom, opened the cabinet, and looked at the contents. Antidepressants, acetaminophen, half a bottle of sleeping pills, aspirin, codeine tablets, the scissors she used to cut the hair on her head and under her arms, disposable razors, the old Gillette razor, a couple of suppository tablets from her mother, and licorice-flavored cough mixture that she had had for almost twenty years. If she used this arsenal with care and in the right dose, it would make a deadly cocktail. She emptied out her cotton balls and tampons from a small plastic basket into the wastebasket, sorted out her personal pharmacy, threw out the harmless tablets and potions, and then proceeded to fill the plastic basket with the rest.

She stood there by the sink for five minutes with her thoughts wandering between various deaths and the unpredictability of life. Everything she couldn't deal with was compressed to nothingness and turned on its head. Everything became pointless.

Finally, she grabbed the Gillette razor, which she had taken from her father's belongings after his death with the intention of using it to shave her pubes in disrespect. Something else she had never gotten around to doing.

She unscrewed the dirty blade and looked at it for a moment. Some of her father's stubble was caught in the soap residue, bringing on a feeling of loathing so strong that it almost knocked her out.

Was she really going to end up with the remains of her damned father in her mortal wound? Was her blood going to cleanse that bastard's razor?

Rose was about to throw up but forced herself to clean the blade in the kitchen sink, cutting herself on the blade and leaving her fingers smothered in blood and bristles from the dish brush.

"The time has come!" she said feebly, with tears in her eyes at the sight of the shining blade. Now all she had to do was write a few sentences on the paper she had found so her sisters could be in no doubt that she had done this voluntarily and that they were to have her belongings.

How will I get through this? she thought.

Tears had previously been a comfort to Rose when she grieved over the life she had been allotted, but now that the end was in sight, they only emphasized her feelings of powerlessness, regret, and shame. Now her tears were just rivers of despair flowing throughout her entire system.

She carefully placed the razor blade on the dining table next to the sheets of paper, the pen, and the basket with all the different medications, opened the TV cabinet, and unscrewed the lids of all the bottles of alcohol. The vase on the shelf had never been used for the simple reason that no one had ever given her flowers, but it came in handy now as she emptied all the dregs into it and mixed them together to create an indeterminable and pungent brown cocktail.

While she was gulping down the contents of the vase, her eyes wandered from the plastic basket to the computer screen, and paradoxically her thoughts became momentarily clearer.

She looked around the chaotic sitting room with a smile, knowing that now at least she had spared her sisters the trouble of deciding what to get rid of and what to keep.

She took the first sheet of paper and wrote:

Dear sisters,

There has been no end to my curse, so don't despair over my death. Now I'm in a place where peace can no longer be disturbed. A place my thoughts have longed for. And that's a good thing. Make the best of your lives and try to think of me with a hint of love and friendship. I loved and respected you all, and still do even in this moment of transgression. Pardon my solemnity, but after all it isn't every day I have allowed myself to say these things to you. I'm sorry for all the bad things I've done. Please humbly accept all my worldly possessions and divide them between you. Farewell.

I love you. Rose

She dated the good-bye letter, read it over a couple of times, and placed it in front of her. *What a pathetic letter,* she thought, crumpled it up, and threw it on the floor.

Rose brought the vase up to her mouth and gulped down a few more mouthfuls, which seemed to sharpen her perception.

"It has to be this way," she sighed, picking up the crumpled piece of paper and smoothing it out.

Then she took the second piece of paper and this time wrote in large letters:

Stenløse, Thursday 5.26.2016

I hereby donate my body to organ donation and research.
Best regards, Rose Knudsen

Rose's hands were shaking when she wrote her national health number, signed, and placed the sheet in a visible spot on the dining table. Then she took her phone and dialed the number for emergency services. While the number rang, she inspected the veins on her left wrist, considering how far up the arm she should cut. Her pulse was strong, so it probably didn't matter where she did it. And when she finally got through to the operator, she was as determined and ready as she could possibly be. She was just about to tell the operator what the situation was—that in a brief moment she would be dead—so they had to hurry up if they wanted to use her organs. She wanted to finish by saying that they should bring freezer bags with them, and then hang up and make a deep, clean cut in both her wrists.

At this precise moment, when the operator's voice repeated the question of who she was and where she was calling from, Rose heard a loud bang against the wall in Rigmor Zimmermann's apartment.

Rose gasped for air. What was going on? And why now?

"I'm sorry. It was a mistake," she stammered and hung up. Her heart was beating so fast it made her head hurt. Her calm and resolve had been disturbed. She was in shock, but Rose the investigator took over. What was going on next door? Was she already so intoxicated that her mind was playing tricks on her?

She covered all the pills and her two farewell notes with her jacket and stepped out into the hallway.

From here the unexpected sounds were also clearly audible. Was it laughter or screaming?

Rose frowned. In all the years she and Zimmermann had been neighbors, she had only once heard another voice from in there. Slightly raised voices; that was all. As far as Rose knew, no one in the building apart from her had bothered to have any contact with Rigmor Zimmermann. When they had gone to the supermarket together, Rose had noticed how people actually tried to avoid contact with her.

But if it wasn't Rigmor Zimmermann in there, who was it?

Rose opened the drawer to her hallway cupboard and took out Zimmermann's key. Rigmor had had to get help from her daughter a few times when she had locked herself out, but six months ago she had given Rose an extra key to avoid that situation.

She staggered out of her front door without closing it behind her, and tiptoed over to Zimmermann's apartment. She stood outside for a moment listening quietly. She could hear voices inside. A couple of girls, she thought, based on the way they spoke.

In a haze, she knocked on the door a couple of times. When to her surprise no one answered, she put the key in the lock and turned it.

31

Thursday, May 26th, 2016

Gordon looked weary, but then again the type of repulsive tasks Carl made him do were probably not what his nice upbringing and background made him most suited for.

"And you've got all the information the Simon Wiesenthal Center could dig up?" asked Carl.

"Yes, it seems so. And I've showed Tomas Laursen a couple photos of how Fritzl Zimmermann executed prisoners with a club to the back of the head, like you asked me. Tomas confirmed that the method was probably similar to the way Stephanie Gundersen and Rigmor Zimmermann were murdered."

"Okay, so far, so good. Thanks."

"Stephanie Gundersen was murdered in 2004. Do I need to point out that Fritzl Zimmermann was still alive at that time?"

"Mmm!" grunted Carl, leafing through the atrocious photos. "No, you don't. But he wasn't when his wife was murdered a month ago."

Gordon pointed a chalky finger at him. "No, and hurrah for that," he said. Not an expression Carl would recommend that he use in this context—or any context for that matter.

Carl turned down the volume on TV2 News. "Gordon, the question remains, Who did it, then? Are you thinking about Birgit Zimmermann or her daughter, Denise? They are the only suspects with a motive so far. As far as I'm concerned, you can take your pick."

"Err, thanks. I don't know anything about the granddaughter, but the daughter may well have done it. She certainly has a more than healthy taste for alcohol, according to Assad, and that doesn't come cheap."

Carl nodded. "True. Maybe you think it's likely that she came running down the street in the pouring rain to bash her mother over the head with a club? And that the terrified Rigmor Zimmermann hid from her daughter in a bush full of dog shit? A peculiar scene, when you put it like that, don't you think?"

Gordon looked dejected. That was just part and parcel of police work. Paradoxes, euphoria, disappointment, and pure doubt galore.

"Where do I go from here, Carl?"

"Find Birgit Zimmermann's daughter, Gordon. What was her name again?"

"She was baptized Dorrit Zimmermann but goes by the name Denise Zimmermann."

"Look for both of them."

Carl felt sorry for Gordon as he watched him walk out the door. As long as the situation with Rose remained as it was, things probably wouldn't go his way.

"What's up with Gordon, Carl?" asked Assad a few seconds later. "He looks like cold death."

Carl shook his head. "Death warmed over, Assad. The phrase is death warmed over."

Curly looked puzzled. "Are you sure? Warmed over? That doesn't make any sense. Wouldn't you be cold if you were dead?"

Carl sighed. "Gordon's feeling a bit down, Assad. This Rose business has really hit him."

"Me too."

"Yes, it's affected us all, Assad. After all, we do miss her." Something of an understatement. In fact, Carl felt her absence very strongly.

The only thing Carl didn't miss was Rose's aversion to cigarettes. He took one from the pack before turning to Assad again. "How's it going with finding Rose's old school friend, Assad? Any luck?"

"That's why I'm here. I've found her."

He threw some color printouts on the desk of a smiling, voluptuous, elfin woman with luscious locks, dressed entirely in purple. "Kinua von Kunstwerk" was written above the photo in big letters, together with a paragraph about her latest exhibition.

"She's a painter, Carl."

"With a very creative pseudonym, I'll say."

"I believe she's very famous in Germany, but I'm not sure why." He backed up his opinion by pointing at a photo from her latest exhibition. It certainly packed a punch.

"Shit," Carl said immediately.

"She lives in Flensburg, Carl. Shall I drive down there?"

"No, we'll drive together," he said slightly absentmindedly, caught up with what was happening on the TV screen. The news crawl under the live coverage was more breaking than usual.

"Have *you* been informed about this, Assad?" he asked.

"I had no idea."

"Hey, have you seen that?" Gordon said from the doorway, where he was pointing at the TV screen. "They've been reporting it for about an hour now. And Lis says it's complete chaos upstairs."

He stood restlessly in the doorway like some sort of salsa dancer. "They're having a briefing about it as we speak. What do you think?" He looked at them pleadingly. "Shouldn't we get up there?"

"You know what? I think you should go if you're so keen, Gordon. But remember that they aren't our cases."

He looked disappointed. Clearly he didn't agree.

Carl smiled. Gordon had really come on in leaps and bounds lately. Not only had he started to display fearlessness; he also had ambition.

"I think we should go up there," he continued.

Carl laughed and stood up. "All right, then, come on. We only live once," he said.

At least twenty disapproving faces turned toward them as they burst into the homicide briefing.

"Sorry, folks, but we just saw it on TV," said Carl. "Just pretend we're not here."

Pasgård snorted. "That'll be damn difficult," he said. Some of the investigators around him nodded in agreement.

Lars Bjørn raised his hand. "Your attention, everyone! With respect for our friends from the cellar . . . ," he said, pausing for effect and causing several of those present to shake their heads. ". . . I will sum up briefly."

He looked directly at Carl. "We've found the red Peugeot that in all likelihood was used in the attacks on Michelle Hansen on May 20th and Senta Berger on May 22nd. It was one of our men from the now disbanded unit that used to look for stolen cars for insurance companies who found it with the window smashed on the driver's side and the ignition forced. It was parked around the corner from Rantzausgade on Griffenfeldsgade with an old parking meter ticket on the dashboard and a dozen parking tickets under the wipers. So we can easily establish when it was parked there. The technicians have found traces of blood and hair on the hood, but it appears to have been cleaned for traces on the inside. We will have to wait to hear more on that front."

"Parked for a whole week in central Copenhagen without being spotted. Wow! All credit to our people patrolling the streets," grunted Carl.

"If you could spare us from your sarcastic outbursts, you're welcome to stay," said Lars Bjørn.

He turned toward the flat-screen on the wall and clicked to the next image.

"Two and a half hours ago at approximately twenty minutes to one, the aforementioned Michelle Hansen was killed by a hit-and-run driver on Stationsvej in Stenløse. The image shows the scene of the incident. According to two schoolchildren who came walking down from the station, the vehicle was a black Honda Civic, which immediately after the incident turned right across Stationspladsen and disappeared. The description of both vehicle and driver are very vague, of course, due to the children's age—the oldest is only ten—and the shock caused by witnessing the hit-and-run. But the children described the driver of the vehicle as being 'not very tall,' to quote them directly."

He turned toward his team. "The situation, ladies and gentlemen, is that if we connect the earlier hit-and-runs with this latest one, we are dealing with premeditated murders. The question remains whether he intends to commit more murders. If the answer is yes, then it's a matter of life and death that we stop the killer. Understood?"

Assad looked at Carl and shrugged. Apparently it would take more than a serial killer on the loose to faze him.

"The last twenty-four hours have been more than eventful and I am sorry to say that we will therefore need to pull people off the investigation into Rigmor Zimmermann's murder, and that includes you and Gert, Pasgård."

"Poor Rigmor," whispered Carl, just loudly enough that Pasgård sent him daggers.

"After the latest hit-and-run involving Michelle Hansen, we conclude that the murder was committed with intent, but that the circumstances surrounding the murder point in different directions. Among other things, Michelle Hansen's handbag was found to contain twenty thousand kroner in used notes, and we know from her bank account what a bad state her finances were in. Further, Michelle Hansen is identical to the woman who was standing outside Victoria nightclub last night chatting with her ex-boyfriend, the bouncer Patrick Pettersson, while there was a robbery in the manager's office. So, it is plausible to assume that she might have had a connection to the robbery. Any questions?"

"Is this Patrick Pettersson still in custody?" asked Terje Ploug.

Carl nodded. If Ploug was the one assigned to lead the investigation, then all he could say was, poor Patrick. Ploug knew his job. Yes, he had bad breath, but if you kept a few feet back from him, you couldn't wish for a better or more competent partner.

"No, Pettersson was temporarily released at eleven thirty-two, first and foremost because his explanation of his movements yesterday was confirmed by the security cameras. But of course we aren't just letting him off the hook and have confiscated his passport as a precaution. A search warrant for his apartment is on its way. He remains a suspect on many fronts, but as of yet, we have nothing on him."

"So, in theory, Pettersson could be the driver of the vehicle that hit Michelle Hansen?" continued Ploug.

"Yes, that is correct."

"Do we know if they had been in contact with each other immediately before the attack?" asked Bente Hansen, who on top of being amiable and in possession of a good sense of humor, carried out her investigative work impeccably.

"No. Michelle Hansen's cell phone was crushed along with the bones in her hand. It's with forensics, but the SIM card is a write-off so we need to get on to the telephone company to check her calls. I'm sure I don't need to say that the body was found in a terrible state. According to the children, she was almost pulled under the car."

"And Patrick Pettersson's cell phone?"

"Yes, he was cooperative and let us check his history. Michelle Hansen sent him a text saying she would come over to his apartment but doesn't say when. However, they could have been in contact via other means, and he may have known where she was staying. That is, *if* it was him."

"It was him," grunted Pasgård. He was obviously keen on a quick result.

"Furthermore, we have a strong hunch that Birna Sigurdardottir—the woman who was taken to Copenhagen University Hospital last night at zero thirty-two hours with a life-threatening gun wound to the chest from a shooting that took place in the alleyway directly beside the nightclub—has a direct connection to the robbery."

"What exactly is that hunch based on?" asked Ploug.

"On her criminal record. Her presence at the nightclub. Her aggressive personality, which has resulted in several cases of extreme violence. She had a knife in her hand when she was found, which could indicate that she was involved in a stand-off with one of the robbers. Of course, we know the caliber of the weapon that was used, which was the same nine-millimeter caliber as the Luger that was used to threaten the manager of the nightclub. And finally, we can determine that she was shot ten meters down the alleyway from where she was found. The drag marks from the wall to the edge of the sidewalk are clear, so we can assume that someone wanted to save her. We presume that the perpetrator or perpetrators were probably women, just like we know the perpetrators of the robbery were women, and that they may have had a close connection with the woman who was shot."

"Wasn't that the stupidest thing to do? To leave her for dead somewhere where other people could find her? Wouldn't they be worried that Birna could rat on the perpetrator or perpetrators?" asked Bente Hansen.

"You would think so. But the girls who are suspects—and who make up the rank and file of Sigurdardottir's girl gang known as the Black Ladies—are not the brightest sparks, so to speak."

Several of them laughed, but not Bente Hansen. "Is there anything to indicate a direct link between Patrick Pettersson and this gang?"

"No. And in that connection, it should be noted that Pettersson has a clean record."

"And what about Michelle Hansen?"

"No, we haven't been able to prove any link between her and the gang."

"Do we know if Birna Sigurdardottir will pull through?"

Lars Bjørn shrugged. "It doesn't look that way, but we hope so, of course."

Carl nodded. That would be the easiest way to solve the case.

"If the girl doesn't survive, they're going to have their work cut out up there," said Assad on his way down the circular staircase.

"Yes, but it'll give us a bit of breathing room." Carl smiled cheekily as he thought about Pasgård, who now had to put the Zimmermann case to one side until they had a breakthrough in the hit-and-run case.

The smile was quickly wiped from his face when he saw who was waiting for them at the bottom of the stairs: Olaf Borg-Pedersen from *Station 3* with two of his colleagues. One of them shoved a camera in

Carl's face while the other was holding a light cannon that made his eyes water.

"Turn that shit off," he managed to say before he realized that Borg-Pedersen was holding a microphone two centimeters from his mouth.

"We've heard that there's been a couple of breakthroughs in the hit-and-run case today," he said. "What do you make of the getaway car that was found on Griffenfeldsgade and the murder of Michelle Hansen in Stenløse?"

"That it's not my case," he grumbled. How the hell had they obtained that information? Was it Bjørn?

"The police are working with the theory that the same hit-and-run driver killed both Senta Berger and Michelle Hansen deliberately. Is it also your theory that we're dealing with a serial killer or are you more prone to thinking that it is an internal gang war? Can these murders be linked to last night's robbery and shooting?"

"Ask homicide," he said. Was the man an idiot?

Borg-Pedersen turned toward the camera. "A lot of information in this case is being kept under wraps. Several departments refuse to comment. But the public is left wondering whether they can feel safe when it's no longer possible to walk the streets without fearing for their lives. There are thousands of vehicles on the road every day. Will the next car be a weapon and will you be the victim? These are the questions we are trying to answer. And now back to the studio."

What the hell was he doing scaring people like that? Was he working for the news now?

Borg-Pedersen turned toward Carl. "We're going to be shadowing you for the next three days, so tell me what your plans are," he managed to say before Carl turned on his heel and stormed into his office with Assad and Gordon in his wake.

"We're not taking them with us to Flensburg, are we, Carl?" asked Assad.

"Over my dead body! Everything concerning Rose is to be kept between us."

"But what will you say to the TV crew? They're outside waiting in the corridor," asked Gordon.

"Come with me," he said, dragging him out to the TV crew with a smile on his face.

"You'll be pleased to know that our very best assistant down here, Gordon Taylor, will take you with him on an important round of the Borgergade neighborhood."

Gordon's spun toward Carl. "Buut, I—"

"Gordon Taylor's last round took a couple of hours, but you should probably set aside the whole day tomorrow."

Gordon's shoulders dropped.

"You'll have to make sure that everyone Gordon speaks with gives their consent to being filmed. But you know all the rules in that area, right?"

Borg-Pedersen frowned. "And where will the rest of you be, if I might ask?"

Carl beamed. "Ask away; that's why we're here. We'll be sitting on our backsides most of the day reviewing boring paperwork. Not very TV-friendly."

Borg-Pedersen didn't look happy. "Listen, Carl Mørck. We earn a living from making TV that's entertaining. Your boss in homicide directed us to you lot because you can provide us with the best material. So we need to work together on this, okay?"

"Agreed. I promise you that we'll do whatever we can to keep you happy, Borg-Pedersen. We understand what you need."

The man seemed to notice Gordon shaking his head, but the mood was reasonably good when they left.

"What am I supposed to do with them?" asked Gordon nervously.

"Do the round one more time, Gordon. Visit all the kiosks, restaurants, and people again. Only this time bring photos of Denise and Birgit Zimmermann. Show them to people and ask if they know anything about the women's movements or finances. Whether the mother and daughter went out together. You'll come up with something to ask. Are you with me?"

"I've just been in contact with a foreman at the steel plant," said Gordon. "He's agreed to give you a tour up there with Leo Andresen this Monday. They'll be waiting for you outside the main gate at ten o'clock. Is that okay?"

Carl nodded. "Did he know Rose?"

"Yes, he clearly remembers both her and the dad. But he didn't say much about the accident. Only that Rose witnessed it and that she saw her dad die. He referred to the incident as strange and very terrible, so it isn't a surprise that she became hysterical afterward. The way he remembers it, she was laughing and screaming at the same time. As if she was possessed. He didn't know anything but said he would ask around among the former employees."

"Okay, Gordon, thanks." He turned to Assad. "My office tomorrow at six sharp. What do you say?"

"Of course. The early worm escapes the bird, as they say!"

"Err, no, Assad. It's the early bird catches the worm!"

He looked at Carl doubtfully. "Not where *I* come from, let me tell you."

"Just a second, Carl," interrupted Gordon. "Vigga called. She said that if you don't visit your ex-mother-in-law today, you'll be in for it. She said the old woman isn't well and that she's been asking after you."

Carl huffed.

That put paid to his hopes of a quiet drive home.

In front of the nursing home, a group of demented old fogeys were being unloaded from a minibus, all walking off in different directions as soon as their feet touched the ground. The staff were really being kept on their toes.

Only one of the old people stood waiting patiently, her head shaking as she watched the scene. It was Karla.

Carl breathed a sigh of relief. His ex-mother-in-law was obviously having one of her good days. As usual, Vigga had exaggerated to get him out there.

"Hello, Karla," he said. "You've obviously been out for the day. Where've you been?"

She turned slowly toward him, inspecting him for a moment and throwing her hand out theatrically at her unruly fellow passengers.

"Didn't I warn them? Look how these children are running around. Don't say I didn't tell them how dangerous the traffic is here in Rio de Janeiro."

Whoa, I overestimated her a bit, he thought as he carefully took her by the arm and led her toward the entrance.

"Careful," she said. "Don't hurt my arm."

He smiled knowingly at one of the carers who had managed to round up a couple of the other passengers.

"What's happened? She thinks she's in Rio de Janeiro."

The carer smiled back looking tired. "When Mrs. Alsing has been out on a trip, she's always confused about where she is when we get back. And you'll have to shout if you want her to hear you."

Carl realized that his ex-mother-in-law wasn't quite right in the head as they walked to her room. She regaled him with a picturesque account of the heavy rain, fallen trees on mountain roads, and the driver who had shot himself in the head as the bus had swerved off the road and into the abyss.

When they finally arrived at her room, she sat down and put her hand to her chest. It was understandable after the adventure she had described!

"It sounds like you had a terrible trip," shouted Carl. "Lucky you made it back alive."

She gave him a surprised look.

"I always do," she answered, fishing out a half-smoked cigarette from behind a cushion.

"Greta Garbo doesn't just die before the director tells her to," she corrected him while she placed the cigarette in a cigarette holder.

Carl looked bemused. Greta Garbo? That was a new one.

"Vigga says you've been asking for me!" he shouted to change the subject.

She lit the cigarette and took a couple of deep puffs, filling her lungs to the bursting point.

"Have I?" She hesitated with her mouth open as the smoke swirled out. Then she nodded.

"Oh yes. Vigga's boy gave me this. What's his name again?"

Carl took the cell she handed him. A Samsung smartphone that was newer than the one Jesper had given him two years ago. Where would you be in life without your children's cast-off electronics?

"His name is Jesper, Karla," he bellowed directly into her ear. "He's your grandson. What do you want me to do with this?"

"I need you to teach me to take selfies, just like all the young girls on the Internet."

Despite his shock, Carl nodded approvingly. "Selfies, Karla! You are becoming very modern these days," he shouted. "Then what you need to do is press here, with the camera lens pointing toward you, and hold the—"

"No, no, not that. That Jesper boy showed me already. I just need to know what to do."

Maybe her hearing really was failing her, so this time he decided to use a booming commando voice as if he was dealing with a difficult arrest. "*What to do? You just point it at yourself and then press.*"

"Yes, yes, stop shouting. I'm not deaf. Just give me the basics. Should I take off my clothes now or afterward?"

32

Thursday, May 26th, 2016

Jazmine was dreaming soundly. She was cocooned in lace fabric, the heat from strange men's bodies, and the rays of the sun. Intoxicated by the scent of pine and lavender mixed with fresh seaweed. She could hear the sound of waves and music and feel gentle hands on her shoulders, which suddenly shook her so hard it hurt.

Jazmine opened her eyes and saw Denise's shocked face looking back at her.

"She's done a runner, Jazmine," she said, still shaking her.

"Stop that! You're hurting me." She sat up in bed rubbing her eyes. "What are you saying? Who has?"

"Michelle, you idiot. There was a bundle of thousand-kroner notes on the table and now it's gone. She took some money and packed all her stuff. She must have left in a rush because she forgot her iPad." She pointed at the shelf next to the dining table, where they had also placed the hand grenade.

"How much has she taken?"

"I don't know. Twenty, thirty thousand, I think. I haven't counted all the notes."

Jazmine stretched. "Well, does it matter? If she only took thirty thousand, then that leaves more for us. What's the time?"

"Are you stupid or what? She isn't coming back if she's packed her things. She's gone back to that shit, Jazmine. We can't trust her. We have to go after her. *Now!*"

Jazmine looked down at herself. She was in the clothes she had been wearing yesterday. She had sweat marks on her blouse at her armpits and her scalp was itchy.

"I need to shower and change first."

"*Now,* damn it! Don't you get it? It's already bloody late. We've slept through the day and Michelle could already have fucked up everything for us. We've committed robbery and maybe killed someone. Who knows what Michelle might say to cover her own back. We could end up taking the rap for this alone if she tries to save her own ass. It wasn't her who committed robbery and she wasn't the one to stick a bullet in Birna."

Jazmine shuddered. "It wasn't bloody well me either, Denise," she blurted out, regretting it immediately.

Denise's face froze and her expression became suddenly hostile. Jazmine couldn't tell whether she was just angry at the remark or about to attack her, but it scared her. Hadn't she seen what Denise was capable of?

"No, sorry. That was a stupid thing to say, Denise," she said with emphasis. "I didn't mean it. I saw Birna attack you with that knife, and we didn't know the pistol was loaded, did we? We're together on this, I promise." She made the sign of the cross on her chest. Not because she was religious but because she felt it made her promise seem more serious.

Denise drew a deep breath. Her expression changed from aggressive to scared. "Jazmine, we don't know if that Birna girl is dead," she said. "We know nothing about what's happened to her. If she's dead, we're fucked. If she's alive, we're also fucked. Why the hell did we get so drunk last night when we came home? How could we sleep so late that Michelle managed to sneak off? It's totally fucked up."

"If Birna's dead, they'll mention it on TV2 News," said Jazmine, dragging Denise with her.

The sight that met them in the sitting room came as a shock. Not because the room looked like a herd of elephants had marched through it, or because of the candle wax and red wine stains on every surface, or the potato chip crumbs scattered all over the floor. No, they froze because the TV was already on and the screen was plastered with images of someone they knew all too well. It wasn't Birna, as they had anticipated, but Michelle. And underneath on the yellow text banner, the breaking news was:

> *Woman in Stenløse killed by hit-and-run driver. Same woman was hit in a separate hit-and-run on May 20th. Possible connection between this incident and yesterday's shooting at Victoria nightclub in Sydhavnen.*

They started throwing things at the walls and shouting at each other, and then Jazmine almost went into shock, whereas Denise reacted quite differently. Every part of her being was screaming for action as she impressed on Jazmine what Michelle had said on two different occasions. Hadn't she said that she thought she had seen Anne-Line Svendsen in a car across from the nightclub? And hadn't she said the same thing when she had been hit the first time?

"But when you were with that bitch and tried to make her admit that it was her Michelle had seen, you said afterward that you didn't think it was her after all. What the hell do you think now, Jazmine?"

"What do you want me to say?" she answered, sounding choked up. "Michelle has been killed and the police might link her to us. And if it really was Anne-Line Svendsen who Michelle saw last night, she must have seen us when we came out of that alleyway. Who knows if she'll talk to the police?"

Denise sneered at her. "You really are an idiot, Jazmine. Don't you think that's the last thing she'd do? She's a damn murderer and we might be the only ones who could give her away. So don't you think that's what she's considering just now?"

Jazmine was taking the wrapping off a pack of Prince cigarettes with her long nails. When the pack was open she tapped a few cigarettes out onto the table and lit the first one. Now Denise looked at her with a seriousness Jazmine hadn't seen before. It was hard to believe that this was the same Denise who had partied hard last night and who only the other day had been frolicking in her room with one of her sugar daddies.

"Damn it," said Denise. "I'm just as shocked by all this. That Michelle is dead and that everything on the news is to do with us. It's just too much. And then all this stuff with Anne-Line Svendsen. It's bloody scary. If I was her, I would be making sure that we were her next victims. She must know where we live. What else would she have been doing out here in Stenløse?"

Jazmine could feel the fear in the pit of her stomach. Denise was right. Anne-Line might be out there keeping tabs on them as they were speaking.

"What should we do if she comes here?"

"What do you mean?" said Denise angrily. "There are knives in the kitchen, and my grandfather's pistol is on the balcony."

"I don't think I can do it, Denise."

"I don't think Anne-Line would dare to show her face here so soon after the thing with Michelle. There must be police all over the place. They are probably doing door-to-door inquiries right now. But we need to be extra-careful and keep our eyes peeled: for the police, Anne-Line, . . . and each other," she ended, looking directly at Jazmine.

Jazmine closed her eyes. She wanted to return to her dream. "Denise, I think we have more than seventy thousand each. We can jump on a plane and get out of here. Shouldn't we just do that?" She looked at her imploringly. "What do you say? We could fly to South America somewhere. That's far away. Don't you think that would be far enough?"

Denise looked at her condescendingly. "Yeah, because you're just so good at Spanish, aren't you? You do know that you can't really learn a language in bed, right? There's more to it than just giving someone a good tit wank. And then you will end up having to earn a living flat on your back when the money runs out. Is that what you want?"

A look of despair appeared on Jazmine's face. Denise had hurt her feelings. "I don't know. Isn't that what we do already? At least the police and Anne-Line won't be on our backs if we're in South America."

"Anne-Line won't be on our backs for long if I've got anything to do with it, because we'll get to her first. We're two against one. We'll make a plan and get her. Maybe we could do it in her home late at night when she least expects it. We can threaten her and make her write a confession and then kill her and make it look like suicide. And if she has any cash lying around, which wouldn't surprise me, we steal that too. Then we can discuss escaping somewhere."

Jazmine looked puzzled and shushed her. Denise stopped talking and heard someone knocking on the front door, followed by the sound of a key turning in the lock.

"What should we do?" Jazmine just managed to whisper before a woman staggered into the apartment, as pale as a corpse and wearing so much eye makeup that you could hardly see her eyelids.

"Who the hell are you?" asked the woman aggressively as she looked around the room.

"None of your business," answered Denise. "Where did you get those keys?"

"I don't know you. Tell me who you are or I'll arrest you for unlawful entry."

Jazmine tried to catch Denise's eye. Despite the state of the woman, she sounded like she meant it. But Denise didn't seem fazed. Rather, she looked like she was ready to attack the woman.

"The fuck you will," she hissed. "I'm Rigmor's granddaughter. I've got every right to be here, but you don't, do you? So give me the keys and beat it or I'll punch you in the face and call the police."

The woman frowned, swaying on her feet, trying to find her balance. "Are you Dorrit?" she asked in a more neutral tone. "I've heard about you."

Jazmine was confused. Dorrit?

"Hand them over," said Denise, stretching out her hand toward the woman. But the woman just shook her head.

"I'm keeping hold of these until I find out what's going on here," she said, her eyes scanning the apartment. "What are you up to? Rigmor has been murdered and there's money lying around everywhere. What do you think a police investigator makes of this? I'll get to the bottom of this, mark my words. And you two stay here in the meantime. Understood?"

She turned on her heel and staggered through the corridor out onto the walkway.

"Damn it," moaned Jazmine. "Did you hear what she said? And about the money?" Jazmine looked around, putting her hand to her mouth in shock. The way the money was lying all over the place was as good as a confession.

Denise was standing with her hands on her hips, fists clenched. Her expression was withdrawn. She looked like a woman who understood the gravity of the situation.

"My grandmother once told me that her neighbor was a police investigator. So that drunkard must have been her," she said, nodding to herself.

Jazmine was shaken. "What should we do, Denise? If she calls the police, they could be here any minute. We need to get out of here." Jazmine looked around. They could gather all the money in ten minutes, and if she threw any old clothes on just now and packed the rest, they would be out the door within fifteen minutes.

Denise shook her head. "No, we need to pay her a visit," she said.

"You mean go over to her place? Why? She saw the money. You won't stop her from checking up on us. I can tell from the way she looked at us."

"Yes, exactly! That's why we need to stop her instead, right?"

Is this chaos really how I want to be remembered? thought Rose, looking around at her apartment.

She caught sight of the jacket covering the suicide note, plastic basket, donor statement, and razor blade, feeling sad about her wasted, lonely life. A few minutes ago she had caught a glimpse of hope when she heard voices from Rigmor Zimmermann's apartment, and for a moment she had felt that she might be able to carry on living.

This is what delusion does to you, she thought. *It creates miracles and drags you into a false sense of security and illusion that immediately changes everything. And then the disappointment of reality always returns with a vengeance.*

Of course the two suspicious women were not supposed to be in Rigmor's apartment, but when it came to it, what business was it of hers? Or that they were stealing from a dead woman? Or that they were living in her apartment?

Rose hung her head and sat despondently on the only chair she hadn't knocked over. Everything had become so messy.

This must be what judgment day feels like, she thought, feeling the urge to throw up. Everything inside her was pleading to get it over with. To call the emergency services and say that she had slit her wrists and that they should come and save her organs. Never mind what was going on on the other side of the wall. If she got involved, she would just end up back where she started. The police would come and that was the last thing she wanted. She certainly didn't want anyone from HQ to come and stop her. And the same went for her sisters and the doctors in Glostrup.

"Screw them, and screw those girls next door. Screw the world," she said out loud, grabbing the jacket and revealing what was underneath. A quick call and two clean cuts and it would all be over.

She had already begun dialing the number for the emergency services when she heard a knock at the door.

Go away! she screamed inside. And when the knocking continued even louder than before, she pressed her hands over her ears. She sat like that for a minute, but when she removed her hands and heard that someone was still knocking, she got up, put the jacket back over the paraphernalia, and staggered over to the door.

"*What?*" she shouted through the mail slot.

"It's Denise Zimmermann," answered the voice outside. "Can we come in for a minute? We just want to explain—"

"Not now!" Rose shouted back. "Come back in half an hour." Then it would all be over anyway.

While she stood staring at the front door, she realized that it might take the paramedics too long to gain entry if the door was locked. That it would be too late for them to use her organs. How could she know how those things worked?

She heard them saying "okay" and the sound of their footsteps as they moved away from the door. When it was silent outside, she unlocked the door to enable the paramedics to get in.

She had not even turned around before the door was kicked in behind her—and a hard bang to the back of her head made her pass out.

33

Thursday, May 26th, and Friday, May 27th, 2016

Who are you, Anneli? she thought when she caught sight of her demonic reflection in the mirror. She had just killed someone and yet she was smiling like someone in love. She had violated the strictest law of God and man, taking someone's life, and yet she had never felt better than in the wonderful moment when Michelle Hansen disappeared under the car with a force that crushed her body and made the car jump half a meter in the air. Of course she had expected some form of pleasure like last time, but nothing like this all-consuming euphoria that ran through her whole body like an elixir of life.

After she had stopped the car for a few seconds to make sure that Michelle's twisted body would never get back up again, she had calmly put her foot down and sped off in the direction of Ølstykke, where she had decided to park the car. She had shivered with excitement all the way. Never before had she laughed so much with relief. The job was done.

But almost as soon as she was home on the sofa with her feet curled up underneath her and a glass of cool white wine in her hand, she had to acknowledge that certain events sometimes developed more quickly and unpredictably than expected.

After the murder of Senta Berger, the media had been divided. Was it an accident or a murder? Was there a concrete link between Berger and the previous hit-and-run attempt on Michelle Hansen? The TV stations and one of the tabloids had mentioned the possibility, but that was all it had come to.

This time, things were different. Not only was Michelle Hansen's death plastered all over the front pages of the online newspapers, but when Anneli turned on her TV she saw that it was being covered by all the TV news channels.

Thankfully, the police didn't seem to have much to go on about the driver, but as usual that didn't stop the news anchors from peddling their theories, and as the day went on, their analyses and theories grew wilder and wilder. Eventually, Anneli was overcome by a rather irrational feeling of being overlooked. Weren't they sitting in the studio linking the robbery the night before with the hit-and-run murder today? Were they completely blind?

She poured herself another glass of wine and considered the situation.

Of course she ought to be pleased that they were looking in the wrong place, but that didn't change the fact that Anneli's mission was not accomplished. Her power over life and death had entered her like a drug, and her desire to continue exterminating these superfluous existences was almost greater than her excitement at the thought that she might have gotten away with it.

Would she be able to stop killing? *That* was the real question.

Last night she had followed the girls' taxi closely from the parking lot in front of the apartment in Stenløse to the nightclub, even though a couple of red lights should have stopped her. She had parked the car across from the nightclub and waited patiently for the girls to come out of the club. As the events of last night came to light, she had a pretty good idea of what she had witnessed. These vain, smug tarts had without doubt committed crimes so serious that they would have been executed in any dictatorship. She had seen Denise and Jazmine sneak into the nightclub while Michelle had distracted the bouncer, whom she recognized as Michelle's boyfriend.

Later, she had seen the girls reappear and hide in the alleyway behind the club. So it wasn't hard to put two and two together when the TV stations said that the robbery was committed by two young women.

She also knew something about the shooting of Birna. She had been surprised when the terrible girl turned up at the club and had watched her reaction as Jazmine and Denise shortly after disappeared into the alleyway. Birna had followed them, and Anneli had seen Michelle walk in the same direction a little later. There were a few minutes when Anneli didn't know what was going on. She had tried to hear their conversation, but the noise from the nightclub drowned out their voices, and the only sound that rose above the beat was a dull sound that Anneli couldn't place. When Denise, Michelle, and Jazmine reappeared, they were having a heated discussion while dragging Birna's lifeless body and leaving it under a streetlamp.

After that, the girls had crossed the street in the direction of Anneli's car, so she had to lean back in the seat to avoid the light from the streetlamps. Close-up, she had noticed how expressionless their faces were. It seemed as if Michelle had looked straight in her direction. But had she? And had she noticed who was in the car? Anneli didn't think so because the windows were steamed up and her face was well-hidden in the dark.

And yet, could she be sure?

They say that the order of the factors does not affect the product, but was that also true in this case? What if she decided to put a stopper in her plans and left it to the news sharks and police to work themselves into a frenzy, linking this stupid group of girls to something larger and more organized? It wasn't too hard to imagine them interpreting the deaths of Michelle Hansen and Senta Berger as the result of internal fighting. That would certainly nullify her involvement. But if she just remained passive, didn't she run the risk of Denise and Jazmine talking to the police if they were caught? And wouldn't they tell the police that Michelle had named the driver of the red Peugeot who had tried to kill her the first time? That was what Jazmine had hinted at last time she came to Anneli's office.

No, it wouldn't do. If the girls said anything, the police would develop new theories about the course of events and come to the conclusion that the crimes were in fact not connected.

Suddenly, all Anneli's euphoria was replaced by doubt and an increasing pain in her breast, which had otherwise subsided somewhat. Anxiety could suddenly manifest itself physically. She had heard about that before, but what did it mean that she was suddenly in so much pain? Was something wrong?

She took more painkillers than she was meant to and gently massaged the scar from the surgery. When that didn't help, she added to the calming effect of the painkillers with a few more glasses of wine.

Anneli did not like the dilemma she had ended up in at all.

The following morning her head felt woozy and heavy—the result of too much wine and a sleepless night. And what was even worse was her complete lack of resolve.

Most of all, she wanted to pop some more pills and just stay in bed. At the same time, she also wanted to jump about and vent her frustration. Smash some crockery on the kitchen floor, tear a few pictures off the wall, and throw everything off her desk.

Basically, she wanted to do anything other than what she knew she ought to do: take it easy and let things run their own course before making any new decisions.

I'll go to work today after the radiation therapy and see what happens, she decided after considering all her options.

Her colleagues greeted her relatively politely when she turned up at the office. There were a few awkward smiles, but mostly she was met with neutral expressions and reserved nods.

She informed the reception desk that she was ready to see her clients, as they were expected to call the scroungers.

Anneli looked around her office. She could tell that someone had been there because her table had been cleared of paperwork and the flowers that had been withering on the windowsill were now in the trash can. Had they thought that she would just quietly disappear?

Anneli smiled. They weren't wrong. Once she had completed her quest of justice with a few more murders, she would disappear from the face of the earth. A plan that Jazmine, Denise, and Michelle had unknowingly speeded up. The news on the Internet mentioned that the haul from the Victoria robbery was one hundred and sixty-five thousand kroner, and she intended to get her hands on that money. It would be easy enough once she had killed Denise and Jazmine. And despite the fact that it wasn't a huge amount of money, she reckoned she would be able to live off it for at least ten years somewhere in central Africa if the cancer didn't get her first. A train to Brussels, a flight to Yaoundé in Cameroon, and she would be gone without a trace. No one could convince her that Interpol or the like could find her once she had been swallowed up by the jungle.

Occupied with these thoughts, and dreams of young black men and eternal sunshine, she didn't hear what the young woman who stepped into her office wanted, only her name.

Anneli briefly inspected her. Mid-twenties, feminine, and a predictable small tattoo of a lizard on the back of her hand between her thumb and index finger. Same tart, different name. Just another sponger with braids.

The girl was strangely polite in an old-fashioned way, bordering on the servile, and was subdued in both appearance and tone. Therefore, Anneli was totally unprepared for what came next.

"Like I said, I'm no longer eligible for student support because I've dropped out of my classes," she said with kitten eyes. "So I can't pay for my room, food, or clothes. Of course, I'm aware that you don't get benefits just like that, but if I don't, I'll kill myself."

Then she went quiet. Just sat there fiddling with her hair like all the other cows, as if having beautiful hair was the most important thing in the world. She was staring at Anneli with a provocative arrogance, probably imagining that her demand was absolutely indisputable. She was obviously as thick as two short planks. Probably the type who had flirted and sucked up to her teachers all through high school in order to get good grades and into college. She had probably realized now that the demands were too high. Failed to turn up to lectures and subsequently been thrown out of school. That would be the real reason her student support had been stopped.

Anneli's expression became stern. Annoyance, resentment, hatred, and contempt were only the tip of the iceberg.

She looked up at the young woman. Was she really threatening to commit suicide, the stupid cow? What a shame for her that she had come to the wrong person.

"I see, so you're going to commit suicide! You know what? I think you should hurry home and get it over with, sweetie," she said and spun around to show the girl her back. This meeting was over.

Anneli could hear the indignation and shock in the girl's voice behind her. "I'll report you to your boss for encouraging me to commit suicide," she said threateningly. "I know that's against all the rules, so for your own sake, I think you'd better find a way to award me five thousand kroner here and now, you b. . . . !"

Had the little brat just called her a bitch?

She slowly turned back around in her chair and directed an icy look at the girl. She had just moved to the top of Anneli's death list. In fact, she would take great pleasure in seeing the horror in her dolled-up eyes and her pretty face smashed to a pulp.

Anneli took her phone from her handbag and pressed the record button.

"The time is ten minutes past nine on May 27th, 2016," she said. "My name is Anne-Line Svendsen and I am a caseworker for Copenhagen municipality. Sitting in front of me is a twenty-six-year-old client, Tasja Albrechtsen, who has demanded a payment of five thousand kroner. She has stated that she will commit suicide if the payment is not made immediately." She pushed the phone in front of the girl. "Would you mind repeating your demand, Tasja Albrechtsen, and state your social security number so we have something for your file?"

Anneli couldn't tell whether it was the recording, the accusation of blackmail, or the overall development of the situation that caused the girl to adopt a worried expression, because at that moment they were interrupted by the telephone. And as Anneli took the receiver, the girl quietly stood up and slipped out of the door.

Anneli smiled. Just a shame that she hadn't managed to get more information out of the tart. Her address, for example. That would have made it easier when her turn came.

"Hi, Anne-Line. It's Elsebeth," said a familiar voice on the other end. "I'm glad I got hold of you."

Anneli pictured her former colleague from Gammel Køge Landevej. She was one of the good ones who took her work seriously enough to challenge her superiors. It was a shame, actually, that they never saw each other anymore.

After a few pleasantries, she stated her business.

"You remember Senta Berger, don't you?"

Anneli frowned. "Yes, Senta. Who could forget that little diva?"

"I took over her case after you, and now she's dead. Had you heard?"

Anneli thought before answering. "Yes, I read about it in the newspaper. An accident, wasn't it?"

"That's the question. The police have just been here to question me about her. Whether she had any enemies, whether I had any problems with her, and whether I knew anything about a red Peugeot or a black Honda. It was really quite awful, almost as if I was a suspect and they expected me to blurt out a lot of information. Luckily I don't even have a driver's license, but all the same."

"Phew, that's understandable. But why are you calling me, Elsebeth?" she asked feeling unease in her stomach. Had the girls already been arrested and told the police about her? She wasn't ready for this at all.

"They asked me who her caseworker was before me, and I had to say it was you. They also asked if you've had any disagreements with her."

"God, no. She was just one of many clients. What did you say?"

"Nothing. How would I know?"

Idiot! thought Anneli. *You could have helped me out a bit. Would it have hurt to say no? It's only a word.*

"No, of course you couldn't know. But we haven't had any disagreements."

"They're on their way over to see you now, I heard them saying to my manager. So now you're warned. That was all, really."

Anneli sat staring at the receiver after Elsebeth had hung up.

Then she pressed the intercom. "Just send in the next client," she said. They weren't going to catch her slacking off.

Apparently the two policemen had been there for a while, probably to state their business to Anneli's manager. She certainly looked at Anneli with reproach when they marched into her office.

"Sorry for the interruption," said the manager to the client, "but we'll need to ask you to wait in reception for a moment."

Anneli nodded to the policemen and then to the client. "That's all right. We were just about finished here, weren't we?" She smiled at the client and they shook hands.

She sat down, calmly collected her notes, and put them in a folder before turning her attention to the two men.

"How can I help you?" She smiled inquisitively to the one who appeared to be in charge. Then she pointed at the two chairs in front of her.

"Please take a seat." The bitch could stand.

"My name is Lars Pasgård," said one of the policemen, handing her his card. Anneli looked at it. "Inspector" was written on the front.

She nodded approvingly. "I see you're from police headquarters. How can I help you?" she asked with chilling calm.

"They're investigating two murders committed by a hit-and-run driver," said her manager with a cold stare.

The inspector turned toward her. "Thank you, we'd prefer to talk to Miss Svendsen alone, if you don't mind."

Anneli kept a straight face, but it was difficult. When had she last seen her manager humiliated, and when had someone last called Anneli "miss"?

Anneli caught the inspector's eye. "Yes, I think I know what this is about."

"I see."

"I received a call half an hour ago from a former colleague at Gammel Køge Landevej. I believe you have just spoken with her. Elsebeth Harms. Isn't that right?"

The two policemen looked at each other. Had they asked her to keep quiet? That was her problem if they had.

"I wish I could help you, but I don't think I know anything."

"I think you should leave that to us to decide, Miss Svendsen."

That brought a smile to her manager's face; she was standing behind them. Now the score was 1–1.

"You own a Ford Ka, is that correct?"

She nodded. "Yes, I've had it for nearly five years. A good economical car, and it can almost be parked anywhere." She laughed without it resonating with any of them.

"Senta Berger and Michelle Hansen are both former clients of yours, is that correct?"

She gave a knowing smile. "Yes, but I assume that Elsebeth and my manager would have confirmed that already."

"Do you have anything to say about these two murders?" asked the other man.

What a stupid question, she thought, looking at the man. Was he new to the job?

She took a deep breath. "I've been following the news, and obviously it made me very sad when Michelle Hansen was hit the first time. After all, she is my client—or rather, was—and she was a really nice girl. It came as a great shock when I then read about Senta Berger and now Michelle again. It's really affected me. Do you have any leads?"

The Lars Pasgård man looked annoyed at the question and didn't answer. "Yes, the media have been busy," he said. "Your manager tells us that you've had quite a lot of absences lately. Dates that fit well with the incidents."

Anneli looked up. She didn't like her manager's attitude.

"Yes, I've had to take some time off lately. That's correct. But now I'm back."

"And the reason for your absence is a little unclear. Have you been ill?"

"I *am* ill."

"I see. And what's wrong with you, if I may ask? Something that might explain your whereabouts?"

Any minute now and they'll ask me about exact times, and I don't want that, she thought.

Anneli stood up slowly. "I haven't been very forward about my illness, no. I can see now that I should've been. But it's been a very difficult time for me. I've been in a lot of pain and have been very depressed. But things are better at the moment."

"So what . . . ," her manager blurted out before Anneli pulled up her blouse.

She stood like that for a moment so they could see the bandage that showed under her bra before pulling that up as well to bare her chest area.

"Breast cancer," she said pointing as the three people in front of her instinctively pulled back.

"It was just recently that I was told that I have a chance of surviving, and that's what pulled me out of it. I'll probably still have to take things easy, but I hope to be back full-time within a week or two, even though I'll still need treatment in the coming weeks."

She gently pulled her bra and blouse back down again.

"I'm sorry," she said to her manager. "I just couldn't talk about it."

Her manager nodded. If there was anything that could make women humble, it was experiencing breast cancer close-up.

"We understand," said the inspector, looking a little shaken. The two policemen looked at each other. Anneli didn't know what to make of their expressions, but it didn't look bad.

Pasgård took a deep breath and Anneli sat down. Behind them, the manager was leaning up against the bookcase. Was she about to faint? She was welcome to.

"I've thought a lot about this," said Anneli, "and I'm actually glad that you came today. I am aware about client confidentiality, but I don't think what I'm about to say will violate it." She bit her upper lip. Hopefully they would interpret it as a sign that she was having an inner struggle.

"I saw on TV yesterday that Michelle Hansen might have been involved in a robbery. I also saw that her boyfriend was a bouncer at the nightclub that was robbed. I recognized him as the Patrick Pettersson who Michelle sometimes dragged along here with her. A rather provocative young man, if you ask me. An electrician with tattoos up and down his arms and huge muscles. He definitely looks like he's taken steroids, which would also explain his violent temper. Last time Michelle brought him here, he shouted at her to get a grip. It was something about Michelle having messed up by moving in with Patrick without informing anyone. Patrick was fuming that they would have to pay back the housing benefit she'd been claiming and that she had committed fraud behind his back. The latter I didn't believe. He comes across as a very cunning type."

Pasgård looked pleased while taking down notes. "You think he might have something to do with the murders?"

"I don't know, but I do know that he's crazy about cars and that he was going to confront Michelle about the situation. It was about money, no doubt about that. He was very keen to get his hands on more of that, and he had complete control over her."

"Do you know if Senta Berger and Michelle Hansen knew each other?"

His tone was suddenly friendlier. Were they finally on the same wavelength?

She shook her head. "I thought about that, but I don't think I know anything. Certainly nothing I can remember at the moment." She paused to emphasize what she had said.

"But there's something else I should probably mention now you're here."

"Yes?"

"Birna Sigurdardottir is also one of my clients. She's the one who was shot . . . outside a nightclub, I believe."

The inspector leaned in over the table.

"She was, yes. We were just about to ask you about that." She nodded. Her timing had been right.

"I believe Michelle Hansen and Birna Sigurdardottir knew each other."

"What makes you believe that?"

Anneli turned to her computer and began typing.

"Look here. Last time Michelle was here she came in immediately after Birna. I'm sure they must have waited together in the reception, and I also seem to recall that it's happened before, but I'm not quite sure about that."

"And what do you make of that?"

She sat back in her chair. "That they maybe arrived together. That they maybe knew each other more than I was aware."

Inspector Pasgård nodded with a satisfied look on his face. In fact, he looked almost exhilarated.

"Thank you for the information, Anne-Line Svendsen. It's been a great help. I think that'll be all for now, and pardon the intrusion." Pasgård got up before his assistant. "We'll be checking up on Patrick Pettersson's movements over the last few weeks. That should be simple enough if his boss has kept his paperwork up to date."

Anneli tried to contain her relief. "Oh, I forgot to mention that Michelle Hansen and Patrick Pettersson were planning to go on holiday. That was one of the reasons Michelle came in to see me. Of course, I couldn't give permission when I had just discovered her fraud. But he might not have been at work lately."

The other policeman whistled and looked knowingly at Pasgård.

Poor Patrick Pettersson.

"Anne-Line, I'm devastated that you've been through all this without speaking to me. It was really embarrassing for me that you had to expose yourself like that. I'm terribly sorry."

Anneli nodded. If she played her cards right, she could probably get a few more days off out of this.

"You don't have to apologize. It was my own fault. You never know how you're going to react before you actually get ill, do you? So I'm the one who needs to apologize. I should have told you everything. I can see that now."

Her manager smiled, looking touched. It was the first time that had ever happened.

"Well, why don't we put that behind us and move on. I can understand you, Anne-Line. I certainly don't think I would have been able to deal with everyone getting involved if I was in your shoes." She smiled, still looking sheepish. "Are you all right?" she added.

"Thank you. I'm a little tired, but I'm doing okay."

"Take things easy until you feel better, okay? Let's agree on that. Just let reception know if you need a day to yourself, okay?"

Anneli tried to look touched. Feelings like those were always better if you shared them.

Emotional bonding, she believed they called it.

34

Friday, May 27th, 2016

Whose damn idea was it to leave so early? Wasn't it Assad's? he asked himself as they were driving south. Now the unshaven bandit had been snoring next to him for the last one hundred and fifty kilometers. The cheek!

"Wake up, Assad!" he yelled, causing the guy to hit his forehead against his knees.

Assad looked around, appearing disoriented. "What are we doing here?" he asked drowsily.

"We're halfway there and I'll fall asleep if you don't speak to me."

Assad rubbed his eyes and looked up at the signs above the glistening wet motorway. "Are we only in Odense? I think I'll take another nap, then."

Carl elbowed him in the side, which still didn't stop him from nodding off again.

"Hey, wake up, Assad. I've been thinking about something. Listen up."

Assad sighed.

"I went to see my ex-mother-in-law yesterday. She'll be ninety soon and has become strange and withdrawn, and yet she wants to involve me in something new every time I see her."

"You've mentioned this before, Carl," he said, closing his eyes.

"Yes, but yesterday she wanted me to teach her to take selfies."

"Hmm!"

"Did you hear what I said?"

"I think so."

"I was thinking that Michelle Hansen's phone must be full of photos. I wouldn't be surprised if she'd taken selfies with the girls who committed the robbery. That is, if it's true that she was an accomplice."

"You seem to forget that it's not our case, Carl. Anyway, the phone was smashed. A total write-down, Carl."

"Write-off, Assad. But that doesn't matter. It was an iPhone."

Assad reluctantly opened his eyes and looked at Carl sleepily. "You mean . . ."

"Yes. Everything can be found in the cloud. Or on her computer or iPad or whatever we can find. Or on Instagram or Facebook or . . ."

"Don't you think the team have already figured that out?"

Carl shrugged. "Probably. Terje Ploug is on the ball with most things, but maybe we should give him a heads-up. What do you say?"

Carl nodded to himself and turned to face Assad. The big lump had fallen asleep again.

After years with Vigga and more than his fair share of years on the streets surrounded by prostitutes and pimps, Carl thought he'd built up a fairly good level of tolerance, but as he stood in Kinua von Kunstwerk's raw gallery down at the harbor in Flensburg, his open-mindedness was put to the test. You couldn't exactly call it porn, but it was a close call. The enormous walls were covered in huge and extremely detailed clinical depictions of female genitalia in bright colors.

Carl caught a glimpse of Assad's bulging eyes as an extraordinary woman waltzed into the room wearing an outfit that perfectly illustrated her eccentricity. Like a bird of paradise, she walked toward them in her ultra-high heels, and Carl saw that Rose had certainly retained some influence from her childhood friend.

"*Willkommen, bienvenue,* welcome, my friends," she said loudly enough that the suspiciously engrossed visitors in the gallery couldn't avoid noticing her entrance.

She kissed Carl and Assad on both cheeks a few times too many for normal north German standards. Carl was worried that Assad would fall to his knees as she stared at them alluringly with her big brown eyes.

"Are you okay?" he whispered to make sure when he saw the veins pumping on Assad's neck, but Curly didn't answer. Instead, he invested all his energy in squinting at the woman as if he was looking directly at the sun.

"We spoke on the phone," said Assad in a voice so smooth that it would give a Spanish crooner a run for his money.

"It's about Rose," interrupted Carl before the sultry mood completely took over.

Karoline, alias Kinua, nodded with a look of concern. "Yes, it doesn't sound like she's doing too well," she said.

Carl glanced over at a promising-looking Nespresso machine, placed on a glass display cabinet underneath a scarlet-and-purple painting of a vagina during labor.

"Do you have somewhere else we could talk?" asked Carl, slightly distracted. "With a cup of coffee, that is. It's been a long drive from Copenhagen."

Surrounded by the less invasive decor of the office, the self-proclaimed artistic icon assumed a more normal demeanor.

"Yes, it's been several years since Rose and I lost touch, which is a real shame because we *were* really good friends, but also *very* different." She stared straight ahead for a moment, lost in her memories, and then nodded. "And we have very different careers that take up a lot of our time."

Carl understood. She didn't need to underline that difference.

"As you have probably figured out, we really need to get to the core of Rose's current situation," he said. "Perhaps you can provide us with a bit more detail about what happened with Rose and her dad? We know that he tyrannized her and that it must have been bad. But *what* did he do exactly? Can you give us some examples?"

Karoline looked surprisingly normal while she tried to find a way to put her thoughts into words.

"Examples?" she finally said. "How much time do you have?"

Carl shrugged.

"Just fire away," said Assad.

She smiled—but only for a second.

"It wouldn't be a lie to say that Rose never heard one positive or kind word from her dad. He was as cold as ice when it came to her, and what was worse, he made sure that Rose's mom didn't dare say anything kind to her either."

"But he wasn't like that with her sisters?"

She shook her head. "I know that Rose tried to placate him in different ways when she was a bit older. But if she cooked for the family, she could rest assured that he would empty the water jug over his plate in disgust after the first bite. If she vacuumed, he would empty his ashtray on the floor if she had missed just one speck of dust."

"That doesn't sound good."

"No, but that's nothing. He wrote notes to her school principal saying that Rose made fun of the teachers and spoke badly about them at home, asking them to instill some respect in her."

"And it wasn't true?"

"Of course it wasn't. When her mom bought her clothes, he burst out laughing, pointed his finger at her and called her an ugly piece of shit, and said the mirror would crack if she looked in it. He threw her things off the shelves if a book was slightly out of place so she would learn to keep her room tidy. He ordered her to eat her dinner in the utility room if she withdrew into herself when he was bullying her. He called her a stinking tart if she dared to borrow a little splash of Yrsa or Vicky's perfume."

Assad said something in Arabic under his breath. That rarely indicated anything favorable about the person in question.

Carl nodded. "So what you're saying is that he was an asshole."

Karoline hung her head. "An asshole? I don't have the words to describe him. When Rose was being confirmed, he made her wear an old dress because he didn't want to spend money on her. They didn't have a party for her because why spend money on presents when she didn't look after her things anyway? Do you think 'asshole' is strong enough for a man who treats his daughter like that?"

Carl shook his head. There are many ways to knock a child's confidence, and none of them justifiable.

"I hear what you're saying, but does that explain what I told you earlier? That she expressed her hatred for her dad every day in her notebooks?"

Kinua von Kunstwerk was in no doubt. "You have to understand that as soon as he came home from work, there wasn't a moment when he wasn't bullying her. For example, he loved to ask her impossible questions, which of course she couldn't answer, and then mock her for being stupid. And if he could get away with doing it when there were other children around, all the better. She told me that when she was learning to ride a bike, which she had to because she had been moved to a new school, her dad pretended to help her keep her balance, but of course he let go of the bike as soon as she swerved, causing her to fall off and hurt herself badly."

She looked at Carl, trying to compose herself. "It's difficult to remember, but now that I've started, it's all coming back to me. I remember clearly that her dad forced her to stay at home when the family went on trips because he didn't want to look at her grumpy face when they were supposed to be having fun. And he favored her sisters to the point of her disappearing entirely.

"When she had a rare opportunity to forget about her trauma, he would corner her, like the time before her final high school exams when he made a racket all night to stop her from getting any sleep. She also said to me that he told her she would die if she had the slightest cold or was feeling a bit unwell. And when he was most cunning, he would pretend to be kind. For example, he would point at the strawberry bed in the vegetable garden and tell her which row she could pick from, only to shout like a maniac afterward that she'd picked them from the row that had been sprayed with insecticide and that she'd die in immense agony."

Carl stared blankly in front of him. Poor Rose.

"Don't you remember anything redeeming?" he asked.

Karoline shook her head. "He *never* apologized, but forced Rose to do it over and over whenever she made the slightest mistake."

"But why, Karoline? Do you know?"

"Maybe because Rose's mom was already expecting her when they met each other. At least that's my theory. Apart from that, he was a complete psycho and hated her because she never, ever cried when he provoked her."

Carl nodded. It definitely made sense. He wondered if her sisters knew all this.

"And then you came into her life?" said Assad.

She smiled. "Yes, I did. And I made her laugh at her so-called dad when he bullied her. That made him furious, but it also dampened his attacks a little bit. He wasn't the type to put up with being the laugh-ingstock. I also told her that she could just kill him if he started again. We laughed a lot about that idea one summer."

Then she went quiet, as if in hindsight she could see it all with more perspective.

"What are you thinking about, Karoline?" asked Carl.

"I'm thinking that he did get her in the end after all."

Carl and Assad looked at her quizzically.

"She wanted to continue studying, but he got her into the steel plant instead. Of course it was where he worked himself. Where else? He wasn't about to give up his control over her, was he?"

"Why didn't she just move to another city, away from her tor-mentor?"

Kinua von Kunstwerk pulled her kimono tighter around her. Now she was back in the present, where this was no longer her problem, and where the doorbell in the exhibition room had suddenly became very active.

"Why?" She shrugged. "When it came to it, he had just worn her down."

"He's broken her for life, don't you think?"

Carl frowned. How he wished that he had known years ago what they had learned today.

"Do you think Rose killed her dad?" continued Assad.

"If she did, it hasn't been proven."

"And what *if* we could prove it?"

Carl glanced out of the side window at a sea of yellow. Wasn't it a bit early for the rapeseed fields to be in full bloom? He could never remember.

"What do you think, Carl? What's the plan?"

"You heard Kinua. Maybe the best thing to do for Rose is to keep this to ourselves."

"Agreed, Carl. I feel the same way." He seemed relieved.

They sat in silence for a long time before their thoughts were interrupted by the telephone ringing. Assad pressed the green telephone icon on the screen.

It was Gordon.

"How did it go on your round?" asked Carl. "Did you manage to lose the TV crew?"

It sounded like Gordon laughed, but you never knew with him.

"Yes," he answered. "They left after twenty minutes because nothing was happening. They said they couldn't be bothered to plod around on a route I'd already done before. Apart from that they kept asking me about the nightclub and hit-and-run cases. I don't think they're really interested in the Zimmermann case."

Carl smiled. All according to plan.

"But they left too soon, because I bumped into a guy in a café on Store Kongensgade. He lives on Borgergade and I'd spoken with him earlier. Since then, he'd discussed our talk with his girlfriend, who had her birthday on the day Zimmermann was murdered. She remembered seeing a big guy on Borgergade on that specific day who was shuffling along the street and seemed a bit . . . she couldn't really describe it but said he seemed very intense. As if he was agitated or worked up about something or other."

"So why didn't they contact us?"

"They intended to but just hadn't gotten around to it."

Carl nodded. Every investigator knew the situation all too well.

"Did she remember what time of day it was?"

"She did. She was on her way to see a friend who had invited her for a birthday celebration around eight o'clock."

"And what was this man doing?"

"He was just standing on the sidewalk a couple of doors down from where Birgit Zimmermann lives. And it was odd because it seemed like he didn't notice that it was pouring down."

"Was she able to give you a description?"

"She described him as relatively well dressed but dirty and with long greasy hair. Perhaps that was why she noticed him. The combination seemed a bit off, she said."

"Does she remember him well enough to give a description to our sketch artist?"

"Not his face, but she can describe his body posture and clothes."

"Okay. Sort that out, then, Gordon."

"I already have, but there's more, Carl. I found another witness. Someone who saw Rigmor Zimmermann just before the murder. In fact, he had spoken to the investigators in homicide but hasn't heard back since."

"When did he contact them?"

"The day after the murder."

"Is that in the report?"

"No. I can't find his witness statement."

Assad rolled his eyes and Carl was with him. If would be a miracle if Pasgård's team managed to solve this case.

"What did this witness see?"

"He saw Rigmor Zimmermann stop at a street corner and look over her shoulder before suddenly starting to run."

"Where exactly?"

"It was on the corner of Klerkegade and Kronprinsessegade."

"Okay. That's only a hundred meters from the King's Garden."

"Yes, and she ran off in that direction. But he didn't see any more because he was walking in the opposite direction down Kronprinsessegade. He lives in Nyboder."

"What did the man make of it?"

"That maybe the rain was too much for her or that she'd suddenly remembered that she was late for something. He didn't know."

"Where did you find him?" asked Assad, putting his feet up on the dashboard in a position that would anger any yoga instructor.

"He found me. He heard me questioning some people where he works."

"Good job, Gordon," said Carl. "Bring him in so we can go through it all one more time, okay? We can be back within thirty minutes. Do you think you can get him down to HQ by then?"

"I can try, but I don't think you have time, Carl. The commissioner himself has just been down in the cellar snooping about. He said you have to report to him as soon as you're back. He looked pretty serious, so I think you'd better do it. Something about the TV crew needing something to be getting on with."

Carl and Assad looked at each other. Suddenly it might take much longer than thirty minutes for them to get back.

"Tell him we had a puncture and drove into a ditch."

There was a long pause. Apparently Gordon wasn't down with that.

35

Friday, May 27th, 2016

The first thing Rose noticed when she regained consciousness was a cutting feeling on the backs of her thighs. Jumbled sounds and images rushed through her head in snatches. A blow, hands struggling with her body, piercing voices, and a ripping sound as if something was being torn.

She slowly opened her eyes and saw a faint white glow creeping in from under a door next to her.

She didn't recognize the room and couldn't work out what she was sitting on.

Then the throbbing pain and pressure from the back of her head kicked in. Was it because of the alcohol or had something else happened? She didn't understand it. She tried to call for help but no sound came out because something had been tied around her face, stopping her from opening her mouth.

With one attempt at maneuvering her upper body, she immediately knew her situation. She didn't know how it had happened, but she had been tied up in a sitting position with her arms pulled up above her head and her hands fastened to something cold. Her ankles were tied together, her back was pressed up against something smooth, and something or other around her neck was stopping her from moving more than a few centimeters forward.

She had no idea what had happened.

From the other side of the door, she could hear the sound of two clear voices arguing. The women sounded young and shrill, and there was no mistaking what they were saying. They were arguing about her. About whether she should live or die.

Just kill me, whoever you are, she thought. It didn't matter how it happened. The result would be the same: She would find peace.

Rose closed her eyes. As long as her headache was so intense, she could keep the persistent thoughts in her head at bay. All the unavoidable images of her father's mangled body. The arm sticking out from the huge slab, still with an accusing finger pointing right at her. The deep red blood flowing toward her shoes. And she recalled the smile on her mother's face when the paramedics dropped her off later that same day. The police were already outside the house, so she had obviously been informed about what had happened. So why was she smiling? Why did she only have the energy to smile? Why was there not a single word of comfort?

Stop! she screamed inside. But these thoughts were inside her. And Rose knew better than anyone that if she wasn't careful, this would just be an overture to even worse images and words that could come at her like a flood any minute.

Darker images than before, words that hurt more than the previous ones, and unstoppable memories.

She fought against whatever it was restraining her arms. Moaned behind the material that was covering her mouth and making her mute.

Then she pressed forward as hard as she could against the restraint around her neck, but even these few centimeters choked her. She stayed like this until the pressure caused her to lose consciousness again.

When she came around, the two women from earlier were standing watching over her. One of them, Rigmor Zimmermann's granddaughter, had a penetrating expression and was holding a sharp object that looked like an awl in one hand, while the other one was holding a roll of gaffer tape.

Are they going to stab me to death? she wondered, but rejected the thought straightaway. Why would the other one be holding gaffer tape if that was the case?

Rose let her eyes wander and recognized the room now. They were in Rigmor's bathroom and she was taped tightly to the toilet. That explained the sharp pain in her thighs.

Try as she might, Rose couldn't look down at herself because of the restraint around her neck. But if she glanced to the left toward the sink and mirror, she could just catch a glimpse of what they had done to her.

Her pants and underwear were pulled down around the backs of her knees, and there was gaffer tape tied tightly around her thighs and the toilet, and around her waist and the cistern behind her. Her hands were elevated, tied with a couple of Rigmor's belts to the grab rail screwed into the wall. She recognized one of the belts as a present she had given Rigmor for Christmas. It was a slim yellow belt that Rigmor had used more out of politeness than pleasure over the Christmas period and then never used again.

There was gaffer tape around Rose's mouth, and a rope made from silk scarves around her neck, tied at either end to the two grab rails on the wall.

Now she remembered that she had tried to strangle herself but had to concede that it was impossible, however hard she might try. Every time she managed to lose consciousness, she would just fall back again, loosening the grip around her neck and allowing the blood to flow back to her brain.

If she had been capable, she would have told the two girls that they could let her go. That she was totally uninterested in them, and that she couldn't understand why it was necessary to do this to her. So she tried to signal with her eyes that she was willing to cooperate, but they ignored her.

What could they have done that she was such a threat to them?

"Should we just leave her sitting there until we make our getaway, Denise?" said the one with the gaffer tape.

Denise? Rose tried to concentrate. Wasn't her name Dorrit? Or had Rigmor once mentioned that her granddaughter had changed her name? Rose seemed to recall that she had.

"Do you have a better suggestion?" asked Denise.

"We'll call someone and say where she is when this is all over, right?"

Denise nodded.

"But if she's staying there, where are we supposed to pee?" asked the other one.

"You'll have to use the sink, Jazmine."

"While she's looking at me?"

"Just pretend that she's not there. That's the general idea anyway. *I'm* in charge of her, okay?"

"But I can't do a number two in the sink."

"Then you'll just have to go next door. The door isn't locked."

Denise looked directly at Rose. "We'll give you something to drink once in a while, and you'll stay calm; otherwise, I'll knock you out again. Got it?"

Rose blinked a couple of times.

"I mean it. And it'll be harder this time, okay?"

Rose blinked again.

Then she held the pointy object toward the tape around Rose's mouth. "I'm going to poke this through to make a small hole. Part your lips if you can."

Rose tried her best, but as soon as the awl was poked through the tape, she could taste blood.

"Sorryyyyy!" said Denise as the blood seeped out of the hole. "But it's for this, so you can drink," she said, holding up a straw of the type used in hospitals.

She stuck the straw through the hole. Rose winced in pain as the injured skin from her upper lip was pushed into her mouth. She swallowed blood a couple of times before she could suck up the water from a toothpaste-stained glass.

As long as they gave her water, they would let her live, she reasoned.

Even though the weather had been so hot lately that it was regarded as a heat wave in Denmark, it was cool in the bathroom. After a few hours, Rose began to feel cold. Perhaps mainly due to the restraints on her blood flow.

If I can't move I'll develop blood clots, she thought, tensing her calves so that her calf muscle pumps wouldn't stop completely. All in all, her situation was terrible. She knew that much. In this position, she would probably survive for a few days, but maybe the girls didn't need longer than that before they disappeared. And they had said that they would call someone and let them know where she was. What would happen then?

Would she be committed again? The person they called was likely to find her mother or sisters, and then her sisters would come rushing, and who could then prevent them from finding the suicide note and the razor blade? That wasn't good. If she had reached the point where she was going to commit suicide, the psychiatrists wouldn't let her go willingly this time. So wasn't it better to die in here?

I'll keep perfectly still. Then I'm bound to get a blood clot sooner or later. Those girls don't know anything about that sort of thing.

She waited with her breath wheezing out from the straw, wondering why the otherwise persnickety Rigmor had left her dirty laundry in the washing machine, and why despite her age she still kept sanitary pads on the shelf above the tumble dryer, and why she had some old panty hose on a hook even though they were ripped down one side. Did she repair her ripped panty hose? Was that even possible?

She closed her eyes to imagine skilled hands threading the thin fabric, but the image was interrupted by one of her father's face frothing at the mouth and with hate emanating from his eyes.

"You come with me when I tell you to, girl," he hissed. "You will come with me and if I tell you to leave, you'll do that too. Understood?"

The face grew larger and larger, and the words hung in the air in an eternal repetition. The image made Rose's heart pound violently in panic. Her cheeks filled with air, and the wheezing in the straw hit a note like the scream Rose wanted to let out but couldn't.

And right there on the toilet she relieved her bladder. Exactly like on that terrible day when she had felt the vibrations from the pager in her pocket.

The next time Denise brought her water, Rose was dripping with sweat. "Are you too hot?" she asked, turning the thermostat on the radiator all the way down before leaving the bathroom with the door ajar.

There was still some daylight in the hallway, although it was dim. At this time of year it was hard to determine what time it was because it didn't really get dark until around eleven. And it couldn't be that late yet.

"They keep going on and on, Denise," said Jazmine a bit later from the sitting room. "They've shown that clip with Michelle all day now," she continued.

"Then turn off the TV, Jazmine!"

"They know that she was at the nightclub when we committed the robbery and Birna was shot, and they know that she was there with two other women. They seem to suspect that Patrick guy, and he knows our names, Denise. He heard them at the hospital."

"Did he? But it isn't certain that he can remember them, is it?"

"He can describe us—I'm *dead* certain about that. The police are looking for us. I just *know* it, Denise."

"Cut it out, Jazmine. They don't know where we are and no one will recognize us when we've finished with this, will they? Let's go to the bathroom now."

The conversation slowly made sense to Rose despite her inner chaos. Her experience as an investigator blocked out the terrible thoughts, and she was only too eager to let them go.

Jazmine had mentioned a robbery and someone called Birna who had been shot outside a nightclub. Did the girls in there think she knew anything about it?

Rose thought back to the moment when she had first stepped into the apartment and found them. What was the last thing she had said? That she would report them for breaking into Rigmor's apartment.

So that was why. They were afraid of her. She was the enemy and that was why she was sitting here. They would leave her here when they made their escape. No one would call anyone. That was the most obvious conclusion.

The two girls came into the bathroom together, and Rose closed her eyes, pretending to be asleep. The last thing she wanted just now was for them to think she had overheard their conversation.

Denise immediately sat in the sink and peed while Jazmine took off her clothes and got in the shower.

They had both cropped their hair. It was a complete transformation.

"I hate this, Denise. It's taken me more than five years to grow my hair this long. I want to fucking cry," said Jazmine as she squeezed hair dye over her scalp and drew the shower curtain.

"Once we're in Brazil, you can have all the hair extensions you want for next to nothing. So stop whining," Denise said, laughing as she jumped down from the sink. She took a couple of sheets of toilet paper from the roll next to Rose, wiped her crotch, and threw the paper in the basket where Rigmor used to keep her laundry. So that was why her laundry had been thrown in the washing machine.

Rose followed Denise's every move through her half-closed eyes, but Denise didn't look in her direction. Was she already dead in their eyes, or did Denise actually think she was asleep?

Then Denise turned toward the mirror and looked at her short hair while shaking the bottle of hair dye. Rose opened her eyes a little more. There were three scratches down Denise's back—not a pretty sight on such a perfect body.

"Are you sure that Anne-Line won't recognize you, Denise? And what if she doesn't let you in?" came Jazmine's voice from behind the shower curtain.

"I've fooled smarter people than her, Jazmine. I'll bring her down before she knows what hit her," answered Denise, spinning around.

She was staring directly at Rose as if she had sensed her eyes on her.

Rose didn't have time to shut her eyes.

36

Sunday, May 29th, and Monday, May 30th, 2016

Marcus Jacobsen waved a hand to decline the can of beer Carl placed in front of him on the garden table at his home in Rønneholtparken. "No, thank you. I've gone cold turkey, so no cigarettes or alcohol for me. I'm trying to look after myself these days."

Carl nodded and lit a cigarette. Statistically, miracles were bound to happen once in a while. But this was a Carl's Special beer. Could it get any better than that?

"Well, Carl, have you looked at my notes?"

Carl clenched his teeth, shaking his head. "I haven't really had time, but I will do it. I promise. I have them on my desk."

Marcus looked disappointed, and he had every reason to be. After all, he was the one who had taught Carl all he knew about investigative work, and then Carl hadn't taken his advice seriously. It really wasn't okay.

"Okay, Marcus, I might as well confess. I had my doubts about you and the case. You were so obsessed with it back then that I thought it might be wishful thinking on your part to link the two cases. But as I said, I promise to look at them now. That's actually why I've invited you."

"Hmm! So it wasn't just for my sake you invited me. What are you after, then?"

Carl sighed more than he had intended to, but maybe the effect would be beneficial. "As you know, we're a bit worked up at the moment because of Rose, so I thought that you might be able to lend us a hand."

Marcus smiled. "With a case that isn't yours, I assume?"

Carl watched as his cigarette smoke rose in the air. Of course he knew that Marcus wouldn't stab him in the back, but the question was still a bit too forward for his liking.

"You know the drill, Marcus. You get all these conflicting and confusing gut feelings, and I for one hate that. And then there's the business with Rose. We normally rely on her when we need to delve deeper into a case, but she's not able to help us now, is she? We need her more than any of us could have imagined."

Marcus smiled. "So what is it you'd like me to 'delve deeper into,' Carl? What are your gut feelings telling you?"

"That I need to know everything about the Zimmermann family and their background. We already know a good deal about Rigmor's husband, and he definitely wasn't a saint." He told Marcus what they knew about Fritzl Zimmermann's shady past, his later life, and his demise.

Marcus Jacobsen nodded. "No, not what you'd call a role model. But now that you mention it, I think our department had some dealings with the case about the man who drowned in Damhus Lake. So that was him, was it?"

They heard a faint humming sound from the hallway. Morten and Hardy were home.

Marcus smiled. It was a reunion he had been looking forward to. He stood up to greet them in the doorway. It was moving to see their former uncompromising boss bending down to hug his old investigator.

"So, how was your trip, old boy?" asked Marcus when Hardy had finally managed to maneuver his electric wheelchair over to the garden table.

"Well . . . ," he answered almost inaudibly as the red-eyed Morten came out to them and asked in a tearful voice if there was anything he could do for them.

"We're fine, Morten, thanks."

"In that case . . . I think . . . I'll go and lie down," he said, sniffling.

"What's the matter with him?" asked Marcus when they could no longer hear footsteps leading down to the basement.

Hardy looked tired. "A broken heart. It's not a good idea to go out in the sunshine in May if you want to avoid seeing people in love everywhere. He's been wailing like an orphaned seal all the way."

"Well, it's hard to remember that feeling of rejected love!" Marcus shook his head and turned to Carl. He was already back in his role as an investigator. "What do we know about Birgit Zimmermann's husband?"

"Nothing. But it's one of the things we hope you'll be able to tell us about when you've done some digging."

As agreed, they arrived at the steel plant Monday morning at ten and were met at security just left of the main gate. An elderly man and a younger woman were standing behind Leo Andresen, so apparently they were taking the tour seriously.

Leo smiled and pointed at the skinny man. "Yeah, Polle P. is the oldest former employee from here, I worked here for thirty years before retiring, and Lana here is the newest recruit at the plant, so together we should be able to answer any questions you might have about the place over the years."

They all shook hands.

"Polle and I will lead the tour, and Lana is our security officer, so in a minute she'll provide you with hard hats and safety shoes. Dare I ask your shoe sizes, gentlemen?"

All three of them looked down at Assad's and Carl's feet.

"May I suggest a size forty-five for you, Carl, and a forty-one for Assad?" continued Leo.

"You may," said Assad, "but if I don't get a forty-two, you might as well kill me straightaway." He was the only one to laugh.

They left security, and Carl filled them in about their meeting with

Benny Andersson. Judging by their reserved expressions, Andersson didn't require any introduction.

"He was one of the people who received compensation for manganese poisoning," snarled Polle. "I don't know about the others, but Benny definitely didn't have manganese poisoning, if you ask me."

"Who cares? It got rid of him," added Leo, understandably.

"No, he's certainly no heartbreaker," said Carl. "But I have the impression that he was fond of Rose, so he can't be all bad. Do you know what their relationship was with each other?"

"Nothing, I think. He just liked women and *really* hated Arne Knudsen."

"Do you know why?"

"Most of us did, to be honest. Arne wasn't nice to anyone, and especially not Rose. That was clear to everyone who came in contact with them. She shouldn't have been working so closely with her dad," said Polle, throwing out one arm in presentation as they turned a corner and the vastness of the plant appeared before them.

The open areas around the buildings were orderly and surprisingly empty considering the enormous amount of steel that passed through the plant. Where were the three hundred and forty employees? There was no one in sight. Even though the area was the size of a small island and the buildings as huge as aircraft hangars, capable of accommodating thousands of people, three hundred and forty people couldn't just disappear. Carl had imagined mountains of scrap, noise from every corner, and strapping men in coveralls swarming around the place.

Leo Andresen laughed. "It's probably not like you imagined it. Things have changed now. The plant is run electronically nowadays. Highly skilled employees sitting with joysticks, pushing buttons, and looking at monitors. That's the way it's been since we stopped melting scrap metal ourselves. Now it's an export company owned by the Russians, and—"

"And how was it in 1999 when Arne Knudsen died?" interrupted Carl.

"Very, very different, and yet not," said Polle. "First of all, we were more than a thousand employees. There's another company out there on the peninsula now, but back then we were all part of the same organization owned by the investment companies A.P. Møller and EAC. And then came that damn manganese case and a lot of other stuff at the same time, making the company less profitable. In 2002, we went bankrupt. That was the end of an era."

He pointed at a row of stacked, thick steel slabs lying on the concrete floor in the open air.

"Back then, we were a recycling company that bought eight hundred thousand tons of scrap metal a year, melted it, and processed it into sheets, bars, and reinforcing steel. We provided material for bridges and tunnels and all sorts. Today, we receive those Russian slabs you can see lying there, with the one aim of rolling them into sheets."

He opened the door into one of the production areas, which was so huge that Assad put his hand to his hard hat in shock. Carl couldn't take in the sheer size of the place.

"Did the accident happen here?" He pointed at the conveyor belt where the slabs were brought into position, lifted up by cranes with enormous magnets, and transported to other positions. "Was it a whopper like that which killed Arne Knudsen?" he asked.

Polle shook his head. "No, and it didn't happen here either. It was down in the old part of W15. This one is a twenty-ton slab, but the one that killed Arne was only half as heavy." He shrugged. It was still more than enough.

"If Rose still worked here, she'd probably be in that office now," he said as they reached the corner of the hall where a glass partition separated the imposing raw area from a typical factory office. He pointed inside at a pretty young woman wearing blue coveralls looking at a computer screen. They waved at each other. "That's Micha. She's a feeder operator—the same job as Rose was apprenticed to with her dad. He was a feeder operator too. They're the people responsible for the numbered slabs being processed in a specific order. *Everything* in here is preordered. We know exactly when and what to deliver, and who it's for and where it's going. We mark the individual slabs with white numbers and letters, heat them up, and roll them into sheets in the desired dimensions. But you can see all that in a minute."

As they neared the end of the hall, the light changed from cool and efficient to dim and yellowish.

This part of section W15 was much more primitive and more like Carl had imagined. Ingenious iron constructions, bridges, pipes, steel staircases, hoisting devices, slide bars, and a furnace that almost looked like a futuristic miniature version of the silos on his father's farm.

Leo Andresen pointed up at one of the cranes above their heads, hanging from a mass of steel wire, a huge machine by Demag. "It lifts the slabs up from the ground and over to the conveyor belt, which transports them directly into the pusher furnaces. Look, the hatch is opening now so you'll be able to feel the heat. We heat it up to twelve hundred degrees, enough to produce molten slabs."

The group were all silent as they watched the magnet. "That's the one that dropped the slab on Arne Knudsen," said Polle. "It was a chance power cut, they said, but how much you can put it down to chance, I don't know."

"Okay. And who operates a machine like that?" asked Carl as he stepped back from the almost unbearable heat emanating from the furnace. Now he understood why the end wall in the hall led directly out into the open air.

"The people who operate the control panel in the control cabin on the other side of the pusher furnace."

"And who was sitting there on that day?" asked Assad.

"Yes, that's the question. It was in the middle of a shift handover. To be honest, this shouldn't be possible, but we don't know exactly who was sitting in there."

"We asked Benny Andersson and he says it wasn't him in the control cabin."

"Okay, but I don't remember anything about that. Around that time, he was here and there and everywhere, manning different posts in the plant."

"But if Rose and Arne Knudsen were normally up in the office you just showed us where the young woman was sitting, why were they down here when it happened?"

"Oh, you must have misunderstood. That part of the hall with the new feeder operator office where Micha is sitting hadn't been built yet. Back then, there was only this." He turned around toward a wooden building behind them. "They sat up there in the office. And once in a while they came down to the piles of slabs here and marked the ones next in line for the pusher furnace."

Carl looked around. "What do you think, Assad? Does anything jump out at you?"

He looked down at the police report. "All it says is that the magnet failed and that Arne Knudsen broke the safety regulations by standing under a slab that was being hoisted by a crane. No one was held responsible for the incident, which was determined to be an accident, even though it was incredibly seldom that the power failed. Arne Knudsen was deemed to be solely responsible and paid the ultimate price for not heeding the safety regulations."

"So Rose was in the office when it happened?"

"No. Some people came running over from the front area when they heard his screams, and they found Rose right next to him as he drew his last breath. She was standing in total shock with her arms down by her sides, unable to utter a sound and her eyes staring in horror."

"You weren't here then?"

"No," answered Andresen. "It wasn't my shift."

"I was working down at the dock, which is a good bit away from here," said Polle.

"Can you tell us in your capacity as someone who worked with the power supply, what caused the power cut, Leo?"

"We have computer systems that ought to be able to establish exactly that, but they couldn't in this case. My personal opinion is that it must have been one of the employees who caused it because the cut was so brief that the magnet only just released the slab and not a second longer. If you ask me, the timing was too perfect."

"So you're saying it was done deliberately?"

"I can't know that for sure, but it's not something I'd rule out."

Carl sighed. It was seventeen years ago. How the hell could he expect anything more precise than that when neither the police nor the working environment authority reports could offer anything more?

"There might come a time when we can ask Rose about it all," said Carl when they finally arrived back at his office.

Assad shook his head. "Did you hear that I asked them whether Rose could have pushed her dad under the slab when it fell? Their reaction seemed very odd."

"Yes, I heard you. But they looked stranger when you hinted that she might've had an accomplice. Leo Andresen did mention that the power cut could've been deliberate, so they couldn't really have expected to avoid the question."

"But how did they time it, Carl? There was no intercom where they were standing and no cell phones either. It all came down to a split second, right?"

A tall shadow appeared in the doorway. "Hi there! I'm supposed to ask again from the commissioner when you'll be back. I haven't told him you're already here."

"Thanks, Gordon. Good thinking. Tell him that his TV crew will have something to sink their teeth into later today or tomorrow, and that we'll be ever so well behaved."

He didn't look happy. "Anyway, I've spoken with that guy who saw Rigmor Zimmermann stop on a street corner and look back before rushing off, but there wasn't much more to it than that. He hardly remembered anything."

"That's a shame. But have you managed to discover Denise Zimmermann's whereabouts?"

"No, no luck there either. She disappeared from her home address a week ago, on May 23rd. I spoke to the other people who live in her building: some fairly odd types. And I also spoke with her mother. Well, 'spoke' is maybe not the word, because she's a complete mess. I could hardly understand a word she said."

"You said Denise disappeared?"

"Denise told her mother that she'd moved in with a man in Slagelse."

"Seven days ago?" Carl looked despondent. Would they now have to widen their search to the back of beyond? No wonder you could end up feeling a bit weary at times.

Then his telephone rang. "Can you two post a summary on the notice board of the cases we're working on? We can look at it together when I'm finished here." And then he answered the phone.

"Yes, it's me," sounded a listless voice at the other end. It was Marcus Jacobsen. "Have you looked at my notes, Carl?" he asked.

"Yeah, uh, kind of."

"Well, can you look at them now, then? I'll wait."

Carl rummaged through the paperwork on his desk before finding one of the notes. It was written in Marcus Jacobsen's angular but easily legible handwriting:

Notes on the Stephanie Gundersen Case:

1) Hardy noticed a woman by the name of Stephanie Gundersen in the audience at a school-based crime-prevention talk.
2) Check the parent lists for the 7th and 9th grades again.
3) Parent-teacher meetings led by S. Gundersen together with the regular class teacher twice ended in arguments with parents—and even once with a single mother!
4) What was S.G. doing in Østre Anlæg Park? She was supposed to be going to badminton.

"Yes, I have one of your notes in front of me. It's a list of four points."

"Good. Those are the four things we never managed to get to the bottom of during the investigation. We'd already spent too much time on the case, at the same time as we were being inundated with lots of other important cases. So I had to make the call that we had done all we could in relation to Stephanie Gundersen's murder and wouldn't make any further progress at that time. The conclusion was that we had to shelve the case even though I really hated having to do it. You know how it is. It's terrible to shelve a case, because deep inside you know that it'll eat away at you.

"Anyway, I found the notes when I cleared out my office at HQ, back when I retired, and since then I've had them hanging on my fridge door, much to my wife's annoyance—while she was still alive, that is. She always said, 'Why can't you just let it go, Marcus?' But it doesn't work like that."

Carl agreed. There hadn't been many cases like that which he'd had to shelve, but there had been a few.

"The way I see it, question number four is particularly conspicuous. What were you thinking when you wrote it?"

"Probably the same as you're thinking now: Why would you skip your weekly badminton session for a walk in the park? For romantic reasons, of course."

"But you didn't find out who Stephanie met?"

"No. Strangely enough, there was nothing to indicate that she had a partner at the time. She was a discrete girl, you know. Not someone to shove her love life in other people's faces."

Carl knew the type. "So what about point number one? What was it Hardy saw when he met this Stephanie?"

"He'd been assigned to one of those boring crime-prevention jobs we have to do from time to time in schools, and when he was there he saw the most beautiful woman he'd ever laid eyes on smiling ever so sweetly at him from the far wall of the classroom. He found it difficult to concentrate. And when she was murdered, he felt frustrated, sad, and angry for days because someone had taken the life of such a lovely creature. He was really eager to help, but as you know he had enough to do with his own investigations."

"Stephanie was a beautiful woman. I know that much."

"She could throw any man off-balance, Hardy told me. Ask him yourself."

"Have you saved the parent lists for the seventh and ninth grades that you mention in point two?"

"Hmm, Carl, I get the impression that you haven't looked at the material I gave you at all. You'll find the list of names on the other piece of paper I gave you at the restaurant. Take a look. You might find something."

"I'm really sorry, Marcus. This is embarrassing. This whole business with Rose has been occupying my mind." He looked again at the piece of paper with four points. "And what about the third point on the list? Arguments must be part and parcel of parent-teacher meetings, don't you think? I certainly remember a few when Vigga and I exchanged words with Jesper's teachers."

"Yes, I'm sure you're right. And the two couples—the Carstensens and the Willumsens—who caused the arguments were also very forthcoming when I inquired about it. Basically, both sets of parents had the same issue, and according to the regular class teacher it wasn't a very pleasant discussion, and also rather unusual. In the third case, involving the single mother, it was something of a more personal nature, and there were undertones that the regular teacher couldn't gauge. The mother—Birthe Frank, I believe she was called—was causing a scene because she thought Stephanie was inappropriately influencing her daughter with all the attention she was giving her. The mother seemed jealous, according to the regular teacher."

"So, basically, Stephanie was simply too pretty?"

Marcus laughed hoarsely and coughed a couple of times at the other end. So he was still feeling the effects of quitting smoking.

"You're not as stupid as you look, Carl. The two couples were both parents to boys who were completely besotted every time they came home from school. One of the couples had even caught their son masturbating over her school photo and were of the opinion that Stephanie ought to tone down her feminine charms."

"And what does that tell you?"

"Yeah, what indeed? In more than half of all homicide cases, sex plays a direct or indirect role, as you know. And Stephanie's mere existence was something of a challenge in that area, as I understand it."

"So you think I should look for someone who either had or wanted to have sex with her?"

"No idea. But now it's out there."

"But she wasn't raped, was she?"

"No, she was hit from behind and murdered. Full stop."

"Okay, thanks. I'm sorry I didn't ask more when you gave me the notes, Marcus."

He laughed. "I've had them for twelve years now. So one week wasn't going to make a difference, was it? I knew we'd get to it at some point, Carl."

After their conversation, Carl rummaged a bit more on his desk. Where the hell was the other note?

"*Gordon! Assad!* Come in here," he shouted. He heard grumbling from the corridor before they appeared.

"Marcus Jacobsen gave me two notes the other day, and now I can't find one of them. Do you know anything about that? It was written on the same kind of lined paper as this one."

He held up the list with four points in front of them.

"You know what, Carl? I think you should come with us to the situation room and see something," said Assad. "Gordon's been very busy."

The lanky guy apologized that he had been in Carl's office to make copies of some of the papers on his desk. But he had no idea where the original was for the other note.

"But don't worry, there are copies of everything in here."

Carl followed them, and when he stepped into the room he immediately saw the five sheets of paper lined up on the big notice board.

"Here are the five cases we're working on at the moment," said Gordon.

Had he said *five*? How could it be so many?

Carl looked at all the sheets.

On the far left, Gordon had pinned up a sheet entitled "The Rose Case." The only thing written on that page was "Rose's dad died on May 18th, 1999." Then came "The Zimmermann Case," "The Stephanie Gundersen Case," "The Hit-and-Run Case," and "The Nightclub Case" involving the robbery and the shooting of the Icelandic woman.

On all the sheets there were notes about the victims' times of death and a little additional information.

"What the heck are the hit-and-run and nightclub cases doing there?" asked Carl. "They've got nothing to do with us."

Gordon smiled. "Yeah, yeah, I know. But since I've ended up dealing with the TV crew and answering all their strange questions, I reckoned those cases could also hang here just so I could keep up to date."

Carl grunted. That man was a piece of work. If he was so keen to take part in the investigation of those two cases, why didn't he just move up to the second floor? It wasn't like he hadn't had the offer.

"Well, as long as Bjørn doesn't get the wrong idea, I suppose it's okay. Where are Marcus's notes?"

"I've pinned the two sheets of notes under "The Stephanie Case," you'll notice," said Gordon proudly.

Assad couldn't contain himself any longer. "Before you look at the list of names, Carl, take a look at this photo." He placed a blown-up color photo in front of him. "Look. We've just received this school photo. It's a photo of the ninth-grade class at Bolman's Independent School from 2003. Have a good look at it."

Carl did as he said. It was one of those usual class photos that one hated a few years later and that many years later one regretted having thrown out. What was special about it?

"Stephanie Gundersen is standing lined up behind the students with the other teachers," said Gordon, pointing at her.

Carl nodded, now recognizing her. "She was really the prettiest of them all," he said. "But where are you going with it?"

"It's not her you need to look at just now, Carl. It's the girl in front of Stephanie—with Stephanie's hands on her shoulders."

Carl squinted. It was a girl wearing her hair up, blue lipstick, and with an expression that was both cheeky and happy at the same time.

"Her name is Dorrit Frank, as far as I can make out from the names underneath."

"Exactly." Assad smiled.

What was he smiling about? "Out with it. I can't quite . . . Do you mean that . . . ?"

"Yes, Dorrit is Denise. She changed her name at some point."

Carl felt a shiver down his spine. "Really? But what about the surname?"

"Denise is called Denise F. Zimmermann. The 'F' stands for 'Frank.' We've checked. And now look at the list of these kids' parents on Marcus's note."

He quickly scanned the list. There it was. Not Birthe Frank, as Marcus remembered it, but Birgit Frank. Birgit Frank Zimmermann.

"I noticed it on the buzzer for her apartment when I was doing my rounds of the Borgergade area, Carl. A single initial for a middle name can be more important than it seems."

Gordon was right. This was a real game changer, possibly linking two seemingly unrelated cases. Motive, people, and murder weapon. But to what and how?

"I need to tell Marcus about this immediately."

He dashed to his office and already had Marcus on the other end of the phone after three rings.

"Marcus, listen to this! The single mother who had an argument with Stephanie Gundersen at the parent-teacher meeting wasn't Birthe Frank but Birgit Frank, and her daughter was called Dorrit before she later changed it to Denise," he said without so much as a hello. "So the mother's full name was and remains Birgit Frank Zimmermann, regardless of whatever mysterious reason lies behind her only using Frank back then—it might even have been just in the context of the school that she only used Frank."

There was a sigh at the other end. The relief was audible.

"So *now* you have the connection between the three women: Stephanie Gundersen, Birgit Zimmermann, and her mother, Rigmor Zimmermann. Satisfied? All three women had some sort of connection with each other. And two of them end up being murdered years apart in exactly the same way. Do you think we should just call that a coincidence, boss?" asked Carl.

For a moment it was deadly quiet at the other end, and then came the outburst.

"Birgit Zimmermann has a middle name that begins with 'F'; of course she bloody does. How did we miss it back then? So in some way she was already in our sights when we investigated the Stephanie Gundersen case."

37

Anneli had had luck on her side once again. She had managed to commit yet another atrocity without being seen by witnesses or passing cars in the neighborhood.

With a ferocious thud, the heavy-footed girl had banged her head against a lamppost and clearly broken her neck, because the angle of her head didn't look like it should.

In many respects, Bertha, alias Roberta, Lind had proved to be a creature of habit. Her bicycle route and the twice-weekly circuit training she no doubt hoped would help her squeeze into a size fourteen were as routine as always, just as Anneli had anticipated.

It had been hot that Sunday, and everyone in Denmark felt the heat. Accordingly, Bertha had worn a minuscule top that slid up her sweaty back, revealing a figure that wasn't the result of good eating habits. At least ten times while cycling, she had alternated between sending text messages and pulling down her top at the back, and the eleventh time proved to be once too many. Taking a wide left turn, she completely lost concentration and overcompensated with the handle bars, making her turn too sharp.

Anneli had driven in second gear, maintaining a speed of eighteen to twenty kilometers an hour to ensure that she didn't get too close to Bertha and remained out of earshot. But when Bertha's bike unexpectedly veered off course a little, she really put her foot down and swerved into Bertha with the side of the car.

Strange, how far a body that heavy can fly, thought Anneli as she hit the brake and watched the helpless course of the body in the side mirror.

"I didn't see her eyes, but mission accomplished, all the same," she said to herself immediately after. Then she parked the little red Renault in a deserted side street off Amager Boulevard, abandoning it after wiping down the interior and taking her rubbish with her.

As Anneli had expected, the TV news didn't describe this hit-and-run incident in the same way as the others. But there was still quite a lot of publicity, because once again it had involved a driver who had left a victim to die. However, in this case, it was believed that the woman may have been hit by a larger vehicle whose driver probably hadn't noticed what had happened.

The morning after, Anneli heard on the radio that the police technicians believed that Bertha had swerved too far off the bicycle path onto the road and been knocked off by a passing truck, and that the strength of the impact when she landed combined with her body weight had caused her death rather than having been hit by the truck. As with all accidents occurring when someone was making a turn, it was tragic but couldn't be compared with the more frequent right-turn accidents that were a constant risk for cyclists in Copenhagen.

Anneli was immensely pleased. Up until now, she had stuck to her plan and remained steadfast to her mission to rid the world of human scum. Of course, the novelty had worn off, as had the immediate intoxication and exhilaration. After all, she was a seasoned killer now. And three strikes in just eight days gave a certain confidence.

This Monday morning, it seemed like everyone had decided to leave her alone. Nobody spoke to her, but it was obvious that they all knew how ill she was and that she had come to work directly after her radiation therapy. So much for her manager's discretion.

Anneli didn't care. The most important thing for her was to dedicate herself to her upcoming missions and assess their risk.

Just now, when parliament was about to break for its summer recess, the media quickly found other news to write about. Apart from the hit-and-run case, which took up several pages in all the newspapers, the main story was Birna's death last night at Copenhagen University Hospital. The hunt for what was being called the Nightclub Killer was already in full swing.

Even though it might feel tempting and logical, there were two things that stopped Anneli from immediately turning in the girls who had killed the young woman. More than anything, she wanted to kill them, but she wouldn't be able to if they were in prison. On top of that, she would run the risk that if the girls ended in police custody, they might voice their suspicion about Anneli's involvement in Michelle's murder in order to secure a reduced sentence. So no matter what, Birna's death could tighten the rope around Anneli's neck. During the questioning of Michelle's boyfriend, Patrick, the police would ultimately put two and two together and link the three girls. And once the police caught up with them, Anneli would be in potential danger.

Anneli looked at the clock. She had just finished with a nice client who had asked for a modest amount to help her through the next ten days until she was back to work and so had been granted a crisis loan. And now Anneli awaited this client's complete opposite. It had become something of a habit for this client to just turn up roughly every five days with new requests, all of which, strangely enough, cost fifteen hundred kroner, and which Anneli had no authority to grant her. It wasn't that she was a bad person, but at the moment Anneli had more important things to deal with. The developments in the cases concerning the robbery and Birna's murder were unpredictable and had to be stopped. So she had to direct her focus on ridding herself of these two loose ends: Denise and Jazmine.

She didn't think a car was a suitable murder weapon any longer. The girls were probably already on their guard, so it was unlikely that she would have the opportunity to get close enough to them. Lucky for her, there had been quite a few shootings in Copenhagen and those suburbs most ravaged by gang crime. If she could get her hands on a gun and make the executions look like a gang shooting, the police were bound to begin looking in other directions than hers. And if everything went sideways anyway, at least she would have a weapon she could use to kill herself quickly and painlessly.

Anneli went to the reception area and informed the two clients waiting for her that she would unfortunately have to ask them to reschedule their appointments. They looked dissatisfied and disappointed, especially the one who had probably come to beg for the usual fifteen hundred kroner. Anneli didn't care.

"I have someone threatening suicide on the phone," she just said and turned on her heel before slamming the door to her office. She searched for a minute before finding the number of a client who had an appointment later in the week. His name was Amin, and he was one of the many Somalians living in the Vesterbro district of Copenhagen who had found a way to supplement his benefits in order to provide for his hastily growing family.

Amin had been in jail a couple of times for being in possession of an illegal weapon, theft, and dealing cannabis, but he had never displayed any violent tendencies. When he attended his appointments with Anneli, he exuded only happiness and gratitude for the little help she could offer.

He turned up just after lunch and placed two well-worn guns on her desk so she could choose. She took the one that looked newest and easiest to use, as well as receiving a whole box of bullets. He apologized that he couldn't get hold of a silencer but gave her some useful tips on other ways to muffle the sound. After a short introduction in releasing the safety, loading the gun, taking out the cartridges, and cleaning the barrel, they agreed that on top of the six thousand kroner in cash, she would also grant him money for clothes for his entire family, and Anneli would try to postpone the compulsory work placement that was looming over him. They swore that this meeting had only been about his family's need for clothes and that the true purpose of the meeting would remain between them.

She had hardly managed to hide the gun before her manager waltzed into her office to offer her crisis counseling.

"I'm devastated that you've had to deal with this on your own, Anne-Line. Not only the terrible cancer diagnosis, but also losing two clients in such awful circumstances over the course of a few days."

Had she said crisis counseling? thought Anneli. Who the hell needed crisis counseling when the reality was that what she needed the most was a silencer?

When the manager left again, having given reassurances of her support, Anneli informed the secretary that she had unfortunately discovered that quite a few of her case files needed to be updated after her absence and so she would have to dedicate the rest of the day to admin work.

Knowing that she wouldn't be disturbed, she spent a couple of hours surfing the Internet reading articles about gang executions. When she felt she had read enough, she decided how she would imitate them. Most important, a gang execution was about moving in and out as quickly as possible. One shot to the back of the head of each girl and then ditch the gun in the harbor. That was all there was to it.

The problem of the missing silencer would be more difficult to deal with, but the Internet even had advice about that.

Webersgade was noted for its small, charming association houses, which had formerly accommodated two to three working-class families. But over the last few decades they had become increasingly attractive, and their prices had soared to ridiculous heights because the middle classes found them appealing despite the fact they were small in size and had tiny rooms and impractical staircases between the floors. The reality, however, was that the Webersgade houses were badly located due to the busy traffic that connected the center of town with Lyngbyvej and North Zealand. Anneli knew all about these houses, which were so patinated from pollution that they could easily have been mistaken for dusty houses in English mining towns. She had rented a damp attic and half the first floor of a house like this for half her life. She never saw the owner, who lived on the ground floor. He was a mechanical engineer and preferred tropical heat, which had the unfortunate result that he didn't invest any money in the upkeep of the house.

When Anneli got home later today, she would let herself into the mechanical engineer's apartment, where he stored all his boxes of junk and long metal shelves covered in all manner of engine and machine parts. In this treasure chamber, she would look for an oil filter whose construction made it well suited as a silencer, according to the Internet. Of course, an oil filter didn't have an exit hole, but once she had pushed it down on the barrel and fired the gun, the bullet would find its own way out. At least that was what had happened in the video she saw online.

When she was finished there, she would drive to Stenløse, park her Ka in the usual parking space, and keep a close eye on the girls' apartment to see if there was any sign of life behind the curtains. If there was, she would ring the doorbell, force her way in when they answered, make them kneel, and quickly finish them off.

38

Monday, May 30th, 2016

They were sitting in front of a woman who in the space of only a few days had gone from being on the verge of going to the dogs to actually completing the transformation.

The stench of tobacco and alcohol was brutally invasive. If the alcohol didn't get her soon, then all the cigarettes she had smoked would.

"I don't understand what she's saying," whispered Assad. But Carl had questioned worse. At least she answered.

"You say you don't remember a Stephanie Gundersen who was a substitute teacher for your daughter's class. But according to what we've heard, you two had a serious run-in. We've heard that you had a big fight at one of the parent-teacher conferences. Don't you remember that, Birgit?"

She shook her head in bewilderment.

"She was the substitute teacher at Bolman's who was murdered in Østre Anlæg Park. My former boss actually questioned you in connection with that back in 2004."

Birgit Zimmermann held up a finger in the air and nodded. Finally they had a connection.

"Do you remember why you were so agitated at the meeting? What happened between you and that Stephanie?"

In her drunken stupor, she shook her head and pointed her finger in the air again. "I know what you're up to, ha-ha. You must think I'm an idiot and that you can pin something on me. But let me tell you, that if you want to know anything about that, you'd be better off talking to my mother."

"That will prove difficult because your mother is dead, Birgit."

"Oh, oops, I forgot. But then you can ask my daughter. And you can also ask her who killed my mother."

"What do you mean? Are you hinting that Denise killed your mother?"

"Ha-ha, you're at it again," she said, laughing hoarsely. "So you *do* think I'm an idiot, but I didn't say what you just said. They're your words."

"May I say something?" asked Assad. As if he would keep quiet if she said no.

She looked at him a little confused, as if she had only just noticed he was there, and almost appeared to be trying to remember where she knew him from.

"It seems that your daughter didn't have the best relationship with her grandmother. Is that right?"

She smiled. "Well, aren't you the clever one. They hated each other, to be blunt."

Assad kept direct eye contact so she couldn't avoid looking at him. "And why was that, Birgit? Was it because Denise suddenly turned her back on her family—something Stephanie Gundersen helped her with?"

He had expected a reaction, that much was clear, but not that she would hold her breath for a moment after having sprayed him with saliva when she laughed in his face.

"Let's say that, chocolate man," she said with a sniff. "That sounds perfect."

And then she collapsed backward on the sofa and went out like a light.

Their audience was over.

"We didn't do too well there, Carl," said Assad back at the station. There was no reason for him to say "we."

Carl nodded to the security guards.

"I can see it in your faces," he said to them. "Do I have to report to Lars Bjørn's office again?"

They shook their heads. "No, this time it's the police commissioner's office," one of them said, laughing.

Carl turned to Assad. "We're agreed that we're going to take this case to the end, right, Assad?"

He nodded.

"You and Gordon dig up all you can find about the Zimmermann family, okay? I want to know everything. When was Birgit married? What happened to her husband? How long had Denise been at Bolman's Independent School? Where is the teacher who was at the meeting with Stephanie and Birgit Zimmermann? What is there of any worth in Rigmor Zimmermann's estate? Anything like that so we can build up a better picture of this odd family. And one more thing: Find Denise Zimmermann even if it means you have to drive all the way to Slagelse."

The police commissioner was not alone. Marcus Jacobsen was already sitting at the glass table on one of the strange leather chairs with three legs, nodding in a friendly manner.

"Take a seat," said the commissioner.

Carl felt strange. The time had finally come after many years at HQ when he was sitting in the sanctuary with all the portraits of the commissioner's predecessors staring down at him.

"I'll get straight to the point, Carl Mørck," said the commissioner. "I apologize that I was misled in relation to the percentage of solved cases in your department. It was based on a misunderstanding that has now been rectified, and your department will continue as before." He nodded to Carl. "I want you to establish a better relationship with the TV crew here to make a program for *Station 3*. They will be shadowing you for the rest of the day. And I recommend you give them something to make them happy."

Carl nodded. He would damn well give them something.

"Marcus here tells me that the old Stephanie Gundersen case and the murder of Rigmor Zimmermann have been linked to each other down in your department."

Carl looked at Marcus with slight reproach, but he shook his head dismissively.

"While the case technically belongs to Lars Bjørn's department, and I seriously doubt that he will hand it over willingly, the situation is that his department have their hands full with the hit-and-run murders. Apart from that, I'm in charge of who does what, and I am assigning the case to you, Carl."

Pure revenge for the embarrassment Lars Bjørn caused him in front of the judicial committee, thought Carl. And the man responsible for this turn of events was sitting right next to him.

He winked at Marcus to thank him.

"Bring the TV crew up to speed with how you linked the cases and make sure they get some good shots, because we want to be able to see the efficiency of the police when the show is broadcast. Finally, I would like to add that Marcus Jacobsen has agreed to join HQ as an external consultant. I have no doubt that that his experience will prove more than beneficial when the need arises."

Carl nodded to Marcus. Brilliant news. But Marcus signaled that Carl would need to take the initiative now. Carl didn't understand immediately what he meant, but Marcus managed to make him understand that they weren't finished here yet with a few jerks of his head in the direction of the commissioner.

Carl cleared his throat. "Well, thank you, and we will do everything we can to solve the Stephanie Gundersen and Rigmor Zimmermann cases. I'd also like to apologize for my behavior the other day. It won't happen again."

A rare smile spread across the commissioner's face.

The desired balance had been reestablished.

It felt great walking past Lars Bjørn's office. They say revenge is sweet, but that was an understatement. Revenge was amazing.

He nodded to Lis and Mrs. Sørensen in recognition of their indirect role and was still smiling as he almost bumped into Mona. They stood for a moment only half a meter apart, and Carl noticed how tired she looked.

"Have you made any progress with Rose?" she asked politely, but her mind was clearly elsewhere. Her skin was pale and once again she emanated vulnerability and the form of melancholia brought about by wasted opportunities.

"Are you okay, Mona?" he asked automatically, hoping that she would break down crying in his arms and confess how unhappy she had been every second since they broke up.

"Yes, thanks," she said dryly. "But I probably shouldn't have eaten the prawns in the canteen. Prawns have never agreed with me."

He could feel that his smile had frozen as she walked over to her office.

"Her daughter is very ill, Carl," said Lis. "She's got a lot on her plate."

39

Monday, May 30th, 2016

Olaf Borg-Pedersen's TV crew had already lined up and turned on a couple of cameras in the middle of the corridor, capturing Carl's tired descent to the cellar. There was even one in his office, and behind Carl's desk sat the TV producer himself with his sound technician and photographer, waiting like vultures for someone to draw his last breath.

"And Inspector Carl Mørck is a busy man," he mouthed off as soon as Carl walked in. "*Station 3* have been granted access for a few days to follow what goes on behind the scenes as the police work to make society a better place."

He nodded to his cameraman, who hurried over to the camera and dismounted it from the tripod.

"We are faced with terrible actions every day that ruin the lives of innocent people."

They're not all innocent, thought Carl while trying to avoid the handheld camera capturing more images of his already annoyed expression.

"A hit-and-run driver is on the loose and young women continue to fall victim to the killer. *Station 3* would like to contribute to putting a stop to this. Perhaps Carl Mørck has hit a dead end that our viewers can help him out of."

You're the one at a dead end, idiot. It's not even our case, so how about doing your job properly, he thought while nodding and conceiving a new and viable idea to irritate the chief of homicide and the police commissioner even more.

"Yes," he said seriously. "The public is often our best ally. Where would we be without alert members of the public keeping an eye on unusual situations and events?"

He turned to face the camera.

"But as long as our internal system prevents me from working on cases that have been assigned to others, I can't help you with this particular case."

"Are you saying that this case is the jurisdiction of another department?"

"Yes, and here in Department Q we're not supposed to get involved in ongoing cases, even though it might shed new light on them."

"Would you call that shortsighted? Shouldn't the police think outside the box?"

Carl nodded. As the police commissioner had requested, the program finally had something to pursue. Olaf Borg-Pedersen was almost drooling.

"So are we to understand that your hands are tied in relation to the most recent hit-and-run incident?"

The most recent hit-and-run incident? Carl had no idea what he was talking about.

"Just a minute," he interrupted. "Let me get my assistant. You want the recordings to be realistic, right? And he would normally be here when we discuss the latest developments."

He found Gordon and Assad talking in the situation room, apparently unaware of the chaos Carl had been thrown into.

"How did it go with the police commissioner?" asked Assad.

Carl nodded. "Fine, thanks. But what the hell is going on? Has there been another hit-and-run murder?"

"We don't know yet," answered Gordon. "It doesn't resemble the other murders. More like a nasty accident."

"Fill me in quickly. The vultures in there want to—"

"And here we are in the Department Q situation room," came a sudden voice from the doorway, making Carl jump. He turned around toward Olaf Borg-Pedersen, who had a microphone stuck halfway in his mouth and was being closely followed by his colleague with the handheld camera. "As far as we understand, this is the room where the cases are linked together and scrutinized, and where the team try to gain an overview of all the events," he continued. "On the notice board on the wall here, we can see the cases the team are working on at the moment. Can you explain what we're looking at, Carl Mørck?"

"Sorry," he said, doing his best to hide the information on the notice board from the camera. He damn well didn't want the Zimmermann case to be spotted by anyone on the second floor. That would be rubbing their noses in it too much. "To enable us to best solve these cases, we can't go into too much detail regarding our methods in this program."

"That's understandable." Olaf Borg-Pedersen nodded but looked like a man who was determined to get the shots he wanted anyway. "We spoke earlier about the hit-and-run murders. Only four days ago the young Michelle Hansen was massacred in Stenløse, and the incident was witnessed by two innocent children. Before that, Senta Berger was killed under similar circumstances, and yesterday the victim was Bertha Lind on Amager. What do you have to say about that? Can Department Q already at this stage link this latest terrible incident to the others?" he asked.

"Well," interrupted Gordon, "in contrast to the other cases, we still don't know if Bertha Lind was hit intentionally. And in order to link cases like these, there have to be either skid marks with clear tire markings or skid marks indicating the same type of rubber as in the previous cases."

Carl looked disapprovingly at the lanky sod. This wasn't meant to get too serious.

"Yes. The way we see it, skid marks or no skid marks," he interrupted, "there definitely seems to be a serial killer on the loose, and it's probably time for the press to be given more than the spare information we have provided so far. However, that's up to Head of

Communications Janus Staal, so you'll have to go back up to the second floor."

Olaf Borg-Pedersen stood up on his toes. "I couldn't help but notice that you've put up the case being referred to as 'The Nightclub Case' next to this one. Are we actually dealing with a cluster of interconnected cases?"

Carl suppressed a sigh. What an idiot! Why on else would the cases be next to each other? "That's something we can't rule out. The young woman, Birna Sigurdardottir, who has now tragically passed away, was on social benefits like the others and around the same age. Did they know each other? Were they involved in something together? That's the question. But maybe *Station 3* viewers can help us with that. And good luck with the interviews with the communications department. Perhaps you'll have the opportunity to touch on the police policy that sometimes hinders us in working together across departments and cases."

When the TV crew had left, Carl grabbed a well-deserved cup of coffee in his office while laughing out loud with relief. What a load of rubbish he had spouted off. It was hardly what Bjørn and the commissioner had imagined. Some people might even call it an ambush, but the fact of the matter was that it finally enabled him to get rid of those idiots.

Then he heard a commotion in the corridor, and a second later Assad and Gordon burst into his office together.

Gordon was first and sounded out of breath. "The technicians have now concluded that it *was* the red Peugeot that was used to hit Michelle the first time, and it was the *same* car used to kill Senta Berger, Carl," he almost cheered. "Lots of traces such as hair and blood on the hood and the fender."

Assad stood next to him groaning. "Everything is spinning around in my head just now, Carl. Can't you just—"

"It's highly likely that Michelle Hansen was connected with the robbery at the nightclub," continued Gordon. "I've spoken to one of the people who questioned Patrick Pettersson, who was Michelle's boyfriend, and Patrick swears that he wasn't involved and has been extremely cooperative. But Pasgård isn't satisfied and has brought him in for a third questioning. They are squeezing him for more details as we speak. I think Pasgård will let him go anytime now, so I thought we could lure him down here before he disappears."

Lure? thought Carl. Gordon was on a mission, but if it annoyed Pasgård, he was in.

"Do you mind if I say something? Shouldn't we discuss what we've discovered in the Zimmermann case first?" interrupted Assad. "Carl, you had a lot of questions and I'd like to have the chance to answer them, if you don't mind."

Carl nodded. Were these two in competition with each other now?

Assad looked at his notepad. "You asked when Birgit Zimmermann was married. I assume you mean to Denise Zimmermann's father?"

"Yes. Were there others?"

"There were. In 1984, when she was eighteen years old, she married a Yugoslavian migrant worker, but they were divorced three months later. In 1987 she was remarried. This time to a former captain in the US Army who was working as a bartender in central Copenhagen. That year she became pregnant with Denise, who was baptized Dorrit when she was born in 1988. The American was the one with the surname Frank, of course. James Lester Frank to be precise. Born in Duluth, Minnesota, in 1958. He hasn't paid tax in Denmark since 1995, making me assume he moved back to the US. I'll follow up on that if you think it's worthwhile."

He seemed very keen to move on.

"Thanks. I think we should pass this on to Marcus to follow up. He's already looking at the case," said Carl.

"And then there was your second question. Denise had attended a school in Rødovre but switched to Bolman's Independent School in the third grade and left after the ninth grade in June 2004."

"So a few weeks after Stephanie Gundersen was murdered. Am I right?" asked Carl.

Assad nodded. "Yes. And the teacher who was present at the parent-teacher meeting with Stephanie when she and Stephanie argued with Denise's mother a few months before still works at the school but couldn't remember the meeting or Denise's mother. But she remembered their substitute teacher being murdered in the middle of the exam period and how annoying that had been."

"Because it happened during the exam period?"

"Yes, actually. She had to step in and take Stephanie's place as a proctor for the final-year exams and certainly didn't sound like someone who had grieved at the time."

"That's a bit cynical," said Gordon.

Assad nodded. "She really sounds like one of the witches from Ball Mountain."

"You mean Bald Mountain, Assad," Carl corrected him.

Assad looked at Carl as if he was crazy. Did it really matter in this connection what the name of the mountain was?

"It was far too difficult to talk with the internal revenue service or the probate court. To be honest, they weren't very cooperative. But Lis helped me—she's a real spot when it comes to that sort of thing, Carl."

Spot? "You mean a real sport, Assad."

Carl had hit a nerve. "Can you not stop interrupting me all the time, Carl?"

Carl nodded. "Yes, but 'can you not stop interrupting me' isn't quite what you mean, Assad. It would be better if you said, 'can you stop interrupting me all the time.'"

That was the final straw. "It's the same damn thing, Carl!" Paying no attention to the fact that Gordon and Carl were shaking their heads, he continued his tirade. "I've put up with it for many years now, but I have to ask you to stop correcting me *constantly*, Carl!"

Carl raised his eyebrows. Did he really correct him that much? He wanted to protest but said nothing, noticing Gordon patting Assad's shoulder. Two against one on a Monday. Who could be bothered with that fight?

Assad took a deep breath and looked down at his notes. "Lis found out that Rigmor Zimmermann was very aff . . ." He thought for a moment. ". . . afflu . . . ent." He glared at Carl, who wanted to nod but didn't dare.

"As well as the six million we already knew she had in the bank, she had stocks to the value of four million and also owned three apartments. One in Borgergade, which is where Birgit Zimmermann lives, one in Rødovre above the old shoe shop her husband owned back in the day, and then one in Stenløse."

Carl whistled. "A rich lady and no mistake. And you say that she owned an apartment in Stenløse. That's odd. That's where Rose lives."

Assad nodded. "Yes, Carl." He turned toward Gordon. "This will be news to you, too, Gordon, because I've only just found out."

Gordon shrugged. Was he supposed to be impressed?

"You won't believe this. Rose's neighbor is called Zimmermann. Rigmor Zimmermann—to be precise!"

40

Monday, May 30th, 2016

"**Everyone at the plant** hates you, Rose. *Everyone*. They smile at you, but when you turn your back they're bent over double laughing about how bad you are at your job. *Ha-ha-haaaa,* they laugh, but you also make them feel uncomfortable because they know how dangerous it is to have someone like you at the plant. So it's about time you pull yourself together before something goes wrong."

Her father looked at his sheet, marked a couple of slabs with white, and then pointed a yellow finger at her. When he pointed that accusing finger, there was no knowing what it might lead to, because Rose's father had a habit of ensuring that he kept hurting her in new ways. He lived and breathed for the pleasure it gave him to bring her down, and nothing was beneath him.

She knew that most of what he said wasn't true, but she just couldn't take it anymore. The distress of not knowing when he would attack next drained her of energy, and a couple of days ago she had decided that it had to stop.

"You should be grateful that I bother to tell you before you hear it from someone else. But you need to know that I'm the only one who defends you, Rose. Don't forget it. And you do need to earn some money, also for your mom's sake." He seemed genuinely touched by his own lies but changed in a second as always, and his expression hardened. "It's never been cheap to have you hanging around in the house, but that's more than your small brain can grasp, isn't it?"

He took a couple of steps back as the magnet lifted up the next slab, noting that she was about to protest. His eyes began to glare with pleasure and contempt, and his mouth widened to unimaginable proportions. His teeth were like stone pillars and the spray of spit forming a cloud around him washed her away.

"And on top of everything else, I have to do all your work. If only management knew. It's not like they're doing well as it is, so maybe I'd be doing them a favor by telling them how I think you're doing. So what do you think I should do, hmm? And I'll tell you something else . . ."

Rose was clutching the vibrating pager in her pocket, using all her strength to block out his words and fill her lungs to their breaking point so that the words that were always on the tip of her tongue could explode in his face.

"If you don't stop now, you bastard, I'll . . . !"

And as expected, he stopped. The world around him disappeared as a blissful smile spread across his nasty face. Moments like this were the best of his life. Rose knew that nothing could compare with it.

"What will you do?"

When Rose's hallucinations reached the point between unconsciousness and reality, she tried to wriggle free. Since the girls had tied her up more than three days ago, she had relived the same dream over and over again. In this state the words tended to merge together to pure black, while her memories of the sounds from the other side of the furnace at the steel plant took center stage. The same thing over and over for three days. Every time she tried to return to reality, her nightmare continued with the sound of the rolled slab being cooled down quickly with water. It was a high-pitched whistling sound that she had been unable to bear ever since.

"You won't do anything," sneered her father through the steam. "And you never will," he said, pointing at her.

And then Rose touched the pager while for the last time taking in the scorn he threw at her.

That moment would become her ultimate triumph. The happiness of her father's accusing finger freezing as the shadow was released from above.

Afterward, she couldn't remember the sound of the magnet releasing the slab—only the sound of his body when the steel colossus hit him, crushing every bone in his lower body.

She woke up gradually with the feeling of sweat gathering on her eyelashes. She half opened one eye, realizing once again where she was and that her already weakened state was worsening.

Rose's legs hurt terribly. The slightest shiver of her calves shot up through her nervous system like needles. In contrast, she hadn't been able to feel her feet for more than two days, and the same went for her forearms and hands. Of course she'd tried to wriggle herself free. If only she was able to jerk one hand free from the belt that tied her to the railing on the wall, she knew she would stand a chance. But the more she struggled, the more the belt cut into her skin.

The first time Rose felt the full effect of the cold room, she knew how her stomach would react. All her experience told her that if her bare abdomen was subjected to this cold temperature for a sustained period, she would develop diarrhea. It had been the same year after year whenever they had gone to Jægersborg Deer Park when the hawthorn was in bloom and her sisters had begged to go on a picnic. It was usually freezing cold to sit on blankets on the ground at that time of year, and it always made Rose ill, much to her father's delight. He used to use it against her, forcing her to stay seated until she couldn't hold it in anymore. It resulted in days of diarrhea and vomiting, so Rose couldn't go to school, and then *that* was a problem. And here in Zimmermann's bathroom she had been ice-cold from the waist down for days. Even though it had been a long time since she had eaten, so there couldn't be much left in her intestines, something suddenly streamed violently out of her.

As expected, she had developed a burning sensation, so if she had been able to make them remove the gaffer tape from her mouth for a moment, she would have begged them to wipe her behind. But it was clear to her that both these hopes were wishful thinking. The only thing they did for her was give her something to drink when they remembered. The strongest of the girls, the one called Denise, had only allowed the other girl to put the straw in her mouth into a glass of water. Rose had overheard them shouting something about a third girl, but she wasn't sure what because she had been hallucinating most of the time and was never entirely sure what was going on around her.

The previous evening when Denise had been peeing in the sink as she normally did before heading to bed, she had spoken directly to Rose for the first time about something other than giving her water.

"Maybe you're wondering what we're doing here?" she said and told Rose that Rigmor was her grandmother, and that the woman had been a witch and a devil, and that she was glad she was dead.

"So you can understand that it's only fair that we're using her apartment, right?"

Perhaps she had expected Rose to nod, but when it didn't happen her expression changed.

"Maybe you think she was a good woman? Do you?" she said coldly when Rose turned her eyes away from her. "She was a plague, and she ruined my life. Don't you believe me? Look at me."

Her lipstick was bright red and her teeth pearly white, but her mouth looked as repulsive and distorted as Rose's father's. Her hatred seemed just as extreme. Maybe she had killed her grandmother, thought Rose. That sort of crime often took place within families. Parents killed their children and children killed their parents and grandparents. No one knew this better than her.

"Are you listening, pig?" she said from the sink as she dried herself. But Rose wasn't.

She busied herself inspecting the room while there was still light. There was a ventilator in the air vent, which activated only when the light was on. But up here on the second floor of the building, it was as if the world had ended. If there had been an upstairs neighbor, she might have been able to whimper and be heard through the vent, though the chance would have been very slim. But apart from this hypothetical chance, there were no other means of communicating with the outside world.

She twisted her head up toward her right hand, where the belt was least tight around her wrist, but she couldn't twist far enough to make any attempt at loosening it further. In short, she was incapable of helping herself, and there was probably no chance the woman sitting across from her would show any mercy.

"Have I told you about the time when my grandfather took me to an auction and I accidentally smashed a Chinese vase by dropping it on the floor? Do you think my grandmother was happy when we came home and told her that it had cost thirty thousand kroner? And do you think my mother defended me?"

Rose drifted off. She had been overly sensitive to stories like that her whole life. She couldn't watch films in which children were misunderstood. She couldn't listen to adults trying to explain away evil deeds. She couldn't stand men with nicotine-stained fingers, men who parted their hair on the right, and men who started their sentences with "I've already told you . . ."—that damn supercilious "already" that served only to widen the distance between them and you. And most of all, she had always hated women who didn't defend their children like lionesses.

And now this bimbo was raking it all up again. That was the *last* thing she needed.

Then the other girl shouted from the sitting room that Denise should come because there was more news, and Denise jumped down from the sink and threw the used toilet paper on the floor. Apparently, it was something they had been waiting for, because this time Denise was in too much of a rush to shut the door to the hallway.

They don't care about me. They can't even be bothered to watch what they say. Rose opened her eyes and looked blankly around the room.

She knew that they would just leave her to die. And for the first time in weeks, it wasn't what she wanted anymore.

For some time there was no other sound from the sitting room than the faint humming of the TV.

But when they turned it off and moved over to the dining table, she was able, with a lot of concentration, to catch the odd word, and even sentences when Jazmine raised her voice.

She couldn't understand much of what they were talking about, but one thing was clear: that the girls, and Jazmine in particular, had started to feel uneasy—maybe even scared.

It was someone called Patrick who had them worried. They were discussing that the police might now be able to link Birna, Michelle, Bertha, and Senta together because of him. And that Birna's gang members had been questioned and had mentioned someone called Jazmine and the girl Michelle who had been killed.

Rose tried her best to follow. Jazmine's voice began to quiver. Meanwhile, Rose's breathing became heavier, causing small bubbles of spit to be pushed back and forth through the straw she was breathing through. They were talking about a shooting, the dead Michelle, the police, and a robbery at a nightclub. And then she suddenly heard very clearly what Denise said.

"We need new passports, Jazmine. You deal with that. And I'll head over to Anne-Line's place and break in. If she has any money, I'll take it. If she doesn't, I'll wait for her to come home."

Then it went quiet. What they had been discussing was apparently an unexpected development in the case, and now they were going to escape.

And here she was. Doomed.

There was a long pause before Jazmine finally reacted. "Anne-Line will kill you, Denise."

She laughed at that. "Not when I have this with me." Apparently she was showing something to Jazmine.

"You're not taking that hand grenade with you, Denise! Do you even know how it works? Do you even know *if* it works?"

"Yes, it's easy enough. You screw the metal cap off the bottom, releasing a small ceramic ball on a string, which you need to let drop and then yank. Then you have four seconds before it goes *boom!*"

"But you're not going to use it, are you?"

She laughed again. "You're easily fooled, Jazmine. It would make too much noise, and besides, I know what it can do to a human being. My grandfather showed me loads of pictures, and it's a complete mess. No, I'll take the pistol and I've already loaded the cartridge. Now we know it works! So just grab the hand grenade if you feel scared being alone."

"Don't mess with me. I'll come with you, Denise. I don't want to be alone with her out there."

What is she scared of? thought Rose. *That I'll lose thirty kilos in ten minutes and free myself? That I'll suddenly jump out and knock her down with a couple of spinning back fists? That she will be taken down forever with seventeen varieties of kickboxing?*

Rose couldn't help squinting her eyes and laughing behind the gaffer tape, and she stopped only when she could sense one of the girls standing in the doorway looking at her.

Then she grunted a few times as if she was dreaming.

"Stay here and keep an eye on her until I get back," said Denise dryly. "Then I will make sure that we won't be hearing any more from her."

41

Monday, May 30th, 2016

Anneli let herself in the house and in her rush simply threw her bag in the hallway of the ground-floor apartment. She had seen at least thirty types of oil filter on the Internet that could be used as makeshift silencers, and the one she was looking for needed to be fairly large. She turned on the fluorescent lights in the mechanical engineer's sitting room, and having scanned the room for half a second she understood why he only rarely ventured home. The room was stuffed from floor to ceiling with shelves of things that, in her opinion, belonged in a junkyard—components and spare parts that even in her wildest imagination she couldn't believe had any meaningful use.

She found a suitable oil filter on the bottom of a box that contained at least twenty others. It was red and round with a hole at one end that fit fairly well around the barrel of the gun.

She waved the gun around the room and could hardly stop herself from firing it to see how well her homemade silencer worked. Actually, she was just about to pull the trigger while pointing at a sack of packthread or kapok, or whatever it was, when the doorbell rang.

Anneli was puzzled. Was it a door-to-door collection? Doctors Without Borders had just been. Could it be the Red Cross or some other charity? She shook her head. They were a day late in that case, because who in their right mind would knock door-to-door on a Monday? No one!

Anneli frowned because she didn't have any neighbors or friends who called unexpectedly. But perhaps it was someone here to visit the mechanical engineer. In that case, she would advise them to go online and buy the first available ticket to Venezuela, Laos, or wherever the hell he was these days.

She went over to the curtain and lifted it a little to see who was waiting on the doorstep.

It was a woman with raven-black hair and makeup that gave her both a cheap and tough appearance. Anneli had never seen her before, and she wouldn't have opened the door if it hadn't been for the woman's pleated skirt. The absurd combination aroused her curiosity. She put the gun down on a shelf just inside the door to the sitting room and opened the front door with a smile that quickly disappeared.

The woman on the doorstep looked at her coldly, pointing a pistol directly at her chest. Despite the makeover, there was no doubt about who she was now that Anneli saw her close-up.

"Denise," she said, surprised. That was all she could muster.

Anneli staggered backward into the hallway when the girl pushed her with the barrel of the pistol. She came across immensely resolute and determined, far from the lazy and obstinate Denise Anneli had despised for years.

"We know it was you who killed Michelle," said Denise. "And if you don't want to end up behind bars for the rest of your life, you need to listen very carefully. Understood, Anne-Line Svendsen?"

She nodded in silence. "Behind bars," she'd said. So Denise hadn't come to kill her with that very efficient-looking pistol. This meant she could start off by simply playing along.

"I'm sorry, but I don't know what you're talking about, Denise. And why do you look like that? I didn't recognize you at all. Is there something I ought to know? Can I help you with something?"

She knew immediately that she had overdone her act as she felt the pistol handle hit her jaw. She suppressed a cry of pain and tried to look like she didn't understand what was happening, but it was clear that Denise wasn't buying it.

"I don't know what you want from me," said Anneli meekly.

"You're going to hand over your money, okay? We know you've won a lot of money in the lottery. Where do you keep it? If it's in the bank, you'll transfer it to my account online. Are you listening?"

Anneli swallowed hard. Was that old lie really going to cause her trouble all these years later? It would have been laughable if the situation wasn't so serious.

"I'm afraid you've been misinformed, Denise. That story with the lottery is only a rumor. I'll happily show you my bank statement, but you'll probably be disappointed. But what's happened to make you do this, Denise? It's not like you. Why don't you put that weapon down, and I promise I won't take this any further. You can tell me—"

The second blow hurt really badly. A guy had once punched her in the face with his fist, which was the end of that relationship, but this was much worse.

She held a hand up to her cheek while Denise demanded to know where she was hiding the money if it wasn't in her bank account.

Anneli sighed and nodded.

"It's in the room next door," she said, pushing open the door into the mechanical engineer's sitting room. "I have a couple of thousand in here for emergencies. We can start with that," she said as she grabbed the gun with the untested silencer from the shelf.

As she spun around, directed the gun at Denise's forehead, and pulled the trigger in the same movement, she realized with relief that the silencer as well as the gun worked brilliantly.

A muted pop. That was it.

Denise was stone dead.

42

Monday, May 30th, 2016

"Isn't Rose's apartment in Sandalsparken the one closest to the stairwell?"

Carl looked at Assad and nodded, but why in the world was he talking about that?

"Carl, you do know that I'm the one who buys the sugar down here in the cellar, don't you?"

Carl was confused. What the heck was he on about? "Yes, Assad, and I know it's been a long day, but aren't you being a bit random just now?"

"And the one who buys coffee and other stuff, I might add. And why do you suppose I do that?"

"I'm thinking it's probably because it's part of your job. But why are you saying all this? Are you trying to get a raise out of me? Because if that's the case, I'll just go to the supermarket and buy the coffee myself next time."

"You don't get it, Carl. But in the unbearably sharp light of hindsight, things sometimes pop up that suddenly make sense."

Had he really said "the unbearably sharp light of hindsight"? He used to always say "the unbearable cleverness of backlight." He was really sounding more and more fluent with every day.

"Well, you're right. I don't get it at all."

"Okay, but it's really quite logical. I buy the coffee and stuff because Rose doesn't—even though that was the agreement. She just *forgets,* Carl. That's why."

"Get to the point, Assad. We have enough to do. I need to find some way to talk with Rose so I can ask her about Rigmor Zimmermann. Maybe she knows something about her neighbor's movements and habits that could help us."

Assad looked at him drowsily. "That's exactly what I'm talking about. Don't you get it? Rose always forgets to buy things for Department Q, and I've teased her about it and asked if she also forgets to buy groceries for herself at home. So she told me about her nice neighbor who always lets her borrow sugar, milk, oatmeal, and stuff like that when she runs out."

Carl frowned. Okay, so that was where this was going.

"And since we now know that Zimmermann was her neighbor, and Rose only had one neighbor because she lives next to the stairwell, it must be Rigmor Zimmermann she borrowed things from. She was the nice neighbor Rose talked about—the same woman whose murder we're investigating." He nodded as he concluded. "So we know now that Rose knew her well, Carl. Really well."

Carl rubbed his forehead with both hands. This was so strange. Then he grabbed the telephone and dialed the number for the ward where Rose was committed.

"You want to speak to Rose Knudsen?" asked the ward nurse. "I'm afraid she's no longer with us. She left voluntarily back on . . . let me see . . ."

Carl heard her typing in the background.

"Yes, here it is. Her file says it was on May 26th."

Carl couldn't believe what he'd just heard. May 26th? That was four days ago. Why hadn't she called them?

"Was she deemed fit to leave, since she just up and left?"

"I wouldn't put it quite like that. On the contrary, she was very introverted and rather aggressive. However, Rose Knudsen was here voluntarily, and so it was her decision, and hers alone, to leave, but it certainly wasn't something we would have recommended based on her mental state. I'd be surprised if we didn't hear from her again soon. That's usually the case."

Carl hung up quietly. "She left the ward on Thursday, Assad. *Four* days ago, and not a word to us. It's not good."

Assad looked at him in shock. "That's the day she was shouting in the background when I was speaking with the receptionist on the ward. So where is she now? Did you ask?"

Carl shook his head. "I don't think they know." He picked up the phone again and dialed Rose's number.

After a few beeps came the automatic response: *"The number you're calling is currently unavailable."*

He looked at Assad. "No answer," he grumbled, turning toward the door to the corridor.

"Gordoooon!" he shouted.

Gordon seemed totally stunned when they told him what Rose had done. And when they called her sisters, their reaction was the same. This was news to all of them.

Having discussed it among themselves, the sisters decided to call their mother in Spain, who confirmed that she had been informed that Rose had left the hospital. She had called Rose without getting through but almost immediately after received a text message from her.

After some difficulty and guidance, their mother managed to forward the message to the sisters and Carl.

Carl read it out to Gordon and Assad:

Dear Mom, I'm on the train just now to Malmö. The connection is bad so I'm texting instead of calling. Don't worry about me. I'm fine. I discharged myself today because a good friend in Blekinge has offered to let me stay in their lovely house for a while. It will do me good. Will be in touch when back. Rose

"Have you ever heard about Rose's friend in Blekinge?" asked Carl. Neither of them had.

"So what do you make of the message?"

Assad jumped in first. "If she knows someone in Blekinge, it's strange that she didn't mention it when you drove to Hallabro in connection with the case about a message in a bottle."

"Her friend could have moved there since then," Gordon said in her defense.

Carl was of a different opinion. "Do you really think this is Rose's style? She wrote 'dear' to her mom, but we know how much she hates her. Remember what she wrote about her mom when she left them: 'Bitch'! And then Rose writes that she's texting because the connection is bad on the Malmö train. That's just bullshit! She also mentions her friend's 'lovely' house. This is the same Rose who doesn't give a damn about orderliness and aesthetics in her own home!"

"So you think that the text message is a diversion?" asked Gordon. Carl looked out of his tiny window, gauging the weather. Bright sunshine and a clear sky. There was no reason to put his jacket on.

"Come on," he said. "We're driving over to her apartment."

"Could we wait half an hour, Carl?" interrupted Gordon. He looked pained. "We have a visitor in a minute. Have you forgotten?"

"Err, who?"

"I explained that I would try and lure Patrick Pettersson down here after he had been questioned by Bjørn. And I also have this for you."

Carl sat back down while Gordon placed a sketch in front of him of a man in a very big jacket.

"This is what the sketch artist makes of the person who the woman on Borgergade saw on her birthday. The day Rigmor Zimmermann was murdered."

Carl looked at the sketch. Artistically, it was detailed and well executed, but from a police point of view, it was unfortunately useless and anonymous.

"Was that all she remembered about the man? This is just a big coat with a pair of legs underneath seen from behind. It could be any old hobo in a Storm P. picture. But thanks, Gordon, it was worth a try."

Gordon nodded in agreement.

"And one more thing, Carl."

"Yes?"

"It's about the parking meter on Griffenfeldsgade. A brilliant man up in homicide—let's call him Pasgård—had the bright idea that the person who parked the first escape vehicle on the street may have paid the parking ticket with coins. And that is sound enough reasoning given that it would have been rather revealing if the person had used a credit card. So, they've already emptied the contents of the parking meter."

"And now you're going to tell me that they're searching the coins for fingerprints?"

Gordon nodded and Carl couldn't hold back a roar of laughter.

Did supersleuth Pasgård think this would lead him to the killer? That one single fingerprint would have hit-and-run driver written all over it? And on a coin of all things! It was laughable.

"Thanks, Gordon, you've made my day."

Gordon looked flattered and tried to laugh like Carl.

Yes, the people on the second floor were out on a limb in this case. Perhaps they could use some help with a professional questioning.

Carl caught a glimpse of a huge guy through the open door to the situation room, where Gordon had arranged to meet him.

Muscular upper arms covered in tattoos of the type that made goofy TV stars look like they were covered in mediocre graffiti.

Carl pulled Gordon to one side and asked him under his breath if he was completely insane, bringing a possible suspect and accomplice to the very room where they had all their notes and photos on display. But Gordon had taken precautions.

"I stapled a sheet in front of the notice board, Carl. Don't worry."

"A sheet? Where the heck did you find a sheet?"

"It's the one Assad uses when he sleeps here once in a while."

Carl turned to Assad with a questioning expression, as if to ask if he planned to sleep in the office again, but it was apparently not a subject Assad intended to comment on.

Carl nodded to Patrick Pettersson as he sat down opposite him. As could be expected after having been questioned for several hours, he looked somewhat pale, but apart from that he came across as a robust type, and his gaze was steady. Surely that gaze did not indicate the brain of a genius, but he was able to answer all Carl's initial questions quickly and precisely.

"You've probably been asked a hundred times before, but we'll just try again, Patrick."

He nodded to Gordon and placed three photos in front of Patrick while Assad came in and put a cup of coffee in front of the guy.

"It's not your special brew, is it, Assad?" he asked as a precaution.

"No, it's just Nescafé Gold."

Carl pointed. "These are photos of Senta Berger, Bertha Lind, and Michelle Hansen, Patrick. All killed by a hit-and-run driver within the last eight days. I understand that you can account for your whereabouts when these incidents happened, so I would like to stress that you are not a suspect."

Did Patrick look at him gratefully as he lifted the coffee cup to his mouth?

"We haven't found any direct link between the three women, but as far as I understand, Michelle knew two other young women—let's call them friends—who you believe she hadn't known for long. Is that correct?"

"Yes."

"Was Michelle normally good at keeping secrets?"

"No, I don't think so. She was pretty straightforward."

"And yet you say that she left you a few days before she died. Wasn't that a huge surprise?"

He lowered his head. "We had been fighting because I wanted her to see her caseworker and sort out her mess."

"What mess?"

"She'd lied about where she was living without telling me. So she needed to set up a repayment schedule with the municipality and accept the work placement she'd been offered."

"And did she?"

He shrugged. "I met her a few days later at the nightclub where I work as a bouncer, and she told me she'd pay what she owed me, so obviously I thought she'd gotten things sorted."

He stared at the photo with melancholy eyes.

"You miss her?" asked Assad.

He looked at him, surprised, perhaps at the gentle nature of the question or perhaps because it came from Assad. Then he nodded.

"I thought we had something special together. And then those two bloody girls came on the scene."

The little bit of moisture that had gathered in the corners of his eyes dried up. He took a sip of his coffee. "I don't know what they dragged her into, but it wasn't anything good."

"What makes you think that?"

"I've seen the surveillance videos from the robbery at the night-club. They showed me them upstairs. You can't really see the girls because their faces are covered with scarves, but I think I recognize them. And they also showed me that selfie they found."

"I don't understand. What selfie?"

"One that Michelle took of herself and two girls. I immediately recognized them as the same girls I saw at the hospital where Michelle was admitted. The police I talked to earlier said that they've identified the place where it was taken as the canal by Gammel Strand. It was taken on May 11th, which is a long time before she left me. And she hadn't told me about that day, so apparently I wasn't supposed to know anything about it."

"You say you saw the two girls at the hospital?"

"Yes, after Michelle had been run over the first time. It was in the waiting room the day she was discharged."

Carl frowned. "You seriously believe that Michelle knew the two girls who committed the robbery and possibly shot Birna Sigurdardottir?"

"Yeah."

"So what if I suggest that Michelle was their accomplice and that she came to the nightclub to distract you? What would you say to that?"

He looked down for a moment. Reality hit him; it was written all over his face and visible from his clenched fists. With a sudden jolt and a yell of frustration, he pushed himself away from the desk and threw his coffee cup violently against the wall on the opposite side where the bedsheet was hanging.

In other circumstances, Carl would probably have reacted strongly to such an outburst. But when the coffee-stained bedsheet fell down, revealing the entire Department Q investigation, the guy stood up and apologized.

"I'll pay for a new cup and whatever else," he said, embarrassed, pointing at the bedsheet on the floor. "All this has really gotten to me. And sorry for the stain on those pictures . . ."

He froze, frowning, as if he couldn't believe his own eyes.

"I don't think . . . ," said Gordon as the guy walked around the desk toward the notice board.

"There she is again," he said, pointing at the enlarged school photo from Bolman's Independent School. "It's the same bloody girl that was in Michelle's selfie and who I saw at the hospital. And I'd swear on it that she's one of the two girls I saw on the nightclub surveillance videos, even though she's much older now."

They all stared at him as if he'd stepped out of a UFO.

After their talk, Carl asked Patrick to wait in Gordon's office while he tried to analyze the new information. He might have some further questions for him before he could leave.

Assad, Gordon, and Carl looked at each other for a while before Assad finally broke the silence.

"I don't get it, Carl. It's as if all the cases are connected now. Michelle from the hit-and-run case knows Denise and the other girl from the nightclub case, and Denise knows Stephanie Gundersen *and* obviously her grandmother, Rigmor Zimmermann, who Rose unbelievably also knows and lives next door to!"

Carl heard what he said, yet didn't answer. They were *all* in shock. He had never experienced anything like this in his time as a policeman. It was so incredibly strange.

"We're going to have to get Bjørn down here, Carl. You'll just have to face the music," said Gordon.

Carl could picture the scenario. Disciplinary proceedings, revenge, and fury combined with all his colleagues feeling bitter and let down by him. But if they hadn't looked into these cases and put them on the notice board, what then?

Carl nodded to the other two, picked up the telephone, and asked Lis to send Lars Bjørn down to them immediately. And then they waited, trying to figure out how on earth these different cases could possibly be connected.

Bjørn came bursting into the room with such force that they were left in no doubt as to his mood. When he glanced over at the notice board, his expression became even more severe and his presence in the room even more overwhelming.

Carl gave Gordon the nod to bring Patrick back, and when the wannabe gangster was standing in the doorway, Bjørn's face turned bright red. He looked like he was ready to explode.

"What the hell is my witness doing down here? And why the bloody hell do you have the hit-and-run case, the nightclub case, and the Zimmermann case down here in Department Q? So *this* is what that idiot Olaf Borg-Pedersen was rambling on about. I just didn't think it could be true."

He turned toward Carl, pointing his finger right in his face. "You've gone too far this time, Carl Mørck. Don't you understand that?"

Carl took a risk, stopping him in his tirade with a brave hand across his mouth. Then he turned calmly toward Patrick. "Would you please tell Chief of Homicide Lars Bjørn what you told us a moment ago?"

Bjørn waved his arms. "No, he's not getting involved in this, Carl. Get him out of here!"

But Patrick walked right over to the notice board and pointed at the girl in the school photo. "This is Denise," he said.

Bjørn squinted his eyes, trying to focus on the photo.

"It's true, Lars. That girl is Denise Frank Zimmermann, and standing behind her is Stephanie Gundersen, who was murdered in 2004. All the cases on the notice board are connected somehow."

It took them ten minutes to collectively explain all the connections to their boss. And when they were finally finished, he stood paralyzed like a pillar of salt outside Sodom. He might be a stickler, but there was nothing wrong with his inner detective. In that moment he felt exactly like them. He couldn't understand it and yet he saw the facts before him.

"Sit down and have a cup of coffee so we can talk about how to move forward, Lars," said Carl. He nodded to Assad, who left to make the coffee.

"The cases are completely intertwined," Bjørn said. He let his eyes wander from case to case. "What about Rose? Why is she up there?"

"Rose is off sick at the moment, and it now transpires that Rigmor Zimmermann is her neighbor. We'll drive out to her apartment after we've talked and ask her about their relationship."

"Is Rose involved in this, Carl?"

Carl frowned. "No, there's nothing to indicate that. It's just a coincidence that they live next door to each other. So why not get an opinion about the victim from a skilled investigator when the opportunity presents itself?"

"Have you already called her about this?"

"Err, no. Her cell phone just gives an automated answer, so it might be that her battery is dead."

Bjørn shook his head. This was all too much for him.

"Does Marcus know anything about all this?"

"Not the latest, no."

Then Patrick Pettersson tapped Carl on the shoulder. They had completely forgotten him.

"Can I go now? I've been here all day already. My boss will begin to ask questions tomorrow morning if I haven't fixed the cars I'm meant to be working on."

"You don't have any plans to leave Copenhagen now, do you?" asked Bjørn.

Patrick shook his head. "First you tell me I can't leave Denmark and now you're saying I can't leave Copenhagen. What's next? That I can't leave my apartment?"

Bjørn attempted a smile and waved him away.

When he had gone, Bjørn took his phone out of his pocket.

"Lis!" he said. "Get everyone together who's in the building and send them down here. Yes, now, I said! Yes, yes, I know it's late. Yes, down to Carl!"

Then he turned toward Carl. "Two questions. Do you have any idea who the hit-and-run driver might be?"

Carl shook his head.

"That's a damn shame. But do you know then where the woman in question, Denise Zimmermann, is?"

"No, we don't know that either. We haven't had time to focus very much on that yet. But according to her mother, she's not staying at her address. She said she believes Denise is staying with a lover in Slagelse."

Bjørn sighed heavily. "I don't damn well know how I should deal with you and your team. I'm going to the bathroom and will consider the situation while I'm gone."

Carl scratched his stubble and nodded to Assad as he came in with Bjørn's coffee. "We'll have to wait an hour before we drive over to Rose's place. We need to brief all the fools from the second floor first. They're on their way down here now."

"Okay. And then what, Carl? Is Bjørn getting ready to come down on us?"

"You never know what the vicious sod might come up with."

Assad laughed and managed to make Gordon laugh too. "He might be vicious, but at least he's fair."

"How do you mean, Assad?"

"He's equally vicious toward everyone."

43

"I'm starving, Carl. Can't you find somewhere I can get something to eat on the way to Stenløse?"

Carl nodded. He wasn't hungry at all. As long as the situation with Rose was occupying his mind, he had no appetite whatsoever.

He started the car and the radio news came on.

"Well, I'll be damned. They're certainly making sure everyone knows we're looking for Denise," said Carl. Never before had the search for a witness been so extensive. All the TV and radio news channels were broadcasting the call for information, so Lars Bjørn and Janus Staal really wanted to get hold of her. But what the heck: If they could succeed in solving three cases at once, it wouldn't be all bad.

Assad's cell was ringing faintly.

"It's for you," he said and put it on speakerphone.

"Yes, this is Carl Mørck," he said to someone coughing loudly on the other end.

"Yes, sorry, Carl," said the voice. "But since I quit smoking, I've been coughing constantly."

It was Marcus Jacobsen.

"As agreed, I've now looked into the circumstances surrounding Birgit Zimmermann's husband and found some information about him that I think you'll find interesting. Should I tell you now?"

Can't it wait until tomorrow? thought Carl. It was already late and he was exhausted.

"We're on our way out of town just now, so fire away," he said anyway.

Marcus cleared his throat. "James Lester Frank was born in 1958 in Duluth, Minnesota, and married Birgit Zimmermann in 1987, the year before Denise Frank Zimmermann was born. The couple were separated in autumn 1995 and divorced a few months later. The mother won custody of Denise Zimmermann and the father moved back to the US in the same year."

Carl squinted. When would he get to the interesting part?

"I also know that he then rejoined the military and did several tours of Iraq and later Afghanistan. In 2002, he disappeared during a mission where two of his soldiers lost their lives. They thought he was dead, but then he was recognized by a liaison officer in Istanbul, triggering a search for him as a deserter."

Sounds like a sensible man, thought Carl. Who wouldn't rather be on the run than dead?

And then he came to the point.

"About a month ago, a certain Mark Johnson collapsed on the street and was brought to Herlev Hospital with a completely explosive liver count. They also found out that a number of his organs had more or less stopped functioning. The doctors were very direct in telling him that the effects of his alcohol intake had reached a level from which few people survived."

"Mark Johnson? Was he the man who recognized Frank in Turkey?" asked Carl.

"No. But I'll get to that. Mark Johnson was of course asked to identify himself, and when he couldn't the police were called."

"A bit harsh given the man was so ill," interjected Assad.

"Yes, you could say that. But the fact is they need to know who they are writing about for their medical records, Assad."

"Of course. And then what happened?" asked Carl.

"They found a number of tattoos on the guy and most importantly a meat tag tattooed under one arm, which they used to identify him."

"What's a meat tag?" asked Carl.

"It's a dog tag tattooed directly on the skin, Carl," said Assad.

"Correct," said Marcus. "It states the soldier's surname and first name, as well as a middle initial if they have one. And in this case because the man was part of the US Army, also his Department of Defense ID number, blood type, and religion. Many soldiers had tattoos like that done back then before being stationed on the front line. Nowadays, I believe the US Army has a different tattoo policy, so I'm not sure they're still allowed. But for those soldiers who got them, it meant they could be identified if they died in service and had lost their dog tags."

"And this meat tag showed that he was James Lester Frank?" asked Carl.

"Exactly. 'Frank L. James,' which means that Birgit Zimmermann's ex-husband is alive—albeit it would seem not for long. He's been discharged from the hospital and of all places is living in the apartment above the shop that used to be Fritzl Zimmermann's shoe shop in Rødovre. And, wait for it, the apartment is still listed as belonging to none other than Rigmor Zimmermann."

"So, he's in Denmark now?"

Assad looked totally confused. "Marcus, I don't get it. I've been through every possible register and couldn't find him. The man isn't registered in the country."

"No, because he's been living here illegally since 2003 under the false name Mark Johnson. I would've liked to know this back when we investigated the Stephanie Gundersen murder."

"Why wasn't he arrested at the hospital, Marcus?" asked Carl.

"Yeah, I don't know. Maybe because the man is terminally ill and won't run anywhere. Of course immigration are looking into the case because the police handed over the case when they were done questioning him. Current protocol means that you don't immediately deport a person who is in such bad health. And immigration cases take a long time under normal circumstances, but they are also dealing with a backlog—just try for yourself to get hold of someone."

"Do you know what he's been living off all these years?"

"No, and I don't think anyone does except him. He's probably lived hand to mouth like a hobo. I think he's a real pity case. But if you ask me, I don't think he's been involved in any criminal activity, because the last thing he'd want is to be arrested and deported to a country where he's wanted for desertion."

"Yes, we do have an extradition agreement with the US, don't we?" asked Carl.

"Yes, and unfortunately for Frank, the agreement was already in place in 2003. They have a similar agreement in Sweden, but unlike us, they don't extradite people under suspicion for military or political crimes. If we had extradited him, he would simply have ended up in the darkest dungeon the US could find. Deserters have never been popular in God's own country. Basically, there's nothing glamorous about being a war vet, wherever you come from."

Assad nodded. He apparently knew better than most.

Carl thanked Marcus for all his work. Imagine that James Frank was in Denmark.

Following the call, he slowed down for a while. "Can you wait a little longer before we eat, Assad?" he asked without waiting for an answer. "Now we have this new information, I'd like to pay this James Lester Frank a visit. I'm thinking that we might find Denise Zimmermann with her father. That would be one hell of a bonus."

Fritzl Zimmermann's old shoe shop in Rødovre was a shadow of its former self. A run-down building with empty, dirty shop windows and a lot of junk inside. The shop sign painted on the wall could still be made out despite the amateurish attempt at covering it. As far as Carl could count, at least five different types of businesses had been forced to close their doors since Zimmermann's day.

Assad pointed at the apartment above the shop. With a single bay window out to the street, it was probably just a studio—but then again, shop assistants and servants couldn't expect more back in those days.

The name "Mark Johnson" was written with a black handheld printer directly on the flaking paint of the door. They knocked and waited.

"Just come in," said a voice in a strong American accent.

They had expected the place to be a total mess, but they were mistaken. The smell of the type of fabric softener used to wash baby clothes permeated the entire apartment. They walked past a couple of painted beer crates in the hallway and on into the sitting room, where there was a sofa bed, TV, chest of drawers, and not much else.

Carl looked around. If Denise Zimmermann was hiding somewhere in this sitting room, she must have shrunk.

He signaled to Assad to check the rest of the apartment.

"You're from the police," said the man on the sofa. His skin was yellow and he was wrapped in quilts, even though the temperature outside was up to almost ninety degrees. "Have you come to arrest me?" he asked.

A rather surprising introduction.

"No, we're not from immigration. We're detectives from homicide in Copenhagen."

Perhaps Carl had imagined that it would make the man feel uncomfortable—that often happened. But instead, he pursed his lips and nodded knowingly.

"We've come because we're looking for your daughter."

Assad returned to the sitting room and gestured that the girl was nowhere to be found.

"Can you tell me when you last saw Denise, James? Or would you prefer that I call you Mark?"

He shrugged. Apparently he didn't care what they called him.

"Denise? Well, she's still Dorrit to me. But I haven't seen her since 2004. And I heard today that you're looking for her. You can probably imagine that it worried me." He reached out for a glass on the table. Apparently it contained water.

"We're investigating the murder of your ex-mother-in-law, and we have to suspect anyone who she was in contact with immediately before she died. So we need to question your daughter about her movements."

The visibly ill man took a drink and rested the glass on his stomach. "You know I risk being extradited, right?"

Both Carl and Assad nodded.

"When a deserter like me ends up in the hands of the US military, they are thrilled. When I deserted, I was about to be promoted to major. I had received so many medals that I almost walked lopsided. I've lost count of how many missions I've been on because there were also a lot back when I was younger. But none of them were glorious, I can tell you that much. That's why they're so eager to get people like me back and out of the way. They don't want us to reveal anything, and especially not high-ranking decorated soldiers." He shook his head. "And the US military never forgets a deserter. They've just demanded an extradition from Sweden, even though the man has lived there for twenty-eight years and has a family. So what would keep Denmark from extraditing me? My illness?"

Carl nodded. It sounded plausible after all.

"You think so, do you? Well, you can forget all about that, because the US will swear blind that they'll offer me the necessary treatment, and before you know it the plane will be ready to take off."

"Okay, but what does that have to do with the purpose of our visit?" asked Carl.

He wasn't a Catholic priest or spiritual guide.

"The purpose? I'm about to tell you something that will prevent my extradition, and I feel good about that."

"And that is?"

"That I've done something even worse than deserting, which no one seems to really care about in Denmark anyway."

Assad moved closer. "Why did you go back to the US in the first place when you had your family here?"

"I'll get to that too."

"The thing that happened in 1995?"

He nodded.

"You know that I'm seriously ill, right?"

"Yes, but not the details."

"You won't need to save up for my next Christmas present, if you get my drift." He laughed at his own joke. "And that's why I don't want to go back to rot and slowly waste away in an American prison. I'd rather die here in Denmark where you're looked after when you're at death's door. Even in prison."

Carl was unsure what would come next. The guy had really set alarm bells ringing.

"James, I might as well tell you that only a few days ago I kicked a man out of my office for making a false murder confession. If that's your game, I warn you. It's not going to help your case."

He smiled. "What's your name?"

"Carl Mørck."

"Good. I can sense that you're not the dumbest policeman I've met because that's exactly what I'm telling you. I can't be extradited to the US given that I've committed a murder here in Denmark. And that's whether you believe it or not."

It had started as a game between James and his father-in-law. Both were former soldiers and had been active in war—with all that entailed. Their background and history were not for the fainthearted, which made Fritzl Zimmermann all the more fond of his son-in-law. Fritzl considered military service to be honorable and a synonym for virility and power. With undisguised bluntness, he questioned James about the military campaigns he had taken part in, from Zaire to Lebanon and Granada, because Fritzl loved all wars in which resolve and cynicism led to confrontation. And the more detail James went into, the more curious Fritzl became. And that was how the game began.

"If I mention the word 'bayonet,' then we both have to say how we've used one, and then it's the other one's turn to name something," suggested Fritzl. "Interesting words like 'ambush,' for example . . . or 'fire.' Actually, 'fire' is a good one."

In the beginning, James hesitated. No matter what the topic was, Fritzl could match James a hundred times over and relished talking about it. Ruthless abuse became crusades. Hangings became self-defense. He talked about duty of care for his fellow soldiers and the brotherhood of men standing shoulder to shoulder, and much to his surprise James slowly began to recognize himself in Fritzl.

They usually met up for a couple of hours on late Saturday mornings when James had slept off his hangover from the night before. Birgit looked after the child and Rigmor kept house, while he and Fritzl brought the past to life in Fritzl's secret office at the far end of the labyrinth of rooms on the ground floor. Here, he had the opportunity to feel the weight of a Parabellum in his hands and see what effective weapons could be made out of all sorts of objects at hand.

All this could probably have gone on for years if things between James and Rigmor had not blown up one fateful Saturday. It had all begun as an ordinary Saturday get-together with an early dinner, and then came one surprising question from his father-in-law that opened a Pandora's box.

The question was inappropriate with Dorrit sitting at the table, but Fritzl didn't care. "What do you think is the worst thing a soldier can do? Commit random executions or random adultery?"

For a moment, James thought that it was part of their game and told his daughter to go and play in the garden until they called her. It was probably just another one of Fritzl's morbid and crazy ideas, but when James answered after a short pause that of course it was random executions, Rigmor Zimmermann slapped him on the cheek so hard that his head was thrown to one side.

"Bastard," she shouted while Fritzl laughed and slammed his fist on the table. James was in shock, and when he turned to his wife for an explanation, she spat straight in his face.

"You fell right in the trap, you idiot. I've told my father and mother about all your women and affairs and about how you keep letting us down. Did you think you could get away with that?"

Then he lied about the affairs, and cried, and swore that there was nothing to it—that he only stayed away for the night when he was doing the books. But she said they knew better.

"She hates you for everything you've done, James. For cheating on me. For being drunk several times a week. For encouraging Father to talk about things that he isn't supposed to talk about."

That day, Rigmor Zimmermann revealed her true self to James, leaving him in no doubt who the boss was in the family. When she placed the divorce papers on the table, James saw that Birgit had already signed.

James begged her to rip them up, but she didn't dare. And besides, Rigmor and Fritzl had promised to take care of her once he was out of the picture.

And he suddenly was in every sense.

He later tried to pressure Rigmor to have the divorce annulled, threatening that if she didn't he would inform the authorities about Fritzl's crimes committed during the Second World War. And promised that they would catch up with him this time. He had evidence.

The response came a few days later in the form of an offer of one hundred and fifty thousand dollars if he went back to the US and never showed his face again. The money would be paid in three installments to his US bank account, and that was the end of that. James agreed. It wasn't every day a working-class guy from Duluth, Minnesota, came into that sort of money.

The problem, however, was that he neglected to inform the US tax office about the transactions. And after several court cases and fines, the money was gone. And more besides.

So James Lester Frank was left with no choice but to enlist again, and he was rewarded with years of almost uninterrupted missions so close to the Taliban that he and his men began to smell and look like them.

"We were like animals. We shat were we slept. Ate whatever we could kill. And we died like animals. The Taliban saw to that. The last one from my unit I saw them execute had his arms cut off first.

"Then I escaped. For eleven months, I lived up in the mountains, and when I finally managed to get out of there, I was done with killing for the US and the US Army."

"But then you were spotted in Istanbul," said Carl.

He nodded and pulled the quilt all the way up to his neck.

"I was working in a tourist bar where most of the guests were Americans. That was stupid. Even though I'd shaved my head and grown a beard, the officer immediately spotted me. Luckily for me, that day I'd met a Danish couple in the bar who had a camper van and were happy to give me a lift to Denmark. I told them my story. That I had been a soldier and was now a deserter, but it wasn't a problem for them. Rather the opposite, I'd say. You'd be hard-pressed to find greater pacifists than them."

"Hmm, that's a great story," said Assad with a hint of irony. "But where are you going with this?" His stomach was rumbling loudly. The lack of energy was apparently beginning to make him irritable. Carl had almost forgotten about the food. If only he could smoke a cigarette, he could keep going for a few more hours.

"When I arrived back in Denmark, I had no papers or money. So my only option was to contact Fritzl and Rigmor and tell them that I intended to stay and that they had to help me. They were horrified because they and Birgit had told Dorrit—Denise—that I was long dead.

"Hearing that made me furious, so even though they tried to stop me, I forced my way into Fritzl's secret office and stole whatever I could get my hands on so I had something to bargain with. I took photos of the room and of them shouting and screaming. Finally, I took Fritzl's army knife and held it against Rigmor's throat. I told her that I knew what it would sound like when I slit her windpipe. Together with the other threats, this was enough to make them cooperate.

"The deal was that they would let me live in this apartment and cover my expenses, and on top of that they would pay me twelve thousand kroner a month for the rest of my life. Of course, I should have demanded more, but I wasn't that smart." He laughed and sighed at the same time, looking like he was about to fall asleep. His eyes were as yellow as a werewolf's. He clearly wasn't well.

"In return, I promised to keep away entirely from Birgit and Denise. Rigmor assured me that if I contacted them, she wouldn't give a damn about what I told the authorities about Fritzl. She'd make sure I was arrested and deported—and she really meant it. She'd rather sacrifice Fritzl and the good name of the family than the girls."

"But I assume you didn't stick to that promise," said Carl.

He smiled. "Yes, I did, actually, in a way. I have no idea how many times I stood behind the trees by Sortedams Lake and watched the main entrance to Bolman's Independent School without ever contacting Denise. I was just hoping to catch a glimpse of her when she left school."

"And Birgit?"

"Yeah, out of curiosity I tried to find out where she was living, but she wasn't registered anywhere. I planned to follow Denise when she walked home from school."

"So you did?" asked Carl.

Assad tapped Carl on the shoulder, sighing. "Carl, honestly, do you see any humps on me?"

"You'll get something to eat in twenty minutes, Assad. Please, no camel jokes now, okay?"

Assad sighed even louder. Apparently twenty minutes was too long.

"So did you follow Denise?"

"No, it never came to that. But I did see her leave the school several times. She had grown so beautiful and vibrant. It was really fascinating to watch her." He took another sip from his glass. It seemed like he was running out of energy.

"But not as fascinating as watching Stephanie Gundersen, was it, James?"

A little water trickled out of the corners of his mouth, ending up as drops on his chin. His suddenly bright eyes expressed surprise.

"Why did you kill Stephanie?" came Carl's inevitable question.

He put the glass on the table, clearing his throat, as the water had gone down the wrong way.

Then he shook his head eagerly. "Did I say you were good before? I take it back."

Assad giggled. Was that another protest over the lack of food?

"Because?"

"Because I loved Stephanie. I chose her over Birgit and Denise. Simple as that. I saw her leaving the school one day, and we were both smitten. We saw each other for nine months, meeting up in town. In fact, we were together several times a week."

"Why all the secrecy?"

"Because she was Denise's teacher. If Denise saw us together and recognized me, I would . . . They'd told her I was dead. My agreement with Rigmor would be finished. I would be arrested and extradited."

He stared vacantly and suddenly cried quietly. No sound, no sniffling.

"I didn't kill Stephanie. Rigmor did." His voice was quivering. "I'm sure the bitch saw me in town with Stephanie and took her revenge by killing her. When I confronted her with my suspicion, she screamed that it wasn't her, but I didn't believe her. Of course I didn't. I just knew that I couldn't touch her and that she could easily blame me for the murder. That I would be painted as an illegal foreign blackmailer and professional killer."

"So you started drinking and kept your mouth shut while you stayed in this apartment and accepted her money. How pathetic can you get?"

Carl looked at Assad. *Well, that sounds like the conclusion to that story,* said his expression. But Assad was sleeping. The last few hours without anything to drink or eat had taken their toll.

"Fritzl drowned the next day, and after a few weeks I didn't see Rigmor anymore because she sold the shop and the house and moved to Borgergade," he continued.

"And what about you?"

"Me? I had absolutely nothing left to live for, so I just drank my days away."

"And it was years before you got your revenge, is that how it was?"

"I was drunk every day for twelve years. That was all I wanted to do. And with twelve thousand a month, I wasn't exactly drinking champagne." He laughed dryly. That was when Carl noticed that he didn't have a single tooth left in his mouth.

"And what changed that situation?"

He tapped his stomach. "I became ill. I saw the same thing happen to one of my drinking buddies, and he didn't last long. Like him, I was suddenly dead tired all the time. Threw up blood and couldn't be bothered to eat. I developed little red spots all over my upper body and my skin turned yellow and itchy. I bruised easily, my legs cramped up, and I couldn't get an erection. If I didn't sleep constantly, I risked collapsing on the street. Yes, I was damn well aware what was happening."

"So the time had come. Is that it?"

He nodded. "Even though I was ill, I didn't stop drinking. I always had a bottle of cherry wine on me. I knew it was only a matter of time before I kicked the bucket, so I didn't care about the agreement I had with Rigmor. Those fucking army men could do whatever the fuck they wanted with me. That was how I felt. As long as I got my revenge. So I went to the library and googled Rigmor and found out that she was still registered on Borgergade."

"But she didn't live there, though, did she?"

"No, as I discovered. The names on the door were Birgit and Denise F. Zimmermann. Oh, that little 'F' made me so happy because it meant I hadn't been completely forgotten. I considered ringing the bell, but in the end I didn't. I looked like shit and hadn't had a shave or a wash for a week. I didn't want them to see that. So I went over to the other side of the street and looked up at the windows, hoping that I might catch a glimpse of them. For the first time in many years, I was euphoric inside. And then Rigmor came out of the main door."

"Did she recognize you?"

"No, not before I approached her. And then she bloody well started running off in the rain. She turned toward me shouting that I could go to hell and threw a bundle of thousand kroner notes in front of me on the wet pavement. But that didn't stop me. On the contrary, it made me fucking mad."

"So you ran after her?"

"I was wasted, man, and the bitch ran quickly down a side street toward Kronprinsessegade. I only just saw her darting into the King's Garden, but when I reached the entrance she was gone."

Carl nudged his assistant. "Assad, wake up! James has something to tell us."

Curly looked around in confusion. "What time is . . . ," he managed to say before his stomach drowned him out.

"Rigmor Zimmermann had disappeared by the time you reached the King's Garden. What happened then, James?" He looked at Assad. "Are you listening, Assad?"

Assad nodded grumpily and pointed at his phone. It had been recording all along.

"I stopped by the entrance and looked around. Rigmor wasn't on the lawn and she couldn't have reached the opposite end and left the park so quickly. So she must still be there somewhere, I thought. I scanned the park thoroughly. Something I became really good at when I was in the Balkans because the Serbians were so brilliant at hiding. You really had to be wary of bushes, not like Iraq, where it was roads, roadsides, or miscellaneous piles left on pavements or dirt tracks. In the Balkans you risked being killed if you didn't remember that bushes were dangerous places."

"So you found Rigmor Zimmermann in the bushes?"

"Yes and no. I exited the park on Kronprinsessegade, standing by the railings so she wouldn't immediately see me if she appeared from her hiding place. It was about five minutes before I sensed movement in the bushes behind the bicycle stands."

"She didn't see you?"

He smiled. "I quickly sneaked back to the entrance and around the ridiculous sign welcoming people to the King's Garden and reminding them to be considerate toward other visitors so everyone can enjoy themselves. I've laughed at that sign before. I thought to myself that I would be very considerate toward my ex mother-in-law and kill her with one single blow."

"So it was premeditated murder?"

He nodded. "One hundred and ten percent premeditated, yes. I've got no reason to say otherwise."

Carl looked at Assad. "Are you writing all this down?"

He nodded and held out his phone again.

"And the actual murder? You let her run down toward the restaurant?"

"No, I hit her in front of the bushes. She screamed when she saw me duck under the branches, and then I pulled her out and hit her on the back of the head with the wine bottle. It was as easy as that. One blow and she was stone dead."

"But you didn't leave her there?"

"No. I stayed where I was, looking at her, before deciding in my drunken state that it would be wrong of me to leave her in that smelly place where drunkards stop to take a piss."

"You moved the body?"

"Yes."

"Rather risky, if you ask me."

He shrugged. "There was no one in the park because of the shitty weather, so I just slung the body over my shoulder and threw her on the grass near the next exit to Kronprinsessegade, so I could make a quick getaway."

"So you killed her with a bottle of cherry wine?"

"Yes." He flashed a toothless smile. "It was almost full at the time, but it wasn't an hour later, so I put it in a trash can on Frederiksborg-gade. Then I just walked home. I say walked because I had built up so much energy by that time that you wouldn't believe it. That lasted about twenty minutes, and then I collapsed. That was where they found me."

"You haven't drunk since. Why?"

"Because I'm not going to be brought before a judge and come across as mentally unstable. I want to be sober and make my statement in front of a Danish court. I don't want to go back to the US."

"Why didn't you just confess to the police who questioned you at the hospital?" interrupted Assad. It almost sounded like he thought that would have saved him from his imminent death by starvation.

James shrugged. "Because they would have arrested me then and there and I wanted to find Denise and talk to her first. I owed that to myself and her."

Carl nodded and looked at Assad. He had already taken quite a few notes, and the voice recorder indicator on his smartphone was still red. This was being served to them on a platter. How often could you say that? He smiled, and not without good reason. They had come to find Denise but ended up solving one or two murders.

Yes, Assad could soon replenish his humps.

"What did you do then?" asked Assad. He wanted all the details.

"I went over to Birgit's building yesterday. I saw her come out the main door with several empty wine bottles in her hands. She was staggering down the sidewalk and didn't recognize me because she was so pissed out of her head. I wanted to tell her that I still care for her but I couldn't bring myself to do it when I saw her."

No doubt the feeling is mutual, thought Carl.

"That's all," he said. "Now you know everything. I'll stay here until someone comes to pick me up."

The shawarma wrap almost made Assad's eyes pop out. Watching him shove this Middle Eastern treat into his mouth was like watching a child eating an ice pop on a hot day. Even if he had won a yacht, he couldn't have been happier than he was right now.

Carl picked at his kebab. It was probably one of the best you could find in Rødovre, but the fact was that a man from Vendsyssel would always be more at home with a hot dog.

"Do you believe everything James Frank told us?" mumbled his chewing partner.

Carl put down his kebab. "I think he believes it himself, but it's up to us to make sense of it all now."

"So do we think he killed Rigmor Zimmermann? Or is it just something he's made up to avoid being deported?"

"Yes, I do believe he killed her. I'm sure it can be confirmed by traces on her clothes. They still have them in forensics. And perhaps there are also traces from Rigmor on the clothes he was wearing that night. I'd be surprised if there weren't."

Assad raised his eyebrows. "So what's the problem with the story?"

"I don't know if there is one. But don't you find it an odd coincidence that Fritzl Zimmermann died the day after Stephanie Gundersen? I'm wondering what happened in the time between those two deaths."

"And you think Birgit Zimmermann might have an idea?"

Carl looked at his partner, who was ordering another shawarma. It was a good question, and hopefully time would tell once Assad had finished eating. First he would call Marcus, and then they would head out to Stenløse.

44

Monday, May 30th, 2016

It was just before seven o'clock and Anneli had been working like crazy for at least an hour cleaning blood from the walls, shelves, machinery, and floor. After that she sat and watched Denise's body for some time. Lying there among the discarded machine parts with a dumbstruck expression on her face, Denise's lifeless body gave Anneli a lot of satisfaction. Her intense, stubborn eyes were now completely lackluster, and all the hours she had spent on getting dolled up and showing off were now in vain.

"Where should I dispose of a lovely little thing like you, Denise Zimmermann? Should we leave it up to fate and dump you among the other prostitutes on Vesterbro, or should we play it safe and put you in one of the upper-class parks where nobody goes after eight? How about Bernstorff's Park, Denise? We could put you down in one of the well-trimmed corners. Then one of the posh little Charlottenlund dogs can find you when it goes for its morning pee."

Anneli laughed.

It seemed like she had gotten away with this. She had hidden Denise's pistol and squeezed the gun into her hand so both their fingerprints were on it. If anyone had heard the shot and called the police, she had decided to pretend to be in shock and say it was an accident. That the woman had barged in, threatening to shoot her with that gun with the strange thing attached to it. That she was one of those crazy people who blamed their caseworker for their own inability to sort out her terrible situation. And a caseworker who had always done her best to help her, no less. The police would probably know that sometimes disturbed clients murdered those whose job it was to help them. It had happened a couple of times over the past few years. And she would add that the attack had removed any doubt from her mind that Denise Zimmermann was insane.

She would explain to them in detail how they had come to blows immediately when she answered the door to Denise. That they had fought their way into the apartment in a life-and-death struggle, with Anneli using all her strength to try to grab the gun from Denise's hand. And that the gun had gone off by accident.

She would cry a little and say with quivering lips that this was the worst experience in her life.

But the police didn't come.

Anneli laughed, retrieving Denise's pistol from where she had hidden it. She could just leave Denise where she was for now while she drove to Stenløse to liquidate Jazmine.

She looked at the gun with its makeshift silencer in Denise's hand.

Both weapons had been used to kill. She was in no doubt about that. The question was if she could exploit that fact.

Oh yes, Anneli felt good about that thought. Wasn't it just the most brilliant of all her plans? Yes, it was.

When Anneli passed the first road sign for Stenløse, she was almost bursting inside. She was so excited about seeing Jazmine's face when she opened the door.

Anneli imagined that the first thing the idiotic girl would think was that Anne-Line Svendsen was supposed to be dead. She would be completely thrown, perplexed, and surprised that Anneli knew where they lived. And she would wonder what had happened to Denise.

Yes, Jazmine would get a shock when she realized that her time was up.

Anneli would immediately force her into the sitting room and shoot her without further ado at close range using the gun with the silencer. Then she would press Denise's pistol into Jazmine's hand and make it look like there had been a showdown between her and Denise that had resulted in Jazmine's death. The old Luger pistol in Jazmine's hand hadn't helped her, it would appear. And later the police would discover that this was the pistol that had killed Birna.

After this, all she would need to do was pick up Denise's body in Webersgade, prop her up in the passenger seat of her car, and drive her to Bernstorff's Park. And she would place the gun with the silencer next to Denise's hand so that it looked like a suicide. Voilà! One stone, many birds. At some point the police would find Jazmine and discover that the gun she had been killed with was the same one Denise had used to commit suicide.

All the loose ends would be tied. It was simply genius.

Anneli couldn't help laughing insanely at how perfect her plan was. If she played her cards right, she might even be able to pin the hit-and-run murders on Denise. Surely the police would find out that Michelle had also lived in the apartment, bringing them to draw conclusions that would benefit Anneli. And if she really could pull all this off, she would have gotten away with everything. Then she could comfortably take a break from her killing spree and concentrate on her treatments and recovery. A year or two without murders and then she could slowly and steadily resume her mission. Meanwhile, she could keep herself entertained by coming up with new ways to kill. She would read books about how to use poison, fire, electricity, and water to fake accidents that couldn't be linked to one another or the hit-and-run murders.

She turned on the car radio because her euphoric mood demanded music.

Now all she needed to make things perfect was a couple of candles and a glass of red wine. But all in good time. When she had completed this mission later tonight, it would be straight back to the apartment for a cozy night of watching a TV series with her feet up on the coffee table. She had heard *True Detective* was good.

She turned into Sandalsparken parking area to the last ironic stanzas of Coldplay's "Viva la Vida" and parked in the exact same place as last time. She was more ready than ever to embark on the penultimate act in this exhilarating play about life and death that she had set in motion a few weeks ago.

Just as she was about to get out of her car, a rather official-looking vehicle drove in front of her, albeit without the blue siren on its roof activated. It parked so close to her that she could easily tell that the odd-looking pair weren't here on a social visit.

Everything about them screamed police.

She watched them as they went up to the apartment immediately to the left of Jazmine and Denise's.

I need to stay away as long as they're there, she thought, leaning back in a more comfortable position.

"But never mind. Good things come to those who wait," she said to herself as the news on the radio announced that Denise Frank Zimmermann was wanted as a witness in connection with a murder. Anyone with information about her whereabouts should contact the police.

"Then I recommend that you take a look in Bernstorff's Park tomorrow morning," Anneli said, giggling to herself.

45

"Which of the sisters will be there to let us in?"

Assad took his feet down from the dashboard, holding up a key as Carl parked the car. "None of them. But I have the key Vicky gave Gordon. If Rose won't let us in, we can use it."

Carl felt a bit uneasy about that idea.

"It makes me a bit nervous to think what Rose will say when we turn up unannounced," said Carl. Not only was Rose as tricky and special as the situation, but she was also their colleague, and a female one at that. Why did women always have to be so complicated? Hadn't he often been forced to acknowledge that in general he didn't understand women at all? Perhaps it was the lively girls from Vendsyssel who had confused him and made him believe that all women were as forthright as them. Hardy had advised him several times to find himself a coach or a men's group that could help him deepen his understanding of the opposite sex. Maybe that was an idea that was worth pursuing. He just never really got around to it.

"I know, Carl. I'm nervous too," said Assad. "I've been really down since she shouted at me on the telephone."

They rang the doorbell a few times without hearing any sign of life from inside.

"Do you think she's asleep?" asked Assad. "Maybe she's still a bit out of it on her medication."

"Phew, what now?" groaned Carl. Rather two drugged-up pimps going berserk with knives than this, because at least he knew where he was with the former. Who knew what the risks were if they barged in just like that?

"I wish we knew if she was in there. Imagine if she . . ."

"If she what?"

"Nothing, Assad. Knock on the door a couple of times, and made it loud. Maybe she can't hear the doorbell throughout the entire apartment."

"Hang on, maybe we can ask that woman if she's seen her?" asked Assad after knocking.

"Who?" asked Carl, looking around.

"The one who twitched at the curtains a moment ago next door in Zimmermann's apartment."

"In Zimmermann's place? I didn't see anyone. Are you sure?"

"Err, yes. I think so. See, the curtain isn't hanging straight now."

"Come on, then," said Carl.

He rang the neighbor's bell, but nothing happened.

"Are you certain, Assad? Who would be in there? Rigmor Zimmermann hasn't risen from the dead."

Assad shrugged and knocked forcefully on the door, and when that didn't have any effect he knelt down on the doormat and shouted at the top of his voice through the mail slot: "Hi in there. We saw you. We just want to ask you a couple of questions."

Carl smiled. The doormat with the intricate pattern almost made it look like he was kneeling on a prayer rug, praying through the mail slot.

"Can you see anything in there?" asked Carl.

"No. The hallway is completely empty."

Carl leaned forward and looked through the gap in the curtains into the kitchen. He couldn't see much, only some dirty dishes and clean tableware that hadn't been put back in the cupboard. But then again, Rigmor Zimmermann couldn't have known that she would never come back to clean up.

He tapped on the window with his fingernails, and Assad shouted a few more times that they would like to speak to the person he had seen at the window.

"Maybe you didn't see anything, Assad," said Carl after a minute of knocking and ringing the bell in vain. "If we'd been smart we would have remembered to bring the key Birgit gave us."

"I've got a lockpick down in the car, Carl."

Carl shook his head. "We'd better leave that to our colleagues in homicide. They're going to come here at some point anyway to check the apartment again. Let's just let ourselves into Rose's place and see if she's there."

Assad took out the key and pressed down the door handle, but just as he was about to put the key in the lock, the door swung open.

This doesn't bode well, thought Carl.

Assad looked baffled as he silently walked through the door. He called Rose's name a couple of times so she wouldn't get a shock when she suddenly saw them standing there.

But the place was as silent as the grave.

"Bloody hell, she's certainly been here, Carl," said Assad. He looked shocked to say the least, and with good reason. Everything that would normally be on the shelves, other furniture, or windowsills had been thrown on the floor. Soil from potted plants was scattered over the sofa, broken coffee cups and plates were spread here and there, and a couple of chairs had been smashed against the floor. It was complete chaos.

"*Rose!*" shouted Assad while snooping around in the other rooms.

"She's not here," he said after a few seconds. "But come on out to the bathroom, Carl."

Carl tore himself away from the laptop on the dining table and went out there.

"Look!" Assad was standing with a forlorn expression, pointing down at the wastebasket, which was full of bandages, packaging, Tampax boxes, cotton balls, and various medicines.

"It doesn't look good, Assad."

"Is that what you meant before?" He sighed. "That she might have taken her own life?"

Carl was unable to answer. He pursed his lips and returned to the sitting room. He just didn't know.

He sniffed the vase on the table. There had been undefinable mix of alcohol in it. Then he looked at the screen on her laptop again.

"Come in here, Assad. Rose has been on the police website and intranet."

He pointed at the broken screen. "There's no doubt that she took an interest in the Zimmermann case, so she *does* know. I'm afraid that might have pushed her over the edge."

He opened her search tabs one by one.

"These searches are very superficial. It's as if she just wanted to bring herself up to speed with the main details of the murder," he said.

"I think that's good, Carl. Then I think we can safely say she didn't kill Zimmermann," said Assad quietly.

Carl looked at him uncomprehendingly. What was he talking about?

"Not that I had any reason to think that, but it was a strange coincidence that they were neighbors, wasn't it?"

"Damn it, Assad, you shouldn't think like that."

Curly looked sullen. He knew that.

"I'm afraid I also found this in the bathroom, Carl."

He placed a Gillette razor on top of the jacket on the table.

"There's no blade in it. It's been screwed off."

Carl felt a stab to his heart. It couldn't be true.

He inspected the razor and let it fall back down on the jacket. There was a dull click when it landed.

Carl looked puzzled, grabbed a corner of the jacket, and lifted it off the table.

There was Rose's cell phone and a lot of other things that made them freeze: a plastic basket with medicines that could easily be mixed into a lethal cocktail, the blade from the razor, and, even more ominously, a letter written in Rose's handwriting.

"Oh no," whispered Assad and said a short, silent prayer in Arabic.

Carl had to force himself to read the letter out to Assad.

Dear sisters,

There has been no end to my curse, so don't despair over my death, read the first line.

He hardly breathed while reading the rest.

They looked at each other for a minute without speaking. What was there to say?

"It's dated May 26th, Carl," said Assad, finally breaking the silence. Carl had never heard him sound so exhausted before. "That was last Thursday, the same day she discharged herself, and I don't think she's been here since." He sighed. "She could be lying dead anywhere, Carl. And maybe she . . ." He couldn't bring himself to finish the sentence.

Carl looked around the sitting room. It was as if she had tried to reflect her shattered mind with her vandalism. As if she had wanted to make clear to those around her that there was nothing to grieve over and nothing to be surprised about.

"She was too clever for her own good, Carl, so I don't think we'll ever find her." His face looked expressionless, apart from his eyebrows and his lips, which were quivering.

Carl put a hand on his shoulder. "It's very sad, Assad. It really is, my friend."

Assad turned his face toward him with a gentle, almost grateful, look in his eyes. He nodded and picked up the suicide note to read it again.

"There's another piece of paper underneath it, Assad," said Carl. He picked it up and read it aloud:

Stenløse, Thursday 5.26.2016

I hereby donate my body to organ donation and research.
Best regards, Rose Knudsen

"I simply don't get it, Assad. Why would she commit suicide somewhere where she can't be found if she wanted to leave her organs for transplants and her body for research?"

Assad shook his head. They looked at each while they tried to find a logical explanation.

"If you want to donate your organs, you don't poison them with lethal medication, and you certainly don't go into hiding. So what's the deal with this?" Carl waved the piece of paper in the air.

Assad scratched his head as if that could help him work it out. "I don't get it. Maybe she had a change of heart and decided to do it somewhere else."

"Does that seem logical to you? What does someone do who wants to commit suicide and also donate their organs to help others? You make sure you're found quickly, which is what I assume she hoped would happen. But where is she, then? And why didn't she take her phone so she could say where she was? It doesn't make any sense."

Carl picked up the phone and tried to turn it on. The battery really was dead, just like he had suggested to Lars Bjørn.

"I wouldn't mind seeing what's on here. Do you think she had a charger somewhere?"

They searched among the chaos. It was hopeless, like looking for the infamous needle in a haystack.

"She had a charger in her office, Carl."

He nodded. There wasn't much more they could do here.

"I notice you've just been in Rose's apartment. Is she okay?" asked a woman on the walkway when they locked the door.

"Who's asking?" asked Carl.

She gave him her hand. "My name is Sanne and I live a couple of doors down." She pointed.

"Do you know each other?"

"I wouldn't say that, but we say hello. I saw her the other day and told her that Zimmermann is dead. Is she ill? I noticed she'd been away for a while, and she didn't seem like her old self."

"When was this?"

"Last Thursday. The day Kevin Magnussen crashed his Renault into a wall. I love Formula One, and especially Kevin. And I had just heard the news when I met Rose. I remember it clearly."

"Rose isn't at home just now. Do you have any idea where we might find her?"

She shook her head. "No, she didn't really have much to do with the rest of us in the building, except Rigmor as far as I know. Anyway, I haven't been at home all weekend." She pointed at a roller suitcase next to her. "I've been visiting my family."

She smiled and looked like she wanted them to ask her what the occasion had been, but they never did.

"Shouldn't we file a missing person's report?" asked Assad on the way down to the car.

"Yes, we should. But . . ." He hesitated for a moment. Just like Assad, he was shocked by Rose's suicide and organ donation notes. Although there were indications that she might have changed her mind, you never knew with someone who was mentally ill. And Rose was, whether they were willing to admit it or not. Carl looked at Assad with a serious expression. "But if we do it, everything about Rose will come out in the open. And what if she's just sitting in some hotel trying to clear her head? Then we'll have destroyed her career."

"You think so?" He sounded surprised.

"Yes, it'll be more than difficult for her to return to her old job if all her secrets get out. Bjørn would never accept that. He does things by the book."

"That wasn't exactly what I meant, Carl. Do you think there's a chance she's sitting somewhere trying to clear her head? Because if that's the case, Carl, then she might still be considering suicide. I think we do need to file that missing person's report."

Assad was right, and it put them in a difficult position. Carl sighed as they walked past the parked cars. There was a woman sleeping in a small Ka a few cars away from theirs.

He wished it was him.

46

Monday, May 30th, 2016

Jazmine was at her wit's end. Denise had been gone for hours without checking in. What the fuck was she doing? And what did she imagine Jazmine should do? Denise had forbidden her to call because it might give her away if she was hiding. But what about her? The woman out there in the bathroom was moaning. She looked really off-color, had nasty red blotches on her thighs, and her fingers were almost blue.

To be honest, she was really worried that if she gave her water she might choke on it due to her weakened state.

Jazmine didn't like thinking about it because if the woman died they would suddenly be guilty of double murder. They would be facing lifetime sentences and that would mean that life was over. What could she do when they released her at forty-five without an education and with the sort of record she could never shake off? Would she even be able to save up for anything in prison, like a ticket to the other side of the world or something like that? Could she ever become anything other than a prostitute? She certainly didn't want *that,* but what else would there be? If Denise didn't return within an hour or two she would just make a run for it. She would take all the money and get the hell out of here. It would be Denise's own fault.

She gathered the money and put it in a canvas bag of the sort old ladies thought were chic thirty years ago. No one would suspect that it contained anything but crap. And then she would take the S-train to the central station and take the Vejle bus from Ingerslevsgade. There was one leaving at around ten, which she could easily catch.

Once she was in Jutland, she would have many more opportunities to continue south without being caught—and south was where she was headed. Out of the country. Far away. Just disappear and never come back. A discounted green ticket to Berlin with Abildskou Buses cost only one hundred and fifty kroner, and from there she could go anywhere in the world. Right now she was particularly tempted by Italy. It was swarming with beautiful men who liked girls like her, and place names like Sardinia and Sicily sounded spellbinding.

Now the woman out there was whimpering again, but sounding weaker and weaker.

Jazmine tried to focus on something in the room that could distract her from what was going on in the bathroom.

"Should I or shouldn't I?" she said quietly to herself a few times before going to the kitchen to get a glass of water. One last time and then she would leave the rest to fate.

She had just leaned in over the steel sink to fill the glass when she heard someone knocking on the door to the next-door apartment.

Jazmine lifted the kitchen curtain slightly to look out and immediately pulled back when a dark man on the walkway looked in her direction.

Jazmine held her breath and hid in the corner next to the fridge. *Did he see me?* she wondered. Then a shadow slid past the curtain. She could hear clearly what they were saying out there. She was so scared her heart almost stopped. The two voices were male, and one of them said he hadn't seen anything. Then the doorbell rang.

Now the woman was moaning in the bathroom again. It was very muffled but Jazmine could hear it. Could they also hear it outside?

The men on the walkway were having a discussion.

She got such a shock that it made her flinch when they suddenly hammered on the door and one of the men shouted through the mail slot that he had seen someone in there. He wanted to ask questions, he shouted, but Jazmine had no intention of talking to anyone, so she didn't answer.

Go away! she screamed internally when the other man asked if there was anything to see through the mail slot. It was a good thing that she hadn't gone into the hallway, because then the game would have been up.

It seemed as if the shadow behind the curtain was moving again— as if someone was trying to look into the kitchen—and then she heard someone tapping on the window. Jazmine looked at the counter under the window. There was nothing to see except dirty dishes and mugs with cutlery in them. What could he get out of that?

"Maybe you didn't see anything, Assad," she heard him say out there when the other man had stopped knocking. He said it very clearly, and he also said that they should have brought the key for the apartment. The other one answered that he had a lockpick down in the car.

Jazmine nearly fainted in shock. If they went down to get it, her life would be over. Yes, the woman in the bathroom was alive, but still. Jazmine had just imagined herself surrounded by colors and hot-blooded men with black hair, but it turned out none of it was real. That was going to be hard to swallow.

But then the first man said that he would leave it to their colleagues in homicide, after which their voices grew fainter. Jazmine thought she heard them enter the next-door apartment. Yes, now she could hear their voices faintly through the wall. It meant that she was off the hook for now—but maybe not for long. One of them had hinted that there would be people from homicide coming out here. But what did they actually know, since they would do that? Was it something about Denise? Why didn't she just call? It was driving her mad. It had all sounded so simple. Denise was just meant to blackmail Anne-Line and if necessary do the same thing to her as they had done to the woman in the bathroom. Keep her hostage until she gave in and handed over the lottery money. But she could still call, so why didn't she?

Stupid bitch! It was her own fault, because Jazmine couldn't stay here. If she took all the money from the robbery, Denise could keep Anne-Line Svendsen's money. Jazmine didn't care. Weren't they meant to split everything when Denise returned anyway?

She frowned, going over everything in her head again. What did they mean when they said that homicide would be paying a visit? Had something gone wrong at Anne-Line's place somehow? Was that what this was about?

They had agreed that if Denise didn't turn up, Jazmine should make an anonymous call to the police and blow the whistle on Anne-Line Svendsen. But did she dare? They could trace her call and it was even easier if you called from a cell phone. Denise obviously hadn't thought about *that*.

The way things were going, Jazmine didn't give a fuck as long as she could save her own neck. Hadn't she done what she was supposed to? Hadn't she arranged for them to have the names in their passports changed later tonight on their way to the bus station? So it was just tough luck that Denise wouldn't get hers.

Now the woman in the bathroom was moaning again.

"Shut up," she hissed as she walked past the bathroom door. If the police were coming, *they* could give the woman some water. She also stank of piss and shit, and Jazmine couldn't stand it.

It took her only five minutes to pack her clothes.

One quick glance out of the window revealed that the coast was clear. She could still hear the muffled sound of the men's voices through the wall, so she would just have to be quick.

She slung the canvas bag with the money over her shoulder, grabbed the suitcase, and lifted the kitchen curtain again.

Just as a precaution, she glanced down at the parking area. There didn't appear to be any other police, because there was just one car with a siren on the roof. The other cars were just the regular sort you expected to find in the suburbs. Not the type Jazmine would drive when she finally made it to Italy. She smiled to herself thinking about convertibles with white leather seats. She had always wanted a car like that.

Suddenly she heard the two men leaving and locking up the apartment next door. Then they had a brief conversation with a woman on the walkway.

Just wait until they've left and the coast is clear, she thought as she tried to follow what was happening outside.

She heard a few suppressed sighs from the bathroom, as if the woman had started crying. Jazmine did feel sorry for her, but what could she do? Maybe Denise would kill her when she came back and realized that Jazmine had done a runner. She could just imagine how she would react when she realized that there wouldn't be a false passport waiting for her and that the woman in the bathroom was suddenly a threat because she knew too much.

But that was Denise's call, not hers.

She saw the police car leaving and pulled the curtain back a little more so she could make sure they were really gone.

Then she suddenly noticed a figure moving in a small car a few spaces to the right. And when the woman removed her sunglasses and looked up toward her, Jazmine froze.

It was her caseworker, Anne-Line! But then where was Denise?

Jazmine felt sick. What should she do?

The woman in the car was looking directly up at her, and the look in her eyes said it all. Anne-Line Svendsen was not scared. She looked perfectly composed, so Denise couldn't have succeeded in her mission. But where was she? Jazmine thought the worst and was overcome with panic.

She just had to get out of there. And there was only one way out apart from the main door: over the balcony and down.

She ran to the bedroom and grabbed all the sheets from the cupboard.

She tied some sheets together, hoping it would be enough to reach the ground. Then she rushed into the sitting room, tied one end around a door handle, pushed the balcony door to one side, threw the makeshift rope and her suitcase over the side, slung the canvas bag over her shoulder, and climbed down.

The friction from the sheets chafed her hands, but then Jazmine had never bragged about her acrobatic prowess.

She looked around as she clambered down. Thankfully there didn't appear to be anyone at home in the downstairs apartment. Then she saw that the suitcase had sprung open from the fall and that her clothes had been flung in all directions.

I don't have time to pick them up, she thought. So when she reached the ground she just started running.

When she had made it past the buildings and saw that there was no one on the sidewalk leading toward the S-train station, she thought with relief that she was safe.

She noticed a spot where the grass on the roadside had been churned up.

This must be where Michelle was killed, she thought before hearing a car speeding up behind her.

47

Monday, May 30th, 2016

"**Come on, Rose, it's** Vicky! Come out now. Dad *has* left for work. He's on the night shift this week."

Her shivering fingers reached for the key in the door to her room but she didn't turn it. Was he on nights? Was it really already Thursday? And who was shouting out there?

The voice had said it was Vicky, but that wasn't true because *she* was Vicky. So why did the person out there think she was Rose? Who would even want to be Rose? No one liked her, whereas with Vicky . . . it was different.

When I can come out, I'll put a shirt on, she thought. *Today should be a yellow-and-black-checked shirt buttoned down to show off my cleavage.* She giggled. She would make people's eyes pop out.

But I'll just smile when they stare and tell them I plan to marry a certain actor. I don't remember his name just now, but never mind. He knows I'm the one for him. Oh yes, he knows.

They say Vicky is so beautiful, so therefore I'm beautiful. Rose is just Rose. It's a shame for her. She can't help it; it's just the way she is. Dad has said so often enough, and he's right, so I'm glad I'm not her.

Who would want to be her? Have I said that already? Well, I certainly wouldn't. And now Dad is on nights, so I'll just go out dancing. Thankfully, they don't have any say in that. None of them do.

Then the uncomfortable burning sensation in her throat returned. She wasn't really sure whether it was part of the image she had just been thinking about. She certainly hoped not, because it was going so well. Only a moment ago, she hadn't been in any pain at all, but now the pain had returned.

Ouch, I vomited again. When will it stop? Oouuch!

Rose opened her eyes. Everything around her was blurry. Her eyes were dry and her whole body ached. Or did it? Wasn't it only her throat and tongue that hurt?

Somewhere in the distance, she could hear a female voice cursing. Was it real or was it a dream again?

Am I drifting off again already? She seemed to have done that many times over many hours now. In fact, she had no sense of time and only a vague sense of where she was.

The overwhelming facts were that she was tied up, her crotch and throat felt like they were on fire, and she couldn't feel the rest of her body. As far as she knew, it was at least twenty-four hours since she had been able to feel her hands and legs. But how long had it actually been?

Now the woman out there was talking again and sounded very angry. She was swearing and cursing the one called Denise. But then this must be reality, and if it was real she only hoped that she could stay here. As soon as she disappeared, she saw her father lying there on the floor, his flesh and bones crushed and with a wide grin on his face directed right at her. Those staring eyes burning their way into her and never fading. They glowed more and more intensely each time she slipped into the dream. Of course, she knew that her sisters would come to her aid every time. Suddenly, they were inside her and she was inside them, and then she felt at peace. And peace was the only thing she was looking for. Come as it may.

"Where the hell is she?" said the angry voice.

What was the name of the one who was talking? Was it Michelle? No, she was the one they had said was dead. Or was that also something she'd dreamed?

She said, "Mmmmm," from behind the gaffer tape, meaning that she was thirsty, but she was drowned out by the woman's voice, which just continued on. But then it hadn't normally been her who had put the straw in her mouth. That much she could remember. Maybe she had done it once, but that was all.

She felt her stomach cramping up and the burning sensation returned in her throat with a vengeance. At least her body could still react—everything was connected.

Rose opened her eyes wide. Her heartburn had pulled her out of her stupor.

She looked around. The light was already dim in the hallway. Did that mean that it was early morning or late at night? It could be hard to determine at this time of year when it was light almost around the clock. It was that time of year when summer was waiting just around the corner, people fell in love at first sight, and everyone was full of anticipation and joy. She had experienced this once in her life, and the memory made her happy. Falling in love was often described as something that happened by itself and countless times. That wasn't Rose's experience, but she had felt that joy inside even though her father put an end to that too.

Now the woman out there was talking again—almost shouting, in fact.

Rose frowned. No, that wasn't right. It wasn't a woman shouting at all. She looked out through the doorway toward the hallway. There was nothing out there, and still a voice filled the entire space. The voice was much deeper than the woman's, and she recognized it. It was Assad's voice, wasn't it? Why would she suddenly hear *that* voice? And why would he suddenly be shouting that he knew there was someone in the apartment and that he just wanted to ask some questions?

Was she only dreaming, or was Assad really trying to tell her that he knew she was in there? Or did he want to ask her questions? Then why didn't he just come in and ask? She would happily answer him. He was her friend after all.

She mumbled, "Mmmmm," and this time it meant that he should just come in. He should come in and remove the tape from her mouth so she could spit out the vile taste in her mouth and answer his questions. She would love to do that.

Come on and ask me something, Assad, she thought, feeling her dry eyes welling up and her chest heaving. It felt good.

Then she heard another voice far away that almost sounded like Carl's. She felt moved when she heard it. So moved, in fact, that the tears ran down her cheeks. Could this be real? Were they out there somewhere? Did they know she was in here?

If that was the case, maybe they would force their way into the apartment. And finding her there in her humiliation, would they still hold her tight?

She hoped they would.

She listened for a long time, trying to make sounds that were louder and more meaningful than inarticulate groans. She was wide-awake, and the adrenaline pumping through her kept her in the real world.

Then the pain suddenly rushed into her shoulders and back. It was a violent onslaught of insistent protest from her joints and muscles. All her nerves came to life, and Rose groaned in agony behind the gaffer tape.

She saw the silhouette of the woman walk past the bathroom door. She seemed to be moving differently. She seemed hectic and tense. "Shut up," she hissed at Rose as she passed, and a few minutes later she could hear noise coming from the sitting room. A click and a few bumps and then it went quiet.

Deadly quiet.

48

Monday, May 30th, 2016

Anneli had gone through more phases of shock and realization over the past hour than in all her adult life.

If she had arrived at Sandalsparken just a few minutes earlier, it would all have been over. She would have been caught red-handed in Denise's apartment and arrested.

She had been only seconds away from getting out of her car when the police car with the two detectives pulled up in front of her. Anneli slouched down in her seat and watched their every move. At first they stopped in front of the neighboring apartment as if they were going to enter, but then they changed their minds and knocked on the door of the girls' apartment, shouting something through the mail slot and tapping on the window. It looked odd and somehow also very unsettling.

What did they suspect? That the girls were guilty of robbery and murder? But how could they know? Or were they there because they wanted to question someone? Perhaps they had discovered that Michelle had been living there; you could never know. The girl might have had a receipt or a telephone number on her that indirectly led them to the apartment. But then why did they give up and disappear into the other apartment? How did that fit in?

As the men finally left the building and walked a few meters past her car, she held her breath. And when the tallest man, the one who looked Caucasian, turned his head and looked directly at her through the car window, she thought he would stop. That he would ask her why she was still there. She pretended to be asleep and he seemed to buy that.

She saw everything from behind her sunglasses. And when the cops finally left, she saw the curtain in the girls' apartment move and a face peeping out. So Anneli took off her sunglasses, but because of the distance she couldn't quite make out if it was Jazmine. However, the way the face at the window jumped backward, as if something had scared her, left little doubt. Jazmine probably wasn't sure who or what she had seen, but she knew that Anneli drove a Ka because she had told her so herself.

Anneli weighed up the situation. Jazmine had not wanted to reveal herself to the police. But had they been foiled or were they on their way to get reinforcements or whatever it was called?

Sensing that she didn't have much time, Anneli quickly got out of the car. Fate had helped her many times before, so she certainly wasn't going to second-guess it now.

She would have run directly from the stairwell up onto the walkway, but there was a woman checking her mailbox, and who knew if she was on her way up or down. If she went up onto the walkway, Anneli had better wait until the coast was clear.

So Anneli walked straight through the entrance hall and out the back door that led to the large communal grass area between the two blocks.

Just as she walked out, she saw a suitcase lying on the grass with its contents spread everywhere. Anneli dashed out onto the lawn and looked up at the girls' apartment. She wasn't surprised when she saw a makeshift rope of sheets swaying from the balcony.

Anneli looked all around and finally caught sight of a slim woman running as fast as she could at the far left end of the block.

There was no doubt in her mind that it was Jazmine. She dressed and moved exactly like that. It was a perfect match. Anneli cursed her own carelessness and ran back to her car as fast as her unfit body allowed.

She's on her way down to the station, she thought, knowing each twist and turn of the road, because that was where she had killed Michelle.

She saw Jazmine a few hundred meters in front of her, almost in the same spot where Michelle had met her end. But this time the sidewalk was not quite as deserted as last time. A group of rowdy young men were leaving the station. They were already in full summer mood, walking along with their jackets swinging on their shoulders and beers in hand. It would be impossible to drive into Jazmine here.

But that wasn't her intention.

Anneli rummaged for Denise's pistol in her bag and sped up when she found it. In front of her, the young boys started shoving each other playfully, and then suddenly cut over the grass, kicking some of the beer cans on their way.

A second later, Anneli drove past Jazmine and hit the brakes hard ten meters in front of her. She reached straight over to the passenger door and flung it open.

Jazmine looked completely defeated when she saw Denise's pistol pointing directly at her.

"We need to talk, Jazmine," said Anneli as she stepped out onto the pavement. "I have Denise at my place, and as you can see I'm in possession of her pistol. And now I really want to get to the bottom of what you've started."

She gestured to Jazmine to get in the car.

"Get in!" she ordered.

Jazmine transformed into a completely different girl from the contemptuous brat who had not long ago sat backstabbing Anneli in the waiting room, calling her a cow and a ridiculous ugly bitch. A very different girl from the one who used to challenge her in her own office.

"I haven't done anything to you," said the girl in a subdued voice next to her. But Anneli turned the car around and drove back toward the parking area at Sandalsparken.

"I don't think for a second that you have, Jazmine, but now we'll drive back to the apartment and get your suitcase. Then we'll go and put the kettle on and get to the bottom of this before we go and get Denise, okay?"

Jazmine shook her head. "I don't want to go back to that place."

"Well, now I'm the one who decides. So you can protest all you like."

"I didn't do anything. It was Denise," she whispered, rather unmotivated. Anneli wasn't quite sure what she was hinting at, but it didn't matter.

"Of course it was Denise, Jazmine," she answered diplomatically. "After all, I am your caseworker, so it shouldn't surprise you that I know you both well."

The girl was about to say something else but stopped herself, and Anneli didn't give a damn anyway. In ten minutes, the world would be rid of her.

Jazmine stopped on the walkway a few meters from the door.

"I don't know how we'll get in," she said very convincingly. "I climbed down from the balcony and the door is locked. The key is inside the apartment."

Anneli looked suspiciously at her. Was she pulling her leg?

"We'll have to go somewhere else. Can't we drive to your place?"

Was she trying to win time or was it true? After all, Anneli had seen that the key was not in the suitcase when they had picked it up along with all the clothes.

"Empty your pockets," she said. Jazmine did as she was told. A couple of hundred-kroner notes and a condom was all she had on her. Then she asked to see the contents of the canvas bag on Jazmine's shoulder, but Jazmine held on to it tightly and suddenly looked determined, snarling that she didn't have the goddamn key. Couldn't Anneli just believe her?

Anneli did believe her because it all sounded logical enough. She had seen the sheets hanging down from the balcony for herself. The problem, however, was that for the first time she had no idea what her next move should be. Her entire plan of creating a scenario of murder and suicide between the girls was in jeopardy if she didn't kill Jazmine behind that door. Nothing else would work.

Gazing down the walkway, Anneli suddenly thought how bare it looked. No plants outside the doors or along the banister. In fact, no decoration anywhere except a single doormat outside the girls' apartment.

"Step back, Jazmine," she said intuitively and lifted the doormat. And there was the key.

"Did you think you could fool me, Jazmine?" She smiled.

Jazmine looked utterly lost. Almost as if she was more surprised than Anneli.

Anneli unlocked the door and pushed the girl into the hallway in front of her. She immediately noticed the unmistakable smell of feces and urine, but the last few weeks had toughened her up. The cancer, the surgery, the radiation therapy, the whole business of plotting the murders, and not least committing them, had erased her old self. Now nothing could shock her or faze her.

But when she saw that the door to the bathroom was open and that the smell was coming from a woman tied to the toilet in her own shit and piss, she was shocked all the same.

"Who is that?" she gasped.

Jazmine shrugged apologetically. "I don't know. It's something Denise has done. I don't know why."

Anneli nudged the woman without getting a reaction.

"She's dead, isn't she?"

"I don't know," said Jazmine, clutching the canvas bag. It looked very suspicious under the circumstances.

"Give that to me, Jazmine," she said angrily and grabbed for it. But the girl didn't let go. Then she swung the pistol at the girl's face at full force, and the effect was brilliant. Jazmine screamed and let go of the bag, putting her hands to her face. She knew that her pretty face was her last asset.

"You'll do exactly what I tell you, Jazmine. Otherwise I'll hit you again. Understood?"

Anneli picked up the canvas bag from the floor and looked inside.

"What?" she exclaimed. This day was really full of surprises.

"How much is there?" she asked. "If it's the money from the robbery, I know it's a lot."

Jazmine nodded, her hands still covering her face. Was she crying?

Anneli shook her head. What brilliant luck. Everything was coming together nicely. She had managed to get the girl back here and now she had her hands on all this money.

Anneli glanced at the limp figure in the bathroom. How would it affect her plans that this woman was there? If she was dead, her presence would remain a mystery. But if she wasn't, she could become a problem. As one of her ex-boyfriends—the most boring one—always said, "Luck is only there to be taken from us if we don't guard it with everything we've got." Maybe he wasn't as stupid as she thought. Time was really getting on, so she had to hurry up and deal with Jazmine before she ran out of luck.

"Come into the sitting room, Jazmine," she said, rehearsing the scene in her head. Once she had shot Jazmine with the gun, Anneli would press Denise's pistol into her hand. The plan was for the police to conclude that there had been a showdown between the two girls and that Jazmine hadn't had time to fire the pistol at Denise before Denise killed her with the silenced gun. The one they would later find next to Denise's body.

"Sit down over by that shelf, Jazmine," she said as she discretely slid her hand in her bag and replaced the pistol with the gun.

Jazmine's expression darkened and she raised her sharply drawn eyebrows. "What's that for?" she asked nervously. "Weren't we supposed to talk? That's what you said."

"Oh, but we will, Jazmine. And you're going to tell me everything, got it? Why did you think that it was me who ran Michelle over?"

Anneli hid the gun under the table and took out the silencer from her bag.

"She told us that she saw you before you hit her."

Anneli nodded. "But she was mistaken, Jazmine. It wasn't me."

The girl couldn't help but frown, even if it meant she would wrinkle her otherwise perfectly smooth face. "Well, she also saw you when . . ."

"When what, Jazmine? I assure you she was mistaken. It must have been someone who looked like me."

Jazmine's gaze moved back and forth from the edge of the table to her side in discomfort. She clearly knew that something drastic was about to happen. And now that damn oil filter wouldn't fit properly on the barrel of the gun.

"What are you doing under the table, Anne-Line?" she asked. In the same moment, she jumped up and grabbed a club-like thing from the teakwood shelf above the dresser.

She'll lunge for me in a second, thought Anneli, pulling the gun out from under the table and giving up on the silencer.

"*Stop* that, Jazmine!" she yelled. But Jazmine had already unscrewed a cap from the shaft of the club, and before Anneli could react, Jazmine pulled on a small ball hanging from a string at one end before tossing the club across the dining table toward Anneli and throwing herself on the floor for protection.

Anneli looked at the object with horror and instinctively threw herself on the floor while Jazmine crawled out into the hallway.

It was a hand grenade, but not one of those pineapple-shaped ones.

But nothing happened. The junk didn't work.

Anneli got up and held a hand to her shoulder, which was sore from her fall. She could hear Jazmine tugging at the front door handle.

"You can forget that, Jazmine," she shouted toward the hallway. "I locked the door behind me."

She picked up the gun and the silencer from the floor and walked out into the hallway while assembling them properly.

Jazmine clearly understood what was about to happen, darting in fear into the bathroom and locking the door, as if that would help.

Anneli pointed the gun at the door and pulled the trigger. The hole in the door was modest, but the scream from the other side was not.

She's making too much noise, thought Anneli. She fired again and the screaming stopped.

What now? She had to check how badly she had injured the girl, but the door was locked. Of course, she could kick it open—it was as thin as cardboard—but then she'd have to wipe the footprint off it afterward. But then she realized that she was going to have to wipe her prints off everything anyway. Why hadn't she remembered to bring gloves?

Then she kicked the door where the lock was and the door flew halfway open.

Anneli squeezed her way in and looked down at the floor where Jazmine lay gasping. Her eyes were big and black and the terrazzo floor was stained red with her blood.

Handy when the floor slopes in the right direction, she thought as she watched the blood flowing toward the drain under the sink.

Then she turned toward the mirror and saw a full-length reflection of herself.

There she was, Anneli Svendsen, a middle-aged woman with bags under her eyes and a gaping mouth. This was the second time she saw herself looking so cold, cynical, and indifferent. It made her shudder. Who *was* this woman calmly standing here as she watched a little creature bleeding to death? Was she actually going crazy like she had thought before? It certainly felt like it.

She looked down at Jazmine's leg, which was twitching as her life ebbed away. It was only when she lay completely still, her eyes staring blankly at the ceiling, that Anneli turned toward the woman who was tied to the toilet.

Anneli reached around her and flushed the toilet. Judging by the smell, it was long overdue.

"There," she said. "Now I've avenged you, whoever you are and whatever you're doing here," Then she stroked the poor woman's hair, rolled a lot of toilet paper around her right hand, and went around the apartment thoroughly wiping everything she had touched.

Finally, she carefully picked up Denise's pistol with a piece of toilet paper and went out to the bathroom to press it into Jazmine's hand. But which hand should she choose? The blood-soaked left hand or the right hand, which still looked clean? Which hand did Jazmine even use? Had she thrown the grenade with her right hand?

Anneli closed her eyes and tried to picture the incident. She simply couldn't remember.

Then she squeezed Jazmine's clean right hand around the pistol grip and let her hand fall back onto the floor before turning off the light and pulling the door shut.

When she had packed her things in her bag, she rolled some paper towels around her hand, placed Jazmine's suitcase on the bed in the bedroom, and opened it. If anyone had seen them with the suitcase down on the grass, which she didn't think anyone had, they would probably just describe Jazmine as a weird girl who had been helped by an elderly lady. The police would ask who the lady was and they would answer that they hadn't seen her before.

The conclusion would be that she had been unpacking when she was interrupted by the showdown with Denise. Wasn't that a story the police would buy? She thought so because it was sufficiently complex and simple at the same time.

Anneli smiled. Maybe she had watched too many crime shows, but wasn't that an advantage in this situation? She thought so.

She was about to leave the apartment when she caught sight of the hand grenade. What luck it hadn't detonated.

She carefully picked it up and scrutinized it.

"*Vor Gebrauch Sprengkapsel Einsetzen,*" was written in big letters on the metal end.

Insert detonator before use, she translated. But who said anyone had ever done that?

Not doing that cost you your life, Jazmine. What a pity, thought Anneli, laughing at the thought. The lazy girl had probably never bothered to learn German.

Anneli turned the grenade upside down and poked the ball and string back into the hollow wooden shaft. It didn't work, but if it could scare *her,* it could scare others, too.

It might be a bit long, but it's useful nonetheless, she thought while she screwed the cap back on and placed it in the canvas bag on top of all the money.

I'll google the thing sometime if I ever need to know how to install the detonator, she thought. Who knew, maybe one day she would devise a murder plan that would be best served with a weapon like this.

When she stepped out onto the walkway and wiped down the key with a bit of paper towel before putting it back under the mat, she thought for a moment that nothing had been more successful than the mission she had been on over the last few weeks. Now all that remained was a little drive with Denise's body, and then she really deserved a good long holiday.

She patted the canvas bag a couple of times in satisfaction and walked back to the car.

Once her radiation treatment was over, a couple of weeks' cruising in the Mediterranean was a tempting thought.

49

Monday, May 30th, 2016

It took a minute before Carl explained to Gordon what they had found in Rose's apartment. Poor Gordon was as silent as the grave at the other end.

Carl looked at Assad with a desolate expression. Assad couldn't even muster the energy to put his feet up on the dashboard.

It was going to be a long night for all of them.

"Are you still there, Gordon?" asked Carl.

Was that a yes?

"I'm afraid we have no idea where Rose might be, but don't lose hope, okay?"

Still no reaction.

"We're considering filing a missing person's report, but I think we need to look into possible whereabouts first."

"Okay!" he answered almost inaudibly.

Carl brought him up to speed about the visit they had paid James Frank and their breakthrough with his confession in the Zimmermann case.

It didn't seem to lift his spirits at all. Understandably, the news about Rose had hit him hard.

"Unfortunately, Assad and I have one more thing to see to, even though it's hard the way we're all feeling just now about Rose. We're going to see Birgit Zimmermann again because there are a few things we need to check up on. How about you? Are you also ready to keep going?"

"Of course I am. Just tell me what you need me to do."

It sounded like he was already recovering from the shock.

Carl imagined Gordon's face. He knew full well what Rose meant to him. She was perhaps the only reason why he stayed working in the cellar for Department Q. The effect of the one he was dreaming about dating but might never get.

"I want you to call her sisters and bring them up to speed, but don't make it sound more dramatic than it is, if possible." Carl doubted that it was. "Ask them if they have any idea where she might be. Does she have any connections in Malmö or Skåne, for example? Could she be staying at a summerhouse or with a former lover? Yeah, sorry to put you in this situation, Gordon, but the last thing is important too."

Of course he didn't comment.

"Keep me updated, Gordon. Let us know what you discover, and then we'll make a decision about the missing person's report."

Although it was still fairly light outside, it looked like every single ceiling lamp in Birgit Zimmermann's mezzanine apartment was lit. It probably meant she was at home.

They pressed the buzzer and were surprisingly enough buzzed in after a few seconds.

"I was actually expecting someone like you," she said, looking dizzy, albeit this time not necessarily the result of alcohol. In fact, she came across far more levelheaded than when they had visited her earlier in the day to talk about Stephanie Gundersen. She invited them to take a seat before they had even said anything.

"Have you found Denise? Is that why you're here?"

"So you know the police have started looking for her since we were here earlier today?"

"Yes, they've called me a few times. Have you found her?"

"Unfortunately not. We were hoping you could help us with that."

"I'm scared," she said. "She's a terrible brat, but I don't want anything bad to happen to her. Do you think she murdered that Icelandic girl and took part in the robbery like the media are suggesting?"

"I assure you, we know nothing about that, Birgit. But she's a suspect and we need to get hold of her to find out. The police in Slagelse have been all around town asking if anyone has seen her, but unfortunately they didn't get anywhere. We also get the feeling that you don't believe she's actually there. Is that correct?"

"If it was her at that nightclub in Sydhavnen, she can't have been in Slagelse at that time, can she?"

Carl agreed. She was considerably more clearheaded than usual.

"We have some specific questions we'd like to ask you, Birgit. Earlier today, you insinuated that Denise might know something about your mother's murder. I'd like to ask you why you did that."

"And what makes you think I want to talk to you about that? I was drunk, wasn't I? You must know that people say stupid things when they're drunk."

"That's right. Let's leave that subject. Meanwhile, we've located your ex-husband."

The reaction was incredible. The tendons on her neck tensed and her jaw dropped. She inhaled deeply and held her breath, clenching her fists. There was no doubt that she was genuinely taken aback and trying to remain calm.

"He's still in the country, Birgit. You probably thought he had disappeared back when Stephanie Gundersen was murdered, right?"

She didn't answer, but her heaving chest clearly showed the level of shock she was in.

"I assume your mother told you that he disappeared after the murder. That if anyone was a suspect, it must be him. That she was willing to tell the police about him if they starting closing in on you, right? She had a whole story prepared."

Strangely enough, Birgit shook her head.

"James is living in the apartment above your father's old shop, but you probably didn't know that, did you?"

She shook her head again.

"Birgit, I don't want to bore you with James's story, but he told us about an agreement he made with your mother. He deserted from the

US Army when he was in Afghanistan, returned to Denmark in 2003, and promised to stay away from you and Denise. Your mother paid him for it, but you did know that?"

She didn't react at all, so they couldn't be sure.

"James believes that your mother saw him and Stephanie Gundersen together in town. He said it was a coincidence, but I don't believe that. While coincidence does often play a role in crime, I'm more inclined to believe that it was you who saw James with Stephanie outside Denise's school and told your mother about it. I think that your mother decided to follow them and was spotted by James. And do you know what all this is based on? Your argument with Stephanie about her way with men at the parent-teacher meeting. I think this case is about a hurt, insanely frustrated, and in some strange way also jealous woman who suddenly saw her daughter's beautiful teacher with her ex-husband. You already hated Stephanie Gundersen because Denise adored her. And my guess is that it made you completely desperate. Do you understand where I'm coming from, Birgit? Not only did you have to contend with all your anger and jealousy from the past, but you also saw your ex-husband with a respected teacher who could steal your daughter away from you just like that. And *that* was something you weren't prepared to risk."

She fumbled for her cigarettes on the table, but Assad beat her to it, offered her one, and even lit it for her. Smart move.

"We're sorry to have to upset you like this, Birgit," said Assad. "It must be shocking to think that your ex-husband has suddenly popped up in your life again. He actually came to visit you here yesterday. He saw you on the street, but you were so drunk that he didn't want to talk to you."

Assad went quiet and they both watched Birgit's reaction. She was bound to start talking at some point, but for now she just held her elbow in her hand, put the cigarette to her lips, and calmly inhaled the smoke.

"Do you want to hear my version of all this?" asked Carl.

No reaction.

"James often waited for Stephanie outside the school, standing behind the trees by the lakes. That way he could choose who saw him. What he didn't know was that you sometimes walked that way if you felt like picking Denise up from school. You came from Borgergade and sometimes walked along Dag Hammarskjölds Allé and farther along the lake to wait for Denise in exactly the same spot where James was. And one day, you saw Stephanie Gundersen leave the school and kiss James passionately while you looked on in disbelief from behind the trees. Your ex-husband was suddenly back in Denmark and too close for comfort. Can we agree on that?"

Then the unexpected finally happened. Birgit Zimmermann nodded silently.

"Birgit, I can tell you that James was convinced that it was your mother who killed Stephanie. I think it's because of the way it happened. After all, your father was always bragging about the damage that could be inflicted with a single hit with a club to the back of the head. Don't you think your mother also knew?"

She looked away. Were her lips quivering? If they were, Carl and Assad were on the right track.

Then she turned to face them directly. There were tears in her eyes and her lips were quivering. This was it!

"James told us earlier today that he killed your mother. It was simply an act of revenge for her killing Stephanie. But do you know what I think, Birgit?"

She grimaced. He was right, then.

"He killed the wrong person. Do we agree?"

The question appeared to have hit a nerve. It could be a feeling of powerlessness or relief. It could be anger or some form of contentment. Carl and Assad looked at each other and waited until she had wiped the snot from her chin and could look at them directly again.

"You actually thought it was Denise who killed your mother, didn't you Birgit? But what made you think that?"

She hesitated for a moment before answering. "Because my mother and Denise had had a horrible fight that day. They hated each other even though they usually managed to contain it. But that day my mother wouldn't give us the money for rent like she usually did. And that made Denise furious. So when they found my mother and she didn't have the money on her, I thought it must be Denise who had taken it. Partly because I saw Denise leaving the apartment with a bottle in her hand a few minutes before my mother left. It was one of those heavy Lambrusco bottles. And believe me, it wasn't only my mother that my father entertained with his stories about what you could do with one of those. We were all subjected to his tales when we were old enough. My father was a lunatic. He really was."

Carl frowned. If James had returned to the apartment on Borgergade just a few minutes earlier, he would have seen his daughter leave the apartment and then things would probably have turned out very differently: He would have approached her, Rigmor might not have been murdered, and the old Stephanie Gundersen would never have resurfaced.

"Thank you, Birgit," said Carl.

In a way, she looked relieved. But it also seemed as if she thought there was nothing more to say. As if there was no reason to continue with this conversation. She seemed a little too sure.

"Your father died the day after Stephanie, Birgit. He drowned in shallow water, and judging by what we know about him, it seems very unlikely that he would have committed suicide. A man whose cunning helped him evade the worst accusations anyone could face. A man whose survival instinct was strong enough to help him escape the hangman's noose. Can we agree that he of all people was an expert in hanging on to life?"

She took another cigarette. This time Assad didn't light it for her.

"I know the type of person," said Assad. "You'll find bastards like that in any war at any given time."

Carl nodded. "Yes, that's true. But it's also true that a man like your father always lets down his guard when he feels safe. He made a mistake in not leaving the past behind. In still bragging about his evil and cunning so many years later. And teaching his own family how to use that evil at any time with any available means was almost unforgiveable."

She nodded. She agreed.

"Your mother looked after your father, and I think they had an agreement based on discretion. Your mother knew that if he revealed too much in public, they would be doomed. *No one* could know who he was, because that would cost you everything. The business, your comfortable life. Everything."

Carl nodded toward her Prince cigarettes and she nodded back. It was always the same when he was wrapping up a case. The nicotine craving hit him.

"I'm convinced that your mother sacrificed your father for your sake, Birgit. He was old, difficult to look after and be around. He had fulfilled his purpose, which was to provide for his family, and now it was your mother's turn. Maybe he boasted in public about who had killed Stephanie, so your mother made a quick decision and pushed him in the lake. Am I right?"

Birgit let out a deep sigh. There was nothing to add.

"It wasn't your mother who killed Stephanie Gundersen, was it, Birgit? It wasn't your mother your father was boasting about. It was you, wasn't it? Your father was as proud as a peacock. Proud of his daughter who had shown so much resolve, eliminating the person who was poisoning her life."

She looked away, neither confirming nor denying. Then she slowly turned toward them and lifted her head as if she took pride in making one last comment in the case.

"How is James?" she asked rather surprisingly.

Carl leaned forward toward the ashtray and tapped the ash from his cigarette. "He's dying, Birgit. A dying man who wouldn't imagine letting a woman like your mother continue to live in this world."

She nodded.

"When you've found Denise, I'll sign my confession and not a moment before," she said.

50

Monday, May 30th, 2016

When Anneli turned the corner onto Webersgade, she was unpleasantly surprised to discover that there wasn't one single free parking space near her house. What the hell were they showing on TV, since everybody had chosen to stay at home on the same night? It wasn't only a wrench in the works; it was almost fatal.

I can't double-park, drag Denise over the sidewalk and bicycle path, and then in between two cars. It's far too risky, she thought while letting the car run idle at the end of the street.

So she took a chance and drove up onto the bicycle path at the point before the parking spaces started, assessing whether or not there was enough space to let her drive down to her house.

Good thing that the car isn't wider, she thought, continuing on with one pair of wheels on the bicycle path and the other pair on the sidewalk. It was a risky maneuver, but if she managed to drive all the way there she would be able to park just one meter from her door.

Please, neighbors, don't complain, she thought as she slowly rolled along. If they stayed indoors, the only thing she had to worry about was a passing patrol car. She smiled at the thought. Patrol cars in Copenhagen? There certainly weren't many of those left in this permanent period of retrenchment.

She parked as intended, right next to her door, and let herself into the building.

Strangely enough, she had to brace herself before stepping into the mechanical engineer's sitting room, where Denise's body was leaning up against the shelf to the right of the door.

It had been several hours since she had killed her, and one single look at the body was enough to make Anneli worried.

Rigor mortis had already set in.

With a slight feeling of discomfort, she dragged the body away from the shelf to confirm her suspicion. Denise's head was tilted to one side, her neck leaning backward in a fixed position that definitely didn't look normal. Anneli grabbed Denise's head with her fingertips and tried to straighten it. But despite some nasty crunching sounds from the stiff muscles and spine, she didn't succeed. She took a deep breath and grabbed the body under the arms, only to discover to her surprise that even the shoulders were stiffening up. With some difficulty, she managed to press the silencer and then the gun into Denise's hand and gently press her index finger against the trigger. That took care of the fingerprints.

I have to get her out of here before she becomes as stiff as a board. Otherwise I won't be able to get her in or out of the car, she thought.

To her amazement, she felt sad looking down on this awkward corpse of a girl who had once been so full of life and fight.

She wouldn't have liked this sight, thought Anneli in a moment of absurdity. It was almost laughable.

Even though it was almost ten thirty in the evening, it still looked like daytime outside. That was just the way it was in this part of the world.

Did that mean that she ought to wait until it was reasonably dark? That would make it way past midnight and the body would be completely stiff.

No, she couldn't wait.

Anneli dragged the body out of the mechanical engineer's cluttered sitting room and propped it up against the wall in front of the main door so she would be able to move it quickly out into the car.

The traffic on Webersgade was still pretty busy at this time of day. But as long as there were no cops, it would be okay. She would just have to keep an eye out for cyclists and pedestrians. And when there was a lull in the traffic, she would drag the body out to the Ka and stuff it in.

Anneli held the door ajar and from behind the crack in the door she could see that there were still people cycling up and down the street. Why the hell would you be cycling at this time of day? Couldn't people just stay at home?

She heard cheerful laughter down from the corner by Øster Farimagsgade and saw a couple of girls walking directly toward her house. One of them was walking with her bicycle while the other one was walking next to her, chatting away. They didn't seem to be in a hurry.

Stupid bitches, she thought. Now the jabbering brats were heading directly toward her car.

Watch where you're going, she thought. Couldn't they just cross the street to the other side?

She pulled the door closed when the girl without the bike banged her knee against the trunk of the Ka.

"Ouch! Goddamn it! Who the hell parked their car on the pavement?" she shouted, banging her fist on the roof of the car several times while she walked around it.

Anneli stood paralyzed with pursed lips as she watched dent after dent appear on her car roof.

Damn brat! If only she knew what Anneli could do to a girl like her.

Meanwhile, the girls were swearing like a couple of drunken sailors, looking over their shoulders several times and giving the finger. It was only when they reached Fredensbro that Anneli dared to put her arms around Denise's chest and drag her out to the car door.

When she tried to push the body into the car, the upper body had already completely stiffened up, so she had to lean the passenger seat all the way back and use all her might to force the body downward in order to be able to close the door on the stiffened arm.

It meant that the body was almost leaning over the gearshift when Anneli had shut the door and sat in the driver's seat.

It was obvious that given the awkward position the body was lying in, any passerby would react if they saw it.

If anyone spotted her, she would just have to floor it.

She struggled a bit with the stiff arm while pushing the body into a more or less upright position.

She inspected the result. Apart from the almost entangled legs, Denise's open eyes, and the unnatural angle of the neck and the head, it looked fairly normal.

Anneli jumped out of the car and opened the passenger door so she could get the seat belt around the body. But that also proved to be complicated.

When she finally succeeded, she realized that a young guy was watching her from the opposite sidewalk.

They stood for a moment silently watching each other.

What should I do? she thought. *He's seen me struggling with the body!*

She nodded to herself, made a split-second decision, walked around the car, and took a couple of steps toward him with a broad smile.

"Is she okay?" he shouted.

She nodded back. "Yes, but I don't think she can avoid having her stomach pumped," called Anneli with a laugh, her pulse racing.

He returned her smile. "Good thing for her that the University Hospital is just around the corner," he shouted and continued along the pavement.

Anneli held her hands up to her face, wiping the sweat from her cheeks. Then she got in the car and looked down along the row of houses. If she was going to get off the sidewalk and bicycle path and onto the road, she would have to drive a good hundred meters past people's front doors.

If someone suddenly walks out of their door, they'll walk straight in front of the car, she thought, knowing full well the damage that could cause.

She eased the car forward in first gear past the houses and realized for the first time ever that there was a no-parking sign between the bicycle path and the sidewalk exactly where the parking spaces stopped. If she could get her car through the tight space, she would be back on the road.

As she reached the parking meter twenty-five meters before the place where she could get back on the road, a police car driving past honked at her.

Anneli stopped in front of a house with a light-blue door and rolled her window down. She did all she could to remain calm in the ominous flashing blue light from the patrol car siren.

"I know—sorry!" she shouted. "But I'm dropping my mother-in-law off at the next house. She is really unsteady on her feet."

The officer in the passenger seat was just about to get out of the car but was stopped by the other officer. They exchanged a few words and then the first officer nodded at Anneli.

"You won't get away with that again, madam. Just hurry up and get out of here before one of our colleagues sees you."

Anneli watched the patrol car until it was out of sight, and nudged the body to make sure the belt was in place. Then she released the clutch.

She breathed a sigh of relief when she finally reached Lyngbyvej. Now all she had to do was drive up Bernstorffsvej and all the way to Bernstorff's Park, and she would have reached her destination. At this time of day, there definitely wouldn't be anyone out walking their dog, and there was sure to be a free parking space outside the park. Of course, Denise wouldn't be easy to drag, but if she drove around the monument on the roundabout at the end of Femvejen, the car would be facing in the right direction so the passenger door opened out to the park. Then she would just have to drag the body across the bicycle path and sidewalk and onto the path.

She intended to complete her plan in two steps. First, she would drag the body into the nearest bushes and take a break to catch her breath. If the coast was clear, she would then drag it on to the next group of bushes, and when she was far enough away from the road she would leave the body and the gun in the densest undergrowth she could find. It was very likely that a dog would sniff out the body the following morning, but never mind. As long as it wasn't found by an amorous couple or a fanatical jogger before Anneli had made it back to the city, cleaned the car, thrown her footwear in a Dumpster, and wrapped herself in her quilt.

Only a few more streetlights and she would be there. She laughed at how well things were going.

"Now Aunty Anneli is going to take you for a little trip to the park, Denise. Aren't you excited?" she said, giving the shoulder a good strong pat. But she shouldn't have. Defying all laws of gravity, the body fell toward her with the result that the head ended up leaning against her chest with vacantly staring eyes.

Anneli tried to push the body back up with the strength she could muster with her one free hand, but the body seemed to be stuck.

When she made one final attempt, elbowing the body hard in the shoulder, she realized that it was the seat belt that was stopping her from pushing the body back.

Anneli turned a little to the side to enable her to release the seat belt and put the body back in place. When she finally succeeded, she was in the middle of the intersection at Kildegårdsvej, driving through a red light at seventy kilometers an hour.

It was too late when she heard the screeching brakes of the other car and saw the black shadow that rammed into the side of her hood with an unearthly metallic crash. Pieces of glass shattered everywhere, and she could smell the ultimate disaster as the entangled bodywork of the two cars swirled around like a dancing couple. Anneli experienced a momentary blackout as the airbag pushed against her body and the seat belt squeezed her ribs together, pressing the air out of her lungs. She could hear a sizzling sound from the car that had driven into hers, only then realizing the immense trouble she was suddenly in.

Anneli looked instinctively to the side and realized to her horror that the airbag in the passenger side had punctured and that Denise's body was no longer sitting in the seat next to her.

In a panic, she struggled free, undid her seat belt, and forced the door open. The air was thick with the stench of gasoline, burned rubber, and oil.

She stepped directly out onto the sidewalk because both cars had been spun around and were now almost pressed up against the wall of a house.

Anneli looked around in confusion.

I'm on Bernstorffsvej, she remembered. Right now it was deserted, but there was life in the block of apartments above them, and windows were being opened.

She heard several worried voices from above, but Anneli instinctively edged her way along the wall, passing the mangled black Golf that had hit her. The driver, a very young man, was still caught behind the white airbag. His eyes were closed but he was moving slightly, thank God.

There was nothing Anneli could do. She just had to get out of there.

When she turned the corner onto Hellerupvej with the canvas bag over her shoulder, she looked back and could just make out the outline of Denise's body sprawled across the hood of the black car like a dog that had been run over.

51

Monday, May 30th, 2016

Carl was tired, but he also felt good about himself. The long day had really paid off. Three cases had been solved. So despite his worry and concern for Rose, he still had a rare feeling that his job was okay. Assad probably felt the same, but it came across slightly differently. Right now, he was snoring like a walrus in his broom cupboard of an office.

"What do you say, Gordon? Three cases in one day! That's good teamwork." He put down Assad's notes in front of Gordon when the guy sat down on the other side of Carl's desk, looking as white as a ghost.

"Yes, it's fantastic, Carl."

He didn't look particularly elated with the result, but then again it was probably about time to go home and get some sleep so they could get back in the saddle tomorrow morning. As long as they hadn't found Rose, they couldn't rest on their laurels.

"Tell me what you've been working on this evening. Do you have any leads for us?"

He looked a bit embarrassed. "Yes, maybe. I got a guy from IT to hack into Rose's private e-mail account."

"Uh, okay." Carl wasn't sure he wanted to hear the details. The complaints board certainly wouldn't look favorably on this if it came to light.

"Don't worry, Carl. He won't talk. I slipped him a thousand kroner." That almost made it worse.

"No more details, Gordon, please! And what did you find in her e-mails?"

"I wish you hadn't asked me to do it, Carl. I can't bear it, just so you know."

That didn't sound good. "Now you're making me nervous, Gordon. What have you discovered?"

"That I don't know the Rose who . . ."

"Who what, Gordon?"

"Do you know how many e-mail addresses she has for different men? How many e-mails she's exchanged with them? And how many of them she's arranged to visit so they could have sex? She doesn't beat around the bush, Carl." He shook his head. "Just in the time I've known her, she's . . ." He clearly almost couldn't bring himself to say it. "She's had sex with at least a hundred and fifty men, as far as I can calculate."

Carl didn't know what to think. Perhaps he was slightly impressed with the level of activity, but he was puzzled as to how she had found the time. He looked at Gordon, who was biting his cheek to avoid being overcome with emotion.

"I'm sorry to have to ask you, but is it your impression that she could've developed a close bond with any of these people?"

He cringed. "A few, yes. If you mean did she fuck them more than once?"

"I'm not sure what I mean. Someone she went back to for some reason or other."

"Yes, there are a few. Four to be precise. And I've called them all."

"Go on, Gordon."

"They were shocked when I called, I can tell you. I think I interrupted a cozy family evening in front of the TV for a couple of them. They rushed out into the kitchen or somewhere when I questioned them, but they didn't dare hang up when I introduced myself as a police investigator." He flashed a smile at his boldness before his melancholia returned. "She wasn't with any of them, and three of them said, 'Thank God for that!' They said she was a maniac when it came to sex. That she treated them like slaves and was so domineering and rough that it took them several days to get over it."

"And the fourth?"

"He couldn't remember her. 'Hell no,' he said. He'd had so many damn bitches that it would take a bloody big computer to keep track of them."

Carl sighed. The kind of disillusionment he was witnessing just now was heartrending. Here was a man who loved Rose dearly and suddenly felt that he was being pushed off a precipice. He had to pause before each sentence and purse his lips to keep it together. It was clear that he hadn't been the right man for the job, but it was too late now.

"I'm sorry, Gordon. We know how you feel about Rose, so this must be hard. But now you know about the chaos that has raged in her head for years, and I'm sure she's only put herself through this in order to be able to forget."

Gordon looked bitter. "I think it's an odd way to do it. *Goddamn it! She could've just talked to us, couldn't she?*" he yelled.

Carl swallowed hard. "Perhaps, Gordon. Maybe she could have talked to you, but not to Assad or me."

The tall guy looked totally dejected and could no longer hold back his tears. "Why do you say that, Carl?"

"Because people like Assad and me are too dangerous, Gordon. We dig about when we suspect that something is wrong, and Rose knows that better than anyone. But with you it's different because you and Rose aren't just colleagues. You have a different relationship. She can confide in you, and *if* she had, you would've listened to her and tried to console her. And maybe it really would've helped her. I think you're right about that."

Gordon wiped his eyes and looked more alert. "I can tell that there's something about Rose you're not telling me, Carl. What is it?"

"Deep down you already know, don't you, Gordon? It's becoming increasingly clear that Rose might have killed her dad. Whether it was deliberate or not, directly or indirectly, I don't know. But she can't be entirely innocent."

"What do you intend to do about it?"

"Do about it? Discover the truth and help her move on. Isn't that what we need to do? Give her the opportunity to have a better life."

"Do you mean that?"

"Yes."

"And Assad?"

"He agrees."

A faint smile spread across Gordon's gloomy face. "We have to find her, Carl."

"So you don't think she's dead either?"

"No." His lips were quivering. "I can't bring myself to think that."

Carl nodded. "Do you think there's anyone among the other one hundred and forty-six men who can remember her?"

He sighed. "I wondered the same thing when I had spoken with the four guys who stood out the most. But I had no idea where to begin, so I just began from the top and got hold of nearly everyone. One a minute, I think. I just said: 'I'm calling from the police crime division. It's come to our attention that a missing person, Rose Knudsen, might be staying with you. Is that correct?'"

"They could've been lying to you."

"Hell no. None of them seemed clever enough to hide anything from me. Perhaps that's what hurts the most. Apart from the three first men, they all sounded like their brain was attached to their dick. They were total idiots, Carl. They couldn't lie to me."

"Okay." Carl was speechless. He hadn't experienced confidence like this since he had looked at his sixteen-year-old reflection in the mirror and discovered that he had grown sideburns.

"Were there any Swedish men among her contacts?"

"Not one. And no one with an obviously Swedish-sounding name for that matter."

"What about more normal e-mails? Hotel bookings, contact with her sisters, her mom, or Rigmor Zimmermann, for example?"

"Nothing that led anywhere. The few e-mails she had written to Rigmor Zimmermann are insignificant. A recipe that Rose wanted or vice versa, whether Rose knew something about this or that, whether she would keep a key for Rigmor. In fact, there was a lot about keys. Apparently Rigmor Zimmermann was hopeless when it came to her keys. And about the latest movies in the cinema, about the residents' association in Sandalsparken, whether she was coming to the annual general meeting, and if so whether they should go together. Nothing that leads anywhere. Not even Zimmermann's complaining about her daughter and granddaughter and the problems they caused her."

Carl patted his shoulder. The man was consumed with jealousy and sorrow. But it was also in some way the second time within a very short period that he had had to wave good-bye to the one he loved.

Carl had just walked through the door in Rønneholtparken when Morten rushed up to him.

"I've been trying to call you all night, Carl. Have you even charged your cell phone?"

Carl took it out of his pocket. It was completely dead.

"Would you mind charging it? It's really annoying that we can't get hold of you. Hardy's been really ill this evening, just so you know."

Oh no. What now? Carl breathed deeply. He could hardly face more bad news.

"He was complaining about terrible pains in his left arm and the left side of his chest. He said it felt like electric shocks. I had to call Mika since I couldn't get hold of you. I was scared he would have a heart attack, so what was I supposed to do?" He demonstratively snatched the phone from Carl's hand and plugged it in to charge in the hallway.

"What are you two doing so late?" Carl joked as he entered the sitting room. It was obvious that Mika had done anything he could to create a calm atmosphere. Apart from the fact that there wasn't flocked wallpaper on the walls, it might as well have been a Pakistani restaurant on Bayswater Road in London. Incense sticks, candles, and so-called world music with sitars and panpipes galore.

"What's wrong, Mika?" he asked the white-clad athlete, nervously looking at Hardy's sleeping face poking out from under the quilt.

"Hardy almost had a panic attack this evening, which is very understandable," he said. "I'm convinced he really did feel pain this time rather than just phantom pain. And I've seen him move his shoulders as if to ease the pressure from the mattress. And look at this."

Carl looked in silence as Mika lifted up the quilt a little. Small movements like a twitching eye were visible on Hardy's left shoulder.

"What do you think is happening here, Mika?" he asked, concerned.

"What's happening is that tomorrow I'm going to contact two brilliant neurologists that I met during a course I took. Hardy is probably regaining feeling in some secondary, minor muscle groups. Just like you, I don't understand it because in principle it shouldn't be possible given his diagnosis. I had to give him a large dose of painkillers to calm him down. He's been sleeping soundly for about an hour now."

It was almost too much for Carl.

"Do you think . . . ?"

"I don't think anything, Carl. I just know that it's extremely intense and exhausting for Hardy to suddenly be in contact with parts of his body that have been dead to him for nine years."

"I turned on your phone, and now it's ringing, Carl," said Morten from the kitchen.

Ringing at this time? What the hell did he care?

"The display says Lars Bjørn," continued Morten.

Carl looked at his friend lying in the bed. It wasn't easy seeing him there with his face contorted with pain even in his sleep.

"Yes," he said as he put the phone to his ear.

"Where are you now, Carl?" asked Lars Bjørn curtly.

"At home. Where else would I be at this time?"

"I caught Assad at HQ. He's with me now."

"Okay. Perhaps he's already told you about our breakthroughs today? That's a shame. I would have liked to—"

"What breakthroughs? We're at the junction between Bernstorffs-vej and Hellerupvej looking at a certain Denise Zimmermann who everyone has been looking for. She's sprawled across the hood of a black Golf and is very dead indeed. Do you think I could persuade you to get yourself out here, pronto?"

There was a mass of flashing blue lights at the intersection, and according to the police constable who helped him duck under the police cordon, they had been there for several hours.

"What's happened here?" he asked when he saw the group of people gathered by the car wrecks and the technicians everywhere. The group of people consisted of Terje Ploug, Lars Bjørn, Bente Hansen, and Assad standing close by. You'd be hard-pressed to find more competent colleagues grouped together.

Bjørn nodded to him. "An accident of the more spectacular sort, I'd say," he grunted.

Carl looked at the entangled vehicles. The Golf had hit the Ka from the left, leaving the engine block exposed, before they had both spun around together. The windshield of the Ka was shattered, the airbags activated, and the woman lying dead on the hood of the Golf had apparently been flung out through the windshield of the Ka.

"Looks like she died on the spot," said Carl.

Bjørn smiled. "Yes, you might say that. But not this spot. I can assure you that the bullet came first."

"I don't understand."

"She was shot, Carl, and it happened some time before this accident, because the rigor mortis is complete. The accident happened about two hours ago and the doctor believes she's been dead for at least seven."

Shot? Carl walked around the body and the crime scene technician who was taking her fingerprints. He could tell from the way her arm was sticking up in the air that it couldn't possibly be the traffic accident that had killed her. He bent down to get a closer look at the girl's open eyes. She really was very dead.

"Hi, Carl," said Assad. If he had looked any sleepier, he might well be have been dead. He pointed over his shoulder as a form of warning and Carl looked in the direction he was indicating. If it wasn't Olaf Borg-Pedersen and his crew from *Station 3* waving at him.

"Yes, Carl," said Bjørn. "That's why I called you. You need to entertain that little group. And this time I think you should make an effort. Are you with me?"

Bjørn smiled a little too broadly for an inveterate stick-in-the-mud like him. "And you can keep their interest by telling them that the most exciting thing about this case is that the car is registered to an owner by the name of Anne-Line Svendsen. And if you can't remember who she is, then Pasgård, who is standing over there with a smirk on his face, can tell you that she was the caseworker for Michelle and Denise and formerly also for the other two hit-and-run victims. Talk to them and tell Borg-Pedersen that if they keep this to themselves for now, we'll give them more information as it comes to light." He gave Carl an unexpected pat on the shoulder. "When we get back to HQ, we'll go down to your so-called situation room. The way you've linked these cases has really got me thinking. But first the TV crew, Carl."

Carl frowned. Was he really the man to talk to those idiots from the TV? Why not just refer them to Pasgård if he was the man of the hour? Carl certainly didn't know anything.

"One more thing, Lars. What have you told the press about the identity of the deceased?"

"That she's the woman we've been looking for: Denise Zimmermann."

Carl pictured Denise's mother, Birgit Zimmermann, hearing the news that her daughter was dead. Would she still be prepared to sign her confession?

Carl briefly greeted his colleagues and pulled Assad to one side.

"What else can you tell me about all this?"

He pointed into the Ka. "That there is a gun with a homemade silencer on the floor by the passenger seat. They're not quite about the silencer, but it seems to be some sort of oil filter. They also believe the deceased's fingerprints are on it, but we'll have that confirmed in a minute."

"Where's the driver?"

He shrugged. "Some people in that building there saw a woman kick her way out of the driver's side and disappear in that direction." He pointed toward the corner.

"Was it the caseworker?"

"We don't know for certain, but that's what we're assuming at the moment. We sent someone to her home half an hour ago, but she wasn't there. We're keeping the search internal for now."

"And the driver of the Golf?"

"He's been admitted to Gentofte Hospital. He's suffering from shock."

"Okay. What've you told the others about Birgit Zimmermann and James Frank?"

He seemed taken aback by the question.

"Nothing, Carl. Absolutely nothing. Is there any rush?"

They managed a couple of hours' sleep in their chairs at HQ before Lars Bjørn summoned them to his office upstairs. He was also clearly suffering from lack of sleep, but who cared about bags under the eyes and the fact that it was quarter to one in the morning by this stage, when a case was about to be solved and others were pending?

"Have a cup of coffee," he said in a surprisingly friendly tone, pointing at a thermos that probably had more coffee on the outside than the inside.

They both politely declined.

"Out with it, then. I can see it on your faces," Bjørn said expectantly.

Carl smiled wryly. "Then I don't want to get a dressing-down for interfering."

"That depends on how far you've gotten."

Carl and Assad looked at each other. So they wouldn't be getting a dressing-down this time.

They took their time explaining, and Bjørn remained silent

throughout. Only his body language revealed his excitement. Who had ever seen him with glaring eyes and his mouth wide open, on the verge of drooling? He completely forgot about his coffee.

"It's absolutely crazy," he said dryly when they were finished.

He leaned back heavily in his leather office chair. "That's good police work, you two. Have you told Marcus?" he asked.

"No, we wanted to tell you first, Lars," said Carl.

Bjørn looked almost touched.

"But you haven't yet arrested Birgit Zimmermann and this James Frank?"

"No. We thought you'd like the honor."

He looked as excited as a child at Christmas.

"Okay. In return, you can have the honor of arresting Anne-Line Svendsen. One favor deserves another. Or two for one in this case, ha-ha."

"Do we know where she is?"

"No. That's what's so great about it. It leaves you something to get your teeth into." Was he really laughing unashamedly?

There was a knock at the door, and without waiting for an answer, Pasgård was in the doorway.

"Oh, you're here?" he said, sounding annoyed when he saw Assad and Carl. "Okay. But maybe it's a good thing. Now you can see how a real detective wraps up a case."

Carl could hardly contain his excitement.

"Here you are, gentlemen! This is the full confession of the murders of Stephanie Gundersen and Rigmor Zimmermann. Signed and everything. I transcribed it myself this evening."

He slammed an extremely thin report on the desk. Three pages at most.

Lars Bjørn looked at the measly-looking report and nodded in acknowledgment at his inspector. "Brilliant, Pasgård. I'm impressed. So who was the perpetrator and how did you find him?"

Pasgård shook his head in false modesty. "Well, you could say that he found me. But I was quick to put two and two together."

"Well done. And the man's name?"

"Mogens Iversen. Currently living in Næstved but with close ties to Copenhagen."

He was completely bulletproof.

Carl smiled and recalled the look on Mogens Iversen's face when he had promised not to bother them anymore with false confessions. Then he smiled cheekily at Bjørn and Assad, who were already holding their breath, their faces slowly changing from morning pale to red and then purple.

When the three of them couldn't hold it in any longer, they exploded in a roar of laughter never before heard in this office. Pasgård looked more than puzzled.

52

Monday, May 30th, 2016

Anneli cried in shock and frustration.

The seconds during which she had freed herself from the car seat and made her escape were erased from her memory, and now only the sight of the unconscious young man and Denise's lifeless body on the hood remained.

She had sprinted from the scene like never before. It would be untrue to say that she had ever been particularly agile, but it was scary that her body could suddenly feel *so* heavy and limp.

It's the radiation therapy, she tried to convince herself while the sweat was dripping from her and her throat was burning.

How could it happen? How could a momentary lapse of concentration completely shatter her future? It was beyond comprehension. Now all her precautions, intentions, and visions were all for nothing. Her own pride had come back to hit her like a boomerang. And here she was now, standing on a deserted suburban street, completely bewildered.

Why did I use my own car for this? she scolded herself. *Why didn't I pull over and secure the body? Why did I lose my temper?*

She sat down on a grey hybrid network box, frantically searching for solutions that could save her. Explanations that could support her version of the events. Precautions that could lead to solutions.

It was now fifteen minutes since the accident, and the sound of police cars and ambulances rose above the roofs of the houses. She had no time to lose.

She found an old beige van farther up toward Lyngbyvej, broke into it, and in less than three minutes had the engine running by inserting her nail file in the ignition. At least some of her detailed preparation wasn't wasted.

The canvas bag containing the hand grenade and the money on the passenger seat next to her brought her some consolation on the journey back to Webersgade.

I'll make my escape later, once I've been to the hospital. I'll request my medical file and continue with my treatment somewhere else in the world. That was her first emergency plan. Take a flight and create a new life somewhere far away.

Basking in the sun for the rest of my life, she thought, throwing her woolen sweaters back into the wardrobe when she was packing. *Take only the very best with you. You can buy anything you need when you're there.*

She was thinking about this while packing and up until the moment when she took her passport from one of the drawers, only to realize that it had expired.

So many years without travel or adventure brought their own punishment. She couldn't just leave.

Anneli collapsed on her sofa and buried her head in her hands. Now what? As far as she knew, she couldn't even get to Sweden without a passport. Denmark's useless politicians had somehow ruined that option too.

Then it will have to be prison, she thought, trying to mobilize her former indifference toward the prospect but without any real success. Sometimes reality appeared in a very different light when the time came.

But was there any alternative? She didn't even have the pistol or the gun so she could shoot herself.

Anneli shook her head and laughed reluctantly. How comical it all seemed.

Then she straightened up.

She could keep the money for later. If she hid it in the van for now, along with the hand grenade, and then erased all traces in the apartment from the last few weeks when she had been plotting the murders, she might get away with it. She could report her car as stolen. Why not? And if she waited until tomorrow morning, it might seem more plausible. She could say that she was signed off sick and had been sleeping since yesterday because she was feeling ill. Only first noticing the theft in the morning when she looked out of her window.

They would definitely ask her if she had an alibi. She would tell them that she had watched her favorite film for the tenth time that evening just to keep the pain at bay, and then fallen asleep. That she had the DVD and that it was still in the DVD player.

She got up, carefully chose *Love Actually,* and put it in the DVD player. That was her alibi.

Then she looked around. Put the clothes back in the wardrobes and the suitcase back where it belonged. She collected all the cuttings and printouts that could be linked to the hit-and-run incidents and car thefts, and placed them all in the back of the van with the canvas bag and the hand grenade.

She changed her clothes and shoes, putting the things she had been wearing in a bag, and went out to put this in the van too.

If she left the house as quickly as possible, she would have time to drive around and deposit all this undesirable evidence in trash bins all over the town and suburbs. And then she could make her getaway.

Finally, there was her computer. She would have to sacrifice that too. And even if she were to toss it in a lake, she would still have to wipe all the evidence from it first. So she would have to go online one last time to find out how to do that.

When everything had been taken care of one hour later, and Anneli was convinced that there was nothing incriminating left in the apartment, she drove off.

When they ask me if I suspect anyone, I'll tell them the same thing I told the police last time they questioned me. That it is my hypothesis that it must be the girls and probably also their boyfriends trying to pin it all on me, she thought. She would tell them that she was aware that they hated her but not to *that* extent.

Anneli was already back at the house by twenty-five minutes past two and was now lying in bed thinking that from now on, it was only a matter of keeping it together and getting a few hours' sleep so she could endure the challenges that awaited her tomorrow. She put her iPad down next to her on the quilt and repeated to herself: *No, my PC died, unfortunately. That's why I have to go into the office once in a while to update my case files. Otherwise I just make do with this.*

Anneli set her alarm for five thirty. That was when she would call and report her car stolen, and then drive the van far away and take the S-train back to town.

She would rent a bike with a basket so she could bring the canvas bag with the hand grenade and the money around with her. There was a bike rental shop on Gasværksvej that opened at nine. And from there she would cycle around Copenhagen to ask every parking attendant she met if they had seen her car. She would give some of them fifty kroner and her cell phone number so they could call her if they saw the Ka somewhere. And she would make sure to get some of their names and memorize them while she was cycling.

I also need to remember to call work and tell them that my car has been stolen and I won't be in until after my radiation therapy at one, she thought. Would the police be waiting for her in her office? It seemed rather likely.

She smiled at the thought. The policeman who was on the case, and who had questioned her in her office, was certainly not worth worrying about.

If she answered in the right way, he would lap it up. Not least the moving story about a woman with cancer who had cycled all around Copenhagen to find her beloved little car.

53

Carl and Assad were standing outside the main door to where Anne-Line Svendsen lived on Webersgade at twenty minutes past six, pressing the buzzer in the hope that someone would come down and let them in.

It was ten minutes since they had been informed by HQ that Anne-Line Svendsen had reported her car as stolen, and that she was unable to provide any precise information about when it had happened, but that it was probably around eight or nine the previous evening. That was as precise as she could be.

The question remained whether the car really had been stolen.

After Bjørn, Assad, and Carl had stopped laughing at Pasgård's blunder with the false confession, Pasgård tried to save face by telling them that he had had his eye on Anne-Line Svendsen for some time and had actually already questioned her. And although it was true that several things linked her to the four dead girls, there definitely didn't seem to be anything fishy about her. That was the expression Pasgård used, which was rather far removed from police lingo.

Pasgård had recommended that they would do better to take a closer look at the girl who was reportedly connected to Denise Zimmermann and Michelle Hansen. Her name was Jazmine Jørgensen, and according to information obtained during their questioning, Patrick Pettersson had seen her with Michelle Hansen and Denise Zimmermann both at the hospital and on Michelle's selfie.

They also couldn't rule out the possibility that Jazmine was one of the two girls who committed the robbery at Victoria nightclub, as Pasgård said. As he very reasonably argued, there was still a hundred and forty-five thousand kroner missing. No doubt someone would kill for that amount of money, but where was it? All in all, wasn't it logical that Jazmine Jørgensen should be their main suspect?

The problem, however, was that no one had any idea where she was. They had called the address where she was registered as living and spoken to a woman who said she was Jazmine's mother. She told them that she was tired of people asking where Jazmine was when she had no idea. Did they think she was running an information service?

But, as Pasgård admitted, it wasn't as if they had made extensive inquiries to find her. But they would intensify their search first thing in the morning when everyone had had a chance to get some sleep. Now that the search for Denise Zimmermann was no longer relevant, it was only appropriate that they redirected their efforts to finding Jazmine Jørgensen.

"The woman isn't at home, Carl," concluded Assad when they had been staring at Anne-Line Svendsen's buzzer for long enough. "She's certainly up with the lark. Do you think she's gone to work?"

Carl shook his head and looked at his watch again. Why would she go to work so early? And at a municipal office? No, it was more likely that she was home and wouldn't let them in. But if they had to obtain a search warrant, they would have to wait a few hours until the employees at the court registry came in to work.

He mulled over the possibilities. What could her reason be for not wanting to let them in? She had proven to be cooperative before, and as she had now reported her Ka stolen, she was in theory less of a suspect. After all, it hadn't been possible to see who left the Ka after last night's accident. Only that it was a woman.

"Maybe she didn't even come home last night, Carl. She is a grown woman after all," said Assad. "When was it the police tried to get hold of her yesterday?"

"I think they said it was before midnight."

"They didn't put a surveillance team on her house afterward?"

"Nope."

"Well, I'll say it again. I don't think she came home."

Carl stepped back down onto the sidewalk. It was difficult to keep a clear head after only a few hours' sleep.

"We might as well turn our attention to Jazmine Jørgensen while we wait for the public offices to open. What do you think?"

Assad shrugged. He probably imagined himself taking a nap in the passenger seat in about two minutes. But he could forget that—even if it meant that Carl had to listen to those jabbering hosts on Radio P3 at full blast.

"What've we got on that Jazmine?" asked Assad, sounding surprisingly awake as Carl was about to turn on the car radio.

"What we've got? Err, more or less nothing. But Anne-Line Svendsen's manager gave Pasgård a list of her clients the day he went to her office. It's just been gathering dust in his office. However, Lars Bjørn made sure that Pasgård scanned it and sent it out to everyone working on the cases, together with Michelle Hansen's selfie, which the IT department retrieved. Much to Pasgård's annoyance, he emphasized that it should also be forwarded to us. So check your cell phone."

After a few seconds Assad was nodding to himself and scrolling down the document.

"There are actually two Jazmines on the list, but here she is," he said. "The only information is her social security number, a cell phone number, and her address. There's also a note saying that the cell phone number is for her mom, who she also lives with."

"What are we waiting for? What's the address?"

"Borgmester Christiansens Gade in Sydhavnen. But can't we just call her?"

Carl gave him an admonishing look. It was clear that Assad just wanted to get it over with so he could get back to HQ and take a nap until the search warrant was granted.

"No, Assad! Because *if* Jazmine is there, and *if* she has good reason to avoid the police, you can be sure that her mom's answer will still be that she has no idea where Jazmine is. And *if* Jazmine suspects that we might turn up anyway, she'll make herself scarce. So don't you think it would be a better idea to simply go there and ring the doorbell?"

"Well, couldn't she just take the back stairs, in that case?"

Carl sighed. "So we park as close to the main door as we possibly can and keep an eye on it while we call her. She isn't likely to take the back stairs if she thinks we're calling from somewhere else, is she?"

Assad let out a mighty yawn. "Come on, Carl, I'm too tired for all that. Let's just do whatever you think."

That was something Carl had never heard him say before.

It was only twenty-five meters to the main door in the large block of apartments. A distance they should be able to muster up the energy to run if Jazmine suddenly appeared.

What was it she looked like again? thought Carl. He must be more tired than he thought.

"Let me see that selfie, Assad." Assad handed him the phone.

"It's so strange," he said, looking at the photo. "It's only a few weeks old and now two of them are dead. The death of young people is something I'll never get used to with this job." Carl shook his head. "Such lovely sunny weather, and such beautiful young women having a great time together, and suddenly they're not here anymore. It's a good thing we can't see our own future; that's all I'm saying."

"Jazmine is the one on the far right with the longest hair. Do you think it's real?"

Carl doubted it, and Assad was right. They had to be on their guard because girls like them could be like chameleons. Blondes one minute, brunettes the next. Tall in heels and short in sandals. You couldn't even rely on a consistent eye color these days.

"I'm sure I can recognize her no matter what." Assad rubbed his eyes a couple of times. He had a good eye for the ladies—they would just have to hope he could keep at least one of them open.

Carl rang the cell phone number on the client list and waited a long time for an answer.

"Aren't you aware that it isn't even seven o'clock?" said an accusing and extremely annoyed female voice.

"I apologize, Mrs. Jørgensen. You're speaking to Inspector Carl Mørck. I was hoping you could help me with information about your daughter's whereabouts."

"Oh, would you shut up!" she just said and hung up.

They waited fifteen minutes while keeping an eye on the main door, but it remained firmly closed.

"Out," ordered Carl, making Assad's legs twitch. He must have managed to fall asleep anyway.

They found Karen-Louise Jørgensen's name on the buzzer and pushed and held it for a few minutes without any result. That set their alarm bells ringing.

"Go and keep an eye on the gate to the courtyard, and stay there until I give the word, Assad."

Then Carl pressed a few of the other buzzers and was finally let in by someone who didn't dare refuse when he said where he was from.

There were already a couple of women in dressing gowns on the stairs when Carl stood in front of the door with the name "Jørgensen" on it.

"Could I persuade you to ring the doorbell?" he asked an elderly grey-haired woman who was standing with one hand tightly holding the top of her dressing gown around her neck. "We're very concerned about Mrs. Jørgensen's daughter and need her help to find her. But it appears that her relationship with the police is somewhat strained, so it would be a great help." He smiled as well he could and showed the woman his badge to help his cause.

She gave him a friendly and understanding nod and tentatively pressed the doorbell to Mrs. Jørgensen's apartment. "Karen-Louise," she said quietly, with her cheek pressed against the door panel, in the gentlest voice Carl had ever heard. "It's only me. Gerda from the fourth floor."

For whatever reason, it worked. The woman in there must have ears like a bat, because a moment later there was a rattling and clicking sound and then the door was opened.

"He's come to help you with Jazmine," said the quiet woman with a smile that was by no means returned as Carl stepped forward and held up his badge.

"You idiots are incorrigible," she said angrily, with an extra-reproachful look at the old woman. "Was it you who called my phone?"

Carl nodded.

"And pretended that my buzzer was a foghorn?"

"Yes, sorry about that. But we need to know where we can find Jazmine, Mrs. Jørgensen."

"Oh, give it a rest with your Mrs. Jørgensen. Aren't you listening? I do *not* know where Jazmine is."

"If she's in the apartment, I'd appreciate it if you told me now."

"Are you simple? I would know where my daughter was if she was in this apartment, wouldn't I?"

The old woman tugged at Carl's sleeve. "It's true. Jazmine hasn't been here for—"

"Thank you, Gerda. You can go back to your own apartment now." Mrs. Jørgensen looked at the other curious spectators leaning against the bannister. "And the same goes for the rest of you. *Good-bye!*"

She shook her head. "Well, come in if you're coming. Those nosy old buggers can kiss my ass," she said. Obviously Sydhavnen hadn't completely lost the language of its working-class roots.

"What is it Jazmine's done, since you're all on my back?" she asked through the smoke of what was probably the first cigarette of the day.

Carl looked at her with respect. It was highly likely that this woman had carried this family single-handedly. Her hands were tough and her face bore the signs of night shifts, cleaning, working at a cash register, or something similar. The lines on her face weren't the result of smiling. They were wrinkles born of constant regret and frustration.

"We are worried that Jazmine might have been involved in a number of serious crimes, but I have to stress that we don't know anything for certain. We might be wrong—it happens—but just to be on the safe side, and for Jazmine's own good, we—"

"I don't know where she is," she said. "There were a couple of women who called for her at one point. One of them said she owed Jazmine money, so I told her she had moved to somewhere or other in Stenløse. A place called Sandal . . . something or other. That's all I know, and I haven't mentioned it to anyone else."

Carl couldn't help it. The information made him gasp for breath so loudly that the woman looked surprised and lost her tough expression.

"What did I just say?" she asked, sounding puzzled.

"Just what we needed, Karen-Louise Jørgensen. Exactly what we needed."

"Damn it, Carl. I know it was her I saw looking out through the curtains in the kitchen. I just know it. We should've let ourselves in."

"Yes, I suppose we should've." Carl nodded, wondering if they should turn on the siren. "But I'm afraid my instinct tells me it's too late. That the bird has flown."

"Carl, I have a really horrible feeling about this."

"Me too."

"Rose's door was open, damn it. That's not normal, and especially not for Rose. And now she's vanished into thin air. And that Jazmine has been next door all this time. And so has Rigmor Zimmermann's granddaughter, Denise, I bet."

That comment made up Carl's mind to activate the siren and step on the gas.

When they arrived, Carl drove right up onto the sidewalk. Assad was quicker than him and was already standing with the lockpick in the keyhole when Carl reached the walkway, audibly out of breath.

He drew his pistol and poised himself as Assad pushed open the door.

"Police! Jazmine Jørgensen! Come out into the hallway with your hands in the air. You've got twenty seconds," shouted Carl. After ten seconds, they both stormed into the apartment, ready to shoot first.

The place seemed deserted and had a strong smell of urine. There were clothes scattered all over the hallway, and in the sitting room at one end of the hallway they could just make out an upturned chair on the carpet. It didn't look at all normal.

They stood quietly outside one of the bedrooms for a moment. There wasn't a sound.

Then Carl walked over to the door into the sitting room, entered with one fluid movement, and pointed the pistol around the room. Nothing here either.

"You take the balcony, Assad. I'll take the dining room and the bedrooms."

Carl stood in the back bedroom looking at the unmade bed and a lot of dirty laundry scattered all over the floor. He was just about to open the wardrobes when Assad shouted from the balcony that the bird really had flown. "There's a rope made of bedsheets dangling from the balcony, Carl."

Damn it, damn it, and double damn it!

They stood for a moment in the sitting room, looking at each other. Assad's frustration was visible, and Carl knew how he felt. His eyes and intuition had been right, but Carl had stopped him.

"I'm sorry, Assad. Next time, I'll have more faith in what you believe you've seen."

Carl looked around the sitting room and the adjacent dining room.

Blouses and shoes and dirty dishes were strewn everywhere. There were obvious signs of a struggle. A couple of chairs had been pushed over, and the tablecloth was lying on the floor.

"I'll just check the last bedroom." He immediately noticed a small suitcase on the bed, packed and ready for takeoff.

"Get in here, Assad," he shouted.

He pointed at the suitcase. "What do you make of this?"

Assad sighed. "That someone was interrupted in their plans. I just hope it wasn't our fault."

Carl nodded. "Yes, that would be vexatious."

"What does vex . . . Hey, look at that, Carl." He pointed at something under the bed. Carl couldn't see what it was until Assad picked it up with his fingertips. It was a rolled-up banknote.

"Shall we just agree that this five-hundred-kroner bill came from Victoria nightclub, Carl?" he said as he wafted the note in the air.

"Definitely."

"Okay, so what do we do now?" he asked.

"We call HQ and let them know that they need to intensify their search for Jazmine Jørgensen. Everything points to us having a killer on the loose."

Carl took his phone out of his pocket as he walked toward the front door.

If Assad was frustrated, then Carl felt the same ten times over. Not only had they been so close to catching the person they were after, but they could also have prevented the murder of Denise Zimmermann. It was a mystery to him what had happened after the escape from the balcony and what had happened between Denise and Jazmine Jørgensen. He sincerely hoped they would catch Jazmine so they could get to the bottom of it.

"Hang on a minute, Carl. I just need to pee before we go," said Assad. He stopped in front of the bathroom door, which was slightly ajar. Then he froze.

"Look there," he said, pointing at a couple of holes in the door.

Carl put his phone back in his pocket.

Then Assad turned on the bathroom light and pushed the door open wide.

The sight that met them was horrific.

54

Tuesday, May 31st, 2016

There were now at least ten vehicles with flashing lights down in the parking area. The atmosphere was intense and more colleagues kept arriving—some to keep away the curious public, others to go over the crime scene ahead of the technicians.

Assad and Carl looked on helplessly as Rose was carried into the ambulance on a stretcher. The doctor shook his head with a concerned expression. Even though Rose was breathing faintly, there were many indications that this couldn't possibly end well.

Assad was inconsolable, and there was almost no end to his self-reproach. "If only we'd entered the apartment yesterday," he said over and over again.

Yes, if only they had.

"Keep us informed," Carl shouted to the doctor before they took Rose to hospital.

They nodded to the medical examiner returning from the apartment.

"The cause of death is a gunshot, and the woman has presumably been dead for at least twelve hours. The forensic pathologist can give you a more precise time of death."

"So in theory it could be Jazmine who shot Denise. But then who shot Jazmine?" asked Assad quietly.

"Well, there's no hint of gunshot residue on the body. So she definitely didn't do it herself," said the doctor with a smirk. "If you ask me, you'll find the gunshot residue on the outside of the bathroom door."

Carl agreed.

Then he took Assad's hands in both of his and looked intensely at him. "Listen to me, Assad. At least we know it can't have been Jazmine Jørgensen driving around with Denise Zimmermann's body. On the other hand, we know for sure that the driver was a woman. That's all we really need to know. Shall we get going?"

Assad had never looked so defeated before. "Yes. But you have to promise me that we'll drive to the hospital as soon as we can, okay?"

"Of course, Assad. I've called Gordon, who was very shaken by all this, but he's heading out to the University Hospital straightaway to wait for the ambulance. He said we can get him on his cell phone anytime we want."

"I've got four jobs for you, Assad," said Carl on their way to Copenhagen. "Can you make sure that HQ puts someone outside Anne-Line Svendsen's house? Then get hold of Lars Bjørn and give him a detailed update of what's happened out here and tell him to call off the search for Jazmine Jørgensen. Tell him we're on our way to Webersgade and it would help if the search warrant was ready and waiting when we get there. Then call Anne-Line Svendsen's work in Vesterbro and ask if she's there."

He nodded. "And then call one of Rose's sisters, right?"

Carl tried to force a smile. No matter what, you could always count on Assad.

There was already a police constable outside Anne-Line Svendsen's address. It was one of Carl's old acquaintances from Station 1 who had now been transferred to uniform at HQ. He gave Carl a reserved nod and confirmed that the search warrant was in place before keeping a close eye on Assad as he gained entry to the property with the lockpick.

The nameplate on the main door informed them that Anne-Line

Svendsen lived upstairs and a small company called Ultimate Machines was situated on the ground floor.

There was no lock on the door into her apartment, which led straight into the sitting room on the first floor. And there was no one at home. On entering, they immediately noticed how neat and tidy everything was on the upper floor and her part of the first floor. Carl sniffed, noticing an odd smell that reminded him of a couple of bedrooms where he had once enjoyed the company of a woman. He had never managed to figure out if it was the combination of lavender and hand soap.

They noticed that the dishes had been done, the bed made, that everything seemed to have been thought through, and, most significantly, that the apartment had been cleaned of all the clues a detective normally looks for.

"She's really gone to town with cleaning and tidying up, Carl," said Assad. "There's no laundry in the laundry basket, and the wastepaper bin and rubbish bin have been emptied."

"Look here. The room at the back is locked. Want to take a look?"

Assad took out the lockpick and unlocked the door.

"That's odd," said Carl when they were standing in the small room, where all the walls were covered with metal shelves full of screws, nails, fittings, and other metal paraphernalia.

"I don't think this room is part of Anne-Line Svendsen's tenancy agreement. You saw on the sign down there what the other occupant does," answered Assad.

"I'm afraid we won't find anything here, then," Carl said and asked Assad to lock the door behind them.

"When you look around the apartment, does anything spring to mind as missing or do you think there seems to be too much of anything?" he asked when they were back in her sitting room.

"Many things, actually. Firstly, I can tell that there's a computer missing because there's a monitor on the floor down there. And then it's strange that the only untidy thing in the entire apartment is a DVD that's been left out as if she wanted it to be the first thing someone noticed. Normally, you'd place it next to the TV or on the coffee table, wouldn't you? So why did she leave it in the middle of an otherwise tidy desk?"

"I think she's trying to create an alibi. I also noticed that there's a key with her Ka registration number on the bulletin board. It's probably an extra key, but it still makes me wonder whether a key was used in her car last night."

"There was. We actually talked about it, but Ploug didn't think it proved that it was the owner of the car driving. He went on about how stupid and careless some people can be, with car keys being stolen from their handbags or hallway tables while they're sleeping."

Carl was aware of that, but they still had to ask.

They went through her drawers and cupboards, but apart from some doctors' notes, they found conspicuously little of a personal nature. It really wasn't normal.

"I know the search warrant doesn't include the ground floor and that she doesn't live there, but shouldn't we have a look anyway? What do you say?" he asked, looking around for Assad.

Assad was already halfway down the stairs.

They entered the mechanical engineer's sitting room, which was full to the brim with machine parts. Carl didn't understand how a grown man could live like that.

"I don't think he spends much time at home," said Assad understandably.

They rummaged through the piles and were just about to give up when they found a neatly sorted box of oil filters not unlike the one that was attached to the gun in the Ka.

"Well, I'll be damned," said Carl.

They looked at each other knowingly and Assad took out his phone.

"I'll just call her work again. Don't you think people would be at work by now?" he asked.

Carl nodded and looked around the room. Nothing in the world could convince him that Anne-Line Svendsen had not been experimenting with oil filters in here, searching for the one best suited as a silencer. Imagine that he could still be surprised at how cunning and cynical human beings could be. Was it really going to turn out that this anonymous caseworker was the most cold-blooded murderer he had ever encountered?

He could sense that Assad, who was still holding the phone up to his ear, was trying to direct his attention to something over by the door.

Carl turned from side to side. He couldn't see what he was supposed to be looking at.

"Thank you," said Assad to the person on the other end. Then he hung up and turned toward Carl. "Anne-Line Svendsen has just called work to tell them that she won't be in before this afternoon. She's undergoing radiation therapy at the University Hospital and has an appointment at one o'clock."

"Good! We've got her. You did say that this is strictly confidential and that they can't breathe a word to anyone before we give the go-ahead, right?" asked Carl.

"Yes, of course. But strangely enough, Anne-Line Svendsen also told the receptionist that she was currently cycling around Copenhagen looking for her stolen car."

Carl raised an eyebrow.

"Yes, for a second I also thought we were on the wrong track, but then I discovered that."

Assad pointed back down toward the shelf a bit left of the door.

Carl bent down. Now he could see it.

There was a dark stain the size of a small coin on the back wall between two shelves full of motor parts. The experts would be able to tell them what had caused the stain, the angle at which it had hit the wall, and definitely also whether it was fresh blood.

"I think Anne-Line Svendsen missed a spot," Assad said, smiling.

Carl rubbed the back of his neck. "Jesus Christ!" he exclaimed. This really put an end to any possible doubt. So, her bicycle trip around Copenhagen and all her talk about looking for her stolen car was just her playing to the crowd, exactly like the DVD on her desk. She was certainly crafty."

Carl was pleased. They were on to the right perpetrator. No doubt about that.

"Well spotted, Assad." Carl looked at his watch again. "We have exactly three hours before Anne-Line Svendsen's appointment at the radiation clinic," he said, then dialed Gordon's number on his cell and put it on speakerphone.

As expected, the guy sounded sad, but now with a hint of hope.

"They've managed to revive Rose, but unfortunately, there are a lot of complications. Just now they're concentrating on stabilizing her condition. They're very worried about the number of blood clots, and about her legs and arms having suffered permanent damage."

He was breathing heavily on the other end, apparently crying. If only Rose knew the affection he felt for her.

"Can you send us a photo of her, Gordon?"

"I don't know. Why?"

"It's for her own good, so try. Is it possible to communicate with her?"

"Not in the way you'd understand normal communication, no. They have had some communication with her, but they say that she seems to be mentally out of reach. They called in the hospital psychiatrists, who conferred with her therapists in Glostrup. They told them that it was paramount for Rose to work through the traumatic event in her past if she was to avoid falling into an eternal inner darkness."

"'Work through the traumatic event,' you said. Did they say anything about how she should do that?"

"No, not as far as I know," said Gordon. There was a pause. Maybe because he needed to compose himself or maybe because he was thinking. "But I assume it means anything that might take the pressure off her," he said.

Assad looked at Carl. "We need to try and keep a lid on what happened at the steel plant. Agreed?"

He nodded. It was almost like "different minds think alike," as Assad might have put it.

Leo Andresen was standing with a bread roll in his hand when he opened the door. The epitome of retired morning bliss. They could hear a morning TV show blaring in the background, the type that still showed trivial and superfluous cooking features as the main content. When they entered the house, they could also hear the sound of a coffee machine spluttering and his wife shuffling around in her slippers. The entire table was covered in supermarket brochures—perhaps the top entertainment of the week.

"We need to get to the bottom of this, Leo. And let me tell you now that we don't give a damn who you might hang out to dry, because the only purpose of our visit is to help Rose. So out with everything you know. Here and now. Do you understand?"

He glanced over at his wife, and even though she did all she could to hide it, Carl noticed that she shook her head discreetly.

Carl turned toward her and offered her his hand. "The nameplate on the door says Gunhild Andresen. Is that you?"

A small twitch at the corner of her mouth was supposed to resemble a smile and a confirmation.

"Good morning, Gunhild. Are you aware that you just gave your husband away?"

She certainly wasn't smiling now.

"You just warned him that he should keep his mouth shut, and in my world that means he knows more than he's telling us. And now he's one of the main suspects in the murder of Arne Knudsen on May 18th, 1999."

He turned toward Leo Andresen, who looked horrified. "Leo Andresen, the time is ten forty-seven and you're under arrest."

Assad was already rattling the handcuffs hanging from his belt, which had an immediate effect on both of them. They seemed frightened, helpless, and on the verge of fainting.

"But . . . ," Leo exclaimed as Assad handcuffed him.

Then Carl turned toward his shocked wife, reaching for his own handcuffs. "Gunhild Andresen, the time is ten forty-eight, and I'm arresting you for withholding vital evidence relating to a murder case."

And that was enough to really make her faint.

Five minutes later, the two of them were sitting at their usual place in the kitchen, shaking and despondent with their hands cuffed behind their backs.

"This is going to be a very long and hard day for all of us. Do you understand?"

The question didn't revive them.

"Well, the first thing we'll do is drive back to police headquarters in Copenhagen, where I'll read the charges against you. Then you'll be questioned and subsequently kept in custody. Tomorrow, you will be arraigned before a judge, who will decide whether to accommodate our request to keep you in custody. And when he has granted our request and a few weeks have passed, during which we'll have made progress with our investigation, we'll discuss what will happen prior to your trial. Your lawyer will probably want to . . . You do have a lawyer, don't you?"

They both shook their heads. It was all they could manage.

"Okay, but you'll be assigned a court-appointed defense lawyer to argue your case. Have you understood the procedure?"

The wife burst out crying uncontrollably. This couldn't be true. They had always led an upright life and kept themselves to themselves. So why them?

"Did you hear that, Leo? 'Why us?' Gunhild just said. Well, does that maybe mean that there are more of you involved?" asked Carl. "Because if the responsibility is shared, it might reduce your sentence a bit."

That made Leo sing. "We'll do anything you ask us to," he implored. "As long as you . . ." He paused to choose his words carefully. "As long as you both . . . We have three grandchildren. They won't be able to understand this." He looked at his wife, who looked devastated, nodding to herself with a vacant expression.

"If we tell you everything, is that going to help us?" he asked.

"Can you assure us that that everything you've just told us won't happen?"

"Yes, you have my word."

Carl nodded to Assad.

"Yes, if you tell us everything, you have my word too," he said.

"And it won't affect any of the others?"

"No, we promise. Tell us the whole truth and everything will be fine."

"Would you be so kind as to remove these?" he asked. "Then we can drive over to Benny Andersson. He doesn't live far from here."

There was a sound from Carl's cell phone. Gordon had sent a photo of Rose's face.

The sight made Carl forget to breathe. It was absolutely heartrending. Then he handed the phone to Leo.

The man definitely didn't look happy when he opened the door and saw Leo Andresen's pale face in front of the rest of the delegation.

"They know, Benny," said Leo. "Just not how it happened."

He would have slammed the door if he thought he could get away with it.

"Begin with the manganese poisoning, Benny," said Leo when they were sitting down around the sticky, ash-covered coffee table.

"You can speak freely. Inspector Mørck has given his solemn word that nothing will be used against you or any of us."

"What about that one? Does that include him?" he asked, pointing at Assad.

"I don't know if I'd say it's solemn, but you could try and ask me," he said caustically.

"I don't trust them one bit," said Benny. "They can drag me to the police station and do whatever they want. I'm not saying a word and I have nothing to hide."

Leo Andresen had once been a foreman at the plant and it showed.

"Are you stupid or what? You're forcing me to turn you in, Benny," he said angrily.

Benny rummaged in his pockets and eventually found his matches. He blinked a few times as he lit his half-smoked cigar. "It's my word against yours, Leo. You can't prove a damn thing because there *is* nothing to prove."

"Hey!" interrupted Carl. "This isn't about you and what you have or haven't done, Benny," said Carl. "It's only about Rose, and at the moment she's in a terrible state."

Benny Andersson hesitated for a moment and then shrugged as if thinking that it wouldn't help her situation if he landed himself in it.

"What's this business with the manganese poisoning, Leo?" asked Carl.

He took a deep breath. "It was before the millennium, when an occupational medicine physician and a neurologist discovered that working at the plant posed a health risk due to the dry manganese particles in the air. The manganese is added to the steel to fix sulfur and get rid of the oxygen, making the steel stainless and strong. But the doctors said that it was making people ill with Parkinson's-like symptoms, even though it was actually a different part of the brain that was affected.

"It resulted in heated discussions between these two doctors and some of their colleagues, who thought it was sheer nonsense.

"It eventually led to some of the workers receiving industrial injury compensation, including Benny here, which proved too much for the company in the financial climate as it was then." Leo looked at Benny with undisguised skepticism. The discussion about whether he had been exposed to poisoning or not would apparently never end. "Arne Knudsen was already dead by then, of course, but before that he had repeatedly claimed that he had also been affected. And he managed to convince everyone. In hindsight, it was employees like Arne and—pardon my saying so—also you, Benny, who ultimately brought the company down."

Benny Andersson put his cigar down in the ashtray. "That's not true, Leo. You're twisting everything."

"Well, pardon me if I do. But things certainly went from bad to worse with Arne and the manganese case, and that was when Rose was still at the plant. Every time there was a discussion about it and we gave him a piece of our minds, knowing that he never came near the manganese dust, he went back to Rose and took in out on her. He did try to make an ally out of Benny, but Benny couldn't stand the man."

He turned toward Benny. "Would you agree with *that*?"

"Hell yes. I hated that prick. He was an asshole and he *hadn't* been poisoned. He was just a malicious bastard intent on ruining it for the rest of us who really *were* ill."

"And Rose was having a really bad time because of her dad's psychological abuse. We could all see it, so there were many reasons why we all wanted to get rid of Arne Knudsen. Get him the hell out of our lives."

"Did you also want to get rid of him, Benny?"

"Are you recording this?" he asked.

Carl shook his head. "No. But we have two things we'd like to show you before we carry on. I've already shown them to Leo." He slammed a photo on the table of Arne Knudsen's body lying on a steel autopsy table.

"Good God," said Benny at the sight of the man with his lower body completely crushed. No one would have been able to guess what they were looking at if they hadn't been told in advance.

"And then there's this photo. I received it half an hour ago." He showed him the photo of Rose on his phone.

Benny Andersson reached for his pack of cigars while his eyes lingered on the tormented face. It really got to him. "Is it Rose?" he asked, visibly shaken.

"Yes. The time between the two photos has been one long nightmare for her, as you can tell. Every day for seventeen years she has lived with the image of her mangled dad and taken the entire blame for his death. But the situation now is that her condition is extremely bad. And if you two don't help us today, she will die inside. Do you believe me when you see this face?"

Benny and Leo had been gone for five minutes, and when they finally returned, neither of them looked comfortable with the situation.

It was Leo who spoke first.

"We are agreed that we don't regret the part we played in what we're about to tell you, and I'm convinced that the others feel the same. Just to set the record straight. Arne Knudsen was a real shit and the world is a better place without him."

Carl nodded. They were a couple of vigilantes and murderers who had ruined Rose's life. Nothing could justify their heinous crime, but it wouldn't benefit Rose if the truth became public.

"Don't expect me to condone what you've done, but a promise is a promise."

"It's a harsh thing to say, but Rose was our useful idiot. Even though it sounds worse than intended."

"That's one of the reasons why I was against it at first, because I had a more personal relationship to Rose than the others," said Benny. "But I gave in when Arne started to make life hell for everyone. You can't imagine how intolerable he could be."

Carl wasn't so sure. "Out with it and don't beat around the bush. We don't have all day. Assad and I have an appointment in town we can't be late for," said Carl.

"Okay. Well, Rose was the only one who could really get her dad so agitated that he didn't notice what was going on around him. He simply loved those situations. It was almost as if they gave him an orgasm," said Leo Andresen.

"There were five of us who devised the plan," interjected Benny Andersson. "Leo wasn't at work that day but 'coincidentally' turned up shortly after the accident," he said, sketching apostrophes in the air when he said "coincidentally."

"I made sure no one saw me at security and disappeared afterward just as quickly as I had arrived," added Leo. "My mission was to delete all the data regarding the power cut, which one of our colleagues had been instructed to cause at the exact moment he received a signal on his pager. Our problem wasn't the power cut but getting the timing right."

"We agreed that immediately before the incident was due to take place, one of our foremen, who unfortunately isn't with us anymore, should lie to Rose's dad that she'd been slagging him off in the worst possible way, which of course she would never have dared," said Benny. "So her dad was already fuming when the man who was controlling the overhead crane in the old hall gave the signal that he was ready. Then Benny walked over to Rose and explained to her that they wanted to teach him a lesson he wouldn't forget, and that she just had to make sure that she was standing on a specific spot in hall W15, just by the conveyor belt to the pusher furnace, when her dad began to have a go at her. She had been told that when her pager vibrated it would be time for her to take up her position. That was all she knew. She had no idea about what was in store for him. The rest of us called it an accident and said that we hadn't meant it to end like that, but it completely crushed Rose," Leo ended.

"So there were five of you behind this?"

"Yes, five plus Rose."

Assad didn't look pleased with the explanation. "I don't understand, Leo. Last time we spoke, you said you thought it wasn't an accident, but that it was deliberate and calculated. Why didn't you just keep silent about it? You must have known that we wouldn't be able to leave it at that."

He hung his head. "If you don't plan to arrest us, then the best thing that could happen for me is that all this comes out in the open. You might think that Rose is the only one who has been suffering after what happened. But that's not the case at all. I haven't been able to sleep for years, and the others also had their own problems. Your conscience nags away at you when it isn't clean. I told my wife, as did a few of the others. Benny here was divorced, and you can see what that led to." He pointed around at all the rubbish and mess, which didn't seem to bother Benny. "And the supervisor, who was otherwise a really plucky and good guy, committed suicide. You can't run away from the sort of thing we did. And so when you turned up, I was split between wanting to clear my conscience, on the one hand, and hoping to avoid punishment, on the other." He looked imploringly at him. "Does that make any sense?"

"It does," said Assad. He looked away for a moment as if he just needed some distance before he could react to the two men. "How do you propose we convince Rose that she isn't guilty? Give us a solution."

As if he had been waiting for a cue, Benny Andersson stood up and edged his way past a couple of man-sized piles of newspaper and junk, stopping in front of a sideboard and pulling out a drawer stuffed full of cardboard and plastic wrapping.

He rummaged around in the drawer and finally pulled out a small object.

"Here," he said, placing a pager in Carl's hand. "It's the pager used that day. She dropped it on the floor when she saw her dad being crushed. If you give it to her and tell her that Benny Andersson says hello, you can tell her the rest of the story yourselves. Okay?"

55

"Hello, it's Olaf Borg-Pedersen," said the man on the telephone. There was no need for further introduction.

Assad rolled his eyes, which made them look even bigger.

"I'm sorry, Borg-Pedersen," said Carl. "We can't speak just now."

"Lars Bjørn tells me that you've made a lot of progress, so we'd like to get some footage of you and Assad bringing our viewers up to date."

That Bjørn never gave up.

"Okay, but it'll have to wait until tomorrow."

"We're airing tomorrow and will need some time to edit before then. So . . ."

"We'll see," said Carl, about to hang up.

"We've heard that the car that was involved in the crash yesterday has been reported stolen by the owner. So we tried to contact Anne-Line Svendsen at her address to ask her about it, but she wasn't there. And they told us at her work that she's signed off sick. You wouldn't happen to know where she is, would you?"

"Who did you say?"

"The woman who owns the Ka from yesterday."

"No, we don't know anything about her. Should we? As you said, the car has been reported stolen."

"Yeah. But as you know, Carl Mørck, this is TV, so we need footage and interviews, and when the crime affects ordinary people like Anne-Line Svendsen, who lost her car in this violent accident, it's bound to interest our viewers. In a sense, Anne- Line Svendsen is also a victim, right?"

Assad shook his head and, pretending to slit his throat with his hand, indicated to Carl to end the call.

"If we discover anything important, you'll be the first person to know, Borg-Pedersen."

Assad and Carl roared with laughter for half a minute about their lie. Who the hell did the man think he was?

Carl put the cell phone back in his pocket and watched in amazement as they drove past the extensive building project around the University Hospital on Blegdamsvej. Had it really been so long since he had driven past here?

"Where the hell have they moved the radiation therapy section to? The entrance should be just over there." He pointed at a chaos of portable buildings and temporary fencing.

"I think it's in that maze somewhere. I think I can see the sign," said Assad.

Carl pulled in and parked halfway up on the sidewalk.

"We're in good time. Anne-Line won't be here for another fifteen minutes," he said, looking at his watch. "It'll be as easy as taking candy from a baby."

They entered the labyrinth of portable buildings and followed the signs toward entrance 39, where radiation therapy was located.

"Have you been here before, Carl?" asked Assad. The situation seemed to make him feel uncomfortable as they walked a few floors down the spiral staircase to the X-ray section. Carl understood him. It felt like the word "cancer" was hanging ominously in the air.

"You only come here if you really have to," he answered. And he hoped he never would.

They pulled the string to open the automatic door and entered the large reception area. If you could disregard the reason why people were here, it was almost cozy. A large aquarium on the end wall, mint-green concrete pillars, beautiful plants, and lots of natural light softened the impression. Carl and Assad walked up to the reception desk.

"Hello," Carl said to the nurses and produced his badge. "We're from Department Q at police headquarters and are here to arrest one of your patients who has an appointment in a few minutes. It will be a subdued affair to make sure we don't cause any unnecessary stress. But now you know."

The nurse looked at him as if to say that he had no business coming down here and bothering their patients.

"We'll have to ask you to do it outside the radiation therapy section," she said. "We're dealing with patients in a critical condition, so if you wouldn't mind obliging."

"Err, I'm afraid it'll have to be here. We can't allow the patient to catch sight of us from a distance."

She summoned a colleague and they whispered together for a minute.

Then the other nurse turned toward them. "Which patient are we talking about?"

"An Anne-Line Svendsen," answered Carl. "She has an appointment at one o'clock."

"Anne-Line Svendsen is already having her treatment. We had a cancellation so we took her in as soon as she arrived. She's in room 2, so I'll have to ask you to wait. I suggest that you wait over by the entrance and do what you need to do very discreetly."

She pointed at the door where they had entered.

During the following ten minutes the nurses glanced over at them frequently with stern expressions on their faces. Maybe he should have told them what they were arresting Anne-Line Svendsen for. That might have changed their tune.

She came out of the room with a large canvas bag over her shoulder and continued directly toward the entrance. A completely ordinary, frumpy woman with uncombed hair and no charisma. The type of woman you could walk past on the street without knowing if it was a man or a woman, or whether you had even seen her at all. They couldn't know for sure how many lives she had taken, but it was at least five.

The woman looked directly at them without a clue who they were, and if it hadn't been for the commotion behind the reception desk and the nervous looks the nurses sent her, it would all have gone smoothly.

She suddenly stopped ten meters away from them and frowned, looking back and forth between the reception desk and them.

Assad was about to walk over to her to make the arrest, but Carl stopped him. She had killed with firearms before, and the way she looked at the moment, she might do it again.

Carl slowly pulled his badge out of his pocket and held it up so she could see it from a distance.

Then a strange thing happened. She smiled at them.

"God, have you found my car?" she asked with an expression that was intended to convey happiness and anticipation.

She walked closer. "Where did you find it? Is it okay?" she asked. She was really putting on a show. Did she really think they would buy it? That they wouldn't think it odd that she never questioned the fact that two policemen had sought her out here just to inform her that they had found her car?

"Yes, so you must be Anne-Line Svendsen? It was a blue and black Ka," said Carl in order to lure her closer while he watched her every movement. Was her hand in the canvas bag? Was she turning something in her hand? Was all that rubbish she had just spouted off only meant to distract them?

Carl took a few steps forward to seize her, but this time Assad stopped him with a hand on his arm.

"I think we'd better let her go, Carl," said Assad, nodding toward the metal cap she demonstratively let fall into the canvas bag.

Carl stood absolutely still. Now he could see her slowly pulling a wooden shaft out of the bag. At first he couldn't make out what it was but suddenly realized that it was a hand grenade of the sort used by the Germans in the Second World War.

"I have the ball in my hand," she said, holding a small white ceramic ball between her fingertips. "If I pull it, this place will look like a slaughterhouse within a few seconds. Do you understand?"

They certainly did.

"Move away from the door," she said, walking over to the mechanical door opener hanging down from the ceiling. She pulled the black ball-shaped handle, and the door opened.

"If you come anywhere near me, I'll detonate this and throw it at you. Don't even walk up the stairs. Just stay where you are until you're sure that I'm far away. I might just be waiting for you up at the entrance."

She really looked like she meant it. The grey woman from before had transformed into a devil who was capable of anything. Her eyes shone with genuine madness, determination, lack of empathy, and, most of all, a completely incomprehensible absence of fear.

"Anne-Line Svendsen, where will you go?" asked Carl. "Everyone will be looking for you. You won't be able to go anywhere without being recognized. I don't think any disguise will be able to conceal your identity. You won't be able to use public transport or cross borders. You won't feel safe even if you hide in a summerhouse or out in the open. So why not just let go of that ball in your hand before something goes wrong? We will—"

"*Stop!*" she shouted so loudly that everyone looked up. She pulled the automatic door opener once again and stepped out into the stairwell.

"If you follow me, you'll die. And I don't care how many others join you. Got it?"

And then she slipped out of sight.

Carl immediately grabbed his cell phone and nodded to Assad to open the door so they could follow her.

In a matter of seconds, Carl had informed HQ about the situation and hung up again.

They heard the sound of her running at the top of the stairwell, and when they almost couldn't hear her anymore, they nodded to each other and sprinted up the stairs two steps at a time.

When they reached the top, they looked out through the glass doors of the main entrance at a green wooden fence and the side of a blue container. But Anne-Line Svendsen was nowhere to be seen.

Carl pulled out his pistol. "Stay behind me, Assad. If I can get her in range, I'll try to hit her in the leg."

Assad shook his head. "Don't *try* to hit her, Carl. You *have* to hit her. Give me the pistol."

He put his hand around the barrel of the gun and pulled it carefully from Carl's hand. "I won't try, Carl," he said calmly. "I will hit her."

What the hell? Was he a marksman all of a sudden?

Then they rushed out the door and down the narrow passage between the fence on one side and a low stone wall on the other. Of course, the woman was already far ahead of them, but what they hadn't bargained for was that Olaf Borg-Pedersen was waiting at the corner of the fence with his cameraman and sound technician already recording.

Borg-Pedersen smiled at them. "A little sweet talk and an incentive convinced the secretary to tip us off that we might find you out here somewhe—"

"Get out of the way!" shouted Assad, and they did when they saw the pistol pointing straight at them.

Carl and Assad turned the corner and caught sight of Anne-Line Svendsen down at the far end of the fence, where she was lunging at an old woman who was just about to secure her bicycle on its kickstand.

"She's stealing the bike," shouted Carl. "She's going to get away." Carl's lungs were wheezing when they came to a halt at the end of the fence. They stared at the waiting taxis, the traffic on Blegdamsvej, and a mass of frightened people who had come from the direction of the main hospital entrance only to be suddenly confronted with the sight of a frantic-looking brown man with a firearm in his hands. Some of them screamed spontaneously and ran for cover, while others stood paralyzed.

"Police!" shouted Carl, jumping out into the road, followed by Assad.

Borg-Pedersen came running up behind them, his crew in tow, encouraging them to make sure they recorded everything, and telling them that this was live action at its best.

"She's down there," said Assad, pointing toward a side street about a hundred meters down toward Ryesgade.

Then the woman stopped on a street corner and laughed manically and unashamedly in their direction. It was obvious that she thought she was safe now.

"Can you hit her from this distance?" asked Carl.

Assad shook his head.

"What's she doing?" asked Carl. "Is she waving the hand grenade?"

Assad nodded. "I think she's trying to tell us that it's a dummy. Look, she's pulling the ceramic ball and letting the grenade fall. Shit, Carl. It *was* just a dummy, it . . ."

The sudden explosion shattered all the windows on the corner, and while it wasn't exactly deafening, it was enough to make the taxi drivers who were standing chatting at the taxi rank instinctively fall to their knees and look around in confusion.

They heard Olaf Borg-Pedersen let out a satisfied sigh behind them. *Station 3* had their footage in the bag: the remains of the bank notes rising like a mushroom cloud above Blegdamsvej, mixed with particles of the flesh that had once been a woman by the name of Anne-Line Svendsen.

EPILOGUE

Tuesday, May 31st, 2016

Olaf Borg-Pedersen was spluttering with rage through his red beard when Lars Bjørn coldly informed him that even if they were to be dragged through a complaints procedure with the ombudsman, internal investigation, press complaints commission, court orders, abuse from the press, political pressure, and all kinds of obstacles, *Station 3* would never obtain permission to use the last half hour of footage. They would just have to hand over the memory cards immediately.

Carl smiled. So there *were* limits to Lars Bjørn's willingness to cooperate. Was he already thinking about how the police commander and head of communications would react if they were forced to explain on national TV why an unauthorized policeman had threatened a TV crew with a firearm to get them out of the way, not to mention the subsequent downpour of flesh and bank notes?

"Have you arrested James Frank and Birgit Zimmermann?" Carl whispered.

Bjørn nodded.

"And have they confessed?"

He nodded again.

"Then strike a deal with Borg-Pedersen and serve him those cases on a silver platter. Two solved murders have got to be better than nothing."

Bjørn scowled and gestured the man over to him.

"I have a suggestion for you, Borg-Pedersen," he said.

Assad and Carl turned around and looked at the colossal buildings that made up the University Hospital.

"Shall we just go up to her?" asked Assad.

Carl wasn't sure. It was one thing that they had just tried to identify a couple of lumps of meat as the woman they had been pursuing, but it was quite another thing altogether to go up and be confronted with someone they loved and who was now only a shadow of her former self.

They stood silently on the way up in the elevator, trying to brace themselves for the hopelessness of the sight that awaited them.

Gordon was paler than ever when he met them at the elevator. But he also seemed strangely grown up for the first time.

"What's the situation?" asked Carl almost reluctantly. Why ask when he didn't really want to hear the answer?

"I don't think they'll let you see her." He pointed at the intensive care unit. "There are a couple of nurses and a doctor by the monitors outside her ward. You'll have to ask them. Rose is in the first examination room."

Carl knocked tentatively on the glass window of the nurse station and held up his badge against the glass.

A nurse appeared immediately. "You can't question Rose Knudsen. She's very weak and hallucinating."

"We're not here to question her. She is a very dear and valued colleague, and we've come to tell you something that we think might help her."

She frowned in the authoritative way that only people with responsibility for the fate of others are capable of. "I don't think we can allow that at this critical stage. You'll have to wait outside the ward until I come to get you. I need to discuss it with my colleagues first. But don't get your hopes up."

Carl nodded. He could just make out Rose's face in there on the pillow.

"Come on, Carl," said Assad, tugging at his arm. "There's nothing you can do just now."

So all three of them sat down side by side in silence while the elevator went up and down, and all the white-clad people on the ward fought for their patients.

"Carl," said a voice in front of him. He was already about to get up and receive the nurse's verdict when he raised his head only to see Mona's beautiful face and glistening eyes. Were those tears?

"I was here anyway and heard that Rose was here too," she said quietly. "So you found her."

He nodded. "Yes, but it was a joint effort between the three of us," he said, nodding at his two faithful assistants. "I'm afraid they won't let us talk to her. But the thing is, Mona, we've brought something that we think can really help her." He attempted a boyish smile but didn't succeed. "I know I shouldn't ask, but maybe they'll listen to you because you're a psychologist and are familiar with the case. Do you think you could tell them that we only want what's best for Rose, and that what we're here for can only be a help to her? Would you do that for us, Mona?"

She stood completely still and looked him straight in the eyes. Then she nodded quietly and stroked his cheek so gently that he almost couldn't feel it.

Carl closed his eyes and sank into the chair. The touch evoked so many feelings, but strangely enough mostly sorrow and an inexplicable sensitivity.

He felt a hand on his and realized that he was gasping for breath. After the unimaginable successes of the last few days, his body was now reacting irrationally, causing him to shiver and feel like his skin was on fire.

"Don't cry," he heard Assad comforting him. "Mona will help us."

Carl opened his eyes and saw the world through a haze of tears that made it look unreal. He fumbled in his pocket, took out the pager, and gave it to Assad. "I can't," he said. "Won't you go in and tell her everything if they let us?"

Assad stared at the pager as if it was a holy chalice that might evaporate and disappear forever if he touched it. When he blinked, his eyelashes suddenly looked so incredibly long and vibrant. Carl had never noticed that before.

Then Assad let go of Carl's hand and stood up. He straightened his shirt and ran a hand through his curly hair a couple of times before walking over to the ward entrance. He stood outside the door for a moment as if trying to compose himself before disappearing inside.

He could hear voices from inside expressing discontent, but then he heard Mona's voice cutting through and smoothing things over. Then it went quiet.

Gordon and Carl stood up a minute later. They looked at each other in support before entering the ward. Through the glass partition, they could see Mona's back in front of the monitors, but Assad wasn't there.

"Come on, Carl," said Gordon. "I think we can go in now."

They hesitated in the doorway, and when no one reacted they snuck in.

It was clear what was about to happen. The nurse who had tried to put them off earlier was standing in Rose's room keeping a close eye on what Assad was doing. Carl could clearly see the way he was looking down at Rose, and how his lips were constantly moving. His face was expressing all kinds of emotion, and his eyes were as intense as his gesticulating hands. The story about a day a long time ago when Rose's father was killed, turned into a pantomime of words and emotions that Carl could easily decipher and recognize. Assad was amazingly patient in telling the tale, and the nurse looked at him nodding, as if he had spellbound her.

Then he held the pager out toward Rose. Carl could tell that the nurse was moved by his gentleness and care for her patient.

Then something happened that made Mona gasp and Gordon lean up against his shoulder for support.

Suddenly the monitor showed that Rose's pulse increased rapidly, and in the room they could see her raising her arm slightly from the bed. It was clear that she couldn't manage more than that, so Assad took her arm and put the pager in her open hand.

It remained there while he finished his explanation.

Rose slowly pressed her fingers around the pager while her arm fell back down onto the bed. The doctor and nurses observed the monitor that showed her pulse slowly and steadily decreasing.

Everyone in the room nodded at one another in relief.

Assad was ready to drop when he stepped out into the waiting room, where Mona gave him a long hug before he sat down heavily on a chair looking like he could fall into a deep sleep right there and then.

"Did she understand everything, Assad?" asked Carl.

He wiped his eyes. "I'd never imagined she'd be so weak, Carl. I was constantly scared of losing her in there. Scared that she'd close her eyes and never open them again. I was so afraid, I really was."

"We saw her accept the pager. Do you think she understood what it meant? That the others abused her trust? And that the pager was a symbol of her innocence?"

Assad nodded. "She understood everything, Carl. She was crying all the time and I almost didn't dare to go on, but the nurse kept encouraging me, so I did."

Carl looked at Mona. "Do you think Rose has a chance?"

She smiled, tears running down her cheeks. "You boys have certainly given us all hope, Carl, but time will tell. But I think from a psychological point of view that she might be recovering."

He nodded. He knew full well that she couldn't magically produce a different reality than the one they were faced with.

Mona's face suddenly contorted with a pain he had never seen in her before. And then he suddenly remembered. Why hadn't he thought about it earlier?

"Why were you here at the hospital in the first place, Mona? Is it your daughter?"

She looked away, blinking her eyes and pursing her lips. Then she suddenly nodded and looked straight into his eyes.

"Hold me, Carl," was all she said.

And Carl knew that if he was going to hold her, it would have to be close, tight, and long.

ACKNOWLEDGMENTS

Thanks to my wife and soul mate, Hanne, for her fantastic and loving support, and not least for her invaluable feedback.

Thanks to Linda Lykke Lundgaard for her professional insight and inspiration for the subject of the novel.

Thanks to Henning Kure for his skilled overview and speedy preliminary editing.

Thanks to Elisabeth Ahlefeldt-Laurvig for her research, all-round help, and resourcefulness.

Thanks also to Elsebeth Wæhrens, Eddie Kiran, Hanne Petersen, Micha Schmalstieg, and Karlo Andersen for their intelligent preliminary proofreading.

A special thanks to my indispensable and fantastic friend and firebrand at Politiken Literary Agency, editor Anne C. Andersen, for her loyalty and watchful eye and for being so uncompromising.

Thanks to Lene Juul and Charlotte Weiss at Politiken Literary Agency for their unfailing belief, hope, and patience. Thanks to Helle Wacher for her PR work on the novel.

My thanks to Gitte and Peter Q. Rannes and the Danish Centre for Writers and Translators for putting me up during the writing process.

Thanks to Superintendent Leif Christensen for his advice with police-related material. Thanks to Kjeld S. Skjærbæk for bringing a ray of sunshine to every day.

Thanks to Nya Guldberg for our fruitful cooperation over many years, and thanks to Rudi Rasmussen for adopting me and taking over.

Thanks to Laura Russo and her fantastic colleagues in Bilbao, Madrid, and Barcelona for help during difficult circumstances.

Thanks to Johan Daniel 'Dan' Schmidt and Daniel Struer for their IT work. Thanks to Benny Thøgersen and Lina Pillora for new writing space in Rørvig.

Thanks to Ole Andersen, Abelone Lind Andersen, and Pelle Dresler for a fantastic tour and introduction to the workings of a steel plant. Thanks to Tina Wright, Zainap Holm and Erik Pedersen for additional information.

Thanks to Eva Marcussen for the tour of the flat in Sandalsparken. Thanks to Malene Thorup and Cecilie Petersen from the Danish Immigration Service.